To Wed A Highland Bride

To Wed A Highland Bride

Prologue

Scotland, the Highlands
Autumn 1801

Buffeted by wind gusts, Donal MacArthur struggled as he climbed a rocky hill in moonlight. Hunched against the chill, his plaid billowing and snapping against his trousered legs, he walked along the shoulder of the slope to face a tall concavity in the rock, shadowed black in the darkness. He reached up to grope along a natural shelf formed by slate and gray stone.

There, he had it—the bit of crystal he had hidden there seven years earlier. It fit the palm of his hand, the clustered points jutting upward. Pressing it into a small opening in the wall, he felt it slide just so, with a chink and a settle.

He pulled the drape of his woolen plaid closer over his jacket and clamped a hand over his bonnet, for the wind began to whip as soon as he inserted the key—the crystal itself. He waited, knowing this was not his usual appointed time, but they expected him. Every seven years throughout his adult life, he had come here, according to the agreement he had made. Seven years, and seven again, until seven-times-nine was reached. By then, he would be a very old man. Tonight, only a year and a day had passed since his last visit.

She always expected him, and welcomed him into her presence, and into her arms. There, he would lose the sense of time for a bit, the sense of himself, his home, his dear ones at Kilcrennan. Inside the hill, he would revel in the pleasures offered, golden wine and ripe fruits, sweet crystalline music, dancing like joyful madness, the laughter as that of angels. Some said that was what they were, the Fey: fallen angels. He could well believe it, given their sweetness and their cruelty.

And the private pleasures with her—sinful, graceful passions, her body perfect and never aging, fitting exquisitely to his own, still hard despite his years. That lush, sensual feverishness always lured him back again—the craving pulsed through blood and soul, and slowed aging. He could not resist, nor did she ever deny him. Lips, touch, thrust, and magic—the blend was powerful and deep.

Inevitably, she would release him and he would find himself standing outside the rock again, in moonlight or at dawn: just Donal the weaver, tall and handsome, blessed in his friends, fortunate in his business; Donal MacArthur, who as a young man had made a dark bargain with a queen of the fairy ilk.

Now the rock wall shifted, opened like a door. Light glowed within, and he heard the pipes, the laughter. Oh, he wanted to go inside. *Not tonight*, he told himself.

for Jennifer,
who knows all about
fairy stones

AVON BOOKS
An Imprint of HarperCollins*Publishers*
10 East 53rd Street
New York, New York 10022-5299

Sarah Gabriel

To Wed A Highland Bride

AVON

An Imprint of HarperCollins*Publishers*

"Donal, dearest!" She stood before him, and he dared not even think her name for its power. Inside the threshold, she was tall and elegant, glowing like a slender moonbeam. Her garments were gossamer, her face and form beautiful. He caught his breath.

"I have come back, a year and a day from the last time, as we agreed, for the return of my son, Niall. You agreed to bargain."

"Did I? I suppose I did." She laughed, silver music. Glancing over her shoulder, she beckoned. The sound of merriment, the fragrances of wine, apples, and cakes wafted toward the entrance. Donal drew breath, tempted.

Then Niall appeared, his handsome son, brown-haired and strong. With him stood the one who had lured him inside—a girl of uncommon beauty, black gloss hair and silver-green eyes. Sensing sadness in her, Donal wondered if Niall was about to leave.

"Niall, are you well?" he asked, heart thumping fast.

"Very well, and happier than any man ever was."

"You must break their power over you—" he began, but Niall shook his head.

"The Fey have won, what's done is done," the queen of that hillside said, and smiled. "Niall has found true love's enchantment here, which all humans long for. He reminds me of you, Donal." Her eyes gleamed, and lust darkened her lips to rose.

"Do not dare," Donal growled.

She laughed. "Come inside forever. Come with me." She opened her arms.

Though it took effort, Donal ignored her to look at his son. "Come out, Niall."

But Niall shook his head. "I cannot cross this

threshold now. I gave my promise . . . I must remain."
He gathered the black-haired beauty close. "I am
happy, and gladly here forever."

Donal knew that feeling too well, and his heart
seemed to sink. "Och, lad."

The queen, his own mysterious lover, reached toward him. "Forever would be bliss for us, too, my
weaver. Come inside to me."

Though he loved her in his way, he shook his head.
"I will return at my allotted time, as we agreed so long
ago. Every seven years for us." He stepped back.

"Good. Oh, the gift! I do keep my promises." She
beckoned, and a Fey girl appeared beside her, holding
a bundle. Niall's black-haired lover reached out, but
the queen snatched it and pushed down the blanket.
"Donal, take this home with you."

She held an infant swathed in glittering fairy cloth,
a small, perfect creature with dark hair and wide eyes,
so impish and lovely that his heart melted, there and
then. "What is this?" he asked. "A changeling, who
will be not so lovely a thing when I reach home?"

"No changeling. She is half our kind, half yours."
His longtime lover touched the child's brow, and a
blue glow like a beam of moonlight appeared and vanished. She offered the infant to Donal, stretching her
arms through the moonlight. "I have given her a gift.
She will see what cannot be seen."

"The Second Sight, aye." Such gifts were freely
given by the fairies, it was said—though often there
was a hidden cost. Donal accepted the feathery weight
in his arms, and looked at Niall. "She is yours?"

His son nodded. "Your granddaughter. We lend her
into your keeping." His lover bowed her head, and
Niall kissed her hair. Donal understood, then, why

she seemed sad. The Fey had good hearts for their own, and for humans, too, sometimes.

"She is yours now, in place of Niall," the queen said. "This is our bargain. She is called Eilidh—as her fairy name, it holds great power. She herself must tell it to another only once." *Ay-leth*, she pronounced it.

"Elspeth was my wife. I will call her that, and love her as if she were my own." He stepped back quickly, before they changed their capricious minds. The squirming bundle was dear to him already. Tears stung his eyes. "Niall—"

"I will see you again. Father, remember this—the power of the Fey flows through my daughter's veins, and the lure of this world will be strong for her. She will live with you in the Highlands until her twenty-first year. Then we will call her back to us."

"But she will be happy and thrive in the earthly realm," Donal said.

The queen shook her head. "She must return to us—unless you find our treasure, stolen from us long ago by one of your own name. Bring that to us, and the girl may stay with you. Though we will have one of you regardless, I promise you."

"Fairy treasure!" Donal said. "No one knows where that lies, or if the legend is even true." The Fey were given to exaggeration, he knew. *Daoine sìth,* they were called in the Gaelic—the people of peace. Yet they could be anything but peaceful if crossed.

"A MacArthur stole it from us." Her voice was cold as ice. "We will have it back, or we will take souls from this glen, as we have done since its disappearance—your treasure for ours. Somewhere in these hills, or in human halls, it lies," she went on, "and you will need two keys to open it. Here is the first one."

She pointed to the stone he had thrust into the rock. "You hold the other key in your arms."

"This child?" He was puzzled. "But where can I find the treasure?"

"If we knew that, we would not ask your help," she said irritably. "Fetch our treasure to escape our thrall. Return it." Her beautiful gaze held his. She lifted her arms.

Sensing her power igniting, Donal moved backward. "This is a wicked bargain. This child is half human, and should have her choice. There must be some other way to break this agreement."

"Love," Niall said suddenly. "That is the way to break all fairy spells, in the end. Love is the strongest magic in the earthly realm, as the Fey well know," he added, looking down at his own dark-haired lover.

"If our daughter should find true love," the child's mother said, "all spells around her will dissolve. But then she would not return to us. Do not let her fall in love, Donal MacArthur," she begged. "Never allow it. I want my child back."

He could not make such a promise, and he knew he must leave soon to protect the child. "Farewell, Niall," he said, stepping back again. His son nodded sadly. Shielding the infant with his plaid, Donal turned away from the glow of that shining world, toward the cold wind and moonlight.

Elspeth would never go back to them if he could prevent it, Donal thought as he hurried away with his granddaughter. Somehow he would keep her in the earthly realm. Though he himself was bound to return every seven years to the hillside portal, he would keep the little one safe from the glamour of the Seelie Court and the irresistible enchantment of her kind. Someday he would encourage her to find love, and to live with her husband far away from this place, to break any otherworldly hold. But what if love never came to her, and they took her from him, as they had taken Niall?

To spend forever in that realm—ah, no, he thought. Forever was too long.

Kilcrennan House, 1808

Elspeth sat beside her grandfather in a wing chair like his, the two chairs covered in green brocade and flanking the fire. She watched the small blue flames licking around the peat bricks, and traced her fingers over the worn, satiny textures on the chair's arms. Sitting proper and straight, as their housekeeper, Mrs. Graeme, had taught her, she smoothed the pale pink and white gingham of her dress and reached up to pat the green ribbon wound in her dark hair. She crossed her feet, in white stockings and tiny black slippers, and watched her grandfather.

He was studying the pages of a little leather book, the one where he kept all the notes and curious crisscross drawings for his weaving. He marked a page with his pencil, *scritch-scratch.*

"Grandda, will you teach me the weaving?"

"I will," he said, distracted.

She swung her feet like the clapper of a bell. "Tell me about the Fey again."

He smiled, looked up at her. "So beautiful," he replied. "Like you, hey. Quick-witted and joyful, like you. And fickle, which you would never be." She laughed, and he continued. "Remember, if the *daoine sìth* like us and love us, good fortune is ours."

"Only so long as they are pleased," she prodded, for she knew all his tales.

"True, if they become irritated, if they turn their hearts and their backs to us, their blessings and gifts will become curses. And we must never look back once we walk away from them, or we will be in their power forever. Such happened to . . . someone I know."

"Never look back," she repeated dutifully, nodding. "My father looked back."

He nodded sadly. "They love and live joyfully, but if they see a chance for power, they will take it. And they do not forgive easily, if ever. That's the Fey."

"What do they look like?" Elspeth had heard the stories many times and always delighted in them. She wanted to know more about the realm where her father lived. Her grandfather had a storyteller's way about him, so that even a repeated tale sounded new. "Tell me again."

"Some are as golden and sparkling as sunshine, and some as delicate and dark as midnight. You are like the dark ones," he added, reaching over to tap her knee. "Hair like gleaming jet, eyes the color of moonlight, and a small and perfect face. You are like your fairy mother, though you have your father's stubborn chin and his temperament, too, for you do not always listen to me or Mrs. Graeme." He looked stern for a moment.

Elspeth smiled. "I do not always obey you, but I listen very well."

"Like your father. Willful and smart, with a mind of your own."

"I wish I had known my parents," she said wistfully. "Grandda, let me try to guess what page you are looking at in your book." She closed her eyes. She liked this game well, for she often knew the answers. "That page says, *Blue, blue, green, green, and five threads of yellow for the weft threads.* It is MacArthur! You are looking at the pattern for our very own plaidie!" She opened her eyes.

"Very good," he said. "I do happen to be looking at the MacArthur plaid, because my cousin wants a new waistcoat."

She smiled. "Peggy Graeme says I have the Sight."

"Mrs. Graeme," he corrected gently. "And so you do. The fairies gave it to you."

"Perhaps someday if I try very hard, I will see where their gold is hidden, the gold that they want us to return to them. And when I do, they will be grateful, and be our friends forever, and my father will come back to us."

Her grandfather sighed. "I fear Niall and the treasure are lost forever, yet anything is possible." Then he returned to his notes. *Scritch, scratch.*

Elspeth looked into the leaping, delicate flames, and wondered if she could see fairies too, as Grandfather had done. She squeezed her eyes shut. Nothing. Sometimes she had lovely dreams, in which a handsome young man and a beautiful lady came to her, laughed with her, hugged her. She thought they were fairy people, but did not know. She closed her eyes again. Nothing appeared.

Someday she would see them herself, she thought.

Chapter 1

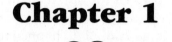

Scotland, Edinburgh
July 1822

F*airies!* You cannot possibly mean, sirs"—Patrick MacCarran leaned forward, knuckles pressed on the lawyers' desk—"that a parcel of blasted fairies stands between us and our inheritance!" He glanced at his three siblings, while the men behind the oak desk, one seated, the other standing, remained silent.

"We need not assume ruination." James MacCarran, Viscount Struan, gave a nonchalant shrug of his shoulders in good black serge as he spoke quietly. He deliberately maintained an unruffled demeanor and casual pose as he leaned against the doorframe of the lawyers' study, though he felt as stunned as the others. "Let Mr. Browne and Sir Walter finish before we decide that we are done for."

His siblings looked grim—his sister, Fiona, pale but

composed, while their younger brothers, William and Patrick, scowled. James preferred distance in most things, actual and emotional, and that served him well today. Scarcely a farthing would come to any of them from their grandmother unless the astonishing conditions of her will were met. Ruination very well could be in store for all of them, James thought.

"What could make this worse?" Patrick shoved a hand through his dark hair.

"A few elves might complement this disaster nicely," William murmured.

James huffed a curt laugh. William, his next younger brother, was a quiet-spoken physician who had hoped to open a hospital with his inheritance; Fiona, their sister, was an independent, serene woman with an academic bent for the study of fossil rock that made her any scholar's equal. Now Fiona stood to calm Patrick, a signet clerk with greater ambitions. The funds could support his younger siblings' dreams, James knew. As for himself, he was content with a professorship in geology; he had few real needs.

But what Grandmother unexpectedly, posthumously asked was untenable.

"Lady Struan's fortune will be divided, with conditions," Mr. Browne said. "Apart from your grandfather's estate at his death a few years ago, which was a modest sum after his considerable expenditures—"

"He helped ease the suffering of displaced Highlanders during the clearances of so many from their homes," Fiona said. "None of us begrudge his decisions."

Browne nodded. "Lady Struan acquired a personal fortune through publications and properties, which she allowed Lord Eldin, her adviser in those matters, to sell for her in the last few years. All but Struan House, which goes to James, who inherited his grandfather's title of Viscount Struan two years ago."

James leaned in the doorway, listening. As eldest grandson, he had inherited the title, for their father had died when he and Fiona had been nine, their brothers younger. Now a titled but less than wealthy peer, James had a modest bank account, and earned most of his living as a professor of natural philosophy at the University of Edinburgh.

He had mourned his grandmother privately, concealing his grief as was natural for him to do, and he had hoped that her fortune would ensure the future for his siblings, particularly his sister, as he himself could not adequately do as a penniless viscount.

But—*fairies*. James felt as bewildered as the others. He glanced at Patrick, who still seethed; Fiona, her air of serenity overcoming what was sometimes a fiery temper; and William, who sat with steepled fingertips, brow furrowed beneath golden hair, as skilled at hiding his thoughts as James. As a boy, James had kept himself to himself while mourning the deaths of his parents and the separation of his siblings into other homes—William and Patrick to uncles, James and Fiona to a great-aunt. He had never entirely emerged from that self-imposed exile of the heart, and he preferred it that way.

William cleared his throat. "Grandmother was fond of fairy tales and scribbled some of her own, but it is surprising that she took it that seriously."

Fiona sat beside William with a graceful swirl of black satin, her bonnet's curved rim highlighting her pretty face and wispy brown curls. Gazing at his twin sister, James suddenly knew what she would say next. *A kerfuffle*—

"It's a kerfuffle," she said, "but we shall resolve it." She smiled tightly.

Did he so often guess her words from sheer logic, or the bond of twinship? A question to ponder another time, he thought, when the scientific reason he preferred could reign cool and supreme. The situation was more than a kerfuffle. It was a disaster.

"I wonder if Grandmother was fully capable when she decided these conditions," Patrick said. "Not to imply that anyone influenced her, for we know she was stubborn. But she was very ill, at the last. William, as one of her physicians, what say you?"

William sat up a little. "Her condition made her increasingly frail, but her mind seemed balanced. I noticed no diminished faculties. James would agree—he saw Grandmother a good bit in the past year, when she was in the house on Charlotte Square."

"She never mentioned the will," James answered, "but she always knew her mind. I never doubted her faculties." He rented a house near his grandmother's town house on Charlotte Square, where she had lived during the last months of her illness, and had seen her a good deal during that time, and they had grown closer than before.

"I regret I was not able to confide in you, though I knew of Lady Struan's plan." Sir Walter Scott smiled a little sadly, James noticed. The poet and author had long been a friend to Lady Struan, and though James did not know Sir Walter well himself, he admired the man's genius and generosity.

"Grandmother so enjoyed your visits, Sir Walter," Fiona said. "We appreciate your attentions to her.

She looked forward to King George's arrival in Edinburgh, too. It is tragic and ironic that she died before the great event."

Sir Walter nodded. "She enthusiastically helped me plan the festivities. I am sure she will be there in spirit for the king's jaunt next month."

"We will be there in her honor," James said. "Let us hear the rest of Grandmother's fairy scheme, if you will, Mr. Browne."

"Aye. Lady Struan's executor, Sir Walter, consulted with her at length, and we know there is no more estimable or trustworthy gentleman in all Scotland."

Sir Walter Scott shook his head slightly, a modest fellow, James thought; all Scotland and indeed England might agree with Mr. Browne. "Go on, sir," James said.

"Now that the will has been read, there are only a few points to discuss further. Each of you has some individual conditions." Browne turned a few pages. "These obligations must be fulfilled. Lady Struan stipulated that if one of you fails to comply, everyone fails to comply."

"What if we do not meet the conditions?" Patrick asked.

"Then most of the inheritance will go to another party." Mr. Browne took up a stack of folded and sealed letters and handed them around with Sir Walter's assistance, the author using his cane as he limped around the desk to present a packet to Fiona with a small bow, while James, Patrick, and William got letters, too.

"Once the conditions are met," Mr. Browne continued, "you will each receive an equal share of Lady Struan's fortune—approximately fifty thousand pounds apiece. However, your portions could be reduced to five thousand pounds if you forgo the conditions of the will."

In the dumbstruck silence that followed, James looked down at his own letter. *The Right Hon. The Viscount Struan,* read the outside of the page. Written in a clerk's hand, not his grandmother's—she would have called him James, or James Arthur MacCarran if she was displeased. He smiled a bit ruefully.

"If you wish, open the letters now, or wait," Mr. Browne said. "Share the contents among yourselves, but please keep them private otherwise. The requests must be adhered to exactly, or the inheritance reverts to the lesser amount."

"Well, I will not wait," Patrick peeled open the seal, unfolded the page, and read quickly and silently. "Ah. I am to help win back Duncrieff Castle, lost to debts ten years past. But—what the devil! I must make a love match for myself, with someone of . . . fairy blood." He looked at the others in disbelief. "It's absurd! How could I do that?"

"Lady Struan asked me to advise you in that," Sir Walter said. "Your grandmother was a considered expert on fairy lore, as you know, having written more than one book on folklore and superstition."

"Given Grandmother's beliefs, it's not surprising," William said. He folded his page and slipped it into a pocket. "I've been asked to do something similar. James?"

Frowning, James held the unopened paper in his hand. He wanted to escape this meeting and return to his geological studies; he had a journal article to complete on evidence of ancient heat at the earth's core, and he had a lecture to prepare for his university classes in natural philosophy and geology. He did not want to wait on this matter of the will any further, though he had little choice.

After the events he had endured at Waterloo years before, he had decided to lead as dull a life as possible—numbingly boring, lacking risk, involvement, and emotion, to the best of his ability. He had experienced enough drama and excess for a lifetime. Safe, dull—he had made himself appreciate its merits, if he could not enjoy it.

Marrying a fairy, even a supposed one, would not be part of the satisfyingly dull bachelor existence he had planned for himself.

Fiona slipped her letter into her black net reticule. "I am to continue the charitable work that I've been doing, teaching English to Gaelic-speaking Highlanders," she said. "I am also expected to marry a Highland gentleman with fortune and breeding. Nothing to dispute there," she said with a smile. "But I must also draw fairy images from life. That's unlikely, either finding fairies, or drawing them well." She laughed. "But the drawings are for James. Why so?"

His siblings, and the lawyers, all looked at him. Sighing, James opened his letter, studied its contents, while a muscle bounced in his jaw. "I am expected . . . to stay at Struan House as its viscount," he said, "and complete the book that Grandmother was working on before her death. I don't know what book it is, though."

"Grandmother's big book of fairies," Patrick drawled. "She was writing something of the sort. Certainly not a topic to suit Professor MacCarran, who has written a thick tome on geologic strata." He smiled wryly.

"What else?" Fiona, as usual, knew when he was withholding something.

"And I am to marry a Highland bride of fairy descent," James admitted.

"Good Lord, all of us," Patrick said, shaking his head.

"What if we cannot meet these requirements, Mr. Browne?" Fiona asked. "Who would inherit the bulk of Grandmother's accounts?"

Mr. Browne glanced at the page. "Nicholas Mac-Carran, Earl of Eldin."

"Cousin Nick," Patrick growled, "that damnable, rotten, scheming scoundrel—sorry, Fiona," he apologized.

"The lying rogue," Fiona continued, "who stole our clan seat, Duncrieff Castle, away from our chief, his own cousin, after his death at Waterloo. Even now Nicholas enjoys the profits of that estate, while we—" She stopped, looking away. James knew that she still felt a keen heartbreak over their cousin's death—after all, their young chief, Archibald MacCarran, had been Fiona's betrothed.

"Nick called it a good business arrangement," Patrick said, scowling.

"So if we do not comply, Eldin inherits all," James said, low and flat.

"But for the lesser funds apportioned to each of you, yes," Mr. Browne said.

"Why would Grandmother do this?" Fiona asked.

"So that we would meet her conditions," James drawled.

"Your grandmother was working on a book about Highland fairy lore," Sir Walter said. "She hoped to restore the legendary fairy luck of the Mac-

Carrans, which she feared had become dilute over generations."

William snorted. "I could find any Highland lass and call her part fairy."

"That is why Lady Struan asked me to help," Sir Walter said. "She wanted you to do this—or it all goes to Lord Eldin. Let that be your incentive," he added.

James stepped away from the door. Write a damned fairy book and find a fairy bride, of all things. He did not want a wife of any sort yet. The fortune itself meant little to him, but his siblings had scant resources for their own plans and futures. And like the others, he wanted to be sure that the funds were protected from Lord Eldin, the only man he had ever truly despised.

He should have shot the blackguard when he had the chance.

"I must go," he said abruptly. "A meeting at the university. And now, it seems, I shall have to request a sabbatical. Until later, then." He bowed his head, made his farewells. Snatching up his cane, he turned and limped away.

Chapter 2

Edinburgh, Scotland
August 1822

Lifting the embroidered, flounced satin of her silver-blue court dress in one gloved hand, Elspeth MacArthur moved with a surge of overdressed, perfumed women, and glanced around for Lucie Graeme. She had lost sight of her cousin in the sea of satins, silks, damask, lace, jewels, feathers, and Highland tartan. The feathers in her own hair felt as if they were slipping loose from her dark curls, held in place by pearled pins. She lifted a hesitant hand to that softness and looked around.

The press of the crowd was unbearably warm and close. Perhaps she should flee entirely, Elspeth thought, like Lady Graeme, Lucie's mother, who only moments before had pleaded faintness, and had been quickly escorted out by Sir John, Lucie's brother. And then Lucie, following them, had been swallowed in the spectacle: more than two thousand ladies and gentlemen were crammed into a few rooms and corridors in Holyroodhouse, while each Scottish lady awaited her chance to be presented to King George the Fourth, lately arrived in Scotland.

With Lady Graeme taken ill, Elspeth wondered how she and Lucie would be introduced to the king, since only those who had met King George previously had the right to introduce ladies to him today. Oh for the gift of vanishing just now, Elspeth thought, looking around—if only such were possible. Her grandfather claimed that the purest fairy blood ran in her veins, and could give her wonderful abilities, but she had her doubts about all of that. To be sure, she did have a touch of Second Sight, but it was inconvenient more than magical, and the Sight was common enough in the Highlands.

No intuition had warned her to keep clear of the palace on this long, hot day, where the waiting had been interminable, and the reason for coming—greeting the king—now looked to be canceled altogether for Elspeth and Lucie.

She was glad that her grandfather had let business meetings keep him away, though he would have relished the event, dressing to the teeth in tartan of his own make, as the Highland laird and weaver he was, and he would have spun exuberant tales of his early smuggling days and his personal encounters with fairies. And he would have soundly embarrassed their Edinburgh cousins, Elspeth was sure; Donal MacArthur was like strong whiskey, best taken in small quantities.

He had insisted that Elspeth go in the company of her cousins. "What other chance will you ever have to meet Fat Geordie?" he had boomed, shushing her protests.

None at all, now, she thought, as she edged through clusters of women dressed like plumed, chattering birds, all waiting to meet Fat Geordie, as many Highlanders called the king, formerly the Prince Regent. The men accompanying the ladies wore either tartaned splendor or austere black and white. Most ignored her as she passed, though she caught several interested male glances as she walked through the crowd until she neared the huge set of doors at the far end of the room. The entrance to the reception room was guarded by Royal Archers in green; inside, the king greeted hundreds of Scottish ladies one by one with their small escort parties.

Elspeth wished he would just greet them all at once and have done with it.

Bumping against the lush, satin-draped curves of a large woman, she stumbled in her borrowed slippers, and clutched the gauzy flounces of her gown to keep from tripping further. The confection of a gown, sheer silk over pale blue satin, the layers embroidered in silver, had been remade from a gown belonging to Lucie. Avoiding another woman, Elspeth turned again, only to connect with the angular jut of a male elbow.

"I beg your pardon, madam," came a deep, murmured apology. A solid arm clothed in smooth black wool brushed her bare shoulder, and a hand came swiftly to her elbow in support, while she leaned inadvertently against the man.

Elspeth looked up at the tall stranger. His broad chest and wide shoulders were clothed in a fine black coat, cream brocade waistcoat, and snowy neck cloth.

Afternoon sunlight, cascading from tall windows, gilded his brown hair. She glimpsed a firm jawline, straight nose, the slant of sideburns. His touch, through her ivory elbow glove, was warm, strong, brief—and made her heart jump a little.

"Pardon," he repeated.

"Quite all right, sir," she answered. "The crowd—"

"So true. Enchanted," he murmured in farewell, as he moved past her. The mingled scents of spicy soap, of green and outdoors, wafted after him. Elspeth closed her eyes, took a breath. Something about the man heightened her senses.

Indeed, for suddenly she felt light-headed, the odd sensation that sometimes preceded a "knowing," when the Sight spontaneously showed her images or told her truths about others. Touch could trigger it, and the gentleman had just grasped her arm.

Oh please, not now, she thought. When the Sight came over her, sometimes her tongue loosened with it, so that she spoke her mind too freely. She could not make a fool of herself here. Rising on her toes, feeling a little anxious, she was relieved to finally see Lucie in the crowd, looking around as she did. Elspeth hurried toward her.

"Oh, Lucie," she said. "How is Lady Graeme feeling?"

"There you are!" Lucie linked arms with her. "Mother is better now that she's out of the crowd. John left her with friends for a few moments and came back with me—but Sir John did not attend the Gentlemen's Assembly the other day, and so cannot introduce us himself. But he's found a substitute. You look as lovely as Cinderella at the ball," she added, patting Elspeth's arm, "and we will find you a prince today!"

"Aye? If it were midnight, I could go home," El-speth said. "Any prince would expect me to live in the Lowlands, and I intend to stay in the Highlands. But Grandfather is determined to marry me off to some Lowlander—that's why he brought me here to Edinburgh, I think. Not for the king, but to find a prince." She made a face, and Lucie laughed.

"You are both stubborn. Come with me. John has arranged for his friend Lord Struan to introduce us."

"Struan?" Elspeth looked quickly at Lucie. "Is he from the Highlands? Struan House sits at the head of our glen—"

"He's a Lowlander I think, but possibly he has inherited there. He is a viscount now." Lucie leaned toward her. "And he could be anyone's prince, if he wasn't such a scowler. Even John says so. Struan teaches at the university, and John attended some of his lectures. Lord Struan is very knowledgeable, says John, though somber. Still, he's a catch, and does not attend many social events, so it is pure luck to see him here."

"I am not looking for a catch. I shall be a spinster." Her grandfather wanted her to make a good marriage in the South, but that went against her own dreams.

"You are not suited to spinsterhood," Lucie said. "But you will never find the right match to please you or your grandfather if you stay in the Highlands weaving your tartan and rarely coming to the city. Nearly two years have passed since we made our debut together here in Edinburgh, and I've gone to many parties, and even had a few suitors, and still no one pleases, quite. Truculent fellows. Look, there's John with Viscount Struan."

"Perhaps you will find a prince instead—" Elspeth stopped, and stared.

Beside Cousin John, whose blond handsomeness, in severe black and white, made him look near angelic, stood a tall gentleman—the same man who had brushed against her earlier, and had made her heart flutter madly. But that was nothing to do with him, she told herself; just the close crowd, the August heat, and too few open windows.

The viscount stood with John, both dressed in black and white, and as she walked forward with Lucie, she studied him a little. He had a classically balanced profile, his hair thick and golden brown, his dark sideburns emphasizing the stern set of his jaw. He was tall enough to lean slightly as he listened, and despite his sober expression, his features had a touch of beauty. But she would not tell Lucie that, and sound like a romantic ninny.

"He is indeed a scowler," Elspeth whispered.

"But so handsome. Let him frown, it suits him," Lucie said.

"The room is full of handsome gentlemen, John among them," Elspeth replied.

Now the strange feeling returned—she felt lightheaded, even breathless. She felt as if a knowing might come over her—either that, or the oppressive air in the room was finally too much. She flapped her painted ivory-and-paper fan a bit frantically.

Lucie, with feathers in her blond hair and wearing a flounced pale pink gown, was not the delicate porcelain doll she appeared as she pulled Elspeth forward through clusters of women, where shawls slipped from smooth shoulders, pearls and jewels flashed, and the wider hooped skirts peculiar to court dress swung gently.

"Ah, ladies," John said, smiling. "Lord Struan, may I introduce my sister, Miss Lucie Graeme, and our cousin, Miss Elspeth MacArthur of Kilcrennan."

"Charmed," Struan said, taking Lucie's gloved hand and then Elspeth's. She offered her fingers to him and looked up.

Breathless indeed. She felt as if she had come face-to-face with a magnificent warrior angel come to life. Standing in a shaft of sunlight, the man was even more attractive than she had realized, with clean masculine features and wavy chestnut hair liberally threaded with gold. His eyes, brilliant blue, seemed cool and reserved.

"Miss MacArthur," he said, his voice deep and quiet, a harmonic comfort in the cacophony of the room. "Kilcrennan sounds familiar."

"Her grandfather, our cousin, owns Kilcrennan Weavers," John supplied.

"Ah. Excellent cloth, I've heard it said. Sir, I would be delighted to include your sister and cousin in my own party until you return." The viscount inclined his head.

"Thank you, Struan," John said, and within moments, took polite leave of them.

"We appreciate this very much, Lord Struan," Lucie said. "We are so excited to be here. King George is the first British monarch to visit Scotland since Charles the Second, I believe," she went on in an overly bright tone. "I wonder how long before we will be admitted to the reception room."

"Not long, Miss Graeme," Struan answered. "The crowd seems to have inched forward in the past hour." Elspeth raised her fan to hide a smile.

"We waited simply hours," Lucie said, "first in that awful line of carriages—miles long, that was—and then these dreadful crowds in the palace rooms. It is taking all day. But we shall soon have our introductions, and our kiss."

Elspeth blinked. "Kiss?" She glanced at Struan— could not help it, though she did not want to, so pointedly. The viscount was watching her with those cool blue eyes.

"Every lady here will receive a kiss of courtesy from the king," Lucie said.

"Are we expected to swoon?" Elspeth said, without thinking.

"Not at all, Miss MacArthur," Struan said, looking mildly amused. He offered an arm to each of them, and Elspeth took his left, noticing that he carried a cane, as did many fashionable men, this one hooked above her hand at his elbow. A slight limp favored his left leg, she saw—unlike many, he required the cane's assistance. She frowned, wondering at the cause of it.

Suddenly she knew why; as her hand lightly touched his arm, Elspeth saw a quick image in her mind of men running, falling, and smoke drifting over a field, while explosions sounded faintly. Then it was gone, and she gasped. "Oh—the war—"

Struan looked down. "Miss MacArthur? Pardon, I did not hear what you said."

"N-nothing," she said, flushing with embarrassment. Lucie leaned to peer at her, puzzled, and Elspeth looked away. Though she had known Lucie all her life, she had told her city cousin little about her gift of Sight. Lucie, with her good heart and practical head, was not very curious about such things.

Struan guided them toward an elderly woman standing with two young women, all silk and feathers, elegance and hauteur. Two gentlemen stood with them, one in somber black, the other in a red plaid Highland kilt, jacket, bonnet, sporran, and socks. The outfit even included the *sgian dubh*, or small black knife, tucked in the top of his sock. Yet Elspeth sensed that he was not a Highlander.

When Struan made quick introductions, Elspeth barely caught the names. "My great-aunt, Lady Rankin of Kelso, my sister, Miss Fiona MacCarran, and Miss Charlotte Sinclair. My brother, Dr. William MacCarran. And Sir Philip Rankin."

"Pleased," Lady Rankin said, not sounding so. She was tall and buxom in cream silk trimmed in chocolate brown flounces, the skirt filled out by wide hoops, though fashion no longer required it in court dress; her white-plumed headdress made her look like an eight-foot tall ostrich, Elspeth thought. Feeling like a pale mouse by comparison, she lifted her chin and smiled.

Both Struan and his brother were impeccably dressed in black cutaway coats and trousers, with waistcoat and neck cloths of white and cream. Not a hint of thistle, heather, tartan, or lightheartedness about them, though Sir Philip wore a bright red plaid. The ladies all wore formal court dress, though Fiona's dress was of somber plum satin with touches of black, as if for mourning. Elspeth tilted her head, wondering who had passed away to affect the siblings and not the others.

Ah, Lady Struan, she remembered, wondering if the kind, elderly lady of that estate, an acquaintance of her grandfather's who had passed away earlier that summer, was related to Struan and his siblings. *Grandmother,* the word came to her then, and she bit her lip to keep from saying it aloud.

"Where is Kilcrennan located, Miss MacArthur?" Lady Rankin asked.

"In the Trossach Mountains, madam, in the central Highlands."

"Oh yes! We are planning a trip there soon, to visit my nephew in his new estate," Lady Rankin said. "We hope to tour Loch Katrine and the other sights described in Sir Walter Scott's marvelous poetry. They say the views are magnificent."

"Truly beautiful," Elspeth agreed.

"I was not aware that you plan to travel north, Aunt," Struan said.

"Did I neglect to mention it? I am quite excited. The Highlands are marvelous to behold in the autumn. I have persuaded Miss Sinclair to accompany me, with perhaps Sir Philip or your cousin Nicholas as our traveling companions."

"Fiona," Struan said to his sister. "If Aunt travels north, do come with her." Elspeth thought she detected a pleading tone in his voice.

"I shall try," Fiona MacCarran replied.

"So you know the area, Miss MacArthur?" Struan asked then.

"Very well. Loch Katrine and Struan House are not far from the glen where I live with my grandfather."

"Then you will not be far from Struan House."

"Not too far—several miles along the same glen. My grandfather knew the late viscountess, and I met her myself. We were distressed to hear of her passing."

"Thank you." Struan inclined his head. "She was

our grandmother." He indicated his siblings in his answer; Fiona smiled, and Dr. MacCarran nodded.

"James is now Viscount Struan." Charlotte Sinclair slipped her arm through his. "But he has so little time to visit there—perhaps for an occasional hunting party, isn't that right, James? He is so busy as a professor in natural philosophy at the university."

Elspeth nodded, smiled, and knew she was being warned away. Miss Sinclair practically glowered at her above the rim of her delicate white fan.

"Actually I have arranged to take a brief absence from my lectures," Struan said.

"What sort of natural philosophy do you teach?" Lucie asked. "There is so very much *of* it."

"Geology, Miss Graeme," he answered.

"Ah. We have rather a lot of rock in the Trossachs," Elspeth said.

Struan suppressed a smile. "Rather a lot of rock sounds intriguing."

"Miss MacArthur, forgive me," Lady Rankin said. "I do not recall your debut."

"It was nothing to notice, madam," Elspeth said. "I attended a hunt ball in Edinburgh two years ago in the company of my cousins, the Graemes of Lincraig."

"I do recall that," Charlotte Sinclair said. "I attended with the family of the Lord Provost Mayor. I remember Sir John Graeme, but I do not remember you." She glanced with a coy smile at the viscount. "Dear Struan was not there. He simply could not attend every ball for every new girl," she told Elspeth in loud confidence, "though he had inherited a fine title, and has an excellent reputation at the university, so he is in great demand at parties and outings. He turns down more invitations than he accepts."

"Because I am not one for social functions," he said, "though had I known Miss MacArthur and Miss Graeme then, I would have made the effort." Struan smiled at Elspeth, and Miss Sinclair frowned. "Ah, we may now advance to the doors."

He extended an arm to Lady Rankin, and offered his elbow to Elspeth. She tucked her hand in the crook of his arm, feeling the solid muscle beneath. Behind them, his brother and Sir Philip escorted Lucie, Fiona, and Charlotte.

They approached the doorway where the Royal Archers stood, bows crossed. Once invitations were shown, the doors were opened and they were waved through.

Beyond the crowd preceding them, Elspeth could see the king, taller than most men there, resplendent in black and white with a sash of red Stewart plaid. Elspeth smiled to herself, aware that the plaid presented to the king that week was of Kilcrennan make, woven by her grandfather, with the help of fairy craft.

Glancing at Lord Struan, she wondered what he, or anyone, would make of that.

He seemed the sort of somber, perfect gentleman who would think fairies utter nonsense, yet she felt a wayward urge to confide in him. Instead, she pressed her lips together in silence, lifted her head, and glided into the receiving room on Lord Struan's arm as if she were a princess, and he, indeed, her prince—just for the moment.

Noticing the increased pressure of the girl's fingers on his arm, James glanced down at Miss MacArthur. "Nervous?" he asked.

"A bit," she admitted. "I do hope my manners are adequate for this."

"Why so?" He watched her, entranced by her beautiful eyes—gray-green, almost silver. Her heart-shaped face was framed by hair so glossy black, silken-rich, that he wanted to touch it. The lovely creature had such a natural allure that he looked at her again and again, as if he could take sustenance from her pure and unassuming beauty. A fragile quality, coupled with a touch of fire, made him feel protective and intrigued all at once. He knew Charlotte, just behind them, must be fuming. "Your manners are perfect."

"I am a native Gaelic speaker," she said. "I do not have the refined English of Edinburgh, let alone England, and I am not accustomed to elegant gatherings."

"I rather like your accent," he murmured. Her soft, graceful manner of speech was refreshing in this gathering of boisterous, Englishified Scots. "You would shine in any gathering, Miss MacArthur, like a diamond. Here we go, then."

They were announced by a footman who led their party forward, heels tapping on the parquet floor. Tall King George was portly in black cutaway and trousers, white waistcoat, and military touches on his costume in plaid sash, badges, and epaulets. James, coming closer, could see the traces of excessive lifestyle in the king's jowly face and doughy complexion; the royal voice was loud, deep, and surprisingly pleasant.

James quietly introduced the ladies in his party, and as each was presented, King George gave the lady a kiss on the cheek, quick passing brushes that barely touched. "Pleased," the king said to Lady Rankin, "enchanted. Charmed."

"Miss Elspeth MacArthur of Kilcrennan," James said. The girl stepped forward and made a pretty curtsy, bowing her head, dark curls teasing her slender neck, feathers bobbing. When she rose, King George leaned to kiss her cheek; James heard the moist smack of it from where he stood.

"Pleased," the king said, his gaze traveling down, then up to her face. "Lovely."

"Your Majesty," she murmured, bowing her head.

James introduced the others, then led Miss Mac-Arthur and Lady Rankin toward the man waiting in the receiving line beside the king. Sir Walter Scott, a tall man with gray-blond hair and an amiable face, greeted James with a nimble smile.

"Struan, excellent to see you here," he said, extending a hand.

"And you, sir," James said. "Sir Walter Scott, you know Lady Rankin. And this is Miss MacArthur of Kilcrennan."

"Oh sir, I am very pleased to meet you," Elspeth MacArthur said, sounding genuinely delighted. "I so admire your poetry and your work on ballads. I particularly favor *The Lady of the Lake,* since I live not far from Loch Katrine. You make it all seem so very romantical." She blushed.

"My dear, I am flattered by the opinion of a true Highland lady." Scott took her gloved hand in his own. Then James saw Miss MacArthur turn pale and gasp.

"Oh dear, oh dear," she said. "The Waverley novels," she blurted. "They are all yours, Sir Walter—"

"I do not claim to be the author of those books, miss. Rather, I am a poet—"

"But sir, they are all yours, and soon the world will know and be glad of it. Your next story will be about . . . Nigel . . . and, aye, Quentin," she said. "It will be some of your best work—oh! I beg your pardon!" She tried to pull her gloved hand away, but Sir Walter held her fingers tightly and leaned toward her.

"How did you know about the books, and the new manuscripts?" he murmured.

"Sir, truly, I did not mean to offend." She looked distressed. James tightened his fingers on her elbow, uncertain what was happening. Beside him, Lady Rankin gasped in horror, and glanced at Charlotte. Lucie Graeme flapped her fan and looked mortified.

"What is it, over there?" the king boomed, looking toward them.

"Your Majesty, only a visit among friends," Sir Walter answered mildly. "My dear," he then whispered fervently, "you have the Sight, am I correct?"

"Sir, I—" The girl looked around, flustered.

"Miss MacArthur, we must go." James tugged gently on her arm.

"Farewell, sir," she told Scott, then let go of James's arm and took up her skirts to hasten away.

"James, were I you," Scott murmured, "I'd pursue that lass. She's a rare treasure."

"Sir," James said. He would pursue her, to be sure—to find out what the devil she had been going on about. Handing his great-aunt over to William, he turned. The girl had slipped through the press of chattering people and into the corridor beyond, but bobbing white feathers and a jet gloss of hair were easy to follow. Catching up to her, he snatched her arm and guided her toward an anteroom he saw just off the corridor.

"Come with me," he said sternly, marching beside her, his cane tapping as they walked. The smaller room was quieter than the other areas. Tall ferns and potted rhododendrons were arranged around the room with large vases of fragrant roses. The room was thick with that mingled, natural perfume.

He pulled her behind some rhododendrons and roses, and glared down at her. "What the devil was that all about?" he demanded.

She stared up at him. "What?"

Glowering, waiting for her to relent, he realized that he was disappointed. She was so lovely, delectable really, yet not the innocent she seemed, having done such a scheming thing. Her beautiful eyes distracted him, but he would not look away. "Miss MacArthur, Sir Walter keeps his identity as a novelist secret. I do not know your game here, but—"

"No game. The knowledge of it just came to me. I never meant to offend."

"Sir Walter seems convinced that you have the Sight. It is a poor joke to play on a gentleman who has such a beneficial passion for Highland lore."

"But I do have the Sight," she said.

"It may amuse you to fool others, but I will not tolerate a mockery of my friends."

"Sometimes I simply . . . know things, and then I say them." She drew a breath and stared up at him, her remarkable eyes flashing. "But you, sir, are rude to accuse and confront me so."

Frowning at her, about to answer, he glanced up

when his party entered the room. "Oh, there you are, James!" Fiona called.

"I am shocked!" Charlotte said, strolling in with Lady Rankin. "Outraged!"

Elspeth MacArthur glanced up at James. "I suppose I am ruined now."

"Nonsense," he said. "I have scarcely touched you." He knew what she meant, but he still wanted to determine the reason for her behavior.

Charlotte and Lady Rankin approached, headdress feathers waving, silk and satin trains sliding like plumed tails. "That was no proper kiss at all from the king," Charlotte said. "I expected something much more genteel and memorable."

"You cannot expect something romantical from the king," Lucie reasoned.

"Struan!" Sir Philip peered behind the rhododendron. "And Miss MacArthur! What are you doing back there? We fellows must make up the deficit for the ladies. Like so!" Leaning toward Charlotte, he kissed her quickly on the lips.

"Oh!" Charlotte swatted him with her fan, but giggled.

"And one for you," Sir Philip said, turning to Fiona, who offered her cheek. William bent toward Lucie, who dimpled and smiled as he kissed her cheek.

Though Lady Rankin huffed indignantly, she laughed when William kissed her cheek next. Standing close beside Miss MacArthur, wrapped in the sweet scent of the flowers, James saw others in the room begin to share kisses, as young women coyly complained, and young men obliged with proper kissing, amid laughter and flirting.

"It seems no one is satisfied with the royal kiss," Lady Rankin said.

"Not Scottish women," Fiona said, and Charlotte and Lucie laughed.

"What of the Highland lass in our party?" Sir Philip asked. "I will do the honors, since I am dressed in proper Highland fashion." He came around the potted plants to kiss Elspeth MacArthur, quick and moist on the lips. He grinned, pleased, and stepped back.

The girl smiled, though James stood beside her and felt himself go still. No reason to feel jealous of that bit of silliness, he told himself—and yet he did.

"Look," Charlotte said, "the Countess of Argyll has accepted a kiss from the Earl of Huntly. No one shall be left out of the game now." They moved off to watch, leaving James and Miss MacArthur alone again, behind a screen of roses and rhododendrons.

"So, was that a proper kiss Rankin gave you?" he asked curtly.

"Not really, but we will let him think so." She looked up to meet his intense gaze. "Not that I am a judge of kissing. Well, there was the draw-lad when I was a girl."

"What in blazes is a draw-lad?" He knew he sounded irritated.

"The boy who pulls the yarn on the big looms. We have both large looms and hand looms at Kilcrennan. But those kisses were not proper, either, I suppose—"

"Hush." The urge welled so quickly in him that he obeyed it without thinking, taking her small chin in his fingers. "This is a proper kiss." He touched his lips to hers.

Surprising. Tender. Breathtaking and heartbreaking all at once, just for an instant, so that something spun inside him like a whirligig. He had not intended it—that simple kiss took him like a storm. He drew back, and felt her quivering hand on his forearm.

"Oh," she gasped. "Oh—" She tilted her face upward for more.

"Aye," he murmured, and leaned down again. This time his lips lingered, warm and firm over hers, and he took her by the small of her waist through the yardage of silks and satins. The big flowering plants shielded them from view, and the girl grabbed his coat sleeve, making a soft little sound in her throat. He felt as if he had stepped off a cliff with his eyes closed, as if he took a small, forbidden moment of hungry bliss.

Drawing in a breath, he pulled her closer to him, and she sighed against his mouth, felt her body press against his, wildly enticing, and she groaned softly as he slid his hand along her back, from the small of her waist upward, until his fingertips skimmed the warm, soft skin over her shoulder blade. She caught her breath, his body surged—

James dropped his hands away. "I beg your pardon. Thoughtless of me."

She still clutched his sleeve. Letting go, she stepped away. "Good day . . . Lord Struan, thank you for"— she did not look at him—"your kindness today."

"Miss MacArthur," he murmured in farewell, knowing full well he craved to pursue the moment, and the girl; his body pulsed, and by her sweet response, she wanted more of this, too. Yet he should never have let things go even this far. Steeling himself, inclining his head, he stepped back. "Good day."

With a murmur, she glided away, then glanced back, her eyes haunting somehow. He would not forget their beautiful color and depth, or their provocative owner. A moment later, she vanished into the glittering sea of people.

Chapter 3

J ames heard the shriek as he stepped over the threshold. Unexpected, unnerving, the sound seemed to come from vaguely overhead in the foyer where he stood. Somewhere in the large, drafty old house, a dog howled as if in answer. James set down his leather satchel, straightened, and looked upward. A creaking door or old floorboards, he thought, or hinges in need of repair—

The eldritch moan sounded again, ending on a shrill note that sent shivers down his neck. Once more the dog howled, and a second one barked. James looked around the dim, quiet foyer. "What in blazes," he muttered.

His introduction as Struan's sole owner and viscount was not particularly promising: ghostly shrieks, dogs baying, and here he stood, drenched by a chill September rain with no staff greeting him. If the work awaiting him proceeded smoothly, he promised himself, he need stay only a few weeks.

Once again, as he had done too often lately, he wondered if he would see Elspeth MacArthur while he was at Struan. She had said that her family home was in this glen, and try as he might, he had not forgotten her. She lingered in his thoughts, his dreams.

He was haunted by the memory of a few simple kisses, of sparkling, seductive eyes. He could almost taste her lips under his, could almost feel her in his arms—not enough to satisfy, and thankfully not enough to fall in love like a damn fool. Yet inexplicably, enough to drive him mad with wanting to see her again.

Sir Walter had not helped the matter any. "Miss MacArthur is an intriguing young lady. When you go to Struan House, be sure to seek her out. Find that one, James."

Well, James told himself, he had come to Struan House for other things, and would have no time to locate or visit Kilcrennan. Pulling off his gloves, he crammed them into a pocket, brushed the rain from the shoulders of his coat, took off his hat and shook it a little. Far too much damned rain lately, he thought.

Eyes gray as rain—there, his mind did it again, made that little leap when his thoughts were nowhere near the matter of the girl. He was obsessed, and disliked it.

Perhaps he would seek her out, he told himself, to ask what mad spell she had put on him, and why she had pulled a despicable ruse on his friend Scott. The poet was the one obsessed with finding her—not James. There. Though seeing her in ordinary circumstances, when she was not all got up like a fairy princess, would certainly dissolve this damnable distraction.

"Halloo!" He glanced around the foyer, a spacious area floored in slate and lined in dark wood paneling. A wide stairway against one wall was balanced by a huge marble fireplace on the other. Above the mantel, the heads of stags and hares contrasted with the angels carved in the fireplace surround. The foyer walls were hung with antique weapons as well, and some small paintings of landscapes and dog portraits.

He thought of the beasts who had howled as he entered, and remembered the stories of ghosts and eldritch creatures he had enjoyed when he had visited here as a boy. He had forgotten how spooky Struan House could seem. But he was an adult now, a thorough skeptic, a calm and unruffled soul who allowed nothing to make him anxious. Not even this place.

"Halloo!" he called again, his voice echoing. When he moved forward, the shrieking came again, a distant, bloodcurdling sound that lifted the fine hairs along his neck. He glanced up, turned around, and wondered what the hell was going on.

Days earlier, he had traveled to Stirling and beyond by landau, entering the foothills of the Highlands to stop at an inn at Callander, where the roads were still good. After a night's rest, he dispatched his driver back to Edinburgh. Then he spent a solitary day walking the countryside, finding some interesting formations of mica-schist which answered to the bite of the small hammer he had carried with him. He made notes on the finds that night and had a quiet dinner, enjoying more than he would admit to anyone the Highland atmosphere. Next morning the ghillie from Struan House had arrived to fetch him in an old but serviceable carriage pulled by a pair of sturdy bays.

Angus MacKimmie was a grizzled, bearded fellow in an ancient and rumpled red kilt and a threadbare brown jacket and bonnet. He had offered to carry James's satchel into the house, but James had released him to the task of tending the horses. When no butler appeared, James had let himself in the front door to stand in the echoing foyer.

That large, dim space was made even gloomier by the silvery sheen of rain through tall windows. "Where the devil is everyone," he muttered.

Somewhere in the shadows past the staircase, a door creaked, and a large gray wolfhound approached on rangy legs. Pausing to give a throaty woof, he then sniffed at the new viscount. James patted the dog's head. "Not only fairies and eerie screeches, but now fairy hounds, hey?"

The dog pushed his head under James's hand to ask for more petting. The eerie sound echoed again, miserable and faint, and the hound whimpered. Was it a creaking floor, or a madwoman trapped somewhere? James could not fathom it.

"'Kirk-Alloway is drawing nigh . . . where ghaists and houlets nightly cry,'" James murmured, quoting Burns as he rubbed the dog's ears. Though he enjoyed poetry and ballads as well, he never recited verses or sang in company; but the dog would not think him of a sentimental bent.

He was about to take his case upstairs and go in search of his rooms when the front door opened behind him, and Angus MacKimmie stepped inside. "Still here, sir?" He picked up James's leather case. "Upstairs I'll be taking this, then. You must make yourself heard here. My wife is a bit deaf. *Mrs. MacKimmie!*" he thundered as he went up the stairs, booted feet pounding. "*MacKimmie!*"

The door beyond the stairs opened again, and a woman came down the hall followed by two terriers, one black and one white. Stocky and middle-aged, the woman wore a plain dark dress, her gray hair wisping beneath a translucent white cap. "Oh, sir! Lord Struan, is it! I'm Mary MacKimmie," she said, dropping a slight curtsy. "Welcome to Struan House. I hope you did not wait long. I was in the kitchen. I'm that surprised to find you here so early in the day—"

"*MacKimmie!*" thundered the ghillie, above stairs.

"I'm here, ye loon!" she called, and turned back to James. "So you've met my husband, and these are the dogs. Osgar," she said, patting the wolfhound, "is a big lad but very gentle. The terriers are Taran—that's the black one—and Nellie. They're good wee pups, though do they see a fox or a rabbit, they'll be gone on the chase."

As she spoke, the shriek came yet again, and a sharp chill with it, as if an outside door blew open, but the front entrance was shut against the cool autumn breeze. Osgar howled plaintively, and the terriers made low, gruff barks. Mrs. MacKimmie glanced calmly upward, as did James, and smiled as if nothing was amiss.

"We expected you later today, with the roads so muddy from the rains. Though Mr. MacKimmie drives like the de'il sometimes, to be sure."

"An interesting ride indeed. Mrs. MacKimmie, I must ask—what is that sound?"

"Oh, that's our banshee. Strange, that. She's glad to see the new laird, I suppose."

"I came to Struan as a boy," he said, "and never heard that sound."

"You weren't the new laird then, were you. I'll take you to your rooms." She led the way up the stairs, while James looked around, bewildered.

At the top landing, Angus MacKimmie met them, having left the satchel. "So you've brought out our *ban-sith*, then."

"An entertaining idea, though it sounds like hinges or floorboards in need of repair," James said. The upper corridor, a wide hallway, turned a corner at the far end, with several closed doors along its cream-colored walls, hung with a few paintings. A worn Oriental carpet ran the length of the hall, with a few items of furniture—a table here, a bench there. He had visited his grandparents here only occasionally for his guardian, Lady Rankin, felt that children should be schooled and kept busy, and not running about like Highland savages. "It's a very nice house," he ventured.

"And without squeaking hinges," Angus said. "Naught needs repair here, sir. I am your factor, caretaker, head groomsman and coachman, and your ghillie, too, do you want to go hunting or fishing. Come find me for all of it."

"I will, thank you. Struan House is quite impressive," James said. "A banshee is an old ghostly hag that prophesies death and disaster, is it not?"

"Aye, some are," Mary MacKimmie replied this time. "The Struan banshee is the sort that belongs to a house and a family. A fairy spirit who makes herself known over deaths, births, anything of importance for the estate or family. Now that she's marked the arrival of the laird, she will be silent." She smiled. "Unless something else of importance happens, for instance, should you marry, sir."

"I see. A sort of weather glass for the family," James said. "I thought fairies were pleasant, harmless little sorts. Small wings, sitting on flowers, and so on."

"There are many different kinds of fairies in the

Highlands, and elsewhere. You will learn more when you read Lady Struan's pages, I expect," she answered.

Angus departed down the stairs, and the housekeeper led James to the laird's rooms, which included bedroom, sitting room, dressing room, and bathing room. He walked past the large, carved bed with its embroidered hangings to look at the view from the windows of mountain crests against a vast, rainy sky.

"Excellent," he pronounced, turning around.

"You'll want to explore the rest of the house, of course. Downstairs is a library and the study where Lady Struan worked. The parlor is on that level, too, along with the dining room. Kitchens are below stairs, and lead out to the back gardens. Normally supper is at half-five, unless you request otherwise." Mrs. MacKimmie turned toward the door. "I'll set tea in the parlor in twenty minutes, as it's past luncheon now."

"Thank you. Mrs. MacKimmie, I'm expecting guests from Edinburgh in a fortnight or so. They plan a Highland tour, and will stay at Struan for a few days." And as soon as Lady Rankin and the others, including his siblings, were gone, he intended to finish Grandmother's manuscript and return to Edinburgh to resume his teaching.

"I'll ready the house for your guests." She paused at the door. "Sir, there is something you should know. Just now, we've very little staff. Only myself and Angus, with a groom and two housemaids, local girls. Last week two girls arrived by post chaise from Edinburgh, sent here by Lady Rankin." She stiffened a little.

"Ah. She means only to be helpful to me." James had assured Lady Rankin that the Highland staff would be capable, but his great-aunt did not trust Highland servants to keep a house the way she would prefer it kept, even if it was not her home. "I hope that is sufficient staff for Struan House." He had no idea.

"Normally, aye, but . . . well, 'tis near time for the fairy riding. It's a local tradition," she explained. "The fairies go riding this time of year. They ride over the lands of Struan, because legend says these lands once belonged to them."

"Why would the household staff be reduced because of this, uh, phenomenon?"

"We keep away at this time of year to allow for the fairy riding to take place. Your grandparents used to close up the house, and no hunting parties could hire the house then, either. It was true of the previous owners also. Already the locals say some fairies have been sighted, or so I've heard. 'Tis unlucky to be about when the Good Folk ride over Struan lands. The rest of the help will return after the fairies return to their own world. Each year, we repeat it. It's how it is done, sir. I hope you understand."

"Remarkable," James said. He must make sure that the odd custom was recorded in his grandmother's book. "My own needs are simple, so a large staff is unnecessary. Whatever you have done in the past for your local holiday, please continue."

"It is no holiday, sir. No one will risk staying here during a fairy riding, with that sort about. I recommend we close the house for a few days. There is a good hotel in the next glen. You would be comfortable there for a bit."

The housekeeper seemed too sensible a woman for all this nonsense, he thought. "I am happy to stay here alone for a few days, Mrs. MacKimmie. I have a good deal of work to do, and the solitude would be useful."

"Oh no, Lord Struan, not that sort of solitude. 'Tis best we all leave."

"Nonsense. I'm a capable bachelor, so long as there is food in the larder and a few simple comforts. The staff may leave, of course. I do not want to disrupt local tradition."

"Very well, sir, but do be warned. And you must always beware the fairy ilk when you walk about on Struan lands at any time of year." Her glance flickered to the cane he had set against a chair.

"I keep a habit of long walks when I can," he said quietly, aware of her interest, "and I will remember your advice."

When the housekeeper left to make the tea, James turned toward the window again, with its spectacular view, even in poor weather. Mist drifted over the hills and draped the treetops like veils. He thought again of Elspeth MacArthur, who lived somewhere in this glen—and he wondered if she thought of Struan's new laird.

When he left the room, he half expected to hear the shriek again. Apparently Mr. MacKimmie had found and silenced that madly squeaking door.

Elspeth rose from her chair and stepped away from the old shuttle loom, pausing to stretch, arching her back a little to ease the strain that sometimes collected there. With one length of weaving half done on the loom, she was already thinking about the next pattern. Preoccupied with that, she left the weaving cottage and strolled across the yard, past two other cottages that held looms as well. The third building was used to store yarn and finished lengths of plaids, and so its walls were of thick stone regularly limewashed against molds and moisture.

Inside, Elspeth went toward the racks, shelves, and baskets where the skeins of yarns and thin woolen threads were kept, hanging in colorful loops on pegs, clustered in baskets on the floor, or spilling in rainbow arrays on a long worktable. The window at that end of the room was usually shuttered to prevent sunlight from fading the yarns and threads. She pulled her green plaid shawl, a favorite one woven years ago by her grandfather, closer about her shoulders, for the yarn room was chilly. Only a small brazier was kept in cold weather for basic comfort, for the smoke of hearth fire and candles could discolor the wool. Nor was Grandfather permitted to smoke his tobacco pipe here.

A large book of patterns sat on the table, but the pattern forming in her mind was an original design, one she wanted to weave just for herself, rather than as a commissioned length, as most of their weavings were now. Opening a writing box to remove paper, quill, and ink bottle, she sketched a grid of crisscrossing lines, counting the warp and weft lines in dot patterns, and labeling her chosen colors.

Then she looked at the yarns in baskets, on pegs and shelves, to see what was on hand. Hearing the cottage door open, she turned to see her grandfather.

"Supper, Elspeth," he said. "Did you not hear Mrs. Graeme calling you?"

"I did not," she answered, smiling. "I was thinking about the next weaving, counting threads for the pattern."

"Well, come ahead, there's lamb pie and boiled

potatoes, and Peggy Graeme's apple tart, which she made just for you."

Elspeth untied the full apron she wore, and leaving it on a hook by the door, walked with her grandfather across the yard between the weaving houses—there were several buildings that contained Kilcrennan's four hand looms, and houses for storing the yarn, preparing wool and yarns, and another separate cottage for storing the completed tartan lengths in rolls before they were transported for sale. The cottage where Elspeth did her own weaving was one of the original weaver's cottages used by generations of MacArthurs, the weavers of Kilcrennan. She preferred using an old shuttle loom that had belonged to her great-grandfather. The old loom seemed almost to know the work itself, having produced tartan cloth for so long.

Kilcrennan House itself was a manse, a large fieldstone structure with three floors, its symmetrical facade of central entrance and rows of windows simple and elegant. A lower wing housed kitchen and servants' quarters, with the other buildings clustered on the acres behind it, including laundry house, smithy, and brew house, as well as the weaving cottages.

"I'm thinking of weaving a lady's arisaid shawl for my next sett on the loom," Elspeth told her grandfather. "We have plenty of the cream yarn for the ground color, and I'll use some of the purple, along with brown and a bit of the indigo. Expensive, that, but there is only a little left, not enough for a longer length."

"We've ordered several color batches from Margaret," Donal said. "The orders for red tartans, especially the Stewart patterns, have increased, with customers wanting to show their Highland colors of late. The dyed yarns are ready. Margaret's eldest son brought some of it the other day."

"I could fetch the rest while you are gone to Edinburgh over the next few days."

"Come with me to meet with the Edinburgh tailors," he said.

"To meet your friend Mr. MacDowell? I know he wants to court me, but I will not marry him, or any Lowland man, though I know you would like that."

"You would be happy there. He's a good man. You could learn to love him."

She glanced up. Donal MacArthur was tall and spare, still a handsome man even approaching eighty, and he looked twenty years younger. His brown eyes still sparkled; his dark hair was scarcely gray. Most did not suspect his true age, and those who knew simply attributed it to good health and good habits. But Elspeth and one other, Mrs. Graeme, knew that his youthfulness included a touch of magic.

"I will not fall in love with a man because you decide that I should," she said gently. "I am happy here. And I have a good bit of weaving to do for so many new orders," she went on briskly. "I'll work on our tartan orders while you travel."

"The king's visit to Scotland was good to us, as weavers of Scottish tartan." Donal's eyes twinkled. "It's fine luck we've had."

"You auld rascal," she said affectionately. "You love having so much work to do, and you love producing it faster and better than any other weaver."

"I'm grateful for our luck." His mood turned sober as they walked on. "Elspeth, do not cross the glen alone if you go to Margaret's. Take a cart and bring someone for company—one of the serving maids or one of the draw-boys to help you fetch the yarn. It's nearly time for the fairy riding."

"I'll be fine. Let them ride their cavalcade over the glen. I won't be stolen away by fairies or anyone else," she reassured him, and tucked her arm in his. "And I intend to stay with you for a long time to come."

"Elspeth, you must marry soon, and may that man watch out for you as well as I have. And may he take you south and away from this glen. That would be best."

"I need no watching over."

"Mr. MacDowell is a good man, and successful—"

"And keen on inheriting Kilcrennan's weaving business through me. You know he would not be so interested in me if he knew the truth," she added.

"Then we will not tell him," he replied. "He need never know. Of course he considers Kilcrennan's weaving business. He is well suited to manage this place after I am gone. I will not be here forever, and I must think about that, and your well-being."

"I can run Kilcrennan Weavers myself someday, you know that." She looked up. "There are few men who would understand the truth about us, that you go off to the fairies every seven years, and that I . . ." She stopped, shrugged.

"That you are half fairy, and they may call you back to them someday? I tell you, if you are not married and away from this glen soon, you will not be here to explain it to anyone. I will allow Mr. MacDowell to court you. I should have done so earlier."

"Grandda, please. I do not want to marry and leave Kilcrennan."

"You are stubborn, but this is best." He looked at her sharply. "Unless . . . is there someone else now?

You mentioned meeting the new Lord Struan at the king's ball in Edinburgh. What a match that would be, hey." He grinned. "My granddaughter and Lady Struan's grandson."

"Oh, stop." She smiled to hide her true thoughts. Last August, she had been kissed and left yearning for a man she might never see again. Those brief, tender kisses had meant far too much to her, and likely nothing at all to him.

"I've heard he's returning to Struan House soon— something to do with his grandmother's effects. Reverend Buchanan heard it from Mrs. MacKimmie."

Elspeth felt breathless suddenly. "Is it so? Well, I expect he would stay but a few days. He does not intend to live here. If we ever met him, it would be outside the kirk on a Sunday morning, once or twice a year. There is no match there, Grandda. A viscount is unlikely to marry a weaver girl."

"Why not? Your grandfather is a wealthy weaver." He shrugged. "I hoped you would be married and away from Kilcrennan by now. It is a worry to me, your approaching birthday, and no solution yet."

"You think me a spinster already?" Elspeth meant to tease him back into his usual bright mood, but she knew he was serious. Though she did not fear any danger, Donal remained convinced. From childhood, she had heard her grandfather's stories of meeting the Fey in his youth, and he claimed to visit them every seven years. She liked the notion that she could be part fairy, but she wondered how much Donal MacArthur had invented about that tale.

Mrs. Graeme, who had been all but true mother to her, always said that Elspeth's mother was dead and her father had run off. But local rumor in the glen

TO WED A HIGHLAND BRIDE

said that Donal and Niall had both gone over to the fairies, with Donal returning, and Niall lost. All her life, Donal had insisted that it was true, including a spell that would come into effect on her twenty-first birthday in mid-October, when the Fey would take her back with them to their realm—unless she found love first.

Was there truth in that, or was it a charming fairy tale, quite literally, from a charming man? She had never been sure of the answer.

At fourteen, she had followed Donal to a hillside near Struan House, and had seen her grandfather set a pretty stone into a rock wall—and had watched as he disappeared into a door that had suddenly opened there. Elspeth had run home frightened. Donal had been gone for two weeks, and upon his return, after Elspeth had persistently questioned him, he had told her his story, including the truth of his weaving talent, a gift from the fairies.

Nearly seven years had passed since then, without incident. Her grandfather was a storyteller at heart, and she loved him, but she did have some doubts about his tales. Of course she believed that fairies existed—few who had grown up in that glen could fail to believe, given the traditions, legends, and strange occurrences that had permeated the area for generations. But she had never felt afraid of the fairies, despite Donal's warning.

She took his arm. "You worry too much about me, Grandda."

"Because you do not worry enough."

"I do believe in the fairy ilk," she said. "But I wish I could tell truth from fancy, with some of these tales."

"In your heart," he said, "you know what is true."

"Grandfather," she said. "With the seven years coming to an end next month, will you go back to the fairies again?"

"I gave my word. But I will come back, unlike you, if they take you."

"Since I've made no agreement with them myself, I've nothing to fear."

"Be wary," he said. "And never look back if you see them. Remember it."

She sighed. Though all her life she had accepted the Sight and the fairies, as she grew older, she wanted a little proof, too. "Grandda, what became of the special blue stone that you said was a key for entering the fairy realm?"

"It stays in its rightful place, hidden in the rocky hill above Struan House."

"With the gardens enlarged at Struan House in the last few years, I wonder if it is still there. Now the stone wall runs up the hill behind the house."

"The stone should still be safely hidden there, but you are right," he said. "I should make sure of it. I will do so when I return."

"If Lord Struan is set to visit the house for a few days, you will want to find out before then. The housekeeper at Struan knows us, and will let us in to look for something we lost there. I will stop there when I go to Margaret's to fetch the yarns."

"I'll attend to it. The fairies go riding through there. You should keep away."

Elspeth frowned. As they walked, she decided to go to Struan's garden herself and look. If she set the stone in the rock as Donal had done, and nothing changed—or if she saw the fairy realm—she would know if all her grandfather said was truthful, and she would know that she must indeed take care. Besides, Donal deserved to possess that very special stone. Once the new viscount was in charge at Struan, her grandfather might have no good chance to find the stone.

What then, if the magic, and Donal's bargain, were indeed real?

Chapter 4

These spritely creatures often inhabit the lush wooded groves of Scotland, particularly in the Highlands, and are to be found in caves and hill-sides. . . . Fairies prefer to reside in hills, mountains, caves, and near natural wells and springs. . . .

What a load of nonsense, James thought. Nonetheless, he dipped his pen in fresh ink and dutifully took notes on creamy paper stock, copying parts of the passage.

A knock sounded at the study door, and James looked up, grateful for an interruption, for he had worked all afternoon. When he called permission, Mrs. MacKimmie peered inside, then entered the study. "My lord, I beg your pardon, but Mary the downstairs maid has just quit your service."

"Another one?" He set down the pen. "Was it the banshee again? That was what sent the other girl screaming from here last week." The thing, or the door hinge, had shrieked through the whole of the night when he had first come here.

"Not this time, sir. It's the haunts and fairies. She

says she canna stay in a household plagued by strange things. She wants to return to Edinburgh today."

He frowned. "That's all the housemaids gone in two weeks."

"Aye, sir." She stood with hands folded, and then James noticed that she wore a long tweed coat and a bonnet, as if she were ready to leave his service, too.

"So it seems that we are infested with fairies as well as banshees, ghosts, boggles, brownies, some nesting doves, and a few mice," he said, pen in hand.

"The fairy ilk—aye, they're here, and soon they will ride."

"Surely you don't believe that, Mrs. MacKimmie, though it's a charming local tradition. What did the maid see? A moth flitting from lamp to lamp?"

"She said there was a fairy in the garden today, a beautiful creature that turned and saw her, then vanished among the bushes. Poor Mary was so upset that she could not stay another day. And those Edinburgh lasses that Lady Rankin sent for housemaids have no head for a good fright, being Southron. Begging your pardon, sir."

"I'm surprised the girl saw anything in the garden with all the rain we've had," James remarked. "Not even the best duck would be out in such a downpour. Not that I believe in such phenomena as phantasms, fairies, and whatnot." He dipped his pen in the ink again to resume writing.

"Struan House is one of the fairies' favorite places, sir. Used to belong to them, so it's said. There is more of the Otherworld in our own world than we know. If I may say."

"Well, if there is a fairy in the garden, we should

invite her inside to dry off and have some tea." As he spoke, he turned pages in the manuscript, and took a few notes, inked nib whispering over the paper. *Fairy riding*, he wrote. *Local custom.*

"I came to tell you, sir, that I would like to leave, just for a day or two."

He looked up. "I hope the fairies have not frightened you away as well."

"Oh no. I always leave the house for a few days to allow for the fairy riding. We all do. My daughter has just had another child, and I'd like to visit her."

"Certainly. As I told you, I am happy to have a few days to myself here."

"If you feel comfortable, sir. Thank you. One of the grooms will drive me, and then return with the gig. And Mr. MacKimmie will take the landau to drive the housemaids to catch the post chaise in Callander to go back to Edinburgh. We'll be gone for no more than a day or two. I beg your pardon for leaving you thus."

"Not at all." *Locals avoid the fairy riding at all costs,* he wrote.

"There's food in the larder, sir, and soup in the kettle today. The groom will be back to see to the cows in the byre, the horses, and the chickens. And I've sent word to a local family to ask if their daughter could come round to see to the housekeeping for you until I return."

"That's very efficient, Mrs. MacKimmie. Thank you."

"Oh, I nearly forgot," she said, entering the room. "The mail arrived just now, very late. The postman said the roads are so muddy that he does not expect to be back for over a week." She set three letters on the corner of the desk. "I'll just leave, shall I?"

He took the letters and smiled at her. "Good day, and safe journey."

"Thank you, sir." She shut the door.

James sat back to open the letters. One was from the lawyer, Mr. Browne, another from Lady Rankin, the last from his brother Patrick. He scanned each one. His great-aunt wrote to inform him—again—of her travel plans, and again fretted about whether Struan House was acceptable for sophisticated city guests, at which James snorted a little. Patrick reported that he would travel to the area with Sir John Graeme, who was interested in a business venture in the north, but they had frantically declined Lady Rankin's invitation to join her own party; James laughed softly at that. The lawyer's terse note made him frown, and he set it aside; it required no response from him at the moment.

Reaching for one of the books stacked haphazardly on the desk, a volume of Scott's work on ballads and legends, James flipped until he found a section on fairy lore, then picked up his pen to jot more notes.

"Fairies and elves," James read aloud, "are interchangeable terms in the Highlands. Ah. So the elfin sort are the fey sort. Right, then." He scribbled that down.

The most formidable attribute of the elves, Sir Walter Scott had written, *was their practice of carrying away, and exchanging, children; and that of stealing human souls from their bodies. . . . the power of the fairies extended to full-grown persons, especially those found asleep under a rock or on a green hill belonging to the fairies . . .*

"Good God, even Sir Walter has succumbed to this nonsense," James muttered, shaking his head. He flipped pages, skimming the essay. A farmer, he next read, had gone out to wait for a procession of fairies, and then heard *the ringing of the fairy bridles, and the wild unearthly sound which accompanied the cavalcade. . . .*

James sat up, finding that of interest, considering the fairy riding that Mrs. MacKimmie had mentioned. He would have to make sure that those details were included in his grandmother's book. Flipping more pages, he came to the old Scots ballad of Tam Lin. Tam had been lured by the irresistible charms of the queen of fairies; appearing to his true love, Janet, he asked her to meet him when the fairies rode in procession. Janet must grab him and hold fast no matter what, so that he could be free.

> *Betwixt the hours of twelve and one*
> *A north wind tore the bent*
> *And straight she heard strange eldritch sounds*
> *Upon that wind which went.*

Outside, the wind and rain picked up fiercely, rattling the windows. He glanced up, hoping that Mrs. MacKimmie and the others traveled in safety, for they would be well on their way by now. Reaching out, he took a stack of handwritten pages from Lady Struan's thick manuscript. More pages were piled beside his right hand, and to his left, stacks of books teetered on the desk and on the floor as well. He slid his own notes among the manuscript pages, planning to revise later with editorial passages.

He stood to fetch another book from a high shelf, climbing an iron stool to reach it, and limped back to the desk, doing without his cane, which he used mostly for distances and on cold or rainy days, when the leg ached, as it had done for days in this dreary weather. He settled in his chair to read again.

"Fairy rings . . . fairy phosphorous . . . now that might prove interesting," he said.

The study walls were lined with books behind mesh-fronted shelves, and the small, cozy library beyond, with its horsehair sofa, wing chairs, and fireplace, was filled with even more books, most of them collected by his grandparents, though some had belonged to previous generations of the lairds of Struan. His grandfather had purchased the property in his middle years, and had been elevated to a peerage for brave service in the military, so that James had become the second Viscount Struan.

He picked up a sheaf of his grandmother's book, the topmost of the handwritten pages with their curling edges and the smell of the ink, even years dry, lingering still. Her handwriting was small and certain, and every page was densely covered, some of them even crisscrossed with sentences. There were at least six hundred pages, he had estimated. He had spent nearly a fortnight just reading, either Grandmother's close, fine handwriting, or various books on fairy lore and social customs in Scotland. All the while, he had taken new notes of his own, so that the pile of papers grew daily.

The scope of the thing was more than he had expected. Lady Struan's handwritten chapters were not fairy tales, but scholarly assessments of aspects of Highland lore. He had to admit that some of it was fascinating, if fanciful. Ever since his arrival, he had applied himself diligently to reading her manuscript and studying reference books, but for long walks for exercise, and to search for rocks to support his geological studies.

Needing a stretch, he rose and walked to the window that faced toward the back. Gazing at the vast, upward-sloping garden—expanded to contain a grotto cut from a rocky hill behind the house—he watched the rainfall, and saw something moving about high up on the garden slope.

For a moment, he thought it was a girl. The fairy the maid had seen was no doubt an illusion formed of flowers, rocks, and atmosphere. Amid the silver rain and twilight, whatever it was moved again—very much like the fleeting form of a girl. Whether wraith, ghost, human, or mist, something was at the top of the hill.

After a moment, he saw her again—definitely a girl. Dark hair, pale face. She looked toward the house, then disappeared behind the wet shrubbery.

He frowned. Rain trickled in rivulets down the hillside. Perhaps it was a tree or a garden statue blurred by the downpour, and he ought to check into it. A garden statue or some of the decorative rocks could dislodge in the mud.

A lightning flash showed the form again—female, or looked that way. The grotto was up there, completed the year before Lady Struan's death. A fairy portal, his grandmother had called the hillside in her manuscript notes.

Fairies, indeed. If someone was mucking about in his grandmother's fairy grotto in this torrent, James intended to find out why.

Turning on his booted heel, snatching up his cane, James marched out into the corridor. Osgar the wolfhound, who lay sleeping in the hallway outside the door, rose and loped after him.

She had to hurry. Two vehicles had left the house in the time since Elspeth had entered the garden, and someone else might still be in the house. She had hoped the place was empty, and thought the storm might hold off, but she had been wrong on both counts. Now she could only hope that the viscount himself was not there.

Given another day, the staff would be gone to avoid the fairy riding, and she would not have had to lurk like this in the garden. But with the poor weather, today had seemed the best chance to look for the stone her grandfather wanted.

She had told Mrs. Graeme that she would stay with Margaret Lamont if the weather got bad. She enjoyed visiting Margaret and her husband and children, for Elspeth loved the company, as well as the chance to lend a hand in the process of combing, dyeing, spinning, and twisting the new wools. But rather than walk the nearly ten miles straight through the glen— like most Highlanders, she was used to walking long distances—Elspeth had stopped at Struan House first. Now she regretted the detour.

But she had to find the stone for her grandfather. According to legend, and Donal, too, a fairy portal existed somewhere in the hill. And she wanted to see for herself if Donal's tales were true. Now, the rain and lightning had set her plans awry.

She even wondered if the *daoine sìth* themselves had taken a hand in this weather, for tradition claimed that they could wield such power. Growing more uneasy, she stood by the rock wall that thrust up at the top of the hill and looked around.

The original hill had been crested by a great cluster of rock, but the work of the last few years had enclosed much of the slope. Elspeth tried to remember where Donal had stood when he had visited this rock, and disappeared into what he said was the fairy world. Where had he hidden the crystal?

In the rain, she pulled up her plaid shawl to better cover her head. Her gown, spencer jacket, and leather boots were already soaked, but she was intent on her task. She could not be discovered here—how could she ever explain that she searched for a precious crystal rock to steal from the garden, a stone that was a key to the fairy world. She would seem mad indeed. The late Lady Struan had been interested in local lore, but she was gone. The others might not be so curious and accepting.

Lady Struan had invited Donal and Elspeth to Struan House once or twice to talk about fairy legends. Donal had told some of his tales, and had warned Lady Struan that certain stories must not be written down, at risk of angering the fairies. Lady Struan had been intrigued; she had also been fascinated by Donal's tale of his son, who Donal said had chosen to stay in the fairy realm forever.

Well, at least the fairies would be dry and out of the rain, Elspeth thought wryly. She stood, wiping a muddy hand over her brow, and studied the high rock. Shivering, she gathered her green plaid shawl snugly over her short jacket. Of the long sort called an arisaid, the shawl covered her head to knee in old Highland tradition. Pinned at the neck, it protected from the elements, but it was growing as soggy as the hem of her dress.

Spanning her hands over the rock, she moved along, the ground mucky under her feet. Thunder boomed then, and she jumped a little. She had to hurry, and find shelter soon until the storm abated. It was not safe, now, for her to travel over open moorland.

Just then she heard a dog bark, and a man call out. She whirled to look through the sheeting rain, stepping forward, her foot placed just where muddy water sluiced down the hill. Her heel went out from under her, and she tumbled and slid downward. Bumping, shrieking, she soon landed at the bottom of the slope, skirts tangled around her, legs sprawled. Slowly she sat up and pushed the plaid away from her face.

And saw black boots standing an inch deep in mud. Looking up, she gazed at buff trousers, a walking stick, gray gloves on strong hands, a brown jacket, and a fine but damp neck cloth—

Lord Struan stared down at her.

No garden statue, no fairy, nor an eldritch hag sprawled at his feet, James realized: just a wet, bedraggled girl in a muddied plaid and gown. Her face was obscured by the green plaid, but he quickly noted that she was slim and well-shaped, from neat ankles and calves encased in soggy stockings and sturdy leather shoes to her slender frame, small waist, and full breasts straining against wet fabric. The rest of her, under the bedraggled tartan, looked to be enticing as well.

"Miss." He leaned down to extend a hand. "May I help you?"

Gasping, she shoved her skirts down rapidly, and pushed back the plaid. He saw a heart-shaped face and black hair in curling tendrils; then large eyes of a gray-green, just now the silvery color of the rain, looked up at him.

"Miss MacArthur," he said, hiding his astonishment behind nonchalance. "How pleasant to see you again. What the devil are you doing in my garden?"

"Lord Struan," she said. "You need not swear."

Stifling his next response, he offered his hand. She refused and stood, wincing. "I'm fine, sir," she said, as he extended his hand again.

He doubted that, judging by the way she favored one foot and hopped about a little. "Are you sure? Well then, what can I do for you?"

They were both drenched, and water ran from the brim of his hat. When she moved, muck sloshed his boots, her shoes. He waited with a polite smile, despite the absurd circumstances.

"Welcome to Struan, my lord," she said, as if they stood in some gas-lit parlor in Edinburgh rather than in a soaking rain while muddy water runneled around their feet, and thunder rumbled. "I hope you are enjoying the Highlands."

James inclined his head. "I'm quite enjoying them now."

"Excellent. I must go. My apologies for intruding." Turning, she stepped, winced again, one arm flailing as her heel faltered in the mud. James snatched at her arm.

"Come along," he said firmly. "I am not about to let you walk off in a thunderstorm." He turned with her toward the house.

As they took another incline and followed the stone

terraced steps that led through the wet, raggedy garden, he noticed that the girl was having real difficulty walking. The rain was lashing nearly sideways now. Elspeth MacArthur drew the plaid over her head, and hurried alongside him toward the house.

Oddly, James realized that they were both limping, almost in a rhythm. But the girl was having trouble— she paused more than once to rest. Lightning cracked nearly overhead, and the wind whirled about them. James felt a sense of something eerie, even dangerous around them that seemed beyond the storm itself.

Snatching her up in his arms despite her protest, he took the garden path in long strides. For some reason his leg hardly hindered him as he rushed over the strip of garden lawn and along a pathway lined with leggy marigolds and late pansies to reach the back kitchen doorway. The girl clung to his neck as he hurried.

When thunder pounded again, for an instant James felt caught again in the nightmare of Quatre Bras. He had been with his Highland Watch regiment, defending ground against an onrush of French cuirassiers. The sensation startled him so that he rushed toward the door and opened it, nearly hurtling inside with the girl in his arms.

In the corridor, the wolfhound and two terriers waited, shuffling back as James entered with the girl. He kicked the door shut behind him and carried the girl down the hall, past the kitchen, and up the back stairs to the parlor. The dogs trotted close and curious on his heels.

Elspeth MacArthur was a sopping bundle, but light-weight and no burden, even on the steps. She fit in his arms like sin itself. Her curves eased against him, and a heavy pulse beat through him. Her face was so close to his, her breath soft upon his cheek, her arm looped around his shoulders, the other resting on his chest.

Heart slamming, he tried to focus on other matters. The slippery steps, the need to get the girl somewhere warm and dry, the slight ache in his left leg from a wound more than seven years old now. He had dropped his cane in the garden when he had lifted her up. And blast it all, he had lost his hat, and the rain had likely ruined a good woolen jacket.

Mundane thoughts, he knew—but he needed them now. Anything to keep his mind off the delicious creature who leaned her head against him as if he were her savior. He, of all men, a rescuer—he almost laughed. These days he went out of his way to keep his life dull. This mad, rain-soaked adventure would soon be over.

But what the devil was the lovely Miss MacArthur doing in his blasted garden?

Chapter 5

Up steps and along a corridor, its polished wood floor reflecting the glow of creamy walls and brass sconces, James carried her into the drawing room. There, upholstered chairs were arranged beside a low fire in the grate. James set the girl down in a wingback chair and angled it toward the fireplace.

The room was dim, and he grabbed a tinderbox to light the wicks of the candles in a brass candelabra. Then he turned. "We'd best get you warmed up. You're soaked."

"So are you," she said. "Sir, I do appreciate this, but I really must go." She half rose from the chair, but shifted to stand on her right foot, favoring the left. "And I should not sit down anywhere. My things are wet and muddy, and will ruin the furnishings."

"My concern is not the upholstery, but you, Miss MacArthur. Sit, please."

She sighed, and sat. "I suppose I could stay until the rain lessens."

"At least that. My housekeeper would have my head if I let you go out again in such weather, and clearly injured."

"Mrs. MacKimmie? Aye, but she knows me, and knows I would leave if I wanted to do so. I'd best take off my plaidie, it's that wet." She shrugged out of the long, damp shawl, and James took it, draping it over a wooden bench beside the fireplace.

"When my shawl dries, I can brush it clean," she said, "but it could take hours for it to dry properly." Looking dismayed she brushed ineffectually at her muddy skirt.

Beneath the plaid, the girl wore a gown of pale cream muslin patterned in small florals with a little green jacket over it. Her bonnet was of straw, its white ribbons and lace ruching pitiful-looking now. Beneath it, her hair was so dark it seemed jet-black, and curled rather than flattened with dampness. Her gown, he noticed, was mud-splotched, and all her garments so wet that the fabric clung to her very enticing curves.

"I'll fetch you a blanket," James said. She nodded and began to remove her jacket. His own coat of superfine was drenched in places, but he could not properly remain in shirtsleeves in a lady's presence. He had to endure the discomfort.

Turning, he looked about for a blanket or a shawl to give her, opening drawers in a highboy to find linens and candles and papers, then opening the front panel of a desk, only to find writing materials, paper stock, inkwell, quills. He was not familiar with much of Struan House beyond the study, the library, and his private rooms. In a low chest under a window, he found a dark tartan lap robe and brought that to her. She tucked it over her, murmuring thanks.

Reaching for a tapestried footstool, he pulled it toward her, and she set her left foot on it. "Where are you injured?" he asked. "If I may inquire."

"My foot." She leaned forward to draw her skirts up, then glanced at him. "Turn away, sir, or your fine city manners might be offended. I must look at my ankle."

He nearly laughed. "I'm hardly offended. I've a little medical experience, if that will help. The first years of my college education were in medical studies before I changed to another science. May I be of assistance?"

She nodded, and James dropped to one knee to ease off her shoe of sturdy laced leather. He looked at her stockinged foot, resting on the stool: pretty little ankle, small toes, muddy stocking. A swelling filled out the inner ankle.

"Are you a doctor like your brother?" she asked. "The one I met in Edinburgh?"

"No, William is better suited to it than I. Though I began medical studies, I later changed my pursuit to natural philosophy. Geological science," he added. He omitted the real reason for changing his mind—a bloody field on the day before Waterloo, when despite his own injury, he had done his best to help in that futile aftermath, though his own cousin and friend had died in his arms. Devastated, he had returned to Scotland and took up the study of rocks and minerals, a subject he had always loved, after that. As it turned out, it suited him.

He looked up at Elspeth MacArthur. "May I?" Complying, she drew her skirts higher. James cupped her heel and turned her foot side to side, running his fingertips along the delicate shape and contour. "It's a bit swollen. I had best compare the two feet."

She lifted the other foot, and he untied the shoelaces to remove her low boot. As he rotated and stroked gently, James felt a deep thrill go through him. Her heel pressed into his palm and her injured foot rested over his bent knee, where he had set it for a moment. Drawing a breath, he let go of her uninjured foot and took up the left foot again to ease his thumb over the ankle, the top of the foot, the bottom. Glancing up, he saw that she had inclined her head backward a little, eyes half closed.

"Oh," she said in a small voice. "Oh."

"Does that hurt?" he asked.

"No." She gathered the blanket closer around her, blushing.

James set her foot down and rose to his feet. "You could use faster warmth than that blanket, and something for the pain," he said. Seeing a decanter and glasses on a table, he went there to open the bottle, sniffing its pale amber contents. "Whiskey. A few sips will do you some good." He poured a little into a glass and brought it to her. "I know ladies generally do not indulge in strong spirits unless they're out on a hunt, or—"

"Whiskey is perfectly acceptable to Highland ladies," she said, taking the glass from him. She tipped it to her lips, swallowed easily, paused, and took a little more, smoothly, without a cough or a tear in the eye, though bright color sprang to her cheeks. She handed the glass back to him. "Sir, your turn. There is an old Highland custom of passing the welcome dram, even between genders."

"Aye then." He drank from the glass quickly, the sweet, mellow burn searing his throat. Glancing down at her, seeing her dulcet smile and radiant gray eyes, he wondered what in blazes to do now. He was alone with the same young beauty who had appeared in his dreams too often recently.

He set down the glass, then knelt and once again took up her injured ankle. "This ought to be wrapped," he said. She laughed. He glanced up, her foot in his hands, and raised a brow in question.

"I feel like Cinderella, about to get a slipper." She giggled a little, then reached for the whiskey glass and took a good swallow.

"Does it hurt when I turn it this way?" He rotated her foot gently.

She winced and jumped. "Ow! Oh, it will be fine." She dropped her skirts to cover her ankles, the soft folds covering his hands as well. "I'm sure it's just a slight twist. I can manage—my home is eight miles from here. I should leave before dark."

"Eight miles?" He looked at her, incredulous. "You walked eight miles to get here?" He still wanted to know why she had been in the garden at all.

"It's not so long a distance to walk in the Highlands. I was going to my cousin's home, another few miles from here. I can walk there instead of home tonight."

"You should not walk anywhere just now." He was still holding her foot. "Your ankle is badly twisted, perhaps sprained, and a doctor should look at it. For now, a bandage for support would help. I advise you to avoid much walking for a week or more, until it heals."

"Perhaps I could borrow a gig or a pony cart."

"I would drive you, but for the weather. Besides, the landau and gig are both in use by the ghillie and a groom, who took the housekeeper and the servants elsewhere. The cart is here, but would not do well in the rain and muck. However, I could escort you home by horseback once the storm lifts."

She glanced through the windows of the drawing room, where rain and winds lashed at the glass. "Who can say when that will be?"

"My ghillie predicted bad weather for days to come." James set her foot on the stool and rocked back on his heels. "Miss MacArthur, I must tell you something."

She tilted her head. "Aye?"

"You should be aware that we are alone here at Struan House just now."

"Alone?" She narrowed her eyes.

"For the present, aye. The ghillie took the maids to Stirling, the other staff have gone to see kinfolk for a few days, and even the housekeeper is gone, called away to tend to family. She left the household in good order and food in the cupboard, and hired a local girl to come in to do some chores. But the girl will not be here for a day or two. So that leaves us alone in the house. I apologize for not saying so immediately."

"We were both distracted." She frowned thoughtfully. "So with this storm, perhaps no one will return until tomorrow, or later."

"It is possible."

"My grandfather, who is my guardian, is away from home at present, and our housekeeper believes I've gone to my friend's home across the glen. But she is not expecting me. So . . . no one knows I am here."

He frowned. His heart thumped very fast, and a peculiar thrill coursed through him. He ignored it. "An unfortunate set of circumstances."

She sat up and smiled. "These are perfect circumstances."

"Miss MacArthur, be assured that you are safe in my company."

"I know." She leaned forward, her head angled as she studied him. Kneeling so close to her, James felt the soft whisper of her breath upon him, and felt the allure of her nearness. "I could be compromised by this," she said.

"Some might think so, but it is not the case. Nor will it be," he said firmly.

"But I do not mind being compromised."

What was this? He frowned. Did she think him a wealthy lord to be caught and then obliged to marry her? "As I said, there is no danger of that."

She smiled, impish and dazzling, her remarkable eyes sparkling. He saw that she had two dimples, darling indentations, to either side of her mouth, and her lips were full, winsome, rose-colored. He knew their taste. "Lord Struan, it would be very convenient for me, at least, if a compromise resulted from this," she said.

A sort of fever shot through him at the thought. He could indeed compromise this delectable female if he were the sort of rascal to do that. James rose to his feet to look down at her. "Tell me what in blazes you are going on about, would you?"

"You swear quite a bit," she said. "Highland gentlemen rarely curse. It is not Gaelic custom. Is it a Southron habit?" When she smiled, it was like sunshine blooming.

But he would not succumb to manipulation. "Do not play coy games with me," he said sharply. "You are not very good at it, pouting like a spoiled child and batting your eyelashes as if there is sand in them."

"Oh." She tipped her head. "What should I do, then?"

"That depends on what you want to accomplish."

"A gentle compromise. That's all." Smile. Sunshine.

Blast. "Miss MacArthur, say outright what you intended by coming here."

"I am here by accident, quite literally. And so long as we are in this situation, I would very much enjoy being compromised."

His heart thundered. "Surely you cannot mean that."

"Gloriously *rrruined*," she said, adopting a broad Scots burr. "That would quite suit. If you do not mind, sir." She took up the whiskey glass, sipped, turned it upside down, and smiled again.

He stared, thoughts and suspicions churning. "Ruination," he drawled, with an edge to his tone, "would necessarily lead to marriage, Miss MacArthur. We need not make that mistake."

"We are alone together. Regardless, there is compromise," she pointed out.

Frowning, James glanced away. Could the girl have plotted this, and not very well at that, to trap the local laird into marriage, believing him wealthy?

The damnable thing was that there was merit in the suggestion. He had come to Struan House, in part, with the decidedly odd mission of finding a woman of fairy descent to marry. With those fey and graceful looks, Elspeth MacArthur could pass easily for a fairy wife. Sir Walter Scott, the judge of this profoundly troublesome scheme, liked her already, he remembered.

It could work. James watched her for a moment. Compromise and its frequent companion, hasty marriage, could come together seamlessly in this situation. Did he have the heart not only to ruin the young woman, but to fool her into believing he wanted a wife?

True, he found her nearly irresistible. Coy, darling, forthright, and seductive all at once. Was it those beautiful eyes, with their luminous color, or the elusive dimples? The gentle bow curve of her lips, the graceful angle of her long neck, the pulse in her throat? Beneath the sodden gown and little jacket, her breath moved her full breasts in enticing rise and fall. He noticed all of it, could not help himself.

What the devil was she doing to him, while merely sitting, smiling, making suggestions that made his heart, his body pound? Despite his wariness, his body was definitely responding, arousing. He was increasingly aware of it—and now his mind was hatching schemes to rival what she herself had concocted.

No, he told himself. Marrying the girl and passing her off as a fairy was preposterous. Yet, if she were willing, it could solve part of his dilemma. Still, she seemed to be proposing compromise without marriage, unless it was all a coy ruse to trap him.

"Miss MacArthur." He stood. "This ordeal has stressed you beyond the norm. We will tend to your injury, and then you should rest. There are bedrooms upstairs—" *Blast it*, he thought, that line of conversation would not do. "I'll find some bandages. I've no idea where they might be kept, but any clean linen will do. The kitchen, perhaps—" He turned, ready to bolt.

"Lord Struan." She rose to her feet and hobbled close, so that he took her arm to steady her. She was fine-boned, and his hand was large on her arm. He felt strong and protective in contrast. Looking up, she batted her eyelashes again, very deliberately, it seemed. Then she reached for him and took his neck cloth.

"What the devil," he muttered. "Stop that."

She tugged. "Your cravat would make a fine bandage, if you will part with it. Then you need not go searching."

"Oh. I suppose so." He reached up to undo the knot in the cloth, his hands brushing hers, and she did not take away her hands, but worked at the soft knot under his fingers. That drove him mad, until she slipped the knot and began to draw the thing away from him. He assisted her in unwrapping it, bowing his head, and his brow brushed the top of her head. Her dark hair smelled divinely of rain and blossoms.

She looked up just as he was looking down, and his nose touched hers.

For a moment, he breathed; she breathed. And he recalled far too vividly a few wild kisses shared behind some potted shrubberies at Holyroodhouse, weeks ago, with this same girl.

"Please," she said, breathless.

A surge went through him, hard and sudden. "Oh. The cravat."

"Of course," she said, and drew it slowly free, soft linen and the air upon his neck as sensual as a caress, setting up a fire in him that only willpower smothered. "Though some men may feel unsettled without their neck cloth, I believe."

"I have a dozen cravats." He could not sound more of a dolt, he thought. Her touch was what unsettled him. Even with his usual composure, he felt whirled off balance, drawn to her like stalwart iron to a curving magnet.

"Miss MacArthur, sit down." He guided her back to the chair, noticing how much she limped. At least that was genuine, he thought. "After we wrap the foot, I will fetch you some tea, and we will decide what to do."

She nodded and sat again, lifting her injured foot to the stool. Bringing up the hem of her skirts, she handed him the cravat. James watched while she removed her stocking, slowly rolling and then slipping it off to reveal her bare foot and slim, neatly muscled calf. His body surged distinctly, uncomfortably.

The sight of bruising startled him out of a haze of desire. Carefully he began to wrap the cravat around her foot and ankle, circling and crossing to provide snug support.

"Thank you. It feels a bit better." She wiggled her toes. "If you did not finish your medical studies, where did you learn to do this?"

"War," he said succinctly. "I learned from the doctors in the regiment. Helped them when I could, while I was in the military." He did not want to talk about that.

She watched him quietly, then sighed. "Quatre Bras was a terrible ordeal."

He looked up, startled and silent.

"The Royal Highlanders," she said. "The Black Watch . . . they were so brave, held their own, the day before Waterloo. But they lost so many men when the French came at them, where they held ground there."

His hands grew still. Then he forced himself to continue wrapping, and to remain calm. "How did you know I was at Quatre Bras?"

"A moment ago, I saw you there in my mind, like a dream image. And then I just knew the name of the place. I have heard of the battle, the day before Waterloo, when the Scots held the day. You were there. The knowing tells me that."

"The knowing?" He glanced up at her silvery eyes, her gaze direct yet mysterious. "Miss MacArthur, do not play me for a fool," he snapped. "Who told you? And to what scheming purpose do you pretend to have a vision about my past?"

"I am not scheming against you." She leaned forward. He tensed and leaned back. "I saw you in my mind just now, on a battlefield, wearing a dark kilt and red coat. I heard the name. Quatre Bras. I did not previously know that you were personally there."

He wrapped and tugged on the cloth a little too hard, simmering with anger. Taking an end of the neck cloth, he tore it fiercely and tied it around her ankle.

"You tried to save him," she said then. "You saw the blinding flash of steel as the blow came down upon him. But then a horseman, a Frenchman, jumped the line of Highlanders, and landed among the Scotsmen. Your leg was trapped beneath the horse . . . and you took a bayonet . . . in your thigh. Just above the knee. You could not move, nor could you save him in time. As you watched, he called to you—"

"Enough," he said sharply, and stood. "Did that nitwit Philip Rankin tell you this?" He was livid, which dissolved the sense of passion he had felt only minutes ago. Anger always burned clean, like a ring of fire about a person, protective, shielding.

Passion, he had found, could muddy things, especially the sort of passion that had to do with women. Passion for a well-stocked stable, or an enviable library collection, or a case of rock specimens carefully labeled, passion for expressing theories in writing— those were safe and solid. Not the muddy emotional sort that whipped like a storm.

"No one told me," she said. "I . . . saw the scene in my mind just now."

"Given that I fought in the war against Napoleon,

it could be assumed that I joined a Highland regiment. The Black Watch is another good guess, and correct. I was a lieutenant in the Forty-second, and so I was at Quatre Bras seven years ago. Very good, Miss MacArthur. I will give you that." He inclined his head. "But to lead me to believe that your clever guesses are Highland divination, and to add grisly detail . . . I hope you have a better explanation for that than 'the Sight.'"

She sat up and pulled her skirts over her feet. "I did not guess it. When I touch someone, or they touch me, sometimes I just know things about them. It comes to me like that. I will admit that at times I speak too quickly, and say more than I should."

"More than enough, and you damn well know it."

"I beg pardon." She looked troubled, biting her lip, frowning. "But—who was he, the friend you lost there? A brother, or a close kinsman?"

"You're the one with the blasted Sight, you tell me," he snapped.

"Your chief," she said quickly. "Chief of your clan."

"First Sir Walter Scott at the Ladies' Assembly," he said, "then you hint at an interest in being compromised, and now this. Whatever your scheme, may it end now." He bowed stiffly. "Rest here, miss. When the weather improves, I will take you home."

She stood, too, fists clenched, facing him. "I thought, being a Highland laird raised in the Highlands, you would be accepting of those with the Sight."

"And who told you I was raised in the Highlands? More divination?"

"*You* told me," she pointed out. "At the Ladies' Assembly. I thought you might have some appreciation for *Da Shealladh*, the Second Sight. But I was mistaken in that, and in speaking out. Do not bother to take me home. I will go myself. Now would be the best time," she muttered, and snatching up her plaid, threw it around her shoulders.

She stood on one foot and the toes of the other, hobbling, fuming. Then she snatched up her shoes and stockings and limped toward the door.

James folded his arms and watched, slightly amused in that moment, still unsure what motivated her. Puzzled by her behavior, he was not entirely convinced she was a schemer. He was wary of minxes who had an eye to a man's fortune, having courted the princess of them all, Charlotte Sinclair, his great-aunt's marriage choice for him, as a niece of the late Lord Rankin. Years ago as a vulnerable soldier returning home, he had fallen for that charm and had found enough to admire and even love in her. Then he realized how manipulative, ambitious, haughty, and possessive she could be. He had not proposed to her, despite expectations, and had cooled his ardor, though Aunt Rankin and Charlotte still held out hope.

James would stake his life that Elspeth MacArthur was not of the same cloth, but he was not sure what she was after. Still, he would give her credit for an imaginative attempt to ensnare the local laird. She seemed innocent of true guile, the sparkle in her eyes and her spirit too genuine to be calculating. Besides, she was so damnably alluring that he did not want to believe ill of her.

But he would not be played for a fool, either. "Miss MacArthur, please sit down. I am not throwing you summarily out the door."

"You will not," she said. "I am leaving."

"If you must know," he said, as he leaned by the

door, "there was a fellow killed beside me at Quatre
Bras. He was my cousin, the young chief of Clan Mac-
Carran. Several people could have told you that. As
for the wound you saw in your supposed reverie—it is
bloody obvious that I require a cane. So I will not bow
to intuition just yet. Please sit, Miss MacArthur." He
went toward her to take her elbow and lead her back
to the chair. "I will not be responsible for your further
injury."

She looked up at him. "Trout," she said.

"What?" He frowned, confused.

"Trout. I heard that word clearly in my head. And
. . . pudding? Do you like trout with pudding, is that
it?" She wrinkled her nose.

"Puddin'," he said, startled. "My cousin loved it
when we were at Eton. The lads teased him merci-
lessly. He was a bit of a pudge then, and handsome
later—Puddin', we called him." Why had he let down
his guard, and told her that much?

"And trout?"

"Enough," he snapped. "I will fetch the tea, if you
will stay here." Stunned, he wanted this game to end.

Sighing, she sat in the chair. "Tea would be lovely,
thank you. I will not bother you further. You may
return to"—she waved her hand a little—"planning
your hunts or adding up sheep revenues, or whatever
it is you do now that you own Struan House."

Despite all, he wanted to laugh. "After tea, while
you rest and I count my vast and princely revenues,"
he drawled, "perhaps if we are lucky, this blasted rain
will stop and I can escort you home."

She smiled a little and nodded. "Lord Struan," she
said. "Please forgive me."

"Of course," he murmured politely, and left the

room, shutting the doors behind him. Out in the corridor, he leaned against the wall to take a deep breath.

Trout. No one knew about that but Fiona, and his sister would not have discussed so intimate and sensitive a topic with a stranger.

How had Elspeth MacArthur learned that, along with the details of his injury? Some of it was known only to himself, and to Nicholas MacCarran, Lord Eldin, who had been there also. Who was low enough to describe for her the death of his beloved friend and cousin before his eyes, while James was unable to defend him? Only Nick, he thought, who had reason to undermine James's bid for the inheritance. Could the two have schemed this?

Yet the girl did not seem keen on marriage. He could not piece it all together.

But—Trout. He sighed. That had been his boyhood name for his cousin when they had been eight years old, when Archie had fallen in a stream while fishing, and had come up with a trout jumping about in his trousers. Both James and Archie had fallen in the water trying to get it out, and had nearly asphyxiated with laughter over it, even years afterward. They had even laughed about it hours before Archie's death, when James had called him Trout. Nicholas had not even been there, then.

How could Elspeth MacArthur have known?

His grandmother's writings were full of references to Highland Sight, he recalled. Fanciful stuff, in sum, but it had begun to influence his thinking. None of it suited a man of science, an esteemed professor of geology.

Still, he could not explain away what Elspeth had

said. Not Trout, especially not Puddin'—she would have had to dig deep to find that one out, too.

He had looked forward to solitude at the house, but now he fervently wished the others were here. If left alone with his pretty visitor, he feared he would either toss her out the window, or throttle her madly and gladly—or quite gloriously ruin her, just as she had suggested.

And too much time alone with the tempting, bewildering, bewitching Miss MacArthur would indeed obligate him to marry her, ruination or none. Finding himself a fairy bride was nothing, he realized, compared to this very real predicament.

Years ago he had decided to skirt risk and live a safe, dull life. Now risk had found him, regardless.

Find the blasted tea, he reminded himself, as he headed for the stairs.

Chapter 6

*R*uination and compromise? Elspeth covered her face with her hand. Had she truly said that, along with talk of visions, death, and battle? Either it was the whiskey or the troublesome tongue loosening that sometimes accompanied her Second Sight. She wondered how to convince Lord Struan that she was neither a hussy nor a madwoman.

Fairy gifts, her grandfather said, came with a price. Her gift of Sight asked a good deal for the privilege. Sometimes she impulsively blurted out whatever came to mind, as she had done with Sir Walter Scott, and now with Lord Struan. No wonder the latter thought her a fortune hunter. Likely he would clear her out of his house quickly, and once she was gone, there might never be a good chance to search the grounds for the stone key.

And by now, Donal MacArthur might have promised her hand to MacDowell; he was determined enough to do that. If he had his way, she and the reliable tailor would stand before a parson soon; her twenty-first birthday was three weeks away.

Yet even a few hours alone with Lord Struan could

render her compromised, at least in reputation, and she could escape marriage offers but from Struan himself, who seemed a gentleman; and she did not have to accept if he did offer. She was just as determined as her grandfather. She would find the missing crystal, and find some way to stay at Kilcrennan, even if it meant living a spinsterish life.

Shivering, Elspeth stood, hopping a little on her good foot to spare her ankle. The rain continued, the darkness increasing, and even sitting by the fire did not warm her; even her underthings were damp through. Slipping the woolen lap robe over her shoulders, she limped to the door to peer out into the dark, silent hallway. Seeing a faint glow from a back staircase, she walked toward it, supporting herself with a hand along the wainscoting.

As she went, she heard a strange sound, a faint, unsettling shriek; she knew it must be the banshee of Struan House. Once she had accompanied her grandfather here for tea with Lady Struan, and she had heard the eerie cry herself. The housekeeper, Mrs. MacKimmie, had been startled, and Lady Struan strangely pleased. Now chills ran down her spine, and she hurried down the narrow steps as best she could.

Despite his injured leg, Lord Struan had carried her up these steps earlier, and she had overlooked that small act of heroism at the time. Down the steps and along a whitewashed corridor, her uneven footsteps tapped on the planked flooring as she headed toward what was surely the kitchen, where more light glowed.

The big gray wolfhound came out of the shadows toward her, shoving his head under her hand. She petted him, and as she moved forward, he pressed close as if offering his tall shoulder for extra support. He almost seemed to lead her to the kitchen door, where light spilled into the corridor. There, Elspeth peered inside to see a long worktable, and she saw Struan standing with his back to her as he placed bread and cheese on a plate.

She entered quietly, the dog at her side. The scrubbed pine table held a bowl of apples, and on the plate were cheese and bread, beside a blue-and-white porcelain teapot. In the huge kitchen hearth, a steaming iron teakettle hung from a hook. A second hook held another kettle, contents bubbling.

"Soup," Elspeth said, sniffing the seasoned air. "It smells delicious."

He turned. "Miss MacArthur. The housekeeper left soup for my supper, and we can share if you're hungry. It's nearly late enough for supper."

"Thank you. No need to take it to the parlor," she added. "We can eat in the kitchen." She helped Struan prepare the tea, and he set the pot on the tray along with other items he found in a cupboard: teacups, saucers, spoons, a bowl of sugar already grated from the cone.

As they worked in silence, Elspeth felt the earlier tension between them dissipate in favor of cooperation. He set the tray on a table beneath a wide window, where chairs were arranged, and he drew out an endmost chair for her. She sat, pulling the woolen blanket closer over her shoulders, teeth chattering a bit. He set a bowl of soup before her, another for himself at the opposite end of the table, and then he sat, too.

"You're shivering," he said.

"My things are still damp," she reminded him. Her bare feet, one of them wrapped in his neck cloth,

touched the cool slate floor. She noticed that Struan
had changed to a dry coat of gray wool, with another cravat knotted at his throat. She stifled another
shiver.

"Forgive me," he said. "I should have offered you
some dry clothing, but honestly I do not know where
to look in the house for something to suit you. I could
offer you my own things, if nothing else."

She shook her head quickly. "The whiskey helped
warm me upstairs, but it is chilly here." Realizing that
he waited courteously for her to spoon up her soup
first, she did, finding it to be excellent, savory and
thick. As they ate, rain pattered the windows beside
the table, and a gust rattled the panes. Elspeth glanced
at the darkened sky. "Will your ghillie and the others
return tonight?"

"I doubt it, judging by the storm. The roads will be
muddy and unsafe in the dark. Most likely they will
arrive tomorrow." He set his nearly empty bowl on the
floor, and the two terriers who had been sitting nearby
rushed for it, nosing at each other. Elspeth set hers on
the floor, too, and the wolfhound came over to lick it.

Struan crossed his forearms on the table. "It would
be dangerous for us to ride out on horseback this evening, for the sake of the horses even more than ourselves. Miss MacArthur . . . you had best stay the
night here."

"I see." Her heart gave a little fillip. She reached for
the teapot and poured a cup for each of them, spoon-
ing sugar into hers, though Struan asked for his plain.
They sipped in silence for a few moments, until he set
his cup down.

"Miss MacArthur, I must ask—why were you in
the garden?"

Hot tea, swallowed too quickly, made her cough. "I . . . was looking for something that my grandfather lost there. He knew Lady Struan. We came here once or twice," she explained. "He is Mr. Donal MacArthur of Kilcrennan."

"Ah. I have seen the name in my grandmother's papers. What did he lose?"

"A stone, something special to him. It was lost when the hill was made into the grotto."

He sat forward. "I see. What sort of stone?"

"It is crystal and . . . chalcedony, perhaps, or agate. One or the other."

"Agate is a form of chalcedony," he said. "A banded variety, very colorful. Chalcedony of itself tends to be grayish. What color is this stone you are looking for?"

"Blue, I believe," she said, frowning. She had not seen the rock for seven years.

"Agate is unusual in this region, and the blue sort is rare anywhere. Did he find it near here?"

She nodded. "It was part of the original rock formation on the hill, before the gardens were altered. The property used to belong to the MacArthurs, when my grandfather was a young man. He left the stone there, but he . . . would like to find it."

"Perhaps it holds some sentiment for him. Of course he must have it, if it can be found. On my walks around the estate, I've noticed massive beds of sedimentary rock in these hills, such as granite and sandstone, with crystalline deposits. But agate is generally found in volcanic rock, which I have not yet seen in this area."

"Volcanic?" She looked surprised. "There are no volcanoes here."

"Not currently, but there may have been many

thousands of years ago. My own research addresses that question, since layers of volcanic rock implies tremendous heat long ago in the terrestrial past. Geologists are still investigating Scotland's mountains, and indeed much of Europe, for the signs. Why did you come back today to look for it?"

"My grandfather remembered it." She could hardly explain that her grandfather needed the thing to open a gate to the fairy world. Struan could not even accept Highland Sight, let alone bargains with the Fey in otherworldly hillside palaces.

He frowned. "Struan House once belonged to your family?"

She sipped her tea, then nodded. "The estate and much of the glen belonged to my great-grandfather. When my grandfather was young, he was often here. The grotto in your garden was once a large hill with a rocky precipice."

"I know the stone wall was extended up the slope. My grandmother was pleased with the result, an ongoing effort over several years, but unfortunately she did not live to enjoy it. Miss MacArthur—why not come to the door and ask about your missing stone?"

He was a persistent and practical man, she realized. "I did not think anyone was in residence. It is the time when the fairies go riding through Struan lands."

"Mrs. MacKimmie explained something about that."

"And my request seemed so mad that I decided to look for myself, believing the house empty. I apologize for the inconvenience."

"Not at all." He swallowed more tea. Elspeth noticed how delicate the cup looked, cradled in his long fingers. She imagined those hands turning a beauti-

ful rock over and over, holding it up to sunlight . . .
and then she imagined his hands upon her, warm and
agile in their caressing. She shivered, not from cold,
and sipped her own tea to hide her sudden flustered
reaction.

"You study such stones as I'm looking for," she
blurted then. "You're writing a book, something to do
with volcanic rock." A strange word sounded clear in
her head. "Geo . . . nosey. What is that?"

He lifted his eyebrows. "Geognosy? It means earth
knowledge—the study of the earth as a complete
structure, interior and exterior. I did not realize that
you were familiar with the work of Werner."

"I never heard of him. The word just came into my
head."

He stared at her, teacup halfway to his lips. "Good
God, how do you do that? How did you know that I've
begun a book about geognostic science? A few years
ago I studied in Freiburg for half a year with Abraham
Werner, who developed the theory of geognosy, which
looks at the earth as a whole. Either someone told you,
or—"

"Or I just knew," she supplied softly.

"Aye," he said, and seemed about to say something
else. He poured himself another cup of tea, and added
to her cup when she held it out. "While I'm here in the
glen, I intend to explore some the rock formations in
these hills. If agate was found nearby, that could have
real significance for my work."

"If you wander these hills, you may even encounter
the *daoine sìth*," she said.

"The—*dowin-shee*?" He looked at her, puzzled.

"The people of peace, in Gaelic. It is one of the
many names we use for the fairy folk. They live in

various places in the earth, but the caves and hills are their special territory in this glen. Do geologists ever take into account the Otherwordly creatures who inhabit the subterranean earth?" She smiled.

"Not if they value their reputations. Fancy and science do not mix well in academia, I assure you." He sat forward. "For now, though, I have agreed to study fancy on behalf of my grandmother and her legacy of work."

"Perhaps you will learn something about rocks to surprise you. Fairies are plentiful among caves and live inside hills," she said, feeling a little mischievous.

"I do not expect to encounter any. But I've made a promise, and I will honor it. Tell me about this curious fairy riding custom. I suppose you know all about it?"

"I do. They ride at the time-between-times, when the curtain between our world and theirs is very thin—dawn, twilight, midnight, mist, and so on."

He tapped fingers on the table, thoughtful. "At times when visibility is poor enough to allow for tricks of the eye and mind. I see."

"I think you do not, actually," she murmured. "Though you could if you want."

"Well, the custom seems to have frightened the living wits out of some of my staff. Between the banshee in the foyer, the ghosts in the house, and the garden fairies, two of the maidservants packed up in haste and left for Edinburgh."

"Southrons," she said with a little huff. "Highlanders do not mind such things."

"Even the Highland staff has gone, now. Apparently they avoid the place this time of year."

"They are not foolish enough to risk being taken

by the Fey folk. You should not be here yourself, nor should I."

"I am not intimidated by nonsensical tales." He smiled then. "It is no surprise that you are an authority on this, being part fairy yourself."

Elspeth nearly gasped. "What do you mean?"

"One of the housemaids must have seen you in the garden, and took you for a fairy. She packed her things and departed."

"Me? She might have seen one of the Struan fairies, but not me, unless it was just before you came outside."

"Of course there's some explanation." He sat back. "Entertaining stories are part and parcel of folklore, but no more than that, to my mind. By the way, Lady Struan mentioned your grandfather in her notes. She respected his knowledge concerning local tradition, and I thought it would be good to speak with him myself regarding the book."

"She and my grandfather discussed fairy lore several times. Will you speak with him before or after he learns that I spent tonight at Struan House?" She smiled.

"Well said," he muttered. Elspeth laughed a little. Sitting here with him, quiet and peaceful, she liked him quite a bit, despite his stubborn skepticism.

She stood. "The dishes need cleaning, but there are no servants here. I will be happy to do it." When she began to carry her dishes to the table and washbowl, Struan took them from her. He willingly did his best to help, though Elspeth suspected he had rarely washed or dried a dish before. Within minutes, all the things were cleaned and set away, and Struan took the lamp from the big pine table.

"I'd best close up the house. There are no servants here to attend to that, either."

"A Highland laird often sees to the shutting of his house personally, with or without a house full of servants. Even in fine houses it is the laird's responsibility to bolt the doors."

"I hope locking up is custom rather than necessity in this glen," he said.

"We have not had cattle raiders or feuding clans for two generations and more. There are some smugglers in the hills, but they stay to themselves except for bringing whiskey along the lochs and rivers to the sea." She paused. "What disturbs the peace of a house in this glen, sir, is not kept out by bolts, but by iron."

"Iron keeps the fairies away." He nodded. "I read about that just recently."

"If the wildfolk want to come in, they will find a way."

He laughed softly. She knew he thought it all harmless superstition, yet she did not resent it. Rather, she found his practical approach intriguing—wholly masculine and a bit of a challenge. She tilted her head, watching him, wondering about him. Standing in that cozy, quiet kitchen while rain pounded at the windows, she felt an unexpected sense of ease and comfort in his company. She did not want this night, this visit, to end quickly.

Tender, unforgettable kisses shared weeks earlier came to her mind, and as she gazed at him, she could almost feel his hands upon her again. An urge to be in his arms again, to experience not only the kisses but the passion and the cherishing that had been part of them, made her breath deepen, made her yearn.

Love, the thought came to her then: *Love feels like this.*

She saw him tilt his head in question at her silence. "What—where shall I sleep, sir?" she asked hastily.

"You may have your pick of the guest rooms." Holding the lantern, he led the way, taking her arm to escort her. A thrill went through her like small lightning. He had a restrained masculine power, tempered by courtesy and an inner control that she found compelling. She walked beside him, limping a little, her heart pounding.

The wolfhound rose from his place to nudge between them, setting Elspeth off balance so that she stumbled against Struan and set a hand on his chest. He caught her with a hand to her arm. The plaid slid from her shoulders, and he caught it, and for a moment she looked into his eyes, very blue in the low light. Through his clothing, his heartbeat under her hand felt strong and hard.

"You've made a friend in Osgar." He smiled as she stepped back.

"His breed are called fairy hounds. They take readily to those with fairy blood. They are true to their kind—though he seems to have taken to you," she said, as Struan reached down to pet the dog. "Do you have a trace of fairy heritage?"

"I was about to ask the same of you, since he likes you so well."

"Oh," she said, shrugging. "We have some legends in the family, like many Highland clans. My grandfather likes to say that my mother . . . had fairy blood."

"I could see that in you . . . in your eyes. Beautiful," he murmured, and reached up to brush back her hair where it had sifted over her cheek. Every part of her felt aware of his touch; wonderful shivers went through her body. He dropped his hand away. "But of course such things are not possible."

"I'm surprised that you acknowledge any claim to fairy ancestry, as much as you disdain such things."

"The legend exists. I did not say I believed it," he said. "Family lore holds that long ago, a MacCarran ancestor saved a fairy woman from drowning, and they were married. Her blood runs through all who are connected to the main branch, including myself and my siblings. They even claim that some MacCarrans have strange abilities because of this mythical ancestor," he added with a little twist of his mouth. "Come along, you lot," he called to the dogs. As they trotted around his heels, he took Elspeth gently by the arm and helped her up the stairs.

"Saved a fairy woman?" Elspeth asked with interest.

"Charming Highland hogwash," he said.

Chapter 7

"There are guest rooms on this level," James said as they walked along the upper corridor. "And the next floor up, but you do not need to climb more stairs just now."

He liked the pressure of her hand tucked in the crook of his elbow as she limped beside him. He understood, having lived with an injured limb for years, the concessions needed, and he was glad to offer support. But his body responded with an intimate tightening each time she changed the position of her hand, or leaned toward him a little. The feeling was strong and best ignored.

He would show her to a guest room and in the morning, drive her home. Between then and now were too many hours filled with temptation. But he would not take advantage of the circumstances, even if she wanted that—and had boldly stated so.

"All the rooms have been freshened for use," he said. "Mrs. MacKimmie set the housemaids to it, since some guests are expected next week."

"And I am unexpected," she said.

"Quite." He opened a door and stood back. The lantern light spilled into the room.

She stepped inside. "I'll need to light the fire—the hearth is cold."

"Let me." James followed her into the room, as did Osgar, while Taran and Nellie plopped down in the doorway. Limping slightly, he crossed the space; he had left his cane in the garden, and between the rain and the exertion, he felt the ache in his injured leg. Kneeling, he found peat bricks already stacked, and lit a match from the lamp that Elspeth held out. Patiently he coaxed the peat to catch. "The room will warm up soon."

"Thank you." She bent a little to warm her hands by the small flames. James stood, his gaze flickering down her body, taking in the lush curves beneath her damp gown. In the rising firelight she was lovely, and as she straightened, he leaned closer.

She looked into his eyes in a way few women he knew had done with him: clear and compassionate, yet enticing and mysterious. The girl knew his past without being told, so far as he knew, and that had shaken him—*she* had shaken him. He had not forgotten those lightning kisses in Edinburgh. Though it had been a public and acceptable flirtation, he had felt a deeper impact that he did not quite understand.

"I remember the first time we met," she said, echoing his thoughts in that damnable way she had. She looked up at him, petite enough to tilt her head. "We kissed." Said so softly, the sound a caress in itself.

"We did." A mere cushion of air warmed between them, and he felt drawn down. He could easily kiss her again, and wondered if she invited that now, and

if so, why. She confounded him with this mix of in-
nocence and possible ruse.

"I must go," he said, straightening. "I have paperwork waiting in the study."

"The fairy lore? I could help you."

"Perhaps another time. The less we are together
here, the better."

She sighed. "If we are discovered here, it will
not matter what we did or did not do. Others will
make their assumptions. Only we two will know the
truth."

"*We* will know. That is more important than the
rest of it."

She tilted her head thoughtfully, and James realized
that he felt off balance, uncertain of his way here. "I
have been honest with you, Lord Struan," she said. "If
I am even slightly compromised, I will be content. And
I will hold you to nothing."

"It is not my habit to ruin young women, however
willing, and abandon them."

"I do not mean the actual deed, sir. A tainted reputation will do." Despite the preposterous subject, she
looked serious.

He huffed a laugh. "Few men would respect the
difference."

"You do."

"And you," he said, "cannot know what I would do."

She watched him, eyes crinkling. "I do know."

"A blithe statement from a bonny girl," he murmured, "can signal disaster." And impulsively he
kissed her, swift and powerful, surprising himself.
The answering touch of her lips fed a flame in him,
deep and intense, and then he was caught—

He slid his fingers into the silken mass of her black hair, and cupped her head in his hand; slanting his mouth over hers, he felt her buckle against him, heard her sigh. She opened her lips beneath his, and he grazed his tongue over the delicate shape of her lower lip. That contact shuddered through him—he was no novice by any means, and had initiated the kiss with the intent of showing her what risk she invited. Yet he himself felt overwhelmed, as if he had taken hold of a new flame and wanted to know what it was to be burned. He made himself draw back, and saw that her eyes were closed, her lips full with a rosy bloom, her cheeks slightly flushed.

"Lovely," she said in a dreamy voice. Her eyes opened. They sparkled.

"Oh no," he said, putting her away from him. "Soon this will be no game, but something with very serious consequences."

"You think I mean to trick you," she said, "because you are a wealthy man."

She knew his thoughts too easily. But she had not guessed that he was not particularly wealthy, though anyone might assume so. "You are a charmer, Miss MacArthur, and something of a minx. That kiss," he said, stepping back, "will accomplish an adequate compromise, since we are alone here. Aye, something happened between us. Tell the world if you will. But let us leave this be, here and now."

She teetered on one foot and grabbed the fireplace mantel. "I am not a vixen, though I can understand if you think so. Very well. Still, the kissing was very nice."

He blinked. "Very nice," he repeated. No face slapping, no huffing away from him, no coy attempt to invite more and entrap him. "Just . . . nice?"

"Wonderful," she said softly.

"Miss MacArthur, explain to me why you do not insist on marriage in return for the delights of this, ah, willing compromise," he said. "Or will that insistence come later, when the fish is well and truly caught?"

"I would rather be ruined, a disgraced spinster," she replied, frowning, "than marry where my grandfather wishes for me."

"Surely your guardian is concerned for your welfare." Or else the old fellow had sent her to snare a wealthy and titled husband.

"He wants me to marry a Lowlander."

"What in thunder is wrong with a Lowland man?" He felt almost insulted.

"Nothing. But I intend to stay in the Highlands. If it takes compromise and disgrace to send away the Lowland suitor my grandfather has chosen for me, then so be it." She lifted her chin. It was a lovely chin, above an elegant throat.

"Interesting," he said, not yet convinced.

"It is true, though you think otherwise."

"You do not know what I think, Miss MacArthur," he murmured.

Her long glance said, indeed, that she did. Then she turned to the fire. "I must ask you something, Lord Struan."

"And that is—?" Was it the entrapment he dreaded? Yet his heart pounded.

She drew out the skirt of her dress. "May I borrow something for the night?"

"Ah." Bewildered, he glanced around the room, saw a tall wardrobe, and went there. He opened the doors to find shelves with folded garments and a few gowns hanging on hooks. "There must be something here."

She joined him, catching at his sleeve to keep her balance. James drew out one of the folded things and held it up: a short corset meant to hold the breasts snug. With it fell a lightweight chemise. He grabbed them and crammed them back. He knew how to undo such things when the time was right, but now he felt himself go red-faced.

"Er, you may look for yourself," he said.

Elspeth took a white folded garment from the shelf, lifting its full, lace-trimmed sleeve and high-necked bodice. "This is a night rail. But whose things are these? Oh dear, did this wardrobe belong to your grandmother?"

James regarded the white, billowy thing, which would no doubt swallow the girl. His grandmother had been a big woman. "She must have stored some of her things here."

"Oh, then I should not borrow these."

Elspeth wearing his grandmother's night rail—that ought to make the girl less appealing, James told himself. Perhaps then he would not feel keenly, intensely tempted; perhaps he would be unable to conjure images of her with nothing on at all. He thrust the thing toward her. "Take it. I insist."

She caught it against her, and James saw the curves of her breasts beneath his grandmother's delicates: a very good deterrent. He stepped back. "Good night, miss."

In shadows and firelight, her eyes were wide and silvery, so that she looked innocent as well as wanton. Though it was wrong to be so very alone with

her, and inconceivable to take advantage of an injured,
stranded girl wearing his grandmother's nightgown—
he wanted to do just that. He hastened for the door
in uneven strides, neatly making his way around the
dogs.

He rushed down the corridor toward the main
stairs as if all the hounds of hell were after him. In
reality only a pair of curious terriers scampered at
his heels. The wolfhound had stayed in the girl's bedchamber. The fairy hound would know its kind, James
remembered.

Only magic could explain the temptations he felt toward the girl, James thought wryly. His usual reserve
was more than enough to keep him aloof and controlled in any situation. Yet when this fey and fetching
creature appeared asking blithely to be compromised,
he had very nearly acted the fool over her.

Hurrying through the shadowed house, he saw a
lamp he'd left burning on a side table and snatched
it up for its light, then crossed connecting rooms into
the study. There he sank into the wide leather chair to
take up the pages he had set down hours ago, before
his life had changed.

What an odd notion, that one, and he dismissed
it. But he could not keep his mind on his grandmother's papers, constantly distracted by thoughts of that
quaint night rail and the delectable girl who wore it
right now. Tapping his fingers on a stack of unread
pages, he gazed through the window as the rain lashed
the glass with renewed force.

He had walked away from a Highland beauty virtually offering herself to him. He was neither a coward
nor wary around women, as some men could be. He
did not care a whit for society's opinion, but he had to

live with himself, and he would not satisfy urges that were blatantly ungentlemanly in this situation, even if a powerful delight in better circumstances. He had kept a mistress years earlier, and had dallied about with other women before and after; but he was not about to further compromise this girl, no matter how willing she claimed to be.

His Belgian mistress had been a pretty creature, the widow of an esteemed and forward-thinking geologist, a man he had corresponded with but who had died by the time James had traveled to the area with his regiment. The scholar's young widow, soft-spoken and buxom, had granted James access to her husband's scientific papers while he was on brief periods of leave from the Black Watch—soon she had offered access to her person as well. Being young and hungry for passion, knowledge, adventure, with the underlying fear that he would face battle soon, James had let the dalliance develop and continue. They had parted without desperation or regret, friends more than lovers. And he had gained an increasing interest in geology and a diminished desire to study medicine.

Only his first lover, when he had been barely twenty and studying medicine and natural philosophy at University of Glasgow, had stirred genuine love in him. He never intended to be that hurt again. The red-haired daughter of a Glasgow shopkeeper, she had an interest in botanical sketching and spent many afternoons wandering the hills above the town; James met her while he was collecting rock samples in pursuit of his personal hobby. Soon they met there by arrangement, working diligently to help each other's efforts; sometimes they played sweetly, privately, in the grasses, or met elsewhere when they could.

She took a chill that winter, and by the time James called at her house, she was seriously ill, with her family unaware of her beau. Turned away, he had not spoken up, thinking to hear from her soon. But he never saw her again. Fostering the reserve he had learned as a boy, he later regretted not revealing himself that day, but he had been young. A few of her drawings were tucked in a drawer at his home on Charlotte Square, and he would keep them always. He had gone to war after that, giving up medicine for the study of rocks. Dull to others, perhaps, but well-suited to him.

Wind whipped past the house then with such strength that for a moment James heard a faint shrieking—that pestering banshee again, he thought wryly, though he knew it was just the moaning of the storm.

Again he thought of Elspeth, alone upstairs, and wondered if she was alarmed by the groans and creaks of the old house. He sighed, rowing fingers through his hair, and told himself that she was a tough Highland girl, after all, and used to such things. Setting aside a recurrent urge to walk upstairs to see if all was well, he took up another stack of handwritten pages to resume reading.

A local weaver, Mr. MacArthur, an abundant source of history and traditional tales for this account [his grandmother had written in her small, careful script], claims to have been abducted by the fairies when he was a young man. However, the gentleman politely refuses to elaborate on the details of his experience except with a trusted few. He believes the fairies will show their wrath

*to those who say too much about them or
reveal their true ways. It is this author's
fervent hope that the Highland weaver will
share his fascinating story with the world
someday. . . .*

James sat straight up, and read the passage again.

Something was not right. The wolfhound was
growling.

Elspeth woke, quick and alert, from sleep, hearing
Osgar's low rumble. The hour had to be very late, she
thought, with the darkness and quiet so deep. Even
the sounds of the storm had faded. "What is it, Osgar?" she asked.

The dog padded over to the side of the bed, looked
at her through the darkness, and whimpered. She
reached out to pat his head, then lay back again.

The bed was soft, the pillows plump, the linens
cool and fresh; she was exceedingly comfortable, yet
she could not sleep. A sound, faint through the walls,
sounded like her name. Sitting up, she saw the room
lit only by sparse light of the peat fire, flickering blue-
gold, all else in shadow. Had James, Lord Struan,
called her name, or had he knocked?

Eilidh . . . The sound came again, softly, and then
again, like an echo. *Eilidh* . . .

Osgar whimpered again, and was pacing, padding
impatiently around the room. Gasping, she drew
her knees to her chest, drew the covers snug to her,
kept still and silent. In a dark corner of the room, she
saw flitting lights—a pale green glow, a shimmering

blue, a streak of violet. Sitting straighter, alert, she wondered if the fire's reflection was dancing on some surface. When she looked again, a cluster of shapes formed in that same corner—and she saw the tall, graceful contours of heads and shoulders, long draped robes.

Shivers rose along her neck, arms. "Who is there?" she called, but it came out as a whisper. "What is it?"

Eilidh . . . The shadowy lights—for both they seemed—moved closer. Ghosts? She felt a chill all over. From the shadows, she clearly saw a hand reach toward her. Elspeth scrambled off the bed and leaped down. Pain stabbed through her ankle and she winced, leaning on the side of the bed, staring toward that side of the room.

"Who are you?" she asked in a hoarse whisper. Moving back, she snatched up her plaid from the back of a chair and edged toward the door, her heart pounding hard. The dog bumped against her, startling her so she cried out, then she rested a hand on his shoulder.

The lights had vanished, whatever they were. She breathed out, telling herself it was foolishness or fatigue. Yet she did not want to go back to the bed. Setting her hand on the doorknob, she turned it, about to step into the corridor.

Then she heard a roll of thunder mingled with distant hoofbeats. Osgar gave a loud, commanding woof and stood tall and alert. When her name sounded again—spoken by voices in soft chorus—she knew. *They* were here.

"Leave me be," she gasped, and limped out into the dark corridor in bare feet. She was not sure where to go, but she had to get away from her bedchamber. Remembering that Lord Struan had a room at the other end of the hallway, she ran that way, wincing, and knocked on the door.

No answer. She knocked again. A crash of thunder shook the walls, and she shrieked, opening the door to step inside. In firelight and darkness, the room was empty—shadowed furnishings, the bedcovers undisturbed. Osgar bumped against her hip as she turned and left.

Holding the dog's collar, she hobbled along the shadowy corridor toward the main staircase, realizing that Struan might be still working in his study. She had to find him, for his safety might be at risk—and she could not bear to be alone just now. But how could she explain to him that she had seen the wildfolk themselves in her room, and had heard the pounding of their horses' hooves through the very walls. The Fey rode tonight, and they knew she was inside Struan House.

She stopped, gasping a little as she realized that the tales her grandfather had told her all her life were true after all. Either that, or she was a little mad, and hearing things.

But she knew better. She knew, deep down now, that this was true, and she was not sure what to do about it. How had they found her inside, with the iron locks bolted? Had Struan shut the house as he had promised? She went as quickly down the stairs as her ankle would allow, grasping her plaid around her shoulders.

Eilidh . . . Soft as a whisper of wind, that sound. They used her fairy name, the one that she herself could tell only once, for the power in it. A crack of lightning came so suddenly that Elspeth leaped, shrieking as a blue-white light filled the stairway. The dog hastened downward ahead of her, reaching the main floor first.

Hearing her name again, she froze for an instant, and hurried on. Despite a strong temptation, she did not glance over her shoulder.

Never look behind you in a fairy-held place, her grandfather had said, *for in that moment they will have you.*

Chapter 8

When the scream sounded, lightning blazed through the windows, and James ran from the study into the main hallway. The terriers ran barking alongside him. The shriek was not the banshee this time, but light and feminine. *Elspeth.* Alarmed, he rounded the corner for the stairs, and a shadowy figure—the wolfhound—hurtled past him. A ghostly figure in white followed. James stepped forward, straight into the arms of the slender wraith that leaped at him, arms looping about his neck—

"What in blazes! Elspeth!"

"Oh!" She sank against him and he gathered her to him as another whipcrack of lightning flickered through the hallway. She felt so good, too good, in his arms, and he embraced her, smoothed her tousled hair, his heart beating heavily with the fright she had given him. "What is it? You're scared—"

"I am not," she said hastily, yet she clung to him like a squirrel on a tree.

"Well, I was bloody frightened," he said. He held her close, felt her relax, and then she set her feet down, hopping a bit. "I thought you were a ghost. What happened?"

"I could not sleep, and came down to find you."

"Was it the lightning?"

"I am not a ninny to be scared of such things," she said. "I thought perhaps I might sit and do some reading while you worked in the study." She still clutched the lapels of his waistcoat; he had been working in shirtsleeves for comfort, and had left his coat behind in the study.

James covered her hand in his own. "Nothing so mundane as that would send you flying down here as if demons were after you. I thought you were the resident banshee when you came down in that floaty white thing—"

"Hush!" The fingers of her free hand pressed his lips. "Do not call the *ban-sìth*!"

"It's only the storm, or creaking hinges, or rain on the roof."

She shook her head, clutching his lapel. "It is not that—oh, James—"

Suddenly, for no good reason that came to mind, he kissed her. Tender and fervent, one kiss melted into another. He tilted his head to hers, caught her face in his hands, pushed his fingers into her hair, savored what she returned. She moaned a little and sank against him, slanting her mouth beneath his, driving him onward when he knew—and surely she knew—they should not do this. Yet he wanted her so keenly in that moment that his mind seemed foggy. Catching her by the waist, he pulled her hard against him, her body pressing against his own through the thin fabric of her gown. He thought he might go mad with the wanting that pulsed so hard through him; he already seemed a bit lunatic where she was concerned.

Not this way. That thought sobered him. He took her by the shoulders and set her a little apart from him. "Enough, before we both regret it."

"I do not regret it," she said, breathless.

"One of us has to be practical."

"Neither of us does," she said, "really."

"Good God," he said. He stepped back, tugged on his waistcoat, heart pounding, and turned away. "If you cannot bear to be upstairs alone in a thunderstorm, I am still working in the study. You can sit there if you wish, or in the library. And cover up a bit more, will you," he added irritably. "I am not a strong fellow."

"Oh you are," she said with a little laugh, as he walked away.

He glanced at her over his shoulder. She seemed a lucent glow in the dark hallway, her pale face, the long whip of her black braid, the white billow of his grandmother's gown. Her eyes were large and luminous, and he stared, entranced.

"Never look over your shoulder at the fairy ilk," she said, inexplicably. Then she came toward him, bare feet over the bare floor in an uneven *slap-pat*, her limp still evident. James crooked out his arm, and she took it.

"Where in botheration did the dogs go?" he asked irritably, glancing around for any distraction. He was painfully aware that Elspeth wore only the night rail and the plaid over her shoulders. Moments ago, he had felt the smooth, warm curves of her body beneath soft fabric. His grandmother's night rail, yet he could not keep his hands off the girl beneath it. "Blast," he muttered.

"Lord Struan," she said. "Please." She sounded amused, relieved.

"We hardly need a banshee in the house with you here," he said. "You've cast your own lunatic spell over the laird. He cannot seem to act the gentleman, and begs your pardon, Miss MacArthur."

She laughed and held his arm as formally as if they entered a ballroom instead of the doorway of the dark library. Both of them were partly clothed and in disarray, and they were alone in the house at midnight, in a fierce storm. Her lush allure and her delightful willingness, together with the passion he could feel for this girl—all of it had the makings of a disaster.

And he wondered how they would get through this night without a necessary obligation of marriage. Truth told, it could benefit both of them. Meanwhile, he was drawn to her like iron shavings to a magnet, holding back every moment he was with her. The infernal thing was that she did not seem to mind the circumstances at all.

The dogs materialized from the shadows to accompany them into the library, and James led Elspeth through it to the study. There, with the oil lamps turned up, things seemed more ordinary. But Elspeth did not relax as he expected. While he returned to his paperwork, she stood in the center of the room with her head cocked, looking wary, as if she listened for something. Thunder boomed distantly, and she jumped.

"Sit down," he said. "Read a book." He gestured toward the volumes available on table surfaces, on shelves. Contrary to the inherent restraint and control in other areas of his life, he was not particularly tidy in his work. Digging about for rocks could make one less fussy about dust and piles of things.

"I am fine," she said, standing in the middle of the room, arms folded, the plaid wrapped over her generous breasts. He lifted a brow and glanced away.

"Miss MacArthur, I cannot seem to think if you stand there like that," he murmured, sifting through some papers. Where the devil was that piece he had read earlier?

She went to the window seat tucked beneath an expanse of paned glass that overlooked the back garden, now all darkness and whipping rain and wind. "The roads will be flooding; the bridge will wash out."

"Is that a prediction?"

"Just familiarity with the glen. In bad storms, the old bridges sometimes crumble and the roads, which are not good to begin with, go to mud. The local men repair what they can afterward, but it is difficult to keep ahead of the weather in poor seasons."

"New bridges should be built, and the roads resurfaced."

"Should be, true. But no one has the wealth for it."

Nodding without answer, he wondered if she truly believed that the laird of Struan had the generous pockets needed. He scarcely had enough funds to keep his house and grounds in order, let alone pay for bridges in the glen, or make a wife wealthy. Unless he finished his grandmother's book and wed a fairy bride, he would have only a modest inheritance.

Fairy bride. He looked up.

Well, no matter what came of this unusual situation, he certainly could not concentrate with her curled on the seat like that; her night rail defined the very delightful shape of her hips and bent legs. He could even see a blush of pink skin through the fine lawn fabric. Rising from the desk, he began to put some books away, carrying them to a wrought-iron ladder, climbing up to slide the books onto high shelves.

Had Elspeth MacArthur come deliberately to Struan House in poor weather intending to find the laird alone, hoping events might lead to a marriage to benefit her family and community? She had been frank about her desire to be ruined. Had she been entirely honest about escaping the marriage her grandfather planned for her, and avoiding any marriage?

He glanced down to see her flipping through the pages of a book. She was so lovely—a fey sort with that dark hair, pale features, and delicate frame. Anyone might believe she had fairy blood. Even Sir Walter Scott was convinced of her unique abilities.

If he married her, he could meet the will's conditions.

Preposterous, he told himself. He and his siblings should have disputed the will instead of agreeing to chase will-o'-the-wisps. Still, he was grateful for the chance to work with his grandmother's manuscript. Lady Struan seemed closer to him now than she had been for much of his life. He would honor that, and her book, regardless of its fairy subject matter. What seemed pure nonsense to him might appeal to others.

The wolfhound rose from his spot by the door and loped toward the girl. She patted his great, unkempt head. "Good lad, Osgar," she said.

"That dog follows you everywhere now," James said. "You need not be frightened in this house. He could scare off anything, earthly or unearthly."

"Oh no, he'd probably let them in."

"Them?"

"The Fey who are out riding tonight."

"Come now, Miss MacArthur. Not even a fairy would be out and about in such a downpour. Nor do dogs open doors. Let us put all this pretense aside."

"I would never try to fool you."

"A pretty promise," he answered, easing another book into place.

She looked up at him. "You've closed off your heart from hurt, James MacCarran," she said softly. "You trust no one."

"Life does go more smoothly that way," he said casually, picking up more books from the stack he'd carried with him, and shoving them into their slots. "It eliminates certain complications, like gullibility—" *And love.* He stopped.

"And love?" she asked.

James shoved another book into place. "The world is full of silly notions and sentiment, Miss MacArthur. We need not debate it here."

"Why do you not believe in the Sight, or fairies—or perhaps anything?"

He climbed off the ladder and came to stand near her chair. "Because believing," he said very quietly, "would require that I accept what is fantastical. I would only be disappointed when it is proven wrong. Give me good solid rocks to categorize—I will show you what is real." He stamped his boot heel. "The earth beneath our feet. The air we breathe. What we touch, and see." He wanted to reach out to her, but instead shoved hands into his pockets. "I rely on that."

"You are afraid to believe." She sat up and leaned toward him, and the lamplight reflected in her eyes. "Afraid it might be true, and that you could not explain it, and you might have to trust in something unseen, and powerful."

"What man trusts easily? Certainly not myself." He inclined his head and stepped away to set some books on the desk.

"You are afraid of me a little, I think," she said.

"A slip of a thing like you? Preposterous."

"I am not frightened of you, or of being here alone with you. Nor am I afraid of what might happen . . . to us, or to my heart." She watched him openly.

He glanced at her, keenly aware that she did frighten him a little; she had come into his solitude and stirred up too much. "This situation is what alarms me, Miss MacArthur. Disgrace is not a convenient solution for your engagement dilemma."

"It could be," she answered.

A decanter of whiskey sat on a nearby shelf, and he lifted it to swirl its contents. "Mrs. MacKimmie has placed bottles in every room," he said, changing the subject. He could use a good swallow of whiskey to fortify him against the fetching little wraith in his study. But better to keep his wits about him. He set the decanter back.

"Struan House has a good supply," she said. "It is the laird's house, after all. The smugglers who live in the hills are generous if one looks the other way. My grandfather never wants for whiskey, and never purchases it. If you are pouring some, I will have a taste, as it is chilly in here. It is a night for whiskey, with such a storm."

James poured a little into a glass and brought it to her. She swallowed a little and handed it back to him. "And you?" she asked.

"Not just now. If I got foxed, you might try to compromise me," he drawled.

"I may abandon that idea. You're too unwilling."

"Oh, I'm quite willing," he murmured. The silence pulsed in the very air between them. "But logic and manners prevail. For now," he added quietly.

The wolfhound stood then, whining, just as a distant, eerie shrieking drifted overhead. Elspeth grabbed James's arm as they turned toward the door. A cracking glow of lightning split the shadows, and a rumble of thunder sounded.

"The banshee—" Elspeth said, her fingers tightening on his arm.

"It's an old rusted weathervane," he answered. He was not convincing even himself, but he persevered. "I'll have Mr. MacKimmie investigate it when he returns. Surely you are not unsettled by a bit of iron creaking in the wind."

"The banshee is warning us," she said. "Something will happen this evening."

"Something is happening. We are stranded here alone in this blasted storm."

"It wants to tell us that the fairy ilk are riding on Struan grounds."

James was pondering his next denial, for it had to be a sound one, when a cacophony of thunder shook the walls. "What the devil," he muttered, moving toward the door, Elspeth holding his arm. "It sounds as if the horses have gone loose from their stalls. I'll have to check. Wait here," he told her, letting go. "Osgar, stay with her."

"I am coming with you," Elspeth said. Wasting no time on argument, James hurried toward the back corridor, then down the steps past the kitchen. The girl and the wolfhound followed him.

"Wait here." He snatched a coat that hung on one of the hooks there, and stepped outside into a whipping gust.

"Struan!" Elspeth called behind him. "*James! Wait!*"

He looked back. "It's only rain," he assured her. "I'll be fine."

"Whatever happens," she called, "do not look back!"

He waved briefly and went out into the storm.

Eilidh. Gasping, hearing her name again, Elspeth stepped out into the elements. The Fey were riding that night, and James had gone out unsuspecting. She knew he would find the horses safe, the stable closed, because the sounds had not come from there. And he might be in danger—she had to find him and urge him to return to the house. Whoever encountered the fairy cavalcade on Struan lands might vanish, never to be seen again.

Eilidh . . . come with us. The voices blended with the wind, and the beat of horses' hooves seemed part of the thunder. She knew how serious the risks were—Donal MacArthur had fallen to their mystical lure years before, and paid the price of it every seven years. Now she, too, felt the strange pull of their presence. But if she found James and stayed with him, he was so solid and unbelieving that even their power might diminish before that, and both of them would be safe.

She had never feared the fairies before, but now she felt wary. James had no idea of the dangers involved if he stayed out. Seeing his discarded cane as she limped over the lawn, she grabbed it up to help her walk, and then rushed onward, her nightgown and plaid whipping back, her uncovered hair soon wet.

Then the wolfhound was beside her, bumping against her, and she took his collar, reassured by his strength. Crossing the wet, soggy grass beside him, limping in bare feet, she soon noticed the pain diminishing. She knew that the presence of the Fey could make a person feel good, healed, even euphoric: their magic was in the very air.

Something moved ahead, shapes and shadows in the mist that took on a strange blue glow. She heard footfalls and bells. Moments later she saw a line of horses, light and dark, moving through the night mist just beyond a line of trees. She hurried forward a few steps, and stopped, scarcely daring to breathe, afraid to be heard or seen.

The riders, for it was they, the *Sidhe* of old, glided by on horseback. Some called them the Seelie Court— a marvel, a vision, they emerged sparkling out of the mist, tall men and slender women who sat their horses elegantly. They were impossibly beautiful, the glitter and spark of their jeweled clothing like webs of light and fire. Their cloaks and garments, a rainbow of color, were hemmed with gold and gems, and the reins in their hands were bejeweled, too. Their hair, set with filaments of gold and silver, was softly curled, sun-gold or night-black, braided and beribboned. Rings flashed on their fingers, buckles glinted on belts and shoes, and their eyes glowed like crystal.

As they approached, she saw magical symbols embroidered in shining threads on hems and saddles. Tiny silver bells, dangling on harnesses and braided in the horses' manes, chimed soft and clear in the night.

In the lead rode a woman, with a man and another woman riding to either side of her. Others followed, seven riders in all, with an empty saddled horse. They meant to bring someone back with them this night.

A cold chill flooded through Elspeth. They had come for her. She knew it like the certainty of stars and sunlight. She stepped back into the shadows as the cavalcade headed toward the back gardens of Struan House. They would soon pass the place where Elspeth stood beneath a huge oak tree to one side of the garden. A stone wall stood between her and the riders, who came at a steady pace as if there were no barrier.

She flattened her back against the oak, sheltered beneath its dripping leaves, and watched as the riders passed clean through the stone wall—all of them, as if they were nothing but mist. Their gait made a kind of music: *clip-clop* and bell ring, with the sighing of the wind.

Even as Elspeth shrank against the tree trunk, the Fey lady in the lead saw her and angled the horse toward her. *There! Come to us, Dear One . . .*

They were close now, nearly abreast with her where she stood under the tree, horses passing slowly in front of her, the boughs of the oak trees shaking in the storm winds as they passed. The lady, beautiful in green and gold, her pale hair streaming like moonlight, reached her arm and beringed hand toward Elspeth, who shrank back.

Yet she felt a strong tug that seemed outside herself, and irresistible. She thought of James, disbelieving and unaware of the threat, and she clung to the tree. The true *Sidhe*—if such these were—could steal the very soul from a human.

Come with us, they said in their melodious sing-song.

The dark-haired lady, near her now, reached out her arm. *Sweet One, join us!*

Suddenly unable to stop herself—she felt drawn to this fairy woman, more so than the first—Elspeth lifted her arms, realizing that she was losing strength against their thrall. The outdoors was their domain, the earth, the trees, the rain, the wind, the rocks, the air. Here, their power was strongest. Her hand was up, the fairy reached out, and she heard music in the rain, and smelled the scent of flowers despite the storm. Then she felt herself lifting on her toes—

"Elspeth!"

His voice cut like a brisk wind. She looked around to see James running toward her. Forcing herself to step away from the line of riders, she whirled and bolted toward him over the wet lawn, crossing in front of the cavalcade as it rode toward the house.

A moment later she heard horse hooves behind her, and then beside her, as the riders caught up to her. *Dear One, wait! Eilidh . . .*

"Elspeth, here!" James was not far away, waving to her. The riders passed Elspeth then, and in an almost fickle way, headed for the man. "I'm here!" he called.

"James, no!" Elspeth ran toward him. The riders moved, clopping hooves and silver bells, and when they reached James, the lady in the lead beckoned to him.

Come with me, she called. Elspeth saw him look up at the Fey. The wind blew at his coat, his hair. Then he reached up, and a mist seemed to envelop him, and the horses.

"No!" She ran into the mist, reaching out to grab James so fervently that he stumbled back a step, wrapping his arms around her. The horses were but an arm's length away, their riders reaching toward both of them. Elspeth spun James around so that his back was to them, and she turned her own face away, tucked against him. Bringing up her arm, swathed in her green-patterned plaid, she covered both of them as best she could. The Fey lingered in the mist, calling out. *Come with us.*

On impulse, Elspeth grabbed James's face in her hands to keep him from looking around. He began to speak, and she kissed him, hard and desperate. She gasped against his warm, pliant, responsive lips, pressing against him along the length of her body, as he caught her.

"No, no, you shall not have him," she whispered frantically.

Chapter 9

As the kiss deepened, James took over, his hands coming up to cup her face. Elspeth cupped her hands over his, determined to keep him from seeing the Seelie Court, and the magical lady who wanted to take them both away with her.

"Hold tight, hold me tight," she whispered between kisses.

Long ago, in the many tales of fairy lore that her grandfather had taught her, she remembered that a loved one could be saved from the fairies by a fast embrace, never letting go, never looking back, until the danger passed.

As James kissed her, she sank against him, feeling as if a whirlwind spun around them. Her hair whipped free, his fingers threading into the strands as he tilted her head back, and renewed the kiss with hunger and wildness. The wind shoved them, turned them, and again, yet Elspeth did her best to keep him from looking up to see the riders. Finally she sensed them moving away, and glanced up to see them vanishing into the mist. The man who rode behind the women looked back, and she thought he looked familiar, but in shadows and storm, she could not tell.

Soon you will be with us, Eilidh, the stranger seemed to say.

But she would not follow them—not now that she knew their power, and knew that her grandfather had been right after all. They did intend to take her. But held tightly in James's arms, she felt safe—she felt loved, for that moment. Whether it was real outside this moment, she wanted more of that feeling, wanted to be with him.

The mist and the sound of small bells faded, leaving only drizzle and thickening fog. The danger had passed, and Elspeth had saved him; they had saved each other. And yet she stood wrapped in James's arms, kissing as if it need never stop, fervent and hungry, the rain wetting her face and his, slicking her hair, her hands, their lips in a slippery, delicious blend. He cupped her face in his hands now, his lips caressing hers, coaxing, craving, and she lost sense of all else but him, and the need, and the rain.

"Hold me," she whispered. "Hold fast, never let go—"

"Never," he murmured against her lips, and tightened his arms around her. She slipped her hands under his coat and waistcoat, where the fabric of his shirt felt warm to her chilled, wet fingers, and she felt herself pulling at fabric, starving for more of that wild touch. Then he slid his hand over her arms, along her hips, over the cotton nightgown, and upward until he cupped her breast, and she drew in a breath.

They turned, slow and dancelike, as his fingers cradled and teased, his thumb grazing over the nipple. She cried out softly and took his mouth again in a kiss.

He groaned low, and his tongue glided over hers, his fingers finding the other breast, and then both, until she felt her knees folding under her and she began to sink down into the soft, wet grass. He sank with her, facing her, pressing close, their abdomens tight together, so that she felt his desire for her, hard and sure. She melted inside, desperately wanting more of this. The mist had grown thicker around them, and she felt as if they were alone here, suspended in a place without time, lost to caresses.

Arching, she felt a hot need building within, and she gasped, hungry to touch him, wandering her hands over him—pulling at his coat, his waistcoat, his shirt, shaping his chest, his abdomen, with her hands. He pulled her tightly against him, his breath as fast as hers, and she rocked against him, and he with her, intimate and daring, and altogether what she wanted, here and now.

His lips traced whispery soft at her ear, and beneath his fingertips, her nipples went to pearls, and she moaned. He dipped his head, lips seeking over her jaw and throat, his hand now pushing aside the damp fabric of her gown, and when his lips touched her breast she cried out, an ecstatic gasp, and felt the bolder touch of his hand over her belly, scooping down, finger pads nudging between her thighs. Teasing warmth, and a pressure that took her breath away, and she shaped her hand over his breeches, her fingers easing along between flap and waist button. She felt such heat, such steely solidity there, and when he groaned against her she felt wanton, tingling, wild throughout—and yet it was more than desire and will; she felt something powerful and driven, something she could not deny, and did not want to refuse.

He moaned, kissed her, his breaths ragged. He lifted his hands away and brought them up to cradle her face. He pushed her rain-slicked hair back.

"Dear God," he said raggedly, "what is this?"

"A wild pledge on a fairy night," she whispered, and kissed him, and knew it was so—at least for her part, she would pledge true, though she might never see him again.

He sighed and came to his feet, and clasped her hands to pull her up to stand with him. "Not here— not like this, savage in a garden. My God," he said, leaning toward her. "Wild pledge on a fairy night—I can almost believe it."

"Almost! You saw them yourself."

"Who?"

"The *Sidhe*," she whispered, glancing about. "The Good Folk. We must be careful how we call them when they are so near."

He stared at her. "Near? Has the storm got to you, or the whiskey?"

"You saw them!" She grabbed his coat lapel. "I know you did. They rode past us, the Good Folk of the Seelie Court. They tried to coax us to come with them."

"We'd best get you inside." He lifted her green plaid again, draped it over her shoulders, guiding her with him toward the house. "A fascinating legend, your fairy riders. On such a night as this one, it is easy to imagine all manner of things."

"Are you sure you saw nothing else?"

"I noticed you, my girl." He brushed back her hair. "It's coming down in a torrent again." He hunched his shoulders, putting his arm around her. "Come away."

She hastened with him toward the house, and no-

ticed that her ankle hurt fiercely once again—but the
pain had stopped earlier, she remembered. Beside her,
James, too, had a halt in his step again, though it had
seemed to temporarily disappear as well, when he had
run across the lawn toward her as the fairy riders came
toward him. His gait had been long and even then.

Seeing the cane discarded, she stopped to pick it
up, and he took it without a word, and they went to
the back doorway, shaking off the rain. With the dogs
bounding around them, they entered the dark corridor
alongside the kitchen.

"What did you see out there?" Elspeth asked him
then.

He was brushing rain from his shoulders, and
paused. He had lost his hat, and his thick hair was
dark and curling with the wet. He looked wildly handsome, so much so it wrenched her heart. "What did I
see? A good deal of rain, that's for certain," he said.
"The trees were blowing and bending so that I shall
have to look in daylight for damage. The horses are
fine, though," he finished.

"Nothing more?" She stood very still.

He touched her cheek. "I saw a lovely woman," he
murmured. "Why?"

She stared at him for a moment. "The thrall had
both of us in its power."

"Oh aye, it did." He brushed his thumb over her
cheek.

She batted his hand away, spun, and stomped toward the stairs, limping heavily, her ankle tender.

"Elspeth! What in blazes is wrong?"

Pausing, she looked over her shoulder. "If I tell you
what I saw, you will call me seven kinds of lunatic, and
swear until you turn blue. So be it—I will not trouble

you with talk of Second Sight, and certainly no talk of fairies," she said, spinning away, "and thank you kindly for the compromise."

James hastened after her, reaching out to grab the black terrier by the collar before it could trip Elspeth on the stairs. "What are you blathering on about?" he asked, climbing the stairs behind her. "Watch yourself," he added, catching her elbow when she missed her footing. She shook him away.

"You saw something out there, I know you did."

"A good deal of rain, and two foolish people who stood kissing in a lightning storm," he answered.

"Why will you not admit what you saw? We kept each other safe out there so that we would not be stolen away—we saved each other, you and I!"

"From being snatched by the wind? It could have lifted you away, but not me."

She reached the hallway and turned to face him. "I've heard that when the Fey are near, a madness can overwhelm those who see them. I think that is what happened to us."

"A kind of madness indeed," he said, stepping up beside her. "And I accept the blame for that." He touched her shoulder. Her hair, dangling in black twists and curls, swept over his hand as she shook her head.

"There is no blame. The thrall had us in its power. Do you not understand?"

"Madness or magic, we will call it something else tomorrow. And then what?"

She leaned close, narrowing her eyes. Even in the dim hallway, he could see the beautiful sheen of her eyes. "You did forget," she said thoughtfully. "The thrall happens that way with some. The memory may return."

He brushed a hand through her hair. "I have not forgotten a single moment of what just happened," he murmured, "nor will I."

"Try to remember, James. The queen of the Fey rode past us, and tried to take us both. We held each other tight to keep safe. Try to recall it."

"My girl, you do not need to invent a story to explain this whole thing away. The truth will do. I was worried about you, I found you—and I lost control of myself. You are . . . rather irresistible."

She pushed his hands away. "You were worried because you saw the Fey."

"I was worried because you ran out into a lightning storm in your nightclothes," he said. "When I saw you outside, with the weather so fierce, and that strange fog rising, I tried to wave you away from the trees— they were bending low in the wind, and I thought they might crack and collapse. Then you ran toward me, and whatever happened after that was my doing."

"Both of ours—but—did you not see the horses, or the riders?"

"The horses in the stable are fine, as I said. That mist was odd—thick and swirling in strange patterns. One might easily imagine horses and riders moving through it, but it was just the trees whipping about." He frowned. "Though you did put a sort of thrall over me." He tipped her chin up with his hand. "And I gave in."

"I have no magic. It was not me who did that."

"You," he said, "have more magic than you know. But you should have waited inside for me to come back from the stables."

"They—the Good Folk, the folk of the Seelie Court—called to me to follow, and they called to you, too. The only way to stay safe when the Fey ride by is to hold tight to another, and fear not, no matter what happens. Fear not, and do not look at them. And we had my cloak of green, which is a protective color against the fairy folk."

He stared. Good God, what was she blathering on about? "Are you talking about the ballad of Tam Lin? 'Hold me fast, let me not go—'" He stopped abruptly.

"'I'll be your bairn's father,'" she finished.

"Very nearly, which you and I had best discuss," he drawled.

"You think me a wanton hussy, intent on my own mean purpose."

"I never said that. We are in extraordinary circumstances, you and I."

"Oh, extraordinary!" She was beginning to seethe, he could see, her shoulders tightening, her brow drawn together in a furious frown, yet still she looked like an angel to him, or a fine fairy beauty with that cloud of black hair and those eyes, crystal gray in some lights. "Stop denying this. I saw you stand there and look up at them, and reach toward them, as if you were tempted to ride away with a queen of the *daoine sìth*."

"Elspeth, enough. If this is part of your scheme to be ruined and wed, have done with it. If it's something else—well, you are Donal MacArthur's granddaughter. I read my grandmother's account of his story. He claims to have had some strange encounters."

"What did she write about him?" Elspeth asked.

"He told her that he had been taken by the fairies, and returns every few years."

"So you think my grandfather a daftie, and me as well." She shook off his hands. "Away with you! Believe what you like. I saw the Good Folk ride past us, and *you* saw them, too," she said, poking his shoulder with a finger, "whether or not you admit it."

"I do not think you are daft. Eccentric, perhaps. Superstitious, certainly."

"I am going into the drawing room to rest my foot," she said, "and to get dry and warm. I need a little time to think. Alone, if you do not mind."

"Fine," he said. "I have work to do in the study."

"As for my grandfather," she said, "Donal MacArthur knows whereof he speaks. When he was a young man, he lived with the fairies, their hostage for seven years."

"Seven years," he repeated carefully.

"Well, to be fair," she said, "it felt like a week to him." She spun away and limped down the hallway toward the drawing room.

James stared after her, dumbfounded. Osgar appeared beside him in the hallway, paused to stare up at him, then turned to pad after Elspeth. "Ah, the fairy hound," James said. "Go after your wee mistress. She's one of their ilk, after all. Make certain she stays safe, hey?"

He blew out a long breath, ran a hand through his damp hair, then again, turning about in the deserted hallway as if he did not know quite what to do next. Seven years with the fairies? What purpose could she have in claiming such a thing?

If he had by some miracle found himself a real fairy, she was furious enough right now to resort to spells, he told himself. He smiled then, thinking he might enjoy a little mischief in her hands, once her temper subsided.

* * *

Passing by the library as she went toward the draw-ing room, Elspeth stopped as she noticed the shutting of the light as James closed the door to his study. She stood leaning against the jamb of the open double door, looking into the high, spacious, book-lined room, and she sighed heavily. For a moment she was tempted to go after him and knock on the door—but she knew better than to pursue this now. Nothing could be agreed or decided when both of them were tired, angry, and a little stunned by what had occurred in the garden. She knew the Seelie Court had ridden past—and she was sure that James had seen it, too, but would not admit it or did not remember. But there was no convincing him.

She walked into the library, clutching her damp green plaid around her shoulders, and stood by the fireplace there, drawn by the warm, glowing hearth. Holding out her hands, she glanced around. Rain sheeted against the tall, darkened windows, and the low fire shed a little light. The room was lined with soaring shelves containing thousands of books neatly stored; at the room's center was a long table, and two sets of wing chairs upholstered in red brocade flanked the fireplace. Beneath the bookshelves were arranged various small tables, chairs, and a few glass-fronted cases that displayed small items.

The warmth felt good, and the lawn of her night rail was so fine that it dried quickly, while she outlasted the impulse to knock on the study door. Breathing a sigh, she turned to leave the library, glancing at the glass case nearest the fireplace as she walked past it.

She stopped short.

The shelves held crystalline stones. She leaned closer, and even in the low firelight, she could see the beautiful color striations. One stone, on the middle of the topmost shelf, glinted blue in the darkness. Turning, she found a candlestick and holder on a table, lit the wick at the hearth, and returned.

The size of her palm, the round, crusty stone was split down its center to reveal the rich layers of color and concentric pattern at its heart. On a small gilded stand, its luminous range of cool blues ran from rich indigo to pale mist, with a multipoint crystalline formation in the center.

She could not be certain, but she thought it could be the beautiful blue stone she had come to Struan House to find. Bending close, she examined it in the candlelight. Years ago, she had seen a rock like this one on the day she had turned fourteen years old, the day her grandfather had brought her to the hills and had explained his own ties to the fairy realm. He had shown her a stone that he had plucked from a hiding place somewhere in a rock crevice. That one had been a unique and beautiful thing, its blues ranging from pale to deep.

She jiggled the little bronze handle of the case, but it was locked, with no key in sight. Other pieces on the shelves looked valuable and antique—stones, buttons, arrowheads, a range of stone specimens. If she could hold the beautiful blue stone in her hands, and then try it in the rock wall above the garden, she would know. The stone she sought was like a live thing, full of unique power, so her grandfather had told her.

Perhaps Struan would let her have the stone inside the case. Her grandfather's future visits with the fairies—which she knew he treasured—depended in part on the magic of the stone entrusted to him. The fairy gold that he had promised to find for them, stolen so long ago, was also tied somehow to the mysterious blue stone. Once her grandfather fulfilled the bargain, the *daoine sìth* would be satisfied.

The stone had to come back to the MacArthurs of Kilcrennan.

Chapter 10

Firelight flickered on the curtains of the old-fashioned canopy bed as James lay on the covers, still dressed but for coat and boots. Arms crossed behind his head, he lay sleepless, staring at the embroidered canopy overhead, where vines, flowers, and bees had been intricately worked long ago. He hardly noticed the design.

He had not seen any blasted fairies out in that storm, he thought, and he was beginning to wonder if he should doubt her sanity—or his own. He had walked into Struan House and stepped knee-deep into fairies and whatnot—from the banshee in the foyer to Grandmother's fairy lore, to a fetching, wanton girl who saw kidnapping fairies riding horses. All he had seen were trees whipping in the wind, and a strange mist that took on anthropomorphic shapes. What sort of a place was this—and how much had his grandmother known of it when she had sent him here via her will?

For now he had more immediate concerns. From the moment he had encountered Elspeth in the garden at the bottom of the muddy hill, he had thought of little else—in fact, she had entered his dreams to stay months ago, after he had met her at Holyroodhouse. That was the day he had thought her a lovely, intriguing Highland girl who had played an odd trick on Sir Walter; he had kissed her behind the potted plants in a flirtation, and had been thoroughly caught.

This evening he had nearly taken her on the lawn in the midst of a storm. However blithely she wanted compromise, she could hardly have meant like that.

And now he was irrevocably obligated to her. Staring at the needlework pattern on the old satin canopy, he thought about the knotwork of circumstances in which he found himself. Sighing again, he rubbed a hand over his eyes. His only choice was to marry the girl, and soon.

Well, he had come to Struan to finish the manuscript and find a Highland fairy bride, of all impossibilities. Elspeth was a Highland girl with a decidedly fey nature, and marriage now seemed inevitable, practical, and necessary. He would speak to her about it in the morning.

Though the question seemed settled, he could not sleep. After tossing for a while, he finally rose from bed, still in shirtsleeves and trousers, deciding to go downstairs and read for a while. Fairy lore was a sure soporific, he told himself.

Heading down the hall past the guest chamber where Elspeth presumably slept, he heard her cough lightly. Pausing at her door, he heard soft footsteps in a pacing rhythm. He was not alone on this strange, restless night.

He tapped on the door. "Miss MacArthur." No answer. Knocked again.

"Go away," she answered.

"You need not open the door. Only listen to me," he replied.

"Say what you will." Now her voice sounded close.

Resting his head against the jamb, he composed his words. "What happened tonight has consequences. I am willing to make compensation for them."

"Unnecessary," she replied, quick and cool.

"Miss MacArthur," he said, huffing in exasperation, "I am offering to marry you." His heart slammed. Until this moment, he never thought to say those words without courting, without careful consideration of merit and need. But fate, and his strong male nature—and some wild magic he did not understand—had put him here. Oddly, he felt more certain of this than of other steps he had taken in his life. He felt a deep urge to do this, as if the emotion and intuition he had long stifled had trumped his forte of logic.

"Elspeth." Flattening a hand on the door, he tapped again. A raw need, more of the heart than the body, roiled in him, but he drew back from its brink. "It is what must be done in such situations," he finally said. "We ought to consider it."

"Must be done," she repeated, with a wry twist to her voice. "Ought to be. What a pretty statement of romantic devotion." A taut silence followed, and James wondered why he had not saved the matter for morning and a clearer head.

"I understand you need time to consider. We will discuss it further tomorrow." Yes, he sounded heartless, but he could hardly tell her that he had to meet the conditions of Lady Struan's will. That news would be even colder than the gentlemanly obligation he genuinely felt.

"You need not feel a gentlemanly obligation," she said, in that odd way she had of saying the words that went through his head—only his twin, Fiona, did that.

"But I do," he said.

"I do not regret what happened. Your offer is appreciated. Thank you."

"Do not thank me. I fully intend to compensate for . . . your compromising."

"It will be our secret. Good night, sir."

Our secret. The words sent a sudden plunge of desire straight through him. "Wait," he said. He could not allow himself to say what he felt—it was far too jumbled and incomprehensible to him, and against his personal code of keeping himself close, and others safely apart. Yet whatever compelled him was powerful. "Elspeth—ah—a clear conscience demands an honorable solution."

"Clear conscience? What good union could come of such a beginning? It's best forgotten. A little ruination suits me. Marriage does not."

"You said you would rather be ruined than marry the man your grandfather has chosen for you." The notion of her with another man made him close up his fist. "I offer you a better solution than disgrace, or marriage to some ogre."

"He is not an ogre. He is a reputable tailor with a fine income, and a country estate outside Edinburgh." Through the thick wood of the door, her voice had a soft intimacy. James leaned close to listen.

"Then what the devil is wrong with the fellow?" He felt annoyed. Jealous.

"Nothing. But he does not love me, nor I him. And he lives in the city, while I want to stay in the Highlands. Besides, I think he is more interested in my grandfather's weaving manufacture than in having me for a wife."

"Then he is a fool." James closed his eyes.

"He is not . . . the one for me."

"And who," he said softly, "is that one?"

"Well, no one now that I am ruined," she said crisply. "That is the point."

"You are not ruined, not while I am here to make it otherwise," he said in exasperation. "You could be the new Lady Struan." The more he insisted, the more he craved this marriage. Hope, like some silly, storybook feeling, dawned in him. If he could convince her, his life would be better. So much better. Hers as well, he thought. "This would benefit both of us. I . . . have need of a wife."

"I am sure there are several ladies who would be glad to know that."

"I am not asking any of them to marry me."

"Perhaps you should. They will be happy to keep to the city with you."

"Is that the root of this infernal stubbornness? I have to stay in the city, Elspeth. I am a lecturer at the university. We could spend our summers here," he offered.

Silence. "I cannot leave this glen," she finally said.

"Listen to me. I am a viscount," he said, and began to tick off on his fingers. "I own this fine estate. I have a respectable yearly income, or may have. I have a town house in Edinburgh and a prestigious position at the university. I'm not unpleasant to look at, despite a bad leg, and I have written a volume on geology that weighs nearly as much as you do." He stopped, surprised by his fervor. He was not one to tout himself or reveal his feelings or needs. And he had never courted any girl with the insistence he was applying to one resistant Highland lass. "Surely that counts for something."

"I am impressed. You have very nice qualities. You will have no difficulty finding a bride when you return to Edinburgh."

Shoving a hand through his hair, he exhaled. "It's more difficult than you know."

"Marrying me will not solve your problems," she said. "Legal . . . problems? What does that mean?"

If one factor discouraged him from having Elspeth for a wife, it was her uncanny ability to ferret out his private thoughts. How in blazes she did it, he had no idea. "Marry me and I will tell you the whole of it."

"No."

"Elspeth, I will not beg. Consider it." He leaned his head on the door. "I am not good at this confounded courting business."

"Better than you know," she said. "I am flattered. You are Viscount Struan, and quite pleasant to look at . . . and I do not mind at all the bad leg. I have a bad ankle at the moment myself. In fact, I must rest it now. So good night."

"You know why we must marry. What in blazes is your true objection?"

"You swear too much. It is a plague in your personality."

"Elspeth," he growled.

"Very well. I told you that I want to—I must—stay in the Highlands, but you are a Lowland man. In fact, you cannot wait to be away from here to go south again."

"I never said so." Not in her hearing, at any rate. "You would have a comfortable life in the city with me."

"I know," she said softly. "But let us be done with this, now. It is late."

The more she denied him, the more appealing the prospect grew. She was interesting. Intriguing. Fascinating. "Tell me this, then." He leaned to the door, speaking low. "Do you refuse to marry because you wait for someone else? Perhaps a man who lives in this glen?"

"I wish he did," she whispered. "He is a fine man. We tumbled sweetly, once, with the fairy magic upon us, and he won my heart. But not all of it," she added firmly. "He does not even believe me most of the time."

James went still, heart thumping. He closed his eyes, aware of a sense of passion, excitement—and a lightning strike of hope. "Is he the one for you?"

"So he thinks. Go on, James MacCarran," she said. "Away with you, now."

A moment later, he knew she no longer stood by the door. Still he lingered, a hand on the wall, head bowed. He felt touched deep in a way he could not define. Finally he stepped back and walked down the dark corridor. He felt strangely different, not the man who had knocked on that door a quarter hour earlier, yet not sure how he was changed.

Elspeth smoothed her skirts and straightened her green jacket, her garments dry now, having been draped by the hearth fire while she slept; she had been able to brush away most of the dried mud, though the stained gown was beyond saving. She hurried now, aware that it was well into the morning; she was determined to leave for home soon. Outside, a fine rain pattered the window glass again.

Truly she wanted to stay. Struan's marriage proposal still echoed in her mind; the intimate tone of his deep voice, his words and their meaning had sent quiet thrills all through her. Though she had no choice but to refuse, and could hardly tell him why, she regretted it deeply. Perhaps she always would.

Glancing into the mirror over the chest of drawers, she combed her fingers through her tousled hair and plaited it in a single braid, tied with a ribbon slipped from her bonnet. Her favorite straw hat, like her dress, would never be the same again. She grabbed her green tartan shawl and tossed it over her shoulders. In more serious ways than her gown and bonnet, she knew she would never be the same again.

She went to the door, with a glance for the window, where the landscape was dreary, brown, and sodden. If it was impractical to walk home, she would have to ask James to drive her. He had not returned to her door last night, and it was just as well, she thought, for she might have relented and agreed to marriage, even knowing he only felt obligated. She had no need to marry him, or anyone, she told herself.

What she wanted was to remain at Kilcrennan with her grandfather; perhaps she might never wed. But the real difficulty, she realized, was that she was falling in love. It had not begun last night—though she had enough reason—but on the August afternoon she had first met James in Edinburgh.

If she surrendered to love, that could nullify the

fairy magic that made her grandfather happy and fed his dreams. She could not leave Kilcrennan, not yet.

After last night, she understood the real power of the fairy sort. Donal had tried to warn her, having lost a son to the Fey, and having fallen to their thrall himself. After spending seven years with them as a young man, his own bargain brought him into the fairy world for a few nights every seven years. That had given him a great gift for weaving, but he feared to lose his granddaughter as he had lost his son. Elspeth could not bear for him to endure that again. Her grandfather and Kilcrennan, this glen and those she loved in it, were all that she knew. She would not be the cause of destroying what she held dear. Even love—even marriage to Lord Struan—seemed a selfish choice if it ruined the happiness of others.

She left the room carrying her bedraggled straw bonnet. Taking the stairs, she found that her ankle, though it ached, was better, hurting only with a good deal of pressure. Glad of the improvement, she took the steps cautiously.

James did not seem to be in the house—she had peered into library, study, and parlor, and then made her way downstairs to the kitchen. Encountering the three dogs in the corridor near the door leading out to the garden, she fussed a little over them, and saw through the kitchen windows a fine, steady downpour. Beyond that, she could see the sodden lawn where she and James had fallen to the grass with wild kisses and lush tenderness, while the fairy court rode by.

Drawing a breath at the pull of that memory, she looked around the deserted kitchen, and noticed a tray on the scrubbed pine table. A silver pot and a single china cup and saucer, with a folded note of creamy paper, had been set there not long ago, for steam twirled up from the spout of the pot, with the delicious fragrance of cocoa.

She had not seen his handwriting before. The script was strong and slightly spiked, with a hint of roundness in the vowel like a secret tenderness. The note held only her name, underlined. She traced a finger over the ink. Pouring chocolate from the pot, she filled the cup and sipped, watching the rain, wondering where James had gone. Then Osgar came forward to nudge at her hand, urging her toward the door.

"Very well," she said, and followed. He scratched at the back door with a paw, and the terriers trotted up, watching curiously as she tied on her bonnet and opened the door.

Pulling the plaid over her head against the wetness, she stepped out, limping slightly, lifting her skirt's hems out of the mud. Once again, Osgar butted against her to offer support, and she patted his shoulder. "Good dog," she said. "My loyal friend."

The gardens were windblown and deserted, and she turned to go back inside when she saw James walking toward her from the direction of the outbuildings, where the stables, animal byres, henhouse, and other buildings were located. He wore a greatcoat and hat, one hand engaged with his cane, the other shoved in a pocket of the coat, its tails billowing in the wind.

"Good morning, Miss MacArthur," he said as if they were mere acquaintances, as if this was a polite encounter in city park or village green. "Chilly and wet today."

"Lord Struan," she said with equal coolness, feeling an awkward tension and avoiding his direct glance. "The weather has improved enough that I can return home."

"On foot? I think not. I will drive you as soon as the roads allow. We should wait to see how the day develops. Stay as long as you like." His quick smile was shy, heart-wrenching, and gone too soon.

"I should not stay any longer than necessary." She glanced away. "Have you seen to the animals yet? They will need tending after such a storm."

"Actually I was just doing that, and all is well. Though I am a city lad, as you are eager to point out, I know the basics of country life. Most of the Struan animals are kept on the home farm, a mile into the glen. We have two cows who gave no milk this morning."

"Probably frightened by the storm."

He nodded. "Mrs. MacKimmie keeps several chickens here—they were penned safely. I found a few eggs this morning." He pulled his hands from his pockets to display two or three brown eggs cupped in each hand, then repocketed them out of sight. "We can share some breakfast, if you like."

"Thank you. And thank you for the hot chocolate, too." She turned to walk toward the house alongside him.

"Quite welcome. How is the ankle this morning?" His own gait, with the cane, had the slight rhythm that seemed part of him. "You're in no condition to walk home, as anxious as you seem to be to escape Struan and its laird."

"I do not want to escape," she said. "But I cannot stay here, alone with you."

"Ah. Not now, in daylight," he said.

She shrugged. In silence, they followed the earthen lane to the house. The morning light was pale, the rain soft, the ground beset with puddles and runnels of water. Elspeth picked her way carefully, now and again setting her hand on his arm, for her ankle troubled her over the uneven ground. If her foot was not strong enough even for this, she could not walk home, and would have to wait on his whim for a ride.

"Halloo! Halloo, my lord!"

Elspeth turned, as did James. "Who is that?" he asked, as they both looked around and into the distance. Two men walked along a road that led over the estate grounds. "It's not MacKimmie or the grooms."

One man wore a kilt, jacket, and flat dark bonnet, with a plaid over his shoulders. The other was dressed in a black suit and black hat, with a plaid over his shoulders as well. They waved again, and she felt her stomach sink a little as she recognized the men.

"That's Mr. Buchanan and his son," she explained. "The elder Buchanan is a smith, and his son is kirk minister down the glen." She looked at him. "When they see us here together, they will make their own conclusions, and news will travel quickly. The Buchanans do not guard secrets well, nor do their wives."

"Let us meet our fate, then," James said, and took her arm to escort her toward the stile in the stone fence that surrounded the grounds of the house.

"Och, it's the new laird," the older man said. "And Miss MacArthur!"

She smiled. "Lord Struan, meet Mr. Willie Buchanan, a neighbor in the glen, and our blacksmith.

And this is his son, the reverend of our glen kirk, Mr. John Buchanan."

"Good to meet you," James said, shaking their hands. The Buchanans, looking like older and younger twins, tipped their hats to Elspeth and the viscount.

"A fine soft day." The elder Buchanan looked up.

"Aye." James smiled. "Let us hope it clears soon."

"Not for a while. The clouds are thick yet, and still flying over the mountains to the west. More rain to come," Willie Buchanan said. "Do you have any metals gone to rusting after this, you be sure to send for me." James nodded.

"I would have visited sooner to welcome you to the glen, sir, but for the weather, and my duties in the parish," the reverend said then. "It is a surprise to find you here, Miss MacArthur," he continued. "I thought you would be working your loom at Kilcrennan, or snug by the fireside there. When we stopped there this morning to see if all was well after the storm, Mrs. Graeme said you were away to Margaret Lamont's house, she said. She was concerned for you."

"I set out for Margaret's house, but had some difficultly yesterday due to the storm. Lord Struan came to my assistance."

"Did he now." The elder narrowed his eyes. "What sort of assistance?"

"A dry roof over her head and an offer of an escort home as soon as roads permit," James said smoothly. "May I offer you hospitality, gentlemen?"

"Thank you, sir, and no," the old smith said. "We'd best be on our way. We're walking about to ask after the neighbors after the storm, and off to see that my auld mum is all right. We canna take the pony cart, but must walk, the roads are that bad. The river and stream are gone floody, too. The auld bridge is washed out. Not yet collapsed, but washed out for the time being."

"Oh!" Elspeth glanced at James. "Then I cannot go home that way."

"You can walk the long way over the hills, as we've done," the reverend said. "Neither cart nor gig can take road nor bridge until things dry up again."

"Is Mrs. MacKimmie home, then?" Willie Buchanan asked. "I have greetings for her from my wife, who is her good friend."

"Not at present, Mr. Buchanan, but I will tell her you called," James replied.

"Not home? Perhaps your ghillie, then. Mr. MacKimmie is a fine friend."

"He is not here either. Delayed by the weather."

"Ah," said Mr. Buchanan, glancing again at his son. "Not home. Alone, they are."

Elspeth shivered and drew her plaid higher over her head. The gentlemen adjusted hat brims and jacket collars as they all stood, rather ridiculously she thought, in the drizzle, with the stone fence and iron gate between them. The Highlanders did not seem in a hurry to leave. Shifting her weight to her uninjured foot, Elspeth felt James's hand briefly at her elbow. Again a fast look exchanged between the Buchanans.

"Yer Southron housemaids ran off, I heard," Mr. Buchanan said. "We saw yer groom driving the lasses along the road yesterday."

"Aye, the girls resigned their places here," James said. "Apparently they dislike ghosts and fairies. I have not been much troubled by them, myself."

"Och, Lowlanders," old Buchanan said, nodding. "Though we canna blame them. It is custom in this glen to avoid Struan lands during the time of the fairy riding. You are a brave man to stay here at this time. Did Miss MacArthur not warn you?"

"My housekeeper mentioned the tradition," James said. "It will not bother me."

The elder Buchanan twisted his hat in his hand and glanced at Elspeth. "Are you sure he understands the whole of it?" he asked.

"He does," she answered.

"You will find Highlanders a superstitious lot in general, Lord Struan," the reverend said. "The people of this glen have their own particular legends, of course. Most find the stories entertaining, while some put real credence in them." He glanced at Elspeth, then away. "It is not a matter of religious faith, not paganism or godlessness, as some might suggest, but rather the unique Celtic character. As a pastor, I try not to concern myself overmuch with it."

"Very wise, sir," James said. "The legends are entertaining, and harmless."

"Such stories, along with the ghosts and fairies themselves," Elspeth said, "are more than amusements. They are part of the cultural legacy of the Scottish Highlands, and as such should be given their just due."

"Of course," Reverend Buchanan agreed. "The late Lady Struan was quite interested in the tales of the glen, as I recall. She often drove her pony cart about to interview people about our local customs."

"She loved her work," James said amiably. "This weather looks to become dreadful again. Sirs, are you sure we cannot offer you some tea?"

"No, we are on our way. Miss MacArthur, may we see you home?" the reverend asked. "We would be glad to walk you over the hills to Kilcrennan."

"Thank you, it is not necessary," she answered, smiling. Beside her, James pulled his hat brim low against the incessant drip and said nothing.

"Lass, no need to impose on the good laird," the elder Buchanan said. "Yer grandfather would want ye home. He's expected home this evening, if roads permit."

"I will see Miss MacArthur home myself," James said.

"We can do that," the reverend insisted. "No doubt you will agree, Lord Struan, that this situation is not . . . seemly."

"There is nothing amiss here," Elspeth said. "We are not even strangers," she blurted then. "Lord Struan and I met last summer in Edinburgh."

"Just so," James said. Elspeth felt the warm pressure of his fingers through her jacket sleeve. A sense of support, of security, infused her, and she was grateful for it.

"Ah." The smith glanced at his son, and back again. "Well then, sir, we will move on before the weather worsens." Then he turned to Elspeth and spoke in Gaelic. "A thousand good wishes to you in your future, Elspeth, granddaughter of Donal."

"And to you, sir," she replied in that language.

The men moved on, and turned to wave. Elspeth waved, too. Then, without a glance for James, she picked up her skirt and hurried toward the house, limping with uneven steps. Catching up to her, James opened the door for her, and they stepped inside. Then she whirled on him in the small passageway.

"Now what? Mr. Buchanan spoke a Gaelic blessing to me, as if I was engaged!"

James frowned. "Well, generally a compromise means a marriage. It's less of an uproar for you that way, than poor assumptions and disgrace. If we were to announce our courtship, or better yet, our engagement, that would avert scandal."

"I do not want to be engaged," she said. "I am trying to avoid one!"

"You spent the night alone with me, and now we've been caught out," he said. "An engagement can be broken, creating less gossip around you."

"Why should you be concerned with that?"

"I am," he said, "because I thought you might be." He bent to pet the terriers, who jumped up, panting for affection.

"Highlanders do not fret over scandal the way Southrons do. Some whispering might occur, but few in the glen would judge me unfairly. Even girls who have babies out of wedlock are not severely judged, or often sent away. We know such things happen."

"Aye," James said wryly, watching her. "They do."

She felt herself blush. "My cousin's first child was such a one, and she but fifteen then. Her family treated her kindly, and a few years later, Margaret married a good man. As for my wee transgression," she said, glancing at James, "I would not be expected to marry the tailor, but I could live contented at Kilcrennan, running the household and doing my own work."

He nodded thoughtfully. "What work is that?"

"Weaving." She lifted a bit of the plaid draped around her shoulders. "This is some of my own work. I help Grandda with his tartan business. It is no occupation for a viscountess."

"Not necessarily. My grandmother did as she pleased, driving about in her pony cart chasing fairy legends, and writing her stories. If she'd set her mind on weaving, the walls of this place would be draped in plaid. She never let convention or obligation deter her from what she most wanted. Even after she died," he added low.

"She also spent a good part of the year in Edinburgh. I will not abandon what is important to me to move south and host tea parties and be bored with little to do, while a husband goes about his own business. I would not expect you to give up your work."

"Nor would I ask it of you. Where is the argument, Elspeth? We can marry, and you could live here as much as you like."

Osgar approached Elspeth, and she busied herself ruffling the silky fur of his ears. Then she looked up. "Away from my husband? I could not live like that."

James gazed at her, a little frown between his brows. The man was inscrutable, she thought, and she sensed more in his persistence than gentlemanly obligation. "Keeping two homes is a good solution for our situation," he said.

Nellie, the white terrier, trotted toward her then. Elspeth bent low to rub her snowy head. "Why are you so determined to see this done? Many men in these circumstances would be glad to be freely released."

He shrugged. "You require a husband, after last night. I require a wife."

Require. She felt that word like a blow. "And I," she said, standing, "will never marry a man who does not love me more than his obligations."

James watched her in silence, then glanced away.

"There will be no engagement," she said, hurt and angry. Snatching her skirts, she turned and swept past the kitchen toward the stairs. Her heart beat hard, and raw need made her desperate to turn back to ask why, and ask what more could be done.

Every instinct, womanly and Celtic, told her that she cared deeply about this man, and that he could care about her. But somehow her instincts were wrong. Though he had suggested marriage, it was dispassionate. She hurried away.

"Damnation," James said then.

Elspeth whirled, shaking, hoping.

"I forgot about the eggs." He removed a hand from his pocket, eggshells in his palm, the clear and golden slime coating his fingers.

She laughed nervously, part sob and part giggle. James scowled, then laughed, too, sheepishly. Egg dripped on his coat, his boots, the floor. The terriers trotted over to lick the floor and his shoes clean, and James pushed them away with his foot.

"I've managed to save these few, at least," James said, producing three whole eggs from the other pocket. "Miss MacArthur, would you consider sharing breakfast?"

She sighed, surrender and sadness. "I would. We can agree on that, at least."

Truth be told, she was hungry, and she did not want to leave Struan House and its laird just yet. If ever. The pull she felt toward him was strong, increasing even as she looked at him now. Each moment, each experience with him added more facets to what she knew of him, more to what she wanted to know. Now, with his crooked half grin, his damp hair and blue eyes, the wide shoulders and lean build, she thought of how good those arms, those lips felt. And she yearned to run to him.

But she stayed where she stood. He held his walking stick so casually, yet she knew how much he needed it; he was empirical and factual, little given to impulse, yet he was learning about fairies. He was careful in his appearance, yet left his study in disarray; and now he stood with rain dripping from his fine coat, and egg smeared on his hands, a terrier licking his boot and another lifting up to paw at him in messy adoration. And he laughed, though she had hardly heard him do so. Her heart seemed to melt further.

She guessed he had little idea how to cook the eggs he had gathered, but she knew he meant to try. For her. It was an apology of sorts, she realized.

She sighed. For a while, she must keep her reasons and her fears to herself, though Struan offered hope, even with obligation. If he knew the truth about her and about Donal, he would withdraw his proposal. Better she refused him now, so that he would never discover the truth, or the extent of the eccentricity, at Kilcrennan.

But she wanted more of his company, and some food, too, before she left him. Nodding silently, she followed him into the kitchen, dogs trotting alongside.

Chapter 11

***D**aunting,* James thought as he surveyed the untidy desk piled high with papers and books, then sat to resume his work of reading and annotating his grandmother's manuscript. The distraction—to put it mildly—over the last couple of days had brought respite from the work, but the task remained to finish the manuscript, and wed a girl of fairy blood. An improbable measure of worth, but he knew Elspeth was more than worthy; at the very thought, his body responded with an unbidden surge. Surely she would meet anyone's standards in a wife for him.

But his great-aunt, Lady Rankin, would soon arrive at Struan House, and she would no doubt have a strong opinion on the matter, particularly as she favored Charlotte Sinclair for him. Still, she could be won over by Elspeth's charm, he thought. If only Elspeth would accept his proposal, he felt sure the rest would fall into place.

Yet stubbornness ran as deep in the girl as mountains in the sea, and convincing her would be a challenge. Once he took her home and met her grandfather, he planned to court her. If she refused him after that, he and his siblings might lose nearly everything.

Sighing, he fluttered the pages of the manuscript, which he had nearly finished reading, and he had made inroads with research and notes. The pages with his own jottings sat to the other side, weighed down by a plain rock. The subject of fairy lore still bewildered him, though the accounts themselves—mostly stories of encounters with fairies and the supernatural—were rather entertaining. But he would study the rock formations in the glen, for he was falling behind on his own work. Science still vied with fancy.

Last night, despite Elspeth's insistence that fairies rode in the garden, all he had noticed were strange drifts of fog and strong gusts, explained by the weather. He was somewhat concerned that she imagined fairies, but he realized, thanks to Lady Struan's work, how strong local traditions were in this glen. Elspeth had learned those perceptions.

Cold rain struck the windows, and the chair creaked beneath him as he set the manuscript aside. The scope of the work was challenging, but nothing was as difficult as convincing Elspeth MacArthur to marry him.

He could not wait much longer. Even before he had arrived at Struan, he had decided to offer the estate up for sale, for it seemed his best practical solution. He had sent a letter to his advocate, Mr. Browne, asking him to search for a buyer to discuss a fair arrangement. It seemed his only choice, for the sake of his family.

Mr. Browne had sent a reply within a week. James now removed that letter from a drawer to read it again. *The Right Hon. The Viscount Struan,* it read.

My Lord,

*Rec'd your inquiry and yr request is understood.
Of course this is within yr private right. If so
desired, I can recommend two parties, one Scottish lord, one English gentleman. Both would be
interested and have funds to generously satisfy
any requirements. Pls advise,*

Yrs, Geo. Browne, Esq.

A lucrative sale would provide funds that James
could divide among his siblings. That way, he could
rescue their plummeting finances, and his own, and
save their dreams as well. His own dreams were
more modest—his geological studies, and now his
bride.

Giving up Struan House would be far harder than
he had anticipated, for he was already attached to its
beauty and its unique atmosphere. But his circumstances had shifted dramatically in the course of the
last two days. As preposterous as it seemed, he still
had hope that all could be resolved.

He put the letter away and dutifully returned to his
work. After a while, he heard the click of dog paws
on the wooden floor in the library, and then the swish
of skirts. He glanced up. Through the open adjoin-
ing door between the study and the library, he saw
Elspeth perusing the bookshelves in the larger room.
Rising, he went to the door.

She turned. "Sir, I did not mean to disturb your
work. I came to read a little." She held up a book. "A
volume on fairy stories." Her voice was soft, careful,
her tone formal.

"There are many more like that one. You're welcome to borrow any of them."

"Thank you, but as I will be leaving soon, it is not prudent to borrow. The rain is lessening." She looked toward the window.

"Aye," he murmured. As Elspeth moved, she limped a little, supporting herself by grasping chairs or running her hand along the library table. "You should be off your feet," he remarked, and stepped forward.

"I am fine, Lord Struan. I do not require assistance."

Had they returned to formal terms so completely? He felt a strong urge to take her into his arms. He was not done with this, though she made it clear that she was. Even the space across the room seemed to him a mile or more. He felt as if he had lost her already, having scarcely known her. But he did not want to let go of this dream.

"It's a handsome room, the library," he said, searching for conversation, determined not to let her silence drive him back into his study.

"It is," she agreed. The walls were set with books from floor to ceiling, and the room boasted a fine marble fireplace and the tall windows were hung with blue satin. Oriental carpets covered the wooden floor, and the walls, papered in hand-painted Chinese florals, held oil paintings of landscapes. "This is a house to protect and preserve. You and your kin must be proud of it," she went on.

He nodded somberly. "Aye."

"You would never want to sell it," she said.

"I would not want to," he agreed, wondering again how she knew his thoughts.

She wandered to one of the small display cases.

"Do you know much about the stones in here?" She pointed.

He joined her to look at the shelves in the glass-fronted case. "They look like stones that are easily found in this area. Quartz, some very nice cairngorms, some red jasper. My grandfather collected stones, fossils, arrowheads, and so on, and had cases made to display the interesting pieces. When my grandparents came here, they brought the cases and the whole odd collection. I remember playing with the stones when I was a lad, especially when my grandparents still lived in Edinburgh. It was my grandfather's habit of walking about collecting stones that made my sister and me curious about natural philosophy, the study of nature. I was interested in rocks, and my sister liked fossils."

"Your grandfather taught you to appreciate rocks, and mine taught me to weave. What of this one?" She pointed at a blue one in the center, one of the larger stones.

"Interesting. A Scotch pebble, that—an agate, and a beautiful specimen. We believe that agates formed when pockets of gases and liquids dried and hardened to form beautiful variegated rings of color. They're often found with quartz, in volcanic rock. I haven't heard of many agates found here in the central Highlands. They have a nice range of colors. The blue ones are quite rare," he added thoughtfully.

"The various blues in it almost glow," she said. "It runs like a rainbow, from moonlight to midnight."

"It does," he murmured. "And it has extraordinary luminosity. Agates like this would probably not be found near Struan. This must have come from elsewhere. Odd, there's no label. Grandmother must have added it sometime last year."

"If the case was open, we could examine it more closely."

He rattled the little door. "I do not know where Mrs. MacKimmie put the key. When she returns, I will open it for you."

"I will not be here then," she said.

"Then you must come back," he replied quietly. "Bring Mr. MacArthur." James recalled something she had said. "You said your grandfather had lost a stone. Could it be this one?"

"I am not certain." She leaned down. "I would have to look closer."

He bent, his arm brushing her shoulder, a pleasant warmth and pressure. He glanced at her, at the purity of her profile, the long sweep of her black lashes, the slight blush on her cheek, her lips. He was still watching her when she glanced up.

She smiled. "Not a closer look at me, but the stone. Tell me more about it."

He forced his attention back to the case. "To my knowledge, agates are often found in the Midlands, Perthshire, the Isles, some other places in Scotland. It is a type of chalcedony or quartz, as I said," he went on, "probably formed by cooling gases during a time of tremendous heat in the formation of our planet. They can appear in beds of sedimentary rock, granite, under red sandstone layers, all indicative of very ancient age, and the stupendous amount of heat—volcanic, really—required to create such deposits in the first place. They are not generally found in the Trossachs, so far as I know."

"But I have seen them in the hills here. Like this one." She tapped the glass.

"Fascinating. Can you show me where?"

"In the glen," she said. "And further, in the hills beside Loch Katrine, a few miles northwest. And I saw a stone like this years ago, in the hill at the top of your garden, before it was enlarged—and improved, as they say."

"Very interesting! Are you certain?"

"I think so. There were stones of different colors, striated like this one. These hills once belonged to the fairies. And they say there is a gateway to the fairy realm on this estate." She looked over at him. "The hills have a few such portals, so it is said."

"Probably some fairy legends are based on natural phenomena," he said thoughtfully. "Some geological notes would be an informative addition to my grandmother's book. Perhaps you would kindly assist me, since you have an excellent knowledge of the local legends."

"My grandfather knows more than I do. What I know, I learned from him." She tilted her head. "But you do not really want to know the truth of the fairies, do you."

"I prefer truth to fancy. Where did you see the agates?"

"In the hills behind this house, I believe. I was much younger then. Years ago my grandfather found a stone like this up there, when the property belonged to his family. There was neither wall nor grotto then on that hillside. Grandfather left the beautiful stone in place because he felt it should stay there. It is poor manners to take what belongs to the fairies," she added.

"More fairy magic at Struan? We are rife with it."

"There are many tales of fairy magic in this glen," she said. "It is disrespectful to alter a fairy site, or to take something away that belongs to the other realm. Surely you have come across some of this in your research."

"Aye, fairy sites are claimed in hills, glades, groves, stone circles, wells, natural springs, loch, streams, caves," he said. "One wonders what is *not* a fairy site."

"Scoff if you like. When the fairy hill on Struan grounds was altered into the grotto, it's all very lovely—but I assure you they are not pleased."

"If so, they have made no fuss about it so far," he said.

"If the fairies are angered, they can be spiteful in their curses. For example, for altering the fairy hill with the grotto, your kin could fall under a curse, or lose a fortune, even have unfortunate deaths in the family, and no children born to continue the line."

Lose a fortune? He frowned. "Sounds exceedingly grim."

"Oh, it can be," she answered.

"Then it's a very good thing fairies are only imagination. I need not worry."

She slid him a sour look and strolled away, looking around the room, stopping before the fireplace to hold out her hands to the warmth. She glanced up. "Oh, look!"

"What is it?" He walked over to join her. "The painting above the mantel? A favorite of my grandmother's, I think. I haven't looked at it closely myself." It was a landscape, the design a little busy, trees in a meadow at moonlight, something like that; he had hardly paid attention to it.

"Such lovely detail," she said, gazing up. "The dancers, the horses, the magical light." Smiling, she looked at him. "You have a fairy painting in your library, sir."

"Fairies! I thought it was just trees and such." Puzzled, he gazed upward. The gilt-framed painting was a large, sweeping oil landscape showing luminous moonlight, dark clouds, and billowing trees, all done in a deft hand with some touches of delicate detail. At first glance the moor and woodland seemed empty. Then he noticed the small figures, a few dancers in gossamer veiling around in a ring of light, other figures visible inside an opening in a hillside that glowed with light. In the distance, cloaked figures moved on horseback between the trees.

"An imaginative artist," he said.

"My father painted it," she said quietly. "Niall Mac-Arthur of Kilcrennan."

James looked at her in surprise. "What! You said nothing of it."

"I knew it was in the house, but I did not know where. He had a gift for painting, and did this one a year or so before I was born. At the time, Struan House was still in our family, the property of my great-grandfather, who sold the estate to your grandfather."

"Aye, the record of sale was among some papers I recently saw. Does your father live at Kilcrennan as well?"

"He is no longer with us. I never knew him, or my mother. My grandfather raised me from infancy."

Murmuring in sympathy, James glanced down at her, touched deep, feeling the urge to share something of himself and his past. "I lost my parents when I was nine years old," he told her. "My brothers and sister and I were taken from our Highland home in Perthshire and separated into the care of relatives. My great-aunt, Lady Rankin, raised me with Fiona, my twin, south of Edinburgh."

As Elspeth studied him, James felt true acceptance there, and knew that the warmth in her eyes was genuine. "We are both orphans, then. We have that in common."

"I would hope we have happier things in common than that," he said wryly.

"So you and your sister were twins? I liked her very much when we met," she added. "I am glad that you had each other to rely on during those sad years."

"Aye. She liked you as well." Later, Fiona had agreed with Sir Walter Scott that James should seek Elspeth out—both of them had hopes of a match, he thought.

She tipped her head. "You do not like people to know much about you. Why so?"

"There is safety in secrets," he answered.

"Now and again it is a relief, and a joy, to share them with someone." Her glance was clear and perceptive. He felt again that she understood more about him than he had revealed, and far more than anyone else knew.

"Not everyone is trustworthy," he murmured. He had not started out trusting Elspeth MacArthur, but now he wanted very much to do so. She turned away calmly to regard the painting. *Secrets indeed*, he thought.

"Do you remember your parents?" she asked.

"Not well, but for a few excellent memories," he said. "I try not to think of them. It is best that way,

I find." He preferred to avoid the sharp sense of loss that remained, though sometimes a deep voice might remind him of his father, and he would recall his calmness, his support, his fairness. Lavender and gentle laughter reminded him of his mother, and he always felt her absence keenly.

"Lavender," Elspeth murmured, lifting her head. "Do you smell it? It's lovely."

Startled, he looked away from her. "No."

"I have no siblings," she went on, "and do not know much about my parents. Grandfather says little about them. The loss of his only son . . . hurt him deeply. They are like shadows to me. Sometimes I dream about them, and I wonder if they were like the parents who appear in my dreams. My grandfather says aye. But he wants me to be happy, so perhaps he agrees for that reason."

"Knowing you," he said, "your dreams are very accurate."

Her return glance was bright. "But you do not believe in such things!"

"A little." He was as surprised as she was, just then, and he looked at the painting again. A detail caught his attention, and he pointed. "Did your mother model for your father? One or two of the girls looks like you. There," he said. "And there as well."

With a delighted gasp, she rose on tiptoe, peering upward, but was unsteady on her injured ankle. James took her arm in support and she leaned into him. "I see! This one, that one, and a third—they all have dark hair like mine, and are about my age now."

"More than that, their hair is black, and glossy as silk, like yours. Their faces have the same sort of delicate heart shape. Look at the one on the left. Her eyes are a pale, silvery green, much like yours."

Her smile was enchanting, her features delicate, and her irises were a luminous, remarkable color. She was lovelier than the girls in the painting. "Do you think so?"

"I do. There is something about the features, the shape of the chin, the eyes"—he swept his fingers gently along the side of her face. She caught her breath, closed her eyes, tilted her face toward him. "The resemblance is there."

Touching her was heaven. He lifted her chin with his fingers, bent closer, nuzzled his mouth against her hair. She smelled wonderful, like cool rain and warm woman. The feeling that shot through him was intoxicating, and he wanted it to continue.

"My mother," she breathed, focused on the painting, though her fingers tightened on his arm. "Do you think he did paint her? I have never seen an image of her."

"Not even a portrait? How sad," he murmured. At least he had that, hanging on the wall of his town home in Edinburgh.

"I do not know her family. The circumstances of my birth were . . . unusual."

"I see." He assumed she meant illegitimacy, or a dispute between families over eloped lovers. "If your father painted her here, then she was a beauty, and you favor her."

"Thank you," she breathed. "You have given me something of my parents that I did not have before." Resting her hands on his lapels, she rose and kissed his cheek.

He drew in a quick breath, for the touch was tender and loving. He set both hands at her waist and pulled her toward him, and before he even knew what he was about, he was kissing her fully, overcome by the pulsing heat that moved through his veins, the feelings that so easily overcame him when she was close, and in his arms.

Elspeth did not resist, despite her arguments and protests earlier, but lifted her arms and sighed, and seemed to melt against him. Pulsing heat moved through his veins. She moved her hands up over his coat lapels, sliding her fingers along his collar.

She pulled away. "I must go soon," she whispered, though her eyes were closed.

"You do not have to leave," he said, kissing her mouth, her cheek, her hair.

"I do," she gasped, and pushed at his chest a little. But she stayed in his arms, her hand resting at the back of his neck as she gazed at him. He could lose himself in those eyes—silvery pools, something magical in them.

She stepped back. "I must go, if the weather and the roads allow. They will be worried about me at Struan, and may send word to Margaret's if I do not return today. I am sorry to have been so much trouble to you here, sir, that you felt you needed to . . . to marry me." She twisted her mouth a little. "No need for you to take a bride you do not really want."

"On the contrary. You are not the only one who finds a compromise convenient."

She blinked. "You?"

He shrugged. "In a few days, my great-aunt will arrive here with family and friends to take a tour of the Highlands. They will stay here, then travel elsewhere."

"Lady Rankin?" she asked. "Will your sister come along as well?"

"Aye, and our youngest brother. Miss Sinclair also plans to be with them."

"I remember her. She has set her cap for you. And she has your aunt on her side." Her glance was astute.

"So you noticed. Did you also notice that I am not keen on the match?"

"I thought perhaps—but Miss Sinclair is beautiful, wealthy, and a part of Edinburgh society. She would be an ideal viscountess for you."

"So would you," he said. "Charlotte and I do not . . . suit."

"So both of us want to avoid other engagements." She tilted her head.

"Exactly. Shall I ask you again?"

"Will you drop to one knee?"

"If you want," he said.

She tilted her head. "What do you want? Do not bother with any of this if you do not mean it."

"In all honesty," he said quietly, "I want to mean it. I would not mind at all if we married. I am . . . glad, in a way, to be obligated to you."

She nodded. "Thank you. But do not let me keep you from your work any longer. Soon we can leave, I think. I will read until then. Did you say that you have other books on fairy lore in your study?" She chattered a little too brightly, and stepped back, skirts swirling, hands clasped in front of her.

Wondering what changed her mind when she seemed on the brink of agreement, he led her into the study, with its desk littered with books and papers. "My grandmother's manuscript," he said, and showed her the book. "As a condition of the will, I have agreed to finish it. For the most part it is done, save for some research and annotations."

She traced her fingers over the books, glancing at titles, and then touched the manuscript. "But you do not believe in fairies, or in any part of Otherworld."

"It makes no difference for this project. The book is a compilation of accounts and stories. The readers must decide for themselves what they accept."

"One must believe wholeheartedly in what one does," she said.

Her simple statement gave him pause, knowing she was right. But he shrugged. "If one is a rabble-rouser, true. But anyone may write objectively about a subject with which they do not necessarily agree."

"Just as one may make a marriage without love. Obligation is enough."

He inclined his head. "Touché, Miss MacArthur."

She flipped through the pages of one of the books. "I suppose we could assist each other," she said softly, "in our mutual . . . compromise."

"In our what?" He was studying her lovely neck as she bent her head. Where the glossy ink of her hair gathered in a braid, her neck was small and vulnerable; the pale shell of her ear, her delicate jawline were beautiful. He stood so close that her gown brushed his thigh, and he felt the warmth of her body beside him. "What did you say?"

"Which road shall we take?" Her fingers traced a verse in the open book. "As in the ballad of 'Thomas the Rhymer.'" She drew a breath to read.

Oh see ye not yon narrow road,
So thick beset with thorns and briars,
That is the road to righteousness,
Though after it but few enquires.

Entranced by her quiet voice, James read aloud as he stood beside her.

And see not ye that broad, broad road
That lies across the lily leven
That is the path of wickedness
Though some call it the road to heaven.

"The second road is more interesting than the first." He rested a hand on her shoulder, and when she allowed that, he traced a finger along the line of her neck. Then she turned into the circle of his arms, sighing softly, and he bent closer.

The kiss happened gently this time, expected, deepening with a tenderness that went beyond ruse or agreement. He knew the risk. He could lose his heart, his very soul in the depth of that kiss. He brushed his lips over her cheek, her earlobe, and then, coming to his senses, remembering the passion of the night before, he forced himself to draw back casually, unwilling to show what was truly happening within him.

"We could agree," he said, tracing his fingers over her shoulder, down her arm. "To an engagement, so long as it suits. A wicked sort of bargain, but it may do for now."

She tapped a finger on his chest. "Never make a bargain with the fairies."

""'Tis the road to fair Elfland, where you and I this night must go,'" he said, quoting another line from the poem. "It seems a fair bargain to me."

"I cannot." But she sighed and looped her arms around his neck. He could not resist her then, felt a spinning within, and he kissed her, pulled her close, felt like a man drowning, and she his only hope. The immersion was his own choice.

"Any more of this, my girl, and we had best marry quick."

"Only if we both agree." The door to the study pushed open then, and Osgar entered, with Nellie and Taran trotting behind.

"Enter the fairy hound," James said, reaching out to scratch Osgar's head as he butted between them. Laughing, Elspeth drew back.

"I must go home," she said. "The time has come."

He felt disappointed, wanting their solitary haven at Struan House to last far longer. "There's no need to hurry."

"We will not be alone for long," she said. She closed her eyes, her back to the windows, so that a halo of bright light seemed to surround her. "Someone is coming to the house. A girl on foot. There's a coach not far behind her. And . . . my grandfather is making his way along another road in his gig. He will be home tonight."

Narrowing his eyes, James walked past her to gaze through the tall library windows, where the view spanned eastward. At first glance he saw only drizzle and mist on the hills.

Then, far off, he saw the small figure of a woman walking along the crest of a hill. Within moments, a coach came around the curved base of the hill, slowly making its way along the muddy track. It stopped, and after a moment the female disappeared inside, and the vehicle resumed its course.

"Your ghillie, or perhaps the groom, is driving back here," Elspeth said, joining him by the window. "He saw the maid, who was walking here alone, and is bringing her to the house."

Puzzled, James looked at her. "Even if you had the eyes of a hawk, you could not have seen that from the study. Your back was turned."

"Now will you believe me, James MacCarran?" she asked quietly.

He wanted to, so much—the desire rose in him like a wave, a feeling like hope, rusty yet there. But he would not. Everything had an explanation, and he would not make a fool of himself by falling for nonsense.

"I should get you home soon," he said. He gestured for her to proceed ahead of him. At the door, just as she was about to cross through, the feeling welled up in him again, an overwhelming demand, a mingling of physical desire and an inner craving that he could not, dare not name. He touched her arm. "Elspeth—"

She turned, and they brushed hands, and James took her into his arms to kiss her, long and thoroughly, until he felt her surrender, and heard her sigh. Her eyes were closed and she looked innocent yet alluring. He brushed her hair back from her brow. "Let us agree on an engagement. I will speak to your grandfather."

She opened her eyes, a flash of silvery green. "I think not."

"Fickle," he said wryly. "I was sure you were about to agree."

"That's the fairy blood in me," she said lightly, and swept past him. Osgar came toward them, and the girl put a hand on the tall dog's shoulder. She glanced back at James.

"Fairy blood," he murmured. "If only that were true."

She smiled, and walked ahead of him.

Chapter 12

When they met the ghillie's coach on the road past Struan House, Elspeth waited as James pulled on the horse's lead, stopping their gig to have a word with the driver. James turned toward her as they waited for the other vehicle to halt. "If you are right about the Buchanans, others will soon know that we were alone," he told her. "We cannot change that. Good afternoon, Angus," he said. "And Mrs. MacKimmie! I'm surprised to see you returning so soon."

The housekeeper, who sat in the coach with a maidservant, leaned forward. "My lord! Aye, I'm back. My daughter has enough help, and with the guests arriving next week, I am needed at Struan House. Mr. MacKimmie came to fetch me. This is Annie MacLeod, the lass who will be a maidservant at Struan. Good to see you, Miss MacArthur," she added, nodding.

"Mrs. MacKimmie," Elspeth said, feeling herself blush. "Lord Struan has offered to take me back to Kilcrennan," she went on in a rush.

"Aye," James said, without offering an explanation. Elspeth sensed that the housekeeper was bursting to know, her eyes flickering from the viscount to Elspeth.

"How did you fare on the roads, Angus?" James asked.

"Well enough, sir, though the way is not easy, depending on where you go. Over to Kilcrennan, you may have some trouble at the bridge." He peered toward Elspeth. "Good afternoon, Miss MacArthur," he said, tipping his hat. "Nice to see you."

Elspeth smiled, and an awkward silence followed. "Miss MacArthur had a bit of a mishap in the storm and is unable to walk the rest of the way home," James said then.

"Oh dear!" Mrs. MacKimmie said.

"There's mud gushing doon the hills to swamp the road in some places," the ghillie said, "and trees down here and there. The auld stone bridge is nearly washed over. I wouldna go that way, sir." Again he peered toward Elspeth, as did his two passengers.

James thanked him, and Elspeth was relieved when they parted moments later. As the gig rattled beneath them on the muddy road, she glanced at him. "Thank you for not telling them more than that."

"I saw no need to explain," he replied, his eyes intent on the road.

"The Buchanans were a bit too interested, I know," she said.

"I doubt Mrs. MacKimmie will ask. We will explain only what is necessary."

"I do not know Mrs. MacKimmie well, just through acquaintanceship in the kirk on Sundays, but it's said she's a good-hearted soul. But now that Willie Buchanan and the kirk minister know, everyone will hear sooner or later."

"Then they will soon hear of an engagement, and no harm done. Few things can be kept secret for long in a small glen like this one."

"The fairies here keep their secrets." She laughed when James glanced at her.

"I think you have more secrets than anyone in this glen," he murmured.

"You have a few of your own, sir."

"Have you not sniffed them all out with your Highland powers?"

She lifted her chin, a bit hurt. "Everyone but you takes me at my word."

He huffed. "I am a cautious sort. Now, I have a question for you."

"I will not," she said, "marry you."

"So you've made clear. What I want to know is when you might be willing to assist me with the research and work to be done on my grandmother's book."

She tilted her head to look at him past her bonnet rim. "When do you need me?"

His keen glance told her his thoughts—he needed her. Wanted her. She caught her breath, almost hearing the unspoken words. A small voice within answered that she wanted to be with him more than she would admit.

If she accepted James, he and her grandfather would agree that she should live in the Lowlands. "I could come to Struan during the days," she ventured, unable to resist the chance to see him at least once more.

"Excellent. I can fetch you whenever you like."

"What about the guests that Mrs. MacKimmie mentioned?"

"My aunt and a few others will arrive in a week or two. I intend to work on Grandmother's papers until then, and complete that work as quickly as possible."

"So after you entertain your guests, you will leave for Edinburgh again." She knew his plans without his telling her. The Sight or none, it seemed obvious.

"I have lectures to prepare, and my own work to see to."

She nodded, then bounced on the seat when the gig hit a rut. James murmured an apology. "The roads are poor, just as Angus warned." He guided horse and vehicle around an upward curve in the road, and paused the gig at the top. The descent on the other side was steep, and the road was marred by runnels of mud. A constant drizzle thickened the mist, and dampened everything—her bonnet and shawl, the lap robe tucked around her, the crown and brim of James's hat. The road was dangerously slick, the fog as thick as clouds in places.

James slapped the reins, pulled on the brake a bit, and guided the horse downward in silence, focused and capable. Elspeth gripped the side support and hung on.

"Devilish weather," James muttered. "I have yet to see the glen in sunshine. It's been mist, rain, or the deluge of the Apocalypse ever since I arrived. Perhaps your wee fairies thought to bring us together when they sent you down the mudslide into my arms," he drawled, glancing at her.

"Of course not," she said, but frowned, wondering for just a moment. Her grandfather had taught her to see the meaning in everything around her. Nothing, Donal often said, was as simple as it seemed.

She craned her head to see the bridge through fog and slanting rain. As they rounded another difficult descending curve, James concentrated on his task, while Elspeth looked ahead to see water, rushing and foamy, swirling in the distance.

"James!" she cried out, placing her hand on his arm. "There's the bridge—and the water is even higher than Angus said."

He drew back hard on the reins to halt the horse. "Wait here," he said, and leaped out of the gig to stride along the road.

Not about to wait, Elspeth climbed down, lifting her skirt hems to follow him along the road toward the area where the bridge spanned a gorge. Her boot heels sank unevenly in mud, her walking further impeded by her stiff ankle. Her skirt snagged on wet heather as she walked to the edge of the gorge to join James.

The gap was twenty feet or so, spanned by a wooden bridge only slightly arched, its stone pylons embedded deep in earth and rock. The full stream gushed high enough to lap at the sides of the bridge, splashing water over the planks. The stream was the color of tea with milk, its current swift and foamy.

"Careful, Ellie," James murmured in a distracted tone, taking her elbow. His shortening of the name— just as her grandfather often did—hinted at affection and familiarity. She wrapped her gloved hand over his arm and felt strength there, and surety.

"The burn is rarely this high," she said. "Only once

or twice do I remember seeing it like this." Along the sides of the deep gorge, tree roots and bracken thrust up out of the water, and fallen branches were sweeping along in the current.

James stepped backward with Elspeth. "There must be another place to cross."

"There's a level place a mile or two from here, where the gorge ends. But the burn is wide at that point, and one must step from rock to rock to cross on foot. The going for a vehicle is very difficult."

"We don't have much choice, unless we return to Struan and wait days or even weeks for all this water to subside. Is there no other access to the other side?"

"Not close by. Sometimes people jump the gap," she said. "Downstream there's a leap, where one side of the gorge is higher than the other." She pointed that way.

He laughed. "I won't chance it, and you shouldn't try, either . . . though I suspect you've probably given it a go in the past."

"Ah, you have the Sight yourself," she said.

"Just logic, Miss MacArthur." He tipped his head as he spoke.

She smiled a little. She was learning more about him in each moment, and she knew that he had warmth and heart beneath his cool exterior, and that, despite how staunchly he maintained his skepticism, he did not dismiss her. "It's true, once I did try the Leap with some friends when I was young. They made it, but I fell and broke an arm. I could make it now, I think."

"Out of the question."

She remembered his leg. "Of course," she murmured.

"You have a turned ankle, and the horse can't jump with us. But I wonder if we could walk the horse over the bridge, without the gig." James moved forward to step tentatively on the bridge. He jumped up and down several times to test its soundness, then walked toward the middle.

Elspeth heard the low groan of wood and iron. "No, stop!" she called, running forward.

He stepped back to the grass. "It might hold long enough, but it's not stable, and is too much risk. We'll cross farther upstream, as you said—or else return to Struan."

"The bridge will hold my weight. You can return to Struan with the horse and gig. You need not escort me home from here." Yet she did not want to say farewell so soon.

"The viscount keeps you alone at Struan, and then casts you out to walk home with a poor ankle, in a storm, over an unsafe bridge? My girl, they write ballads about cruel lovers like that," he said. "And your grandfather would be after me to hang me."

Lover, she thought, thrilled at the way he had spoken with such casual acceptance. "Grandda would bring a reverend, not a rope."

"Which is worse, in your opinion?" he asked wryly. Elspeth did not answer, walking with him toward the gig. He lifted her inside, his hands firm through the cloth of her gown, and took up the reins to turn the placid dark mare.

"That way," she said, pointing, and he guided horse and vehicle along the earthen track that ran beside the gorge. So much water and mud rushed down from the higher hills to the west and north that the gap brimmed nearly to its banks.

When they reached the fording place, where the sides of the gorge disappeared, Elspeth saw that the run-off had spilled out to flood the moorland to either side. "Over there is where we usually cross on foot," she told him. "We can walk over the flat rocks without getting our shoes wet. But we have the gig and horse."

"Aye, and the water is too high for an easy crossing of any sort," James said. The burn had overflowed its banks to create a swampy area to either side, and the familiar rocks that Elspeth had looked for were all but submerged. James pointed downstream. "I think the horse can pull the gig across. Hold tight."

He sent the horse forward before Elspeth could protest; under his skilled and certain hands, the gig rattled steadily across the boggy ground. With one gloved hand, Elspeth grabbed the side of the seat, and with the other she grabbed James's sleeve, his arm tense beneath the cloth as he held the reins taut.

Then they were fording the burn, the horse obediently stepping into the flow, the gig following. Elspeth squealed in alarm at the swirl and rush of the current. "James!"

"We'll be fine," he said, and proceeded. Within moments, the water swirled to the hubs, then nearly the tops, of the wheels, splashing over James's boots and soaking Elspeth's hem.

"Turn back," she said, clutching the seat.

"That, my girl, would be worse than going forward." The horse stepped through the surge. As water sluiced over the floorboards, Elspeth shrieked faintly.

Halfway across, the horse stopped, and the wheels seemed stuck fast, the gig shaking with the current.

Water slopped over the floorboards by now, and Elspeth's shoes and skirts were wet. The horse pulled again, whinnied, stopped.

"Stay here," James told Elspeth, and stepped down into water that surged around his boot tops, and then his thighs. The tail of his frock coat floated behind him as he walked toward the horse's head and took the bridle. He spoke quietly to the horse, patting the mare's nose. When he moved forward, the horse followed.

Soon the gig lurched free, while Elspeth bounced and slid on the seat. "Hold on!" James called back over his shoulder, over the rush and swirl of the burn.

Elspeth drew her feet up and bent her legs to sit cross-legged on the seat, pulling up her skirts, her low boots and cotton stockings exposed. The horse, a calm beast, gave a hesitant whicker or two, and plowed steadily through the water.

Holding the bridle, James led the horse cautiously, testing the way first. Once he faltered and went down in swirling water to his chest, his hat tipping off his head as he rose up. Elspeth leaned down and snatched up the hat as it swirled past.

Then James surged out of the water, dripping, the horse behind him, and the gig rolled onto the opposite bank with a great lurch, water draining. James sloshed back to the vehicle and climbed inside.

"Well done," Elspeth said. "Your hat, sir." Grinning, he took it and placed it on his wet hair, water running from its brim. She laughed, and bent to wring her skirts. "Kilcrennan is only a little way," she said, and pointed northward.

"There's something to be said for putting funds into roads,' James said, as they continued along the rutted, muddy road.

"As laird of Struan, you can pay for repairs and not wait for the Crown to fix the roads. They are slow about such things in remote Highland glens."

He nodded, but was silent when she hoped for a reply, and as they rode to Kilcrennan in relative quiet, chilled and damp, Elspeth wondered what she would tell her grandfather when the time came.

Chapter 13

James shrugged into a borrowed tartan waistcoat of dark green and black with thin stripes of yellow, lined in satin and neatly made. He picked up the neck cloth and wrapped it around the high collar of his fresh linen shirt. The borrowed things, which included leather boots, and trousers and frock coat of deep gray superfine, fit surprisingly well. Mrs. Graeme had brought them to him after showing him to a guest room where he could wash, change, and rest. The clothing, she had explained, came from Mr. MacArthur's own wardrobe.

"He will be glad to lend these to you. He, too, is a tall man, wide through the shoulders," she had said. "Lord Struan, I am grateful to you for taking care of Miss Elspeth and seeing her safe home."

She had left, smiling, and inviting him to come downstairs for a hearty tea to be laid in a half hour. *Safe home*, he thought, savoring the phrase. He suspected that Mrs. Graeme knew that Elspeth had spent two days alone with him, yet had made no fuss. Tying the knot in the neck cloth, he wandered to the window and glanced out over the courtyard and modest estate of nearly two thousand acres, so Elspeth had told him upon arriving. Kilcrennan was a respectable house, at its heart a converted old stone tower keep, added to over generations, so that it was a little tilted, a bit shabby, and cramped in places, with a patina of age and respectability. He glanced toward the outbuildings, which included the weaving cottages, as the housekeeper had explained. In the distance he saw blue mountains through a drizzle, beneath a sky that promised clearing in a day or so.

Seeing movement in the yard below, he glanced down and saw Elspeth coming down the steps from the house, the entrance being two floors below the window of his bedchamber. He saw that she had changed to a pale gray dress, with a pale shawl around her shoulders. As she hurried down the steps and away from the house, he wondered where she was going.

Even the sight of her stirred a feeling in him that tugged at him, as if he felt some inexpressible craving of the heart. He knew then how much he wanted to marry her, and that he would never feel right without that fey and fascinating girl in his life. His feelings went so far beyond obligation, or thoughts of his grandmother's will, that he began to wonder if he was falling in love.

He scarcely had courage to acknowledge that, and he was glad when he saw the distraction of a gig and horse riding up the lane from the opposite direction that he and Elspeth had followed. Donal MacArthur must be arriving home. James watched until the vehicle drew to a halt. The man who stepped down was elderly yet robust, in a dark suit and red plaid waistcoat. When he removed his hat, his thick hair and beard shone like copper and silver. He flung his arms wide as Elspeth stepped into them, and he enveloped her in a deep hug that she returned. From his high window, James could hear her laughter, and her grandfather's booming reply.

"You're home, wee girl! I worried that you might vanish on the moor!"

She laughed. "The fairies did not take me, Grandda. I was safe at Struan House."

Mrs. Graeme approached, and rather than the cool greetings for servants that James was accustomed to seeing, she received a kiss on the cheek from the master, and the three of them stood together talking in animated conversation. Donal set his arm around Elspeth, and she put her arm around Mrs. Graeme. They were linked, the three, snug, supportive, loving.

James sucked in a breath. He felt a yearning that had long been there, unsatisfied, and the tug of its rising hurt. Years ago he vaguely remembered such scenes in his own home, the laughter of mother, father, of servants who were cousins, of such ease of affection—a touch on shoulder or head, a warm hand to hold his, and smiles, always those.

Old loneliness with no business renewing, he thought. As the outsider here, he felt it keenly. Then Donal MacArthur looked up, met James's gaze, and nodded. Just once, direct, a silent, respectful, private introduction, perhaps thanks as well. Elspeth looked up and smiled. For a moment, James felt part of their circle.

Then he stepped back, turning away to knot the last of his neck cloth and shrug into the frock coat. With another glance for the sky, quickly darkening in the cool October twilight over a now-empty courtyard, he headed for the stairs.

* * *

Tea was supper after all, James discovered: a simple, generous spread served in the dining room, where he now sat with Elspeth and Mrs. Graeme. He glanced around the small, cozy room with its robin's-egg-blue walls and creaking wood-planked floor, and at the table crisp white linens, delicate china dishes, and a silver service that even his fussy aunt would be proud to lay out. The fare was excellent, too—hot rolls and salted butter, cold sliced beef and lamb, rowan jelly and sweet custard, and a variety of small cakes and biscuits, as well as steaming hot tea. Mrs. Graeme poured, and he noted that all but he added liberal sugar and cream. He had always taken his tea strong, fragrant, and unsweetened.

His Aunt Rankin, James thought, would have her nose out of joint when she discovered that the Highlands was not the crude, backward place she believed it to be, but quite civilized. She had maintained that opinion all her life, even when her sister, Lady Struan, had moved to Struan House. Lady Rankin had refused to send her wards, James and Fiona, to the Highlands to see their grandparents but for a week or two at a time, now and then. "You will catch your death of cold up there, and come home undisciplined and starved for civilization," she had claimed.

That, of course, had never happened. He and Fiona had hunted for rocks, and Fiona had studied Gaelic, and each time James left Struan, he only wanted to go back. By the time he left Eton for Oxford and then University of Glasgow, and finally a teaching position in Edinburgh, he was too busy to visit his grandmother often. Thanks to his great-aunt's overbearing nature, he had not formed a habit of summers spent in the Highlands, though he would not have objected.

Now, seated in the pleasant dining room, he glanced through the window at another stunning view of the mountains, and felt—well, at home, if he dared admit it. Or at least a place he could imagine as home. The warmth of this home and its inhabitants helped enhance that sense.

Mrs. Graeme poured the tea and filled their plates according to their whims—cold meat and rolls for each, rowan jelly for him, custard and a cake for Elspeth. James watched Elspeth, admiring her stunning yet simple loveliness. She had changed her wet things for a gown of pale gray wool, her hair was softly drawn up, and small pearls dropped from her earlobes. Her shawl was of creamy wool crisscrossed with soft green, purple, and rose, with a crocheted fringe.

"A handsome shawl, Miss MacArthur," he said. "My sister would admire it."

She smiled. "It's one of my own weaving pieces. I would be honored if you would accept a similar piece for your sister. I would be happy to show you the loom later, if you . . . if you have time." A blush rose high in her cheeks. He nodded, smiled.

"Please stay the night, Lord Struan," Mrs. Graeme said. "It is going dark, and the roads will be no better on your way home than when you came."

"I'll gratefully accept the hospitality, if it is agreeable to the MacArthurs."

"Of course," Elspeth said quickly, and sipped her tea.

"Mr. MacArthur has just arrived and will join us shortly," Mrs. Graeme said. He learned during their conversation that the housekeeper was a family member as well, a cousin through Mr. MacArthur's late wife.

"Graeme, aye," he said. "I know Sir John, and I met Miss Lucie Graeme at the king's reception in Edinburgh, when . . . Miss MacArthur and I first met. Sir John is a good acquaintance of mine, and a very fine road engineer. Naturally he had a keen interest in geology—" As he spoke, the drawing room door opened and MacArthur entered.

"Ah, Lord Struan! Good to meet you, sir," Donal MacArthur said briskly, coming toward him as James stood to clasp his hand. "Welcome to Kilcrennan."

"Lord Struan will be our guest for the night, Mr. MacArthur," Mrs. Graeme said, sounding more like a wife than servant or even cousin.

"Excellent," MacArthur said, helping himself to food, and accepting a cup of steaming tea, heavily sweetened, from his granddaughter.

"Thank you for the loan of clothing and boots, sir," James said. "Unfortunately my own things got wet as we were crossing some high water."

"Down by the Durchan Water, Grandfather," Elspeth supplied. "It was very floody, but Lord Struan got us across, bravely and competently."

"Then we're further in your debt, sir," Donal MacArthur said. "Souls have been swept away in lesser floods than we've had this week. I had a de'il of a time coming back from Edinburgh—would have been home sooner if not for the high waters and poor roads." He leaned forward. "I understand that you are a professor at the university, sir."

"Aye, Mr. MacArthur. I teach natural philosophy,

specifically the geological sciences, and do my own research as well," James answered.

"Rocks and such, hey! A very good occupation, sir, and a good use of a fine education. Though you do not spend much time at Struan House, from what I've heard. Beg pardon, you've been viscount since your grandfather passed on a few years back, and yet Lady Struan herself told me that her grandson kept to the city."

"Struan House was still my grandmother's home then, and she enjoyed having charge of the estate. And I am much occupied with my lecturing duties, although my research sometimes brings me into the Highlands."

MacArthur nodded, looking pleased. He speared a roll with a two-pronged fork, slathered it with butter and jelly, and glanced at Elspeth. "Stays much in the city, does the laird of Struan," he said, tearing off a bit of roll and popping it into his mouth.

"I know," she said tersely.

In the awkward silence, James gratefully accepted another slice of cold beef, offered by Mrs. Graeme, and turned his attention to cutting it into strips.

"Where's the yarns from Margaret, then?" Donal MacArthur asked next. "Is your cousin well? And how did Lord Struan come to be taking you home? Much appreciated sir," he added.

"I have not been to Margaret's yet," Elspeth said. She was staring into her tea, and then lifted her head, a pink flush on her cheeks. The spark of bravado in her eyes was worthy of anyone, James thought. "I was at Struan House, stranded by the weather."

"Ah." Donal set down his fork and looked from

his granddaughter to James, while Mrs. Graeme sat silently by. Glancing at Elspeth, James felt suddenly like a boy caught out at school. "And Mrs. MacKimmie away and all."

"Why do you say that?" Elspeth asked warily.

"I saw Reverend Buchanan on my way home today. He told me that he and his father met the pair of you under interesting circumstances, were his words." He set down his knife. "Is there something that the kirk minister knows and I do not?"

James sat up. "Sir, let me be frank. Miss MacArthur did stay at Struan House. She had a mishap while traveling over Struan lands and was injured."

"She has a twisted ankle, Donal MacArthur," Mrs. Graeme supplied quietly. "I looked at it myself this afternoon, and made her soak it in a salt bath. She must rest it."

"Injured, aye," Donal said. "Go on." He fixed James with a stern stare.

"I happened upon her when she was injured, sir. Given the storm, I offered her the hospitality of Struan House. My housekeeper was detained elsewhere at the time."

"And the rest of the household staff would be gone then, too," Donal MacArthur said slowly, "due to the fairy riding at Struan."

"Grandfather, none of it could be helped," Elspeth said.

"Alone," her grandfather went on. "Together."

"I was treated cordially as a guest." Elspeth lifted her chin. "Reverend Buchanan has no right to suggest otherwise, if he did so."

James saw signs of temper flaring in Donal, a spark

in the leonine eye, a flaring of the nostrils, though the older man held his composure. He saw, too, where Elspeth got it.

"Elspeth had turned her ankle, Donal," Mrs. Graeme reminded him.

"I slid down a muddy hill," Elspeth said. "It's stronger now, but at first I could hardly walk."

"Aye, the situation could not be helped," James said. "Between the girl's incapacitation, the weather, the poor roads, we were unable to travel until the second day. I was unwilling to risk it, for her safety and that of the horse."

"Two days!" MacArthur thundered, setting down his custard spoon. Mrs. Graeme leaned back in her chair. Elspeth's cheeks flushed bright as she glanced at James again.

"Fortunately, Lord Struan was there to help," Mrs. Graeme said. "Elspeth might have come to real harm if she had tried to make her way home."

Donal MacArthur said nothing, tapping his fingers on the tablecloth. "Well, I will commend you for considering the horse, and my granddaughter's well-being. But what of her reputation?"

"Sir, these were extraordinary circumstances," James said.

"Indeed," Elspeth added. "Grandfather, we saw the riding!"

MacArthur stared. "On Struan lands?"

"Aye. Both James—er, Lord Struan and I heard the horses. And I saw—" She stopped. "I will tell you about it later. It was altogether an exceptional night."

"How exceptional," her grandfather growled.

"Lord Struan was a thorough gentleman," she said

with admirable dignity, though James dared not meet her glance just then.

"I understand how the situation appears, Mr. Mac-Arthur," James said. "And I realize such things can jeopardize a family's reputation. I am prepared to make it right."

"Make it right," Donal MacArthur repeated thoughtfully. He regarded James and then Elspeth, and for those moments, James felt his heart pounding—strong, steady, anticipating. "Normally we would speak alone, you and me, sir," Donal MacArthur said. "But this is not the usual, is it. As I understand it, you are offering to marry Elspeth?"

"I am, and I have already told her so." Still James did not look at Elspeth, but he felt the intensity of her gaze.

MacArthur grunted. "And will you have the man?"

"No," she said, and set down her teacup.

"He's a fine gentleman," her grandfather said, "with a title and property, and clearly good morals. I believe the man has a good heart as well."

"He is and he does, but my answer is no," Elspeth said.

"Certainly he has an estate anyone would be proud to own," MacArthur went on, as if Elspeth had not blatantly refused, "and a generous income—sir, may I assume that your income is excellent?"

"I am . . . comfortable," James said, feeling distinctly uncomfortable.

"There," MacArthur continued in a blustery fashion. "And he has a teaching position and a house in Edinburgh as well."

"I do," James said, looking at Elspeth. "And Highland property."

"Highland or Lowland, the decision was made when you stayed the night at Struan House, poor weather or none." MacArthur smiled. "Besides, it seems to me that the two of you are a fine match."

"We are," James ventured.

"We are not," Elspeth said decisively in the same moment.

"Peggy agrees with me, do you not?" MacArthur boomed.

"Lord Struan is all of a gentleman, and Elspeth is fortunate," Mrs. Graeme said.

Donal MacArthur raised his china cup. "To Struan!"

"Indeed," Elspeth said, and stood. "I have some weaving to finish, having been gone from it for too many days." She headed for the door and turned. "This matter is not decided, by any means, so do not celebrate." She left, shutting the dining room door firmly behind her.

"There," MacArthur said in a satisfied tone, "that's done."

"You must keep from interfering, Donal MacArthur," the housekeeper said.

"As stubborn as yon lass is, we may need to interfere. Eh, Struan?"

"I rather like a stubborn lass," James replied as he stood. "And I'll take the matter into my own hands, if you do not mind, sir. Mrs. Graeme, thank you for the supper." He bowed slightly and went toward the door.

"Hoo hoo," Donal crowed as James left. "A wedding for certain, Peggy dear!"

* * *

The loom clicked and its heddle bars shifted as Elspeth pressed the foot pedals. She threw the small threaded shuttle from right to left, then another left to right, through the gap between the threads, all the while moving her body side to side and back and forth with steady rhythms created by loom, shuttle, woman. She moved quickly, letting thought go, so that the repetition soothed her, erasing all but the moment.

And that was what she most needed.

As she pressed the treadle again, the quick motion shifted a wooden heddle bar bringing one set of warp threads down to create a tunnel between the layered warp threads—then she took up a shuttle threaded with yellow, the weft thread, and tossed it surely through the gap, catching it with her left hand as it sailed through, and the next treadle push dropped the warp threads to snug that new yellow into the weave. She tossed the yellow through again, dropped it and picked up the black. On she went, weaving the weft threads, yellow and black, through the warp threads, red and black. The new cloth grew by inches, its smooth width—no wider than the reach of her arms allowed—turning on the wooden roller that pressed against her taut belly as she leaned into the work.

The layered rhythms seemed to speak to her—*go to him, stay here, go to him, stay here*, and the colors reflected her feelings: red for passion and anger, black for fear, yellow for hope. *Be with James, leave Kilcrennan*, said the loom; *be with James, leave Kilcrennan*. She tossed the yellow-threaded shuttle, pressed the treadle—*all will be well, all will be well*.

Elspeth took up the black-threaded shuttle again and flung it right to left. Catch the shuttle, press the treadle, catch the shuttle, press the treadle; she need not think, need only keep a watchful eye on the process, the warp and the weft, the heddle and the roller, and the rest.

She had to make a decision. For now, she found respite in rhythm, and satisfaction in steadily creating a length of sturdy and handsome plaid, inch by inch. Somewhere, someone waited for this cloth. For now, that was enough.

But it was not enough to fill a lifetime.

Catch the shuttle, press the treadle. Yellow goes over, black comes back; hope flies through, and shadows follow.

James stood in the open doorway, shoulder leaned against the doorjamb, hands in pockets, and watched the weaver absorbed in her work. He had never seen tartan cloth, or any cloth come to think of it, produced on a loom before; he realized that he had always taken woolen fabric for granted, thinking little about how it came into existence—just what it cost per ell, or how it looked and felt, how neatly the tailor cut it, or whether it beaded moisture in rain and kept him dry, or left him chilled and dissatisfied.

Now, though he did not understand the process entirely, a few moments studying the loom in action gave him a rudimentary understanding of how the parts worked together, how the stripes of colored threads interwove, loom and shuttle, to spool a taut and perfect plaid onto the roller. But that was not what held his attention.

She fascinated him, both the girl and her skill. She sat on a wood and wicker chair and leaned into the loom, her back straight, arms out, hands moving, as if she held a great harp sideways in her lap and played a rhythmic melody of clicks and shushes upon it. Every motion she made was practiced, efficient expertise as she leaned and tossed, pressed and caught, while the loom posts shuddered gently.

He noticed how deftly she snatched the shuttle bit with its long tail of color to send it flying through the separated threads; how she caught it on the other side and sent it back again; how her foot pushed the wooden pedal at just the right moment, so that shuttle never caught, threads never tangled, and the loom wove sweetly, steadily, under her sure handling.

Compelled, James watched not only what she did, but *how* she did it: with total focus, her face still and lovely, her gaze peaceful and almost trancelike, but for an occasional glance toward hands, threads, or the loom. The tartan cloth grew beneath her caring and skilled hands, created from simple threads. He listened to the steady, controlled beat she played on the old loom, and saw her deep concentration, her enchanting face in the soft light within.

Being male, he naturally savored the sight for other reasons—the swanlike grace of her body clothed in soft gray, the swell of her breasts pressed against the loom bar as she moved forward, the supple curves of her waist as she leaned; the way her teeth just touched her lower lip sent a shiver through him, as did the sight of her slender fingers, so deft where they shaped and threw the shuttle. What she did was dancelike, reminiscent of lovemaking, and his own body stirred, surged inwardly as he watched her. He knew the feeling of her body moving against his own—he wanted that again, fiercely so, distractingly so.

Yet he saw more than enticing beauty and a beautiful young weaver at work; more than a blur of colored threads and the shifting loom. He saw her gift, and her love, for the work.

Now he understood why she refused to marry a Southron and leave Kilcrennan. Some of his circle of acquaintances in Edinburgh might not appreciate her skills and knowledge, though they would be polite about his weaver lass. In the Highlands, weaving was an ancient and honorable craft; in the South, it was regarded as industry and labor, an outmoded artisan craft that would be highly unsuited to a proper viscountess.

He smiled to himself, thinking that if Elspeth became his viscountess, she would more likely be seen as a charming Highland beauty, and therefore allowed her eccentric hobby. But now he realized that weaving was not just a pastime for her; it was an art, and a devotion. Even a few moments watching her told him that.

With a sudden, deep ache inside, he knew that he could not ask her to leave it, or leave this place.

Silent, he stepped back and turned, walking away.

Chapter 14

"The storms are clearing at last," Donal MacArthur said, as he entered the parlor where James stood by the window.

"Aye," James said. Under the evening sky, the rain had stopped, with thick mist over the far mountains. "I will return to Struan House tomorrow. I'm grateful for the hospitality, sir."

"As we're glad for the company, sir, and for your assistance. My granddaughter mentioned that you're finishing up Lady Struan's final book."

James nodded. "The work should take but a few weeks, and then I'll return to Edinburgh. I've lectures to resume." He did not think he would convince Elspeth to go with him to Edinburgh, though he could not stay always in the Highlands. Now he did not know if he should try; a Lowland marriage might be a disservice to her after all. Shoving his hands in his pockets, he gazed out on the vast scenery, and sighed.

MacArthur walked over to a cupboard, opening that to remove a brown bottle and two glasses. He poured out for each of them and returned. "Whiskey, sir?"

James took the glass, thanked him, and tasted it. "Excellent," he said. The warmth sank and seemed to spread throughout his body. "Is this from a local distiller?"

"It is," MacArthur said, and swallowed.

"Mellow yet with a subtle power—it's extraordinarily pleasant." James sipped again. "I've never tasted the like."

"'Gie us the drink, to make us wink,'" MacArthur recited, and James laughed at the Burns quote. "A cousin of mine makes this. He owns a small distillery in the hills . . . so long as he makes no more than a modest amount for family and friends, 'tis all very legal." Donal grinned, brown eyes gleaming.

"Oh, of course." James knew very well that the manufacture of illicit whiskey, and its smuggling for export, had been rampant in the Highlands for years, despite legal strictures. "I wish your cousin well of his enterprises, with a product this fine."

"He makes several gallons of this particular whiskey every year, and always sends some to Kilcrennan. It's what he calls a fairy brew."

"Aye?" James sipped again. "For its delicate flavor, I suppose."

"It has an unusual ingredient—the dew collected from certain flowers at dawn, said to be the fairies' own drink." He lifted his glass in salute. "There's no whiskey like it."

"Excellent stuff." It warmed like fire yet felt soothing to his throat, even to his spirit, relaxing him beyond any similar drink he'd ever tasted. "Your cousin could become a wealthy man bottling and selling this."

"Legitimately? *Tcha*," MacArthur said. "The taxes would be too high to make the profit worthwhile. He does very well exporting the other whiskey that his stills produce, but he could never make enough of this particular potion to meet the demand, once the news of this got out. He keeps his loyalty to the *daoine sìth*, and will not take a profit from their secret. The fairy dew is necessary for the fairy brew." He winked.

"Fairy brew," James said thoughtfully, studying the glass.

"The *daoine sìth* gave him the knowledge of it." Donal smiled.

"*Dowin-shee*." James attempted the Gaelic, a safer topic than that of fairies making whiskey, in addition to all else they apparently could do. "My sister is fluent in Gaelic, learned from our first nanny, and she's kept up her study, but I do not have it myself. Though I spent my boyhood in the Highlands—I was born in Perthshire."

MacArthur nodded. "Good. Then you have a Highland nature at heart, though you be a Lowlander now, and a man of science."

"I am all of it, I suppose. Sir, you cannot truly believe in this fairy business."

"Oh, I do," the older man murmured, and took a swallow or two of the whiskey.

"My grandmother mentioned you in her notes. She was impressed with your knowledge of fairy lore in particular, and she hoped to interview you in more detail. I believe she meant to devote a chapter to your stories and experiences, sir."

"Did she?" Donal MacArthur carried his glass and the bottle toward the fireplace, where a pair of chairs, covered in threadbare green brocade, flanked the low-burning peat fire. Sitting, he indicated for James to

take the other chair. "Well, I am that flattered. I like
to think Lady Struan and I were good acquaintances,
and I am pleased to be in her wee book." He raised his
glass. "To Lady Struan, a fine lady and a good friend
to the weaver of Kilcrennan."

"To Lady Struan," James echoed. "Sir, she also
mentioned Niall MacArthur."

"Niall," MacArthur said, "was my son. Elspeth's
father."

"So I understand. A painting of his hangs in the
library at Struan House."

"Ah, the fairy grove. He finished that . . . in the
months before he disappeared."

"Fairy grove," James said, nodding. "May I ask
what became of your son, sir?"

MacArthur drank quickly, then filled his glass and
poured more into James's own. "He was lured away
from Kilcrennan by the charms of a fairy lass."

"Some women do have a magic about them, like an
enchantment." James thought immediately of Elspeth,
though he kept that to himself.

"Some do. And some are of the fairy ilk themselves,
whether or not you believe it is possible, sir." MacArthur shrugged. "Niall used to roam out in the hills
sketching from nature, and would come back and
paint what he saw. He worked at the weaving, too,
though he had a talent for the pictures. One afternoon
he went out, and never came home again. He went
over to the fairies."

Unsure how to respond to that, James sipped,
frowning. Perhaps the account was an embellishment
to disguise the shame of a young man abandoning his
family, which MacArthur would not want to admit to
a stranger. "It is a tragedy," he said carefully.

"For us, it is a sad thing, but for him, he enjoys himself where he is. One can lose a sense of time in the fairy realm. A day there could be a year for us. A week could be seven years. I know this, myself."

James nodded, skeptical, remembering something Elspeth had said, and something more he had read in his grandmother's pages. "Miss MacArthur never knew her father?"

"Never seen him. She has seen him in her dreams, I think. She has a gift, you know. The Highland Sight." He tapped his forehead.

"So she tells me," James replied.

"It is very strong in her. Some call it the gift of the fairies." MacArthur sighed. "Mrs. Graeme and I have tried to give her the usual pleasantries a young lass should have, so we took her to Edinburgh for her debut and parties with her cousins, but Elspeth dislikes the city. She prefers to be here, weaving tartan cloth. She's an excellent weaver, but to be honest, sir, I want to see her married, and happy—and away from here." He glanced intently at James.

"I believe she considers your happiness, sir, and that of others at Kilcrennan, over her own future." James did not know that for certain, but suspected her insistence came from love of her family. "She is determined to stay here."

"Do not give up your suit, sir," Donal said.

"I cannot force her to change her mind. She knows what she wants."

"But soon she will turn twenty-one." MacArthur sighed. "Never mind. The fairies have won, what's done is done." The last was almost singsong.

The weaver had imbibed more than that bit in his glass, James was certain, to speak in such riddles and delusions. "What does her age have to do with it? I will turn thirty next May. I do not understand."

"It is time she wed, is all. She would be a fine wife for any man, and I intend to find that man," Donal said. He sipped more whiskey, then leaned close. "Struan, sir, I am relieved she did not want the tailor, for when I saw him last week, I did not like him so well as I had. Now, having met you, I am telling myself, 'Ah, this is the lad for Elspeth!'"

Steadily, James returned MacArthur's gaze, and did not answer.

"Good then," the older man said, half to himself. "You can help us find the gold." He raised his glass high. "I think you are the one."

"I would not object to that." James was certain that the older man had sampled too much of the "fairy brew." His own head was buzzing, even after a few swallows. He looked askance at what remained in his glass, now wary of its potency. "Gold? My grandmother's notes mention fairy gold as a common tale. She states there is a legend in this glen, too. But there is not much detail about it in her account."

"Och, every glen has legends of fairy treasure," MacArthur said. "Let me tell you ours—ah, Elspeth!" He looked up.

Turning, James saw Elspeth in the doorway, and stood. "Miss MacArthur."

"Lord Struan." She approached, limping slightly, her gait improved but the ankle not yet healed. James offered her his chair, and she sat, gray skirts settling around her, feet crossed at the ankle. He slid a footstool toward her, and she rested her foot there; he saw narrow black slippers and a hint of white silk stockings before she dropped the fabric of the gown over all.

"He is a fine man to give you the wee stool for the foot," MacArthur said.

"He is," Elspeth said, sounding curt.

James hid a smile as he leaned against the mantelpiece. The whiskey had indeed made him mellow, so that he could almost believe in fairies, and could well imagine Elspeth as queen of that ilk. He glanced down at the delicate grace of her profile, the sweep of dark lashes above faintly pink cheeks. He wanted to touch her hair, knew it would feel soft, cool, thick. She glanced at him, her eyes sparking—and he saw that she was not content in the least.

"Ellie, have some of Dougal MacGregor's fairy brew. 'Twill take the pain from your foot," her grandfather said. Then he frowned, having inadvertently revealed the name of his whiskey-making—and no doubt smuggling—cousin.

"Your kinsman's name is safe with me, sir," James said.

"I like your new lairdie," MacArthur told Elspeth. "Will you have the brew?"

"A bit, thank you. A swallow—that's enough," Elspeth said as her grandfather poured. "I do hope you warned Lord Struan about the strength of this particular brew."

"Och, he's done well with Dougal's fairy blend. He's had a dram and a bit, as have I, and no sign of weakness. 'We are na fou,'" he said. "'We're na that fou—'"

"'But just a drappie in our ee.'" Completing the Burns line, James raised his glass.

MacArthur laughed. "You should marry this lad, Ellie."

"Aye, Ellie," James echoed, feeling more comfortable at Kilcrennan by the moment. Whether it was the easy company or the whiskey that loosened his usual restraint, he was enjoying it. He raised the glass in a small salute that only Elspeth saw.

"Away wi' you," she said, and her quick, softened gaze melted his heart.

"Never," he mouthed, and a pounding began deep within. *Never.* Surely that was the whiskey, he thought, but however teasing the remark, he had meant it. A strong emotion rose in him, near overwhelmed. He straightened, hid it once more.

"Beware that fairy brew, James MacCarran," she said.

"And the wee fairy herself," he whispered. She laughed, shook her head.

"It's late, Grandfather," she said then. "Our guest will want an early start."

"Women always come up with practical notions when there are good topics and good whiskey to hand," MacArthur complained. "First I will tell Struan about the fairy gold. He must know the truth of it."

Gowd, the man said, as if it were an ancient word. "Go on," James replied, intrigued.

Dear God, not all the truth, Elspeth thought in a sudden panic, as Donal MacArthur sat up and cleared his throat. "Grandfather—"

"Long ago they do say," he began, "the *daoine sìth* of this glen had a treasure so fine it shone like the sun inside the hillside palaces of the fairy ilk. There was gold and silver and precious stones from deep in the earth—there are veins and mines said to be mined only by the fairies—more precious and beautiful than anything imaginable. Well, every glen has its fairies, and every fairy clan has its treasure, but this, oh this, was something special to behold."

Elspeth glanced up. James listened intently, arms folded, one shoulder leaned against the mantelpiece. He looked handsome and comfortable in this room, even in Donal's old suit, as if he belonged here. Her heart beat faster as she studied him, but when he met her gaze, she looked away.

"And long ago, one of our MacArthur ancestors found that hidden cache," Donal continued. "The MacArthurs are the oldest clan in the Highlands, some claim. Likely it is true or we would not be claiming it now, would we?"

James laughed softly, and Elspeth smiled, too, just seeing that. Indeed, the man had some magic about him that made her feel good. All he did was stand there in her home, laughing with her grandfather, and she felt warm and happy, with a precious sort of excitement quickening within. If she married him, she thought, she would have a lifetime of such feelings, and dreams come true. All she had to do was accept his offer.

But the power of fairy in her own life made that impossible, no matter how much she wanted it. She did not know how to explain that to him.

He watched her again, blue eyes narrowed and thoughtful. Even her sense of Highland Sight could not penetrate those inscrutable eyes. The knowledge came to her or it did not; she could not simply summon herself. Did he regard his proposal only as an obligation? Why did he need a bride, as he had hinted?

Yet she had a growing sense, sure and certain within, that he loved her, though he might not know it himself. The sense was warm, open, joyful, like petals blowing open in the sunlight—and yet she could not acknowledge it. Not yet, if ever. And so it hurt.

"This clever MacArthur clansman found the fairy treasure in the hills," Donal was saying. "He hid it away to ransom his kinsman, a piper who had been lured into the hillside by the fairies. They would not give that piper back, just demanded the precious lot returned to them, and they began making havoc in the glen, stealing humans and playing tricks. But the thief himself died of a fairy bolt in his leg, and the gold never went back to the fairies. And they have been stealing humans and making wicked bargains with some in this glen ever since, until the treasure is returned."

"The fairy riding," James said suddenly. "Is that why some are frightened of it?"

"They fear the fairies will take them away, aye."

Elspeth knew that James thought of the night they had both nearly been taken, and she knew it puzzled him. "How long ago was this treasure said to be hidden?" he asked.

"Three hundred years," Donal intoned.

"And how is it to be found? Are there clues?"

"No one has sorted it out yet. Once it is found there are two keys to open it. One is a certain stone. And the other—" He nodded toward Elspeth. She shook her head to silence her grandfather from telling all her secrets.

"You were searching for a stone in the garden at Struan House," James said, turning to Elspeth. "What of the piece in the library case, the blue agate?"

"Did you find the blue stone?" MacArthur leaned forward.

"If it is the one, it is at Struan House," she answered.

"Even so, the key is useless without the treasure. What does it unlock? We do not know."

"A bit of gold, a few gems, a box of ancient gold or silver—treasure is found now and again in the Highlands, left by early cultures," James said. "It could easily be taken for fairy gold. I can see how the legend would arise."

"This is real," Donal said abruptly.

"If so," James said, "how would one know it was, ah, fairy gold? And how could it possibly be returned?"

"Once it is found, I know how to return it," Donal replied.

Elspeth listened, realizing that James puzzled over this, with so little logic applied. She saw him shaking his head slightly, half to himself. "Since this MacArthur fellow was an ancestor, is there family lore or clan legends that might provide clues about the treasure?" he asked.

"This treasure needs two keys, one the blue stone, the other . . . well, Elspeth and I know what that is. Without their treasure, the fairies lack their full power, and they need human help to find what is missing. That ancient MacArthur nearly outwitted them," Donal said. "The fairies of this glen remain unhappy because of it."

"Why is this cache so important to them? That is, if they exist," James added.

"The precious stones and elements come from their own hill, and so contain power for them," Donal explained. "Without it they are not as strong as they could be. They are not at ease."

"A fairy's purpose in life is to be happy, in harmony with all aspects of life and the earth," Elspeth added.

"Living is an art to them, an expression of pleasure and delight and enchantment. They cannot fulfill their purpose if something has been taken from them and they are uneasy."

"They are a temperamental lot," Donal MacArthur said. "They do not forget."

"We often call them the Good Neighbors," Elspeth said. "And they would be better neighbors if they had their gold again." She and Donal glanced at each other, and James saw an understanding there. A secret. They knew something more that they did not share with him.

"Certainly people over the years have looked for this treasure," James said.

"Some greedy souls, aye, especially those who do not believe in fairies," Donal MacArthur said. "But the wrath of the *daoine sìth* falls on those who try to outwit them."

"An interesting tale. I will be sure to note it down for Grandmother's book."

"Oh no, you must not put all of this in the book," Elspeth said quickly.

"I thought local legends were the point of Grandmother's book," he answered.

"The legend of the lost fairy gold is common knowledge here," MacArthur said. "But Elspeth is right—you must not write down all the details. Some part of it must be left out. The fairies will be angry if their secrets are told."

"Grandda, enough," Elspeth said. "Our guest has little patience for the fairy lore. He does not believe a word of it, I think."

"Actually I find the tale of the lost treasure very intriguing," James countered.

"But you do not *believe* it," she answered softly. "There is a difference."

"I believe," he replied, "what is proven to me."

"He'll believe soon enough. He's writing the fairy book, he's drinking the fairy brew," Donal MacArthur said, "and he's very taken with you, lass. He's fallen to the glamourie."

"The glamourie?" James asked.

"It's all over you, sir. Yon lass has the knack of it."

"Ah," James said, and courteously inclined his head. "That she does."

Chapter 15

Stirring in the dark of night, still groggy, James was unsure what had woken him. Though he had not dreamed, he felt as if he had heard voices, seen people around him. Sitting up, he needed some fresh air to clear his head. The fairy brew, as MacArthur had called that exquisite liquor, had been stronger than he thought.

Dressing quickly in trousers and boots, he shrugged on the borrowed frock coat over his shirt, leaving neck cloth and waistcoat aside, and quietly left the house, intending to stroll the grounds. Passing the kitchen garden and a walled flower garden, he followed the long earthen lane that led past stables and outbuildings to three weaving cottages. These backed against a hill to one side, with a sweep of orchards and meadow to the other. The night was cool and misty, and a little moonlight sliced through overhead clouds. Fog curled along the ground as he walked, and he saw translucent rings around the bright moon, the sky clearing overhead after so many days of rain.

His brisk footfalls echoed strangely, and soon he heard the clacking rhythm of a loom. Ahead, faint light showed in the windows of one of the weaver cottages. Was Elspeth up late, too, unable to sleep? The loom clicked and shushed in a fast cadence, as if its weaver was passionate about the work.

Detouring from the lane, he approached the door, about to knock, then realized that it was not the cottage Elspeth had used earlier, but the one beside it. He stepped sideways to glance through the small window beside the door.

Donal MacArthur sat at the loom, lit by the glow of a single lantern, the rest of the room shadowy. Immediately James noticed how quickly the man worked, shifting and moving in the same way that Elspeth had, lacking her grace, but all speed and certainty.

Then James stared. The man worked so fast that his hands, as well as the shuttle and moving parts of the loom, were near a blur. The tartan, a red pattern, gathered quickly on the roller—more quickly than seemed humanly possible.

He blinked, rubbed fingers against his eyelids, looked again. The loom whirred, clicked, and shuddered while the weaver sped through his work. The incredible pace seemed beyond what any man could sustain.

Had the whiskey had been that strong, James wondered, that he was dreaming? Was he in his bed, and not seeing this at all?

"Come away." A hand touched his arm, and James turned, startled to see Elspeth. She pulled on his coat sleeve. "James, please."

He pulled her close so that she, too, could peer through the window. "Look at that," he said. "What in blazes is going on?"

"Hush," she whispered, and touched her fingers to

her lips, then his. The contact sent a shudder through him. He circled his arm around her, felt her arm fit around his waist, felt the silk of her hair as she pressed close against him.

She wore a dark plaid shawl, and he saw that she was in a night rail beneath, the gathered fabric pale in the night. Her dark hair was loose and long, and the tartan covered her nearly like a cloak; his coat was dark, too, and so neither of them could be seen easily. Still, he drew her off to the side with him.

"What are you doing out here?" he asked. "Did you follow me, or did that infernal clacking noise wake you?"

"I woke from a dream," she said, "and knew you were out here. I knew Grandda was here, too, and that I must find you."

"Woke and just knew," he said.

"Just knew. I feel you," she whispered. "It is as if I can sense you, wherever you are, as if you are . . . part of me." She touched his arm, and he saw a soft blue spark go between them.

My God, he thought, stirred and amazed by what she said, what he felt, and what he had just seen. Had she meant love? And had that been a phosphorescent effect? His mind whirled on two paths at once, but the first won out. "Elspeth—" He slipped his hand over her hair. She lifted her face, her willingness echoing desire, matching his own. He wanted to tell her, then, that he loved her. He had only begun to realize it.

"Come away with me," she whispered in his ear. "We should not be here."

"A moment," he murmured, his mouth at her earlobe. He felt her catch her breath, sigh. "I want to sort this out." He meant more than the grandfather weaving away.

"We must not watch this," she insisted.

"Your grandfather is working the loom like the devil himself. Tell me what you know of it."

She hesitated. "It is the secret of the Kilcrennan Weavers that you see here. And Grandda's own secret, long guarded. So we must leave—" She tugged at his arm.

"Secret? It's near inhuman." He glanced again through the window. Caught in the whirlwind of the weaving, Donal never looked up, even as he snatched another roll of cloth from the loom and set the frame again, absorbed in his work at that steady and astonishing speed. "I saw you today at the loom. You were all skill and grace." He brushed his knuckles along her cheek. "But what he is doing in there is unearthly."

"It is not of this earth, what he does."

A chill slid down his spine. "You had best explain that."

"It is the fairy gift upon him. Listen, now. Years ago, Grandda was given the ability to weave a month's work in an evening. I was given a gift, too, but mine is not the weaving. Mine is the Sight."

"You make an art of the weaving. What do you mean, fairy gifts?"

"Abilities bestowed by the fairies," she said, "personally. Like a . . . spell."

"Away wi' you," James said gently. "I did not have that much whiskey."

She was sincere, her eyes wide and earnest. "It is because of the whiskey that you see this tonight. The fairy brew can allow us to see fairy magic for a little while. Without a few sips of the whiskey," she said, "you would simply see a man at the weaving."

Stunned, James had no reply for that. He recalled that Donal had made a similar remark. "The Sight," he murmured. "Your grandfather called it the gift of the fairies. I thought it was simply another term for the Highland Sight."

"Sometimes, but in my case it was bestowed by the fairy ilk."

He wanted to deny what she was telling him, but he had a strange, dreadful sense that it could be true; the small hairs lifted on his arms, on his neck, and he felt an odd warning knell in his gut. Yet he could not accept it unquestioned. "What do you mean?"

"My grandfather can weave dozens of plaids in a long night, when the magic comes over him like this," she said. "Most weavers—I myself, and I am good— can weave a decent length of tartan in a few days. I wonder if he wanted you to know, James. He gave you the fairy brew that he shares only with me, and later he set to his weaving, aware that he might be seen."

"So this is a deliberate . . . revelation for my benefit?" He had almost said *spell*.

"Possibly. Still, I do not want him to catch us here. Donal MacArthur has a fierce pride, and he is always careful to keep the fairy magic secret. But for you," she said, looking up at him thoughtfully. "Just you."

"My dear girl," he whispered, for she stood that close, the night wrapping round them like a cool blanket, "any moment now I shall wake in my bed, with the taste of last night's liquor in my mouth, and a banging in my head. And I want to know . . . if you will be there beside me when I wake." As he spoke, he let his fingers drift down over her shoulder, her upper arm, his thumb brushing past the swell of her breast. "I want you to be there."

"Hush," she said, so softly that he ached to hear it again. She set a finger to her own lips. Then she took his face between her hands, slender and cool on his skin, and she lifted on her toes and kissed his mouth.

Slow, tender, a surprise and a delight—the kiss sank through him, crown to sole, and he felt himself surge, craving instantly. He caught her by the waist, dipped his head, kissed her hard and fast and sure, so that she arched a little, moaned under her breath. And he pulled back.

"That was real," he whispered. "This is real." He snugged his hand against her waist, let his thumb trace under the delicious weight of her breast. She caught her breath, her hands clenching his arms.

"Jamie," she breathed, pressing against him. He stopped for a moment, closed his eyes. Long ago, his mother, his father had called him that—since then, only his twin sister. But it sounded so right when Elspeth said it, too.

He drew a breath. "There is no proof you can give me," he went on, "of fairy magic instead of . . . well, whiskey." His heart pulsed like a drum. Leaning down, he nuzzled his lips over her brow, her cheek, traced down to touch her lips, and kissed her.

Her lips opened naturally under his, and he heard, felt her sigh against his mouth. This time she drew back and then, oddly, pressed her finger to his brow for a moment. "Now," she whispered, "look through the window again."

He did, holding her by the waist. He glanced through the window. The weaver, hard at his work, seemed to glow—a haze of golden light shimmered around him, his hands, the loom, even around the cloth as it spooled onto the roller.

"It is real, what you see there," she whispered.

For a moment, he saw a shimmering around her, as well, and the elusive silvery sparkle that sometimes appeared in her eyes. "I do not understand this."

"Sometimes it is enough to trust, and believe."

Trusting easily was not in his nature. Yet from the moment he had met Elspeth, she had challenged him to believe what he could not easily allow. Certainly she had a sort of magic about her, but he told himself it was her charm as a woman, and his own strong, masculine nature. Elspeth had captivated him as no woman ever had, and now, once more, she was pushing him to think beyond what he accepted as true.

"What you did just then—touching me, and I saw—" He stopped, shook his head, felt something of a fool. Surely that had not happened. "The whiskey is working on me."

"In a way," she said. "I tasted a bit of the fairy brew, too. It allows me a gift that does not come readily otherwise. It is not the spirit, but the fairy dew itself. Tasting the dew of a flower at dawn will do the same thing. I touched you where the fairies bestow the gift of Sight, knowing that you, too, might be able to see what cannot be seen." She smiled. He continued to see a rim of brightness around her.

Enough, he thought, and nearly stepped back, nearly tossed up his hands to dismiss all of it—all but her, solid and real, before him. "All I saw was a man weaving like a lunatic. And here before me, a lovely girl." He brushed his hand over her soft hair, and let his thumb graze over her cheek until he traced the

curve of her lower lip. He lowered his head to kiss
her again, drawing her lower lip out gently, slipping
the merest tip of his tongue over hers. She opened her
mouth a little, inviting him.

Oh aye, that was real and reassuring, touch and response in himself, and her. He needed her more than
he could ever tell her, and wanted her for his wife,
aside from any obligation or responsibility. He wanted
to spend his life with her.

Yet she did not want that, and he did not know
why.

Her passion was as genuine as his own, though,
he was sure, for she caught her breath and pressed
against him, her mouth urgent and vibrant, lush and
soft, against his own. She pulled back a little, looked
up. "Something more is real here," she whispered.
"Your feelings. And my own."

Once again, she knew—he had not said, had only
realized the depth and power of what he was feeling—
and yet she knew. "You," he whispered, "are a conun-
drum to me. And I . . . love that in you." He could not
say more, though his heart pounded.

"Please, come away," she said, and this time he
turned with her to move through shadows and fog.
As they passed her own weaving cottage, James took
her arm to pull her into a dark recess beside the outer
wall, turning her so that her back was to the cottage.
Setting a hand to the cool, damp stone, he tucked his
other hand at the small of her back and pulled her
tightly against him. And there, where they stood
swathed in that blackness and silence, he took her into
his arms and bent his head to kiss her again.

And again, deep and fervent kisses, then slow and
tender. A sort of wildness was upon him, his heart

thudding, hands savoring the feel of her against him.
He told himself to slow, stop, consider. But so long
as she was kissing him like this, with opened lips and
the curious touch of her tongue, so long as she pressed
against him, she had to know. He was filled and hardened and aching for her now, and so long as she had
equal fervor, he followed the craving's lead.

So he stood with her in the lee of the stone wall,
and lost himself in needful kisses and touches. Sliding a hand under her plaid shawl to rest at her taut
waist, he felt the gauzy cloth of her night rail bunch-
ing under his palm. She felt slender and warm, and the
awareness that only the night shift was between his
hand and the fullness of her body made him quicken
all through, like fire. Kissing him, she ran her hands
over his shoulders, then tucked inside the lapels of his
coat, where he wore only the shirt. That warm touch
teased, tantalized him, and he pressed her against the
wall, allowed his hunger, his craving to show. Even
then, he knew he must master the passion, and himself, for he teetered on the brink. He was changing, he
was opening, and it unsettled him.

All he had known, his reliable, routine, dull life, so
carefully constructed over the last years, had begun to
shift in a matter of days. What seemed dreamlike and
fantastical to him was acceptable and unquestioned to
her. And his feelings, too, were expanding somehow.
That scared him most of all, for he had guarded those
so carefully.

So he simply lost himself to the freedom of the moment and her acquiescence, her fervor. She felt so warm
and real in his arms, under his mouth, his fingertips—
he could rely on that. Her elusive magic, whatever it
was in her that lured him like this, he could surrender

to that for now. Moment to moment, kiss and touch and caress, he need not think or question. Not yet.

By nature a thinker, a scientist, a man who questioned and preferred evidence, what he had seen at the weaver's cottage had stunned him. But now he was caught in a force from within, his body demanding, his heart needful, and rational wisdom receding. He resisted for a moment and drew back to look at Elspeth. She tilted her head to invite another kiss, her lips full, breathing ragged, hair sifting and tousled. She felt it, too, as he did, and she was so beautiful and willing that his heart ached.

"What are you doing to me?" he asked.

She laughed lightly. "Whatever you are doing to *me*," she whispered, "I will let you." Then she took him by hand to lead him around the corner to the stone step of her weaving cottage. As she lifted the door latch, James felt the intent of what they would do here surging strong within him. Suddenly he lifted her in his arms, pushed the door open, and stepped inside holding her.

The small dark room smelled of wood and planking, of whitewashed walls and lengths of wool, and held a sense of simple, solid values, of effort and reward. Elspeth slid out of his arms sweet as a kitten, then took his hands and pulled him toward a dark corner where he saw stacks of plaids. She tossed a few blankets down for a nest, then tugged on his hand.

As she drew James down with her to the soft plaids spread beneath them, Elspeth did not care about consequences; only the moment, only her pulsing, yearning body; only being with James. Enclosed in darkness and silence, they would not be disturbed here, at this hour, and her grandfather would be occupied well into the morning. Facing him, she looped her arms about his neck.

He streamed his fingers through her hair, cupped her cheek in his palm, leaned to kiss her, aching tender. And he traced his mouth along her cheek, to her ear, at the same time taking her full into his arms. "Elspeth," he whispered. "What is this, between us? What now, before we go on?" His lips traced, touched, and she melted.

She closed her eyes, bit her lower lip, resisting the urge to say what rushed through her mind. *I love you—I want you to love me.* "I want . . . to feel what we felt the other night. Just that, before you go back to Struan."

"I am only going across the glen," he whispered. "I will see you soon."

"For now we are alone," she answered, touching his jaw, the beard like sand under her fingertips. "We may do as we will."

He sighed, and she felt his desire in the sound. He soothed his hand over her shoulder and the length of her hair spilling there, and shivers cascaded through her. When he bent his head to kiss her, pulling her deeper into his arms, the warmth of his body penetrated through her nightgown. She sighed and pressed close, his heart thudding against her, only lawn and linen between them. Pulling at his sleeves, she helped him strip off his coat, which he tossed aside, and she dropped the plaid shawl away, adding to the thick nest that surrounded them.

He kissed her again, a feeling like a plummeting to be caught safe in his arms; he kissed her breathless, leaning her back, fitting his lips to hers. A quivering ran through her, a sheer delicious thrill as his fingers smoothed over her cheek, her throat, her breasts. Her nipples tightened, tingled, as his fingers grazed past, and she arched to urge for more. She felt as if she would do anything he asked—anything but marry him.

That thought filled her with a poignant sadness. What if she were never in his arms like this again? What if he asked her to marry him again—what if he did not, and left, never to return. Only a fool would refuse him, yet she had no choice. And each time he touched her, she only wanted more, without telling him why she had to refuse the future and the lifetime he offered her.

So she would take joy from these moments. Kissing him, she slid her fingers into the thick waves of his hair, and he dipped his head to kiss her throat again, so that she cried out softly, eagerly. She pushed the collar of his shirt aside to touch him, and felt his heart thumping under warm, bare, firm skin, and a layer of fine hair; she found and traced his small, flat nipples.

He groaned, muted, and brought his hand over her breast, tugging aside the neck of her gown, and then his lips were hot and pliant upon her breast, his breath warming her. He swept his tongue over her nipple, nudged it, and the tightening shot through her like lightning to plunge deep. She gasped, whimpered.

Again he took her mouth in a kiss, his hands cupping her breasts, his thumbs teasing until she moaned and writhed, hot within and wanting more, pleading for more. The urgency of his lips and hands melted her so that she felt buttery and willing, and as he kissed the shell of her ear, she felt a raw need thrumming through her. What she most yearned to say—*I love you, I will wed you*—she somehow kept inside, biting at her lips, moaning soft, asking with her body for that which she could not express in words.

He took her down to the thick bed of plaids, and she lay on her side facing him, slipping her leg over his as she pressed against him. Quickly he slid his hand along her leg, up her thigh, to round over her hip. She ran her fingers through his hair, arched to encourage him to kiss her breasts—she could not get enough of what he did, only wanted more, the beating of her heart untamed, her body moving, rocking, in further plea.

Her fingers found his chest again, and she tore his shirt free of his breeches. With shaking fingers she eased over the panel of his trousers, over the hardness there, a proof of how he wanted her, and she intended to give herself to him. The urge was irresistible now as passion replaced thought and wildness displaced logic. As she tugged at buttons and the cloth flap fell away, she pushed his shirttail aside and found him there, the length of him like warm velvet over iron, and she gasped at the heightening desire in her own body, fueled by touches, kisses in the darkness. She moved boldly against him, pushing her own gown aside, desperate for skin to touch skin, heat to heat.

He sought her breast again, and with her own hand she shaped him full, teasing, until he groaned fiercely against her, his lips taking her nipple so that a strong, peculiar fluttering began deep within, and she gasped. He rose to smother the sound with his mouth. "Let me love you," he whispered, his lips a breath away from her own, his hands skimming over her hips, feeling so warm and so good.

In answer, she moved against him, whimpering, and

he sighed and fit his mouth over hers, the kiss deep and raw, and his fingers skimmed over her flat belly and downward. When he slipped a finger just inside her, tip to cleft, she gasped again, and as he touched her deeper, she burned, melted, her hands seeking over the planes of his belly and his hard, wonderful, warm length. And he touched off a spark in her that caught like a flame, and as he caressed her, she rocked like the familiar rhythm of the loom, rose and cried out, gone to shimmering.

Wild with unspoken, instinctive need, she shifted her hips to take him inside her, every bit of her crying out for sudden thrust and release. But he pushed her hips away and guided her hand upon him again, and with his fingers inside, he stroked her to bring her to that burning, while she stroked and felt him meet his own release against her.

Then she sobbed out, aware of something precious and something missing all at once. "I wanted—I thought we both wanted—"

He kissed her. "My girl," he whispered raggedly, "if we let that happen, there would be a wedding quick, whether or not you agree. So"—his fingers traced over her breasts, her body still tingling at his merest touch—"remember there will be time for that, and so much more, if we marry."

Sighing, she turned away, knowing he was wise to suggest that they hold back and wait, but she yearned for all of it—but he knew that. He knew it.

She stood, legs trembly, feeling ease and heartache all at once. She found a cloth for him, then straightened her night rail, found her plaid. When he was ready he shrugged into his coat, then reached out to draw her close. Wordless and fervent, he kissed her.

Elspeth rested against him, eyes closed, aware that she must tell him farewell. She could not give way to the intense desire and burgeoning love she felt—not until all the fairy debt was settled. She wondered if he would wait for her, if he knew that. She wondered if he would believe it, even after tonight.

He lifted her chin to look down at her. "You know I mean to marry you."

She felt a small thrill, but she glanced away and shook her head in silence.

"You could be the wife of the viscount who owns most of this glen," he said. "Yet you will not. You could marry a wealthy tailor to benefit your grandfather's weaving business, yet you will not. Your own grandfather disagrees with you, and so do I. There is no reason that I know of, and perhaps he understands it more. I only know that you will not be convinced to marry, no matter how—I feel about you."

"Leave it be," she whispered, a catch in her voice. "I have my reasons."

He waited, but she would not look up, or give in, though it hurt to resist. Part of her insisted that she was foolish—but another inner voice agreed with her caution. The human half of her, she realized, was vying with the fairy half. And she could not tell him that. Not now, in this moment.

James released her, stepped back. "So be it. I will spare both of us the unpleasantness of asking again." He went to the door and yanked it open.

"James," she said. He looked over his shoulder. "If I did marry . . . it would be you."

"Then why—blast it, I will not argue it further." He shut the door behind him.

She stood motionless, aching inside, then went to

the door and looked out. Dawn brightened over the mountains, and James walked along the lane up to the house.

And she could hear the incessant clack and *shoosh* of the loom in the next building, driven by the same demanding magic that had made such a shambles of her dreams.

Chapter 16

Good granite was abundant in this part of the glen, James thought, standing atop a high conical hill that overlooked Struan House, with a view of the glen and surroundings for miles. The morning air was fresh, the sunlight invigorating as he turned back to his work. Removing a small hammer and chisel from his pocket, he bent to tap and break off another chunk of the stone ledge that ran under the hillside. A crust made up of sedimentary rock and limestone with patches of red sandstone, it broke away easily in places. James was certain the layers stretched a long way through this string of hills. The tapping had revealed a shoulder of granite close to the surface, the common gray composite stuff studded with a glitter of plain quartz and a touch of cairngorm.

Angus MacKimmie had spoken of a quarry across the glen that produced red sandstone and pale limestone, with pockets of granite and trap rock, the latter so hard it could not be quarried. James was pleased to hear of the variety, for finding large deposits of granite and basalt in this glen, which was set well into the central Highlands, was encouraging for his geological research.

He broke off some bits of limestone that showed traces of fossils, knowing that Fiona would enjoy examining them; his twin shared his interest in geology and collected fossils of all sorts. Dropping them into the leather bag he carried, he set aside his tall, gnarled walking stick, recommended by Angus for strenuous hill climbing, and pulled a small leather notebook and wood-cased pencil from his pocket. Then he sat on a rocky outcrop to jot some notes.

Granite and whinstone formations NW of house . . . 100 ft. plus above level of house, he wrote. *The deposits indicate possible internal heat, fusing masses together to create beds of sedimentary rock . . . molten material extruded from terrestrial core, cooled as crust, becoming volcanic rock. Evidence of such here. Basalt, dolerite, gray granite . . . traces of red sandstone also found in the vicinity . . .*

Excellent material for lectures, he told himself, and for a chapter in the book he had been working on in Edinburgh; that project drew together many theories, including that of a catastrophic development of earth, with stupendous heaving shifts of earth's most ancient land and sea masses; other scientists theorized that early land masses and rocky formations had evolved slowly as a result of gradual erosion. James leaned toward the Catastrophists, himself, while agreeing in some specifics with the Uniformitarianists.

Granite, a rocky mass that required tremendous heat to form, evidenced volcanic activity, and James was pleased to find rich sources of it this far into the Highlands, a considerable distance away from known volcanoes such as those in and near Edinburgh. He was pleased, too, to find the beds on his own property. What he had discovered was worthy of exploration, a potential contribution to the wealth of information accumulating more rapidly every year as geologists pieced together a picture of earth's creation. As well as looking backward, the discoveries pointed toward the future direction that terrestrial evolution might take, as he intended to point out in his next book.

Still seated, the wind brisk around him, he looked into the kit he had brought in the leather bag. It contained not only various chisels and two small geologist's hammers, but a fine loupe—two small hinged magnifying lenses banded in engraved brass, a gift from Fiona—along with other items, including chunks of unfired ceramic clay to test the streaking properties of minerals; and bits of metal, such as gold, silver, and iron, with a few shards of wood for testing the hardness and density of rocks and stones. In addition he carried a small vial of hydrochloric acid, well-capped and protected, to dissolve certain sedimentary deposits, often helpful in cleaning and identifying rock. Today, all he really needed were the chisels, a hammer, and the loupe.

Hearing the dogs bark, he looked around to see Angus climbing the hill with the wolfhound and the white terrier running alongside him. Nellie reached him first, and James rubbed her head as she leaped up to greet him.

"Your guests are arriving, sir," Angus said, pointing southeast.

"Sooner than expected, if so. I had a letter from my great-aunt a few days ago saying they would arrive by Friday afternoon. It's but Wednesday."

"Mrs. MacKimmie has the house more than ready," her husband said.

"She does indeed." Struan House virtually sparkled, from polished furniture and sparkling silver and glass in the public rooms, to the white counterpanes and freshly laundered linens in the guest rooms. James narrowed his eyes as he saw a vehicle approach from two, perhaps three miles away. The black coach and matched four followed the winding road that led through the glen and past Struan House.

"No hired chaise, neither," Angus MacKimmie said. "That's a private coach. I've sent a groom, Davie, ahead to lead them to the house. The roads are still muddy and rutted—and will stay so until they are fixed," he added bluntly. "Yon coachman had best go slow."

James nodded, appreciating Angus's broad hint. He stood beside the older man on the conical peak overlooking Struan House, no more than ten minutes' walk from the house, and so in no hurry to rush to greet the arrivals. He dropped the bits of rock and the chisel and hammer into the leather bag he shouldered, then took up the walking stick to descend the hill. Angus and the dogs went with him.

The young groom came flying back along the road on foot—Davie, one of Angus's nephews, a kilted boy with red hair and an elfin grin. The head ghillie walked quickly to meet him, leaving James to make his way more slowly, using the cane to balance.

The pockets of his rough tweed jacket sagged, for he had dropped some rock specimens into them, hardly thinking about it. The loose, comfortable jacket had been a gift, its sturdy woolen weave handsome, warm, and impervious to damp. Two days after his visit to

Kilcrennan, a boy had arrived at Struan with a package in brown paper. Donal MacArthur had sent the coat with his compliments.

But there had been no message from Elspeth, and no word of her welfare. James had returned a handwritten note of thanks, extending a dinner invitation to the MacArthurs and Mrs. Graeme, and he had inquired politely after Miss MacArthur, adding that he hoped she was still interested in acting as his research assistant.

So far no answer had come back, though over a week had passed. James had contemplated riding to Kilcrennan, but uncertainty as well as pride put him off the idea. He sensed that he was reverting to his previous self, with that familiar shell closing over him again. This time, he regretted it, for the changes he had felt in himself were freeing. Until he had met Elspeth, he had not realized how much he wanted to shake off the past, and step away from the old, restrained, bitter part of himself.

But he would not ask her again to marry him. She had refused repeatedly, and he would not make a fool of himself again, not even to meet the odd conditions of his grandmother's will. Elspeth was perfect for that. Perfect for him.

Fairy or none, he wanted her, desired her endlessly, and now craved the thought of marrying her. He could not imagine his future without her in it. Though daydreaming was not in his character, he had found a little solace, a little lonely contentment, in that habit lately. But if the girl did not want him, that avenue of dreams was closed.

If he had no appropriate Highland bride, he would jeopardize everything—his siblings' inheritance, and his property of Struan. He might have to find other candidates for marriage—he knew Lady Rankin was sure to push Charlotte Sinclair at him—but he wanted only one.

If he had to, he could let go of his dreams of Elspeth. He would recover, as he had recovered from his wounds of the past. The injuries taken at Quatre Bras had left him with a limp. Now he would have injuries that were not so obvious.

He could almost feel the clenching of his spirit in protest. He was accustomed to life as a solitary soul, and he would continue, even if he had to make a marriage of convenience someday. And he would sell Struan House, though he knew it would only break his heart further.

Angus spoke with his nephew and returned, gesturing toward a carriage in the distance. "Davie says there are three gentlemen in the coach, only some of your guests. The rest are following in a second coach, the gentlemen told Davie."

"My brother Patrick wrote to say that he might arrive ahead of the rest, but I've had no word since." He shrugged, puzzled.

"You'll find out soon who they are. That driver is flyin' fast on a poor road."

Chuckling at another hint, James walked downward to stand on the sloping foot of the hillside, watching as the vehicle drew closer. It was a handsome black barouche, he now saw, drawn by four powerful bays with whipping black manes. Angus lifted his arm in salute, and the coach slowed and stopped. For a moment, James thought of the coaches of the devil said to haunt some Highland roads.

But he dismissed that when his brother Patrick

opened the door to leap down as Angus came forward to greet the coachman. James walked down to meet Patrick, who greeted him with a handshake and a thump on the shoulder.

"James, you look well, the country laird and a' that, hey." Patrick grinned. "The others are following us— Fiona, Aunt Rankin, Philip, and Miss Sinclair rode in a second coach. They fell a bit behind, but should be here within the hour."

James nodded. "Very good. Who have you brought with you?" As he walked toward the carriage, the door opened and another man emerged. "Sir John! Excellent to see you," James said, as John Graeme stepped down. James extended his hand.

"Struan, good to see you." John tipped his hat, his blond hair bright in the sun. "I hope you do not mind the intrusion. We had a business endeavor just north of here, and Patrick invited us to accompany him. Lord Eldin was generous enough to offer the use of his carriage for the trip."

"Eldin?" James glanced toward the barouche. A third man sat in the shadows, dressed in black from the crown of his hat and dark hair to his suit of clothes and immaculate boots. He remained inside, though he shifted his long legs to lean forward, tapping the point of his cane.

"Greetings, Struan. I see no reason to get out too soon, with the driver about to take us to the entrance." Nicholas MacCarran, Lord Eldin, nodded and extended a hand.

"Eldin," James said, reaching in to briefly shake the man's gloved hand. He would rather have ignored him, but propriety demanded that resentment and anger remain hidden.

"No doubt you're surprised to see us, particularly myself," his cousin Nicholas said, "but as Sir John and I had business near here—I have a building project near Loch Katrine—we thought it efficient to travel with Patrick in advance of Lady Rankin's party."

"Of course," James said. Seeing Patrick and John watching soberly, he yanked the door open wide. "Will you stay the night at Struan House?"

"Luncheon will be fine," Lord Eldin answered, as if Struan House was an inn. "Sir John and I have business in the north tomorrow, and would like to reach our hotel by this evening."

"Of course. Gentlemen, you may want to ride up to the house. I'll walk and meet you there," James answered, keeping his temper in check.

"I'll come with you," Patrick said, and John Graeme climbed back into the coach with Eldin. Angus and his nephew joined the driver, and they set off.

Patrick glanced at James. "Couldn't be helped," he said. "Nick is persistent."

"True," James said. "He talked our uncle into selling the clan seat, years back."

Patrick huffed agreement. "He and Sir John are going up north to see to the renovation of an old castle near Loch Katrine, a property Nick has purchased. He's going to open a new hotel there. With so many travelers going on tour up there, more accommodations are needed every year. Eldin has hired Sir John as engineer on the estate—private roads to build, a bridge, so forth. They're even talking about a small canal to connect two waterways, from what I heard."

"Impressive, though he might find that the Highlanders feel it is rather too much improvement for their remote area," James murmured. He did not want to discuss their cousin. "I understand Aunt Rankin plans a tour of the Highlands."

"Aye, she's quite enthused about it. She won't stay at Struan but a night or two—she is in a hurry, you know how she can be. Likely she'll breeze through the Highlands and barely appreciate it, but once home, she will be an expert to impress her friends."

"Indeed. I'm surprised you decided to accompany her. You've got little patience for her or her entourage. Who is she bringing with her?"

"Fiona, thank heavens, or I could not have borne the company. Aunt Rankin is dragging along her insufferable nephew Philip and Miss Sinclair—the latter for your benefit, I'm sure."

"No doubt," James muttered.

"I would have begged off the trip entirely, but I have my own reason for coming." Patrick grinned. "I've been appointed to a position in the Highlands as Excise Officer in a northern area. I'm going north to look at the area now, and after the new year, I'm to work with a glen sheriff there."

"Excellent! It's a better use of your talents than clerking documents in the signet courts all day. You do have a taste for adventure."

"Smugglers abound in those hills, so it should prove interesting."

"So I understand." James thought of the elusive cousin of the MacArthurs who made illicit whiskey, some of it supposedly of fairy make.

"I am to meet with a local laird named MacGregor," Patrick said.

"There are a fair number of MacGregors in this part of the Trossachs," James said, without giving away what he knew. "I am glad Fiona decided to come with Aunt Rankin after all."

"She's making arrangements to teach at a Gaelic school, and she wanted to see you before she accepts the assignment. She has her own requirement to fulfill, as do we all, thanks to Grandmother's will." Patrick glanced at James. "Any luck?"

"I am learning a good deal about fairy belief, but I have not found a fairy bride, if that is what you are wondering about."

"I am not surprised." They had reached the stone pier gates that led to the drive in front of the house. "What if you do not find a bride who can fulfill the requirement?"

James sighed. "I have decided to sell Struan House. It's mine to do with as I please. We can divide the profit and need not pursue the fairy nonsense, in that case."

"But we would lose Struan House," Patrick said. "Our grandparents loved this place. The house and estate are as much our family legacy, now, as the inheritance."

"We have no choice," James said curtly. "Fairy brides are scarce." *And unwilling.*

"Selling would solve the financial problem, perhaps. But we would still lose the inheritance to Eldin if we do not meet the rest of the will. We cannot let that happen."

Ahead, the vehicle had stopped in front of the wide entrance steps. Nicholas, Lord Eldin, stepped down. Dressed in black from head to foot, he lifted that haughty, handsome head to survey the house and its immediate grounds.

"Perhaps Mr. Browne can more liberally interpret the will," James said, watching Eldin.

"I doubt it," Patrick drawled. "Jamie, you cannot imagine spending several hours in a coach with Lord Raven, over there. The man is cold and factual. Not a whit of humor or warmth to him. It's as if someone had plucked the heart out of him long ago. Though I do not remember him like that as a lad. He was pleasant enough when we were young."

"He was." James had forgotten the early years, but not the betrayals he and his family had suffered since. He strode forward, determined to honor his duty as host and laird of Struan and uphold Highland hospitality, which dictated courtesy no matter the guest. "Gentlemen, this way, if you please," he said, as he reached the entrance steps.

As they entered the house, Patrick's words echoed in his thoughts. *It's as if someone had plucked the heart out of him . . .* In a way, James felt like that himself, after Elspeth's rejection of his proposal. He wondered, with time, if he would grow as unfeeling as the Earl of Eldin.

A shout from Angus MacKimmie caught his attention, and James turned to see the ghillie pointing toward the road, where a second landau approached. He waited until it entered the drive, then walked forward to meet it. The driver opened the door of the coach, and Sir Philip stepped out first with a mumbled greeting, turning with James to assist the ladies out of the vehicle.

"James," Lady Rankin said as he helped her step down moments later, receiving a kiss on the cheek, "how good to see you. What an absolutely dreadful road we came over. Look who I've brought with me!" She gestured toward the coach. As the driver held open the door, James saw Fiona and Charlotte still inside. His sister stepped out, her gloved hand in his, her smile quick and bright, her kiss light and welcome. Smoothing the creases from her dark gray skirt and short jacket, she moved aside, and James looked up.

Charlotte Sinclair stepped out, twitching the white skirts that fell beneath a pink velvet spencer, her blond hair neat under a white bonnet tied with matching ribbons. She smiled and stretched out her hand. "Dear James, how I've missed you!"

"Miss Sinclair," James said, though they had long used first names. He stepped aside to allow Sir Philip to hand her down to the ground. "How good to see everyone. Welcome to Struan House."

When Charlotte grabbed his arm possessively, he thought of Elspeth and her gentle pressure whenever she took his arm—he had not felt that touch for days, and realized how deeply he missed it.

An hour later, enjoying Mrs. MacKimmie's excellent meal of cold lamb and butter-mashed turnips, James listened, nodding repeatedly, while his great-aunt explained her plans in excruciating detail. The woman scarcely took a breath, despite Patrick and Fiona's polite attempts to interrupt her.

"Miss Sinclair has the headache and chooses to have lunch in her room," Lady Rankin told Mrs. Mac-Kimmie for what was probably the third time. "Send a tray upstairs to her, please."

"Aye, madam, we've seen to it," Mrs. MacKimmie answered as she moved around the room, quietly directing the two housemaids as they brought dishes to the table.

"James, I want you to find us a local guide," she was saying now, as he sliced into another piece of lamb and added a spoonful of rowan jelly. "Sir Walter Scott hoped to join us in our trip, but he was unable at the last moment, a prior obligation of some kind. I was so very disappointed. He would have been a superb guide on our journey through the Trossachs. His poem is set there, you know, *The Lady of the Lake*—"

"I know, Aunt," James said. "I will ask if—"

"—though he did give us a most excellent travelogue for the area, written out in his own hand. Fiona has it—you do have it, you did not forget?"

"I have it," Fiona said, and reached into her pocket to produce a folded letter, which she opened to reveal a page densely covered in hand script that used every available inch of paper.

"We are so excited to see Loch Katrine, described in the poem," Lady Rankin said. "Lady Murray of Calton Hill told me at tea last week that the views there are simply breathtaking and not to be missed. Fiona, you must bring your sketchbook and pencils so that in the future we may all enjoy some pictures of our trip."

"I have that, too, Aunt," Fiona answered.

"Very good, madam. You will enjoy your tour," Eldin said. "The area is quite popular with tourists. In fact, I plan to open an inn there. I've purchased an old castle that is in the process of being refurbished."

"How nice!" Lady Rankin said. Glancing around the table, James noticed that his brother and sister were quiet while Sir Philip and Lady Rankin expressed their interest.

"I would be honored if any of you would choose to stay there once it is ready to accommodate guests," Eldin said. "A reasonable price would be extended to family and friends." James saw Patrick glance at Fiona and roll his eyes.

"Thank you, Nicholas," Lady Rankin said. "Fiona, you might consider Lord Eldin's hotel for your accommodations if your teaching assignment is near there."

"Cousin Fiona would be more than welcome," Eldin said.

"Perhaps." Fiona folded the letter and slipped it back into her pocket.

After Lady Rankin and Fiona retired to their rooms to rest, the gentlemen remained to have coffee, electing to stay at the table. James was relieved, finding the casual choice better than retiring to the parlor. He wanted to return to his study as soon as possible, and had no desire to put forth more effort than necessary toward entertaining Eldin in particular. A housemaid brought a silver server of steaming coffee, and china cups were filled. When John Graeme expressed curiosity about the local Highland whiskey, James fetched a bottle, and though Eldin held up a hand in curt refusal—the man had spartan tastes, James knew—the others accepted small drams. James, meanwhile, drank the strong coffee, dark and bitter, adding a spoonful of sugar when he thought of Elspeth.

She was never far from his mind—even her sweet tooth had influenced him.

Much of the meal had been spent discussing engineering improvements in Scotland, which James would have found a more animated discussion if not for the glowering presence of Lord Eldin, who said little outside of brusquely ending one topic to initiate another that interested him more. James found him cool, polite, and enigmatic. Nicholas seemed keen, though, to learn as much about plans for certain Highland areas as he could.

"The roads in this glen are in very poor condition, Struan," Nicholas said. "I do hope there are plans to repair them."

"A portion of the damage is due to some recent severe storms. I will ask my ghillie, Mr. MacKimmie, to hire a few men to make repairs to a bridge near here," James answered. "Though long-term repairs and replacements are needed."

"The roads planned by the Highland Commission since the first of this century are nearly complete," John Graeme was saying. "The work of Telford and others has made a difference throughout the Highlands. Between those roads and the older ones created under General Wade for the British campaign a hundred years ago, the Highlands are more accessible than ever. I cannot say, though, if this glen was included in the plan."

"Likely not, from what I've heard," James said. "There is a good deal of work to be done, though the costs would be considerable."

"You should submit a report on the condition of the area to the Commissioners for Roads and Bridges in the Highlands," John said, "which will require an engineer to assess the problems. I would be happy to do that for you." He frowned. "But it takes months, if not longer, to gain the commission's approval, and more time for them to find the funds, hire the teams, and acquire the materials."

"You might better pay for it yourself, Struan," Philip suggested, "as the road and the bridge are on your estate. Get the thing designed, hire the laborers and workmen, and have it complete by next summer."

"True, some others have done that, finding it unwise to wait," John agreed.

"Perhaps you are hesitant to part with the funds for the repairs," Nicholas said.

"If it needs to be done, it will be done," James said curtly.

"Indeed. Allow me to offer a donation for the work," Eldin offered.

"Why would you do that?" James responded warily.

Eldin shrugged. "It is a pretty glen, from what I saw as we traveled through. I hear it is a place of fairy legends, too. I'm partial to fairies," he added.

Was the man mocking them, was he outright insulting, or was he serious about the offer? James narrowed his eyes. "There are interesting legends here, as in most places in the Highlands. As for the work on the estate or in this glen, it is no concern of yours, sir."

"I do not offer out of the goodness of my heart," Eldin said. "I intend to open a hotel at the head of Loch Katrine, and this glen would be an easy way for travelers to come north. Naturally I would prefer that these roads and bridges be in good repair."

"Understandable," James said, tight-lipped. Eldin shrugged, sipped his coffee.

"How is your research going, Struan?" Philip Rankin asked. "I understand you are doing some geological exploration here, and some folklore research as well."

"I am making progress with my investigations, thank you. My grandmother requested that I complete her last work, and that's going well also."

"A long while ago," Nicholas said then, "I remember hearing about some missing fairy gold in this glen. Have you encountered such a story?"

"In passing," James answered. "A curious tale. I doubt there is any truth to it."

"Lady Struan may have something in her notes," Eldin said. "Your grandmother was a thorough scholar of folklore. I had great respect for her, and her work. That she trusted you to finish her last book is not surprising."

James inclined his head at the unexpected compliment. "I will do my best."

"Treasure? Interesting," Patrick said. "That bit of gold would solve problems for all of—well, it would be nice if it could be found."

"Certainly anyone with the slightest clue would be looking for it," Nicholas said. "The temptation exists where any legend of gold or treasure presents itself. Only natural."

"Have you seen my cousins by any chance, Struan?" John Graeme asked, and James turned, grateful for a change in subject. "We are to meet the Glasgow architects in the morning, and so cannot stay long enough for me to arrange a visit."

"I have met them," James said carefully. "They are quite well."

"Excellent," John said. "Please give them my best regards."

"You should invite them to dinner while Aunt Rankin is here," Patrick said. "She and the others met Cousin Elspeth at the Ladies' Assembly in Edinburgh, from what I understand."

Sipping his coffee, James nodded. "As did I. Lovely girl," he murmured.

"She seemed quite taken with you that day— though many kisses flowed that afternoon, as I recall." Philip grinned. "You and Miss MacArthur seemed in agreement."

"Met a Highland lass, have you?" Nicholas asked quietly. "Well. Very good."

Sensing an edge in the tone, James turned away. He would be glad when Eldin's fancy barouche took him out of here later, along that rough and rutted glen road. *And may the very de'il bounce him back to hell,* he thought.

Chapter 17

Removing from the loom a full roller of the tartan length she had produced in the last three days, Elspeth set down the heavy bolt. She tugged the wooden roller free and set that once again on the loom. She took time to remove the last yarn sett from the loom, winding the spare yarns into bundles while she thought about the next design. Having completed several lengths of commissioned tartan, she had planned to make another lady's arisaid pattern, but she decided to make a gift piece for James instead.

Although she did not know if she would ever see him again, she wanted him to have a length of yarn from her loom. Then, at least, she would know that part of her would always be with him.

In the past week, a veritable demon of weaving had possessed her, and she had worked what seemed night and day. Nothing like her grandfather's work—that was indeed otherworldly—but her fast pace helped her forget all else, and lose herself to the creating of the cloth. Other weavers in the glen worked hand looms for Kilcrennan, and Elspeth went to their cottages to collect goods and give payment in coin and materials.

She had learned a good deal from them, her cousin Margaret among them. Lately some came to watch her and learn from her facile technique, and so she was further absorbed in her work. Margaret and her husband, Robbie, had tutored under Donal, an expert weaver by anyone's standard. Only Elspeth and Peggy Graeme—and now James—knew the secret that allowed him to finish his work so quickly.

Being busy with the weaving, Elspeth had been able to avoid her grandfather's attempts to bring up any subject involving Struan, marriage, or the future. And she avoided much thought about it, for the matter pressed upon her, heart and soul.

Leaving her cottage, she headed across the lane to the storage house where yarns and supplies were kept. Inside the dim room, bright, slender sunbeams poured through the cracks in the shutters, and motes and woolen fibers floated on the light. From a shelf, she took down a copy of Wilson's *Key Pattern Book*, and sat at the worktable to turn the pages. Published by an Edinburgh tailor a few years earlier, the compilation contained hundreds of tartan designs, each assigned to particular clans. Some were based on old, accepted clan traditions, while many, she and her grandfather were convinced, were simply invented. And all of them had helped feed the current craze for tartan that was of such benefit to the MacArthurs of Kilcrennan and other Scottish weavers.

She was so immersed in studying the various tartans meticulously hand-colored on each page that she hardly noticed a knock, or the door opening, until sunlight poured over the pages of the book. She glanced up.

"Margaret!" Sliding from her stool, she gave her

cousin a welcoming embrace. "I did not expect you here today!"

Margaret Lamont smiled, round face beaming, brown eyes sparkling. Her red hair was swept back in a thick braid wrapped and pinned at the back of her head, and she was tall and a bit heavyset, her hands rough and pink from the work she did, working almost daily with wools and dye baths. "Reverend Buchanan kindly took me here on his way elsewhere," Margaret answered.

Knowing that her cousin was expecting a fourth child, Elspeth saw a difference even over the last few weeks, the girl's figure increasingly full, a pretty flush on her cheeks. "You look healthy," she said. "And I hope you are not working with the dye baths, for it is not good for your back, and you've said the smell makes you quite ill."

"True. My husband has asked me to let others do the dyeing, while I do the spinning and combing. Today I had some free time, with my sister doing the dyeing, my mother watching my children, and so I thought to get some fresh air and visit Kilcrennan, to see what you and Uncle Donal have been weaving with my yarns." She smiled.

"Your yarns are the best, and make wonderful weaving," Elspeth said. "I've just finished several tartans this week, and just now I'm searching for a new pattern."

Margaret came forward to peer at the book Elspeth had opened. "We're very fortunate to have this resource," she said, speaking softly in Gaelic, as she and Elspeth always did. "Tartan is in great demand since the king's visit, and many are ordering lengths from the Kilcrennan Weavers, I hear. The demand will keep you, and myself, busy for a while to come."

"I'm glad," Elspeth said. "Grandda is content when he's busy at the weaving."

"What sett will you do next?" Margaret looked over her shoulder.

Elspeth flipped pages in the book. "I cannot find the one I want, which is, ah, MacCarran," she said.

"Lord Struan's plaid?" Margaret asked. "You met him at Struan House, I know. Reverend Buchanan told me, and your grandfather told me, too, just now, when I arrived. He and Peggy Graeme said . . . quite a bit without saying so directly, Elspeth."

She felt herself blush. "Ah, some secrets Grandda cannot keep for long."

"And some he will keep a lifetime. He has your best interest at heart."

"I know." Elspeth turned another page. "Lord Struan does not have a kilt of his own, so I thought to weave the cloth for him. He can have it made up in Edinburgh."

"Would this be your wedding gift?"

"Now I know you've been chatting with my grandfather."

"It is customary for a bride to make her husband a tartan of his clan. I did that for my Robbie Lamont when we married."

"This is a parting gift," Elspeth murmured.

"Peggy Graeme and your grandfather love you very much," Margaret said quietly. "They fret over you as if you were their own child. And those Buchanans are gossiping now, too, which makes Peggy angry. She does not mind whatever happened between you and

Lord Struan—she likes him. But she fears this will ruin you in the future so that no man will have you for a wife once he hears of it." She paused. "She wishes you would accept the laird's offer. You would be wise to marry him if he has offered, Elspeth. And if you care about him. Only then, mind you."

Turning another page without seeing what was there, Elspeth sighed. "It is all my doing, this kerfuffle. I asked him to ruin me, Margaret," she answered. "I wanted to escape the Lowland marriage that Grandda was so set on arranging. But I never thought—well, no matter." She looked away.

"If you did not like MacDowell, you should have told your grandfather outright."

"I did, but he was determined—if not Mr. Mac-Dowell, then some other Lowland suitor. Now he has set his mind on Lord Struan. I know he wants my happiness. All of you want that." She saw her cousin nod, listening. "But I want to stay here at Kilcrennan. I thought that if no one would marry me, the matter would be settled. But Lord Struan . . . has offered. He is not obligated, however, because it was all my idea."

Margaret sighed. "Oh dear. Still, I can understand. I have not seen him myself, but Peggy says he is a lovely braw man."

"Oh, he is," Elspeth said, and this time she knew she blushed furiously.

"And did he? Ruin you, I mean. Though I should not ask," Margaret added.

"He is a gentleman, and that is all I will say. But I admit that what happened was . . . wonderful, and unforgettable. And I made a mistake, because I never expected—" Her voice caught.

"To fall in love?" Margaret asked quietly.

Elspeth flipped pages frantically, ignoring that. "I cannot find the pattern I want."

"The MacCarrans are a small clan. Perhaps it is not in Wilson's publication."

"My grandfather has notebooks with all the patterns that the Kilcrennan Weavers have made over generations. Wait." Elspeth reached toward a shelf and took down a black leather notebook, much worn, with slips of paper stuck among tattered pages, the whole tied with red yarn. She began to look through that, turning pages quickly. "Ah, MacCarran." She opened the page to show Margaret. "You were right. Here it is."

They leaned together to study two open pages, which were filled with ink and pencil sketches and charted weaving notations. "It says here that the MacCarrans are a sept of the MacDonalds of the Isles. And that one must be the MacCarran plaid," Margaret said, pointing with a fingertip.

"Aye, it is! My great-great-grandfather wrote these notes," Elspeth said. She read the marginal note along the side of the page. "It says, 'Kilcrennan Weavers made this tartan for a laird of the MacCarran clan in the years before the Jacobite Wars.'"

"Ah. Not all the old clan tartans are included in Wilson's pattern book, so you are fortunate to have your grandfather's notes. So many of the ancient plaids were not fixed designs for a clan, but varied from glen to glen, depending on local weavers and the plant dyes available for those who colored the yarns."

"True," Elspeth agreed. Looking at the ink sketch of the tartan design, Elspeth scanned the color names and the penciled numbers that were the weaving instructions. "Twenty warp threads of deep blue . . . twenty warp of forest green . . . ten weft threads of red, five weft of white," she read. Those yarn threads, stretched on the loom in the warp or forward direction and the weft, or crosswise direction, would make up one repeat or "sett" of the pattern, which was then repeated for the width of the plaid. "This would be a very handsome tartan."

"I've heard something of the MacCarrans," Margaret said. "A small clan with a singular history. Do you know their clan motto?"

Elspeth shook her head. "Lord Struan did mention a tradition of a fairy ancestor, but he . . . is not a believer in such himself. It is all fancy, he says."

"Then he should spend more time in this glen, and with the MacArthurs of Kilcrennan," Margaret said. "You must ask your viscount about the MacCarran motto."

"He is not my viscount." Elspeth took a scrap of paper and a pencil from a box on the table, and began to copy the sett instructions. "I may not have occasion to speak with him before he leaves for the city. I may not see him again at all," she said as firmly as she could. "I will send the tartan length to Edinburgh when it is woven, and if he likes it, Lord Struan may take it to an Edinburgh tailor." She copied carefully, her heart thumping as she thought of James in Edinburgh, and apart from her.

"He will love it. And you should deliver the gift yourself."

Elspeth looked up. "Go to Edinburgh?"

Margaret watched her. "Let me tell you their motto, since you are too stubborn to ask him about it yourself. It is something you may want to know."

Elspeth shrugged as if it did not matter, but waited intently.

"The MacCarrans keep a golden cup at their castle seat—it was given to their clan generations ago by their fairy ancestor. Around its base, I have heard, are some engraved words." She paused. "'Love makes its own magic,' reads the fairy cup of Duncrieff."

Elspeth sighed. "That is beautiful."

"I thought you might find it interesting."

"Oh, Margaret," Elspeth said. "What have I done?"

"Only you know that," Margaret answered. "From what I know of this, and of you—I say marry the man. No matter what obstacle exists, or why you refuse, ask your heart, and follow its lead. The MacArthurs of Kilcrennan have some secrets that we, their friends, are wise not to know. But follow your heart, and all will be well, I'm sure of it."

"He proposed out of responsibility, when the situation was mostly my doing. And Grandda needs me here, even if he says he does not."

"What if it could be sorted out? There is always a solution. Surely your Sight tells you something about this?"

She shrugged. "I feel . . . that he cares. A little."

"Listen to me," Margaret said. "Nothing else is as important as loving the one you love. You can find a way, with this."

"I wish it could be sorted through . . . but I am not sure."

"Sometimes we complicate love when it is a simple, beautiful thing of its own nature." Margaret smiled. "If you love him, then tell him so. You may be surprised to see what happens. Give the man, and the future, a chance."

Without reply, Elspeth stood and walked toward the baskets and shelves of yarn. She chose skeins of dyed yarns for the MacCarran plaid, taking the moments with her back turned to compose herself, for her thoughts tumbled. Suddenly she wanted to weep, and to run over the hills to Struan House before he left—and before she turned twenty-one and she belonged, by fairy bargain, to those she did not know. But Margaret had never heard the whole of that story—Donal and Elspeth had kept it close.

Margaret chose some skeins of yarn from another basket. "Elspeth, your grandfather needs more of the red and the yellow for his work." She handed them to Elspeth. "Take them to him. Go on—there are things to be said between you. Start there."

Elspeth took the yarn and gave Margaret a hug. Within moments she crossed to the other cottage and knocked, entering. Her grandfather glanced up as she set the yarns on a table beside his loom, and she saw that he did not really need those colors. There were ample amounts already there. But Margaret was right—there were things that needed explaining. Elspeth faced him. "Grandfather," she said.

"Aye then," he said, stopping his work. "What have you to say?"

"Kilcrennan Weavers is flourishing, Grandda. And that depends in part on your ability to weave tartan so quickly, by virtue of your skill, and your secret."

He nodded. "Go on."

"We can meet the orders for tartan faster than many others, though only we know why. Otherwise, to do this much work, we would need eight or ten more weavers to help us fill our orders. There are not that many to be found in this glen—Margaret's husband has his own small weaving business, and he might join us, but it is not enough to replace the work you do when the magic is upon you."

"I have been meaning to speak to Robbie Lamont about that very thing. I will not be here forever at Kilcrennan."

"Oh you will," Elspeth insisted. "And I will help you. You and I and Robbie can train new weavers. But for now, with so many orders, and the tartan madness upon the city folk, your fairy gift allows Kilcrennan Weavers to thrive and grow."

"Elspeth," he said quietly. "We do not need to fill all those requests ourselves."

"But you love this business, and you have put your life into building it. And we have come to rely on your fairy magic, and the goodwill of the fairy ilk."

"In some ways, it is so," he agreed. "Kilcrennan tartans themselves can cast a bit of a spell, bringing happiness through the wearing of the plaid." He smiled.

"Grandda, if I ever fell in love, all that magic would end. You said yourself that it would break all the fairy spells over us. So I cannot . . . fall in love. All this would end."

"Ellie, you would be happy. That is blessing worth the rest."

"What makes you think I am unhappy now? I love Kilcrennan. I love my work."

"That may be enough for some," he said. "But I think it is not enough for you."

She sighed. "But it cannot be, and that is that. When I was fourteen, you took me to see the place where you first found the fairy portal, and you told me the truth of the fairies of this glen that day. You said that if I found true love, all binding agreements would be broken. You said that love—" She stopped, her throat constricting suddenly.

"Love is the greatest magic humans possess," he finished for her. "It is more powerful than fairy magic, and can undo spells and satisfy bargains."

Love makes its own magic, Margaret had told her—the motto of the MacCarrans. James knew about that. He had to know, and yet he insisted that such things were fanciful. "I cannot bring ill fortune to Kilcrennan," she said.

He frowned. "I made a mistake, those years ago, telling you this when you were too young to understand that your happiness is all that I have ever sought."

"What of your happiness? You would lose your fairy power. And the rare privilege of your visits to the fairy realm every seven years. I will not ruin that for you."

"Is this why you refused the laird?" Donal folded his arms. "For the sake of my rare gifts?" He looked stormy.

She nodded. "As for my birthday coming up, and this lost fairy treasure—which I fear will never be found, certainly not by us—if the fairy ilk wish me to return to them, I cannot stop them. I have no magic of my own against that."

"You do," he said.

"I do not want to be taken by those I do not know, to live forever in someplace that is . . . not my home. Grandda, I have not always believed what you said, until the night I saw the Seelie Court riding through the gardens of Struan House. I saw the Fey," she said. "And I do not want to go with them. Yet I cannot break those spells, for you, or me . . . or for the sake of any of those that we love. And I do not know what to do."

"You have the Sight," he said. "The fairy queen's own gift to you when you were an infant. With it you can see what cannot be seen. Use it to protect yourself."

"I do not understand," she said impatiently. "My gift is unpredictable. I cannot control what I see with the Sight. Often it is weeks, months with nothing, then many things at once. Please understand, Grandda," she pleaded. "I must stay at Kilcrennan. And I can never fall in love."

"It is too late," Donal said, regarding her soberly. "You already have."

Inked pen scratching over paper, James sat at his desk after luncheon, writing a few thoughts on geology before he returned to the task of organizing and annotating his grandmother's manuscript. He would have a new series of lectures to deliver after the Christmas holidays, and though it was only October now, he was not one to fall behind. While his observations upon exploring the hill near Struan were fresh in his mind, he wanted to write more notes about it. He had spent the last hour making pencil sketches of the rocks he had collected, and those were scattered over the desk now, each one labeled with a small tag tied with string.

"The earth is still evolving into its present and future states," he wrote. "Lava, volcanoes, floods and tidal waves, earthquakes and other catastrophes caused massive shifts of land and sea, leaving earthly documents in rock and stone, such as the ripples seen in rocks along the shore, the cracks formed in mud that dried in hot sun, and the imprints of sea surges, raindrops, steady trickles of water, as well as the fossil remains of marine shells, plants, mammals, and reptiles."

He murmured to himself as he wrote. Osgar, who had been napping beside his desk, sat up, looking attentive, enough of an audience that James directed some of his comments toward the wolfhound. After all, he would be delivering these words to a full lecture hall at some point. "Since the Greeks," he said, while the dog tipped his head, "man has noted the evidence of a long-ago sea that surged as high as the mountains, and whole continents that once lay under water. A record of the truth is preserved in rock, and those secrets can be interpreted by astute and educated investigators.

"The present is the key to the past," he read even as he wrote it. He paused, waggled the pen in the air. "And the past is the key to both present and future."

For some reason, the phrase made his think of Elspeth with a sharp, sudden longing. Sanding the ink and blowing that gently over a tray, he put the sheaf of paper away with his other scientific notes. Thoughtful, he glanced at his grandmother's manuscript, stacked high and untidy to the left side of the desk, divided into two piles, the way he had been working on it throughout his weeks at Struan. Then he shifted a few of the labeled rocks out of the way, knowing he must finish this fairy business.

A knock sounded at the door, and Osgar loped to his feet, tail and ears alert. James went to the door and opened it, Osgar at his heels. Eldin stood there.

"Struan," he said, looking grim and unreadable.

"Come in," James said somewhat reluctantly. Yet he realized there was something to be got through here, and not to be postponed. Nicholas stepped inside, and James closed the door. "May I send for coffee or tea?"

"Thank you, no. Your housekeeper has been generous with refreshments, and Sir John and I will be leaving shortly. What a handsome animal," he said, stretching out a hand toward Osgar. "A proud and ancient breed, these hounds."

"Aye." James hoped that Osgar would growl ominously, sensing his master's enemy, but the wolfhound merely nudged his head under Eldin's hand. "Greedy beast," he muttered.

"I will take only a moment of your time, sir. I understand through Mr. Browne that you may decide to sell this house. If so, I am prepared to offer for it."

James stared. "I have not entirely decided."

"Perhaps I should make it clear that Lady Struan's decision regarding my role in her will was wholly her own. I did not influence her in that."

"I am aware that you and Lady Struan corresponded often, with some business dealings in common, from what I understand of her last months."

"In the last few years, she invested some of her capital in certain enterprises—jute, herrings, salt—in order to support Scottish industry. I assisted her in those transactions. And though it may surprise you, she made more than a little profit in the last years in illicit trading as well, mostly whiskey and salt. She believed that Highlanders who already suffered from the clearings of their homes after the landlord's sale of the properties should not also pay exorbitant tax duties on necessary items. It was because I helped her to earn those extra funds," he said, nodding his head a little, "that she included me in her will as a sort of . . . contingency."

"So you know the conditions of Lady Struan's will."

"I do," Nicholas said. "And I wish you the best of luck in your endeavor." His eyes were snapping, so dark a blue that they seemed nearly black. James found the man's cool, neutral, hawkish expression nearly impossible to decipher.

"To be honest, sir, my family are convinced that you exerted a good deal of influence over Lady Struan. But I will say no more on that topic, as there is nothing to be done about it."

"Absolutely nothing," Nicholas responded in a cool tone. "Nor is there anything to be done about other bygones."

"You watched our cousin die on that bloody field, and did nothing to save him," James said in a near growl. He flexed fingers on the doorknob. "It is not forgotten."

Nicholas glanced down, his gaze taking in James's left leg, injured on that same field in his attempt to rescue Archie MacCarran, the young chief of their clan. "Some situations," he said, "are not to be helped. Were they repeated, perhaps circumstances would not change."

"Particularly if one chooses to save himself while a friend and kinsman suffers."

"Subjective interpretation must be one of the basic laws of existence, is it not? As a professor, you must know such things."

"Indeed," James said, fuming. At his side, Osgar pricked up his ears and trotted to one of the large windows in the study; one looked out on the side garden, and the other on the trees and lawn at the front of the house, where Osgar now stood, tall enough to rest his chin on the windowsill. He whimpered a little, tail wagging. James glanced that way, and saw a gig coming past the trees toward the house. The dog woofed quietly.

"Down," James said, watching the approaching vehicle, which carried an older man and a young woman, who wore a plaid shawl and bonnet over her dark-as-night hair.

Elspeth and Donal MacArthur. Nicholas joined him by the window. "Ah. Visitors," he said. "Would this be the potential Highland bride, by any chance?"

James stayed silent, looking through the window. Osgar nudged close to his leg, and he reached down to pat the great, rough head.

"I believe Lady Rankin has it in mind for you to wed Miss Charlotte Sinclair."

"Really? I hadn't heard," James drawled, though it was common knowledge.

"You ought to consider it seriously. Miss Sinclair is a handsome young woman, and moneyed as well, which should appeal to you in your current state. Well, as I said, sir, I will not take up your time. I wished only to extend my offer of purchase."

"Which you have done. Good day, sir."

Nicholas turned for the door. "Your ghillie will bring the barouche around, and Sir John and I will be departing. Thank you for your hospitality." He glanced around. "It is a fine estate."

"It is," James murmured, gazing through the window at the approaching gig. He heard the door close behind Eldin. Calling Osgar to follow, he left the room himself.

In the corridor, he heard a faint, unexpected sound as a shriek echoed somewhere overhead. He glanced up just as Mrs. MacKimmie came around the corner.

"Och, sir, what is our banshee wanting to tell us now?" she said with a half smile. "Our laird is already here. Who else important could be coming to that door?"

The laird's bride, he wished he could say. But he only inclined his head to allow the housekeeper to move ahead of him. "Let us go and see, then, Mrs. MacKimmie."

"Grandda, what are you doing?" Elspeth asked. "When we left Margaret's to take her home, I thought we were going back to Kilcrennan along the glen road. This is not the way!" She saw they were headed for the earthen road that led to Struan House. The manor sat a mile ahead, its profile elegant among autumn hills beneath a blue sky.

"The glen road is in poor condition after the flooding. We'll have to go this way."

"There is no reason to go this close to Struan House."

"I forgot to answer the laird, who sent us a dinner invitation for later this week."

"Send our refusal by post or messenger, like anyone else. Stop, please. I do not want to see Lord Struan now. Not yet," she added miserably.

"The viscount also asked that you work with him in his library. You will have to refuse him yourself, for I will not."

"You've quite an imagination to think I want to see him." She lifted her chin.

"I have done things I am not so proud of, either," he said wryly.

"You are a good man," she said, "except when you do not listen to your granddaughter. Please, turn the gig and go back to the moor road—"

"When I was a young man, when I first met the queen of the fairies of this glen," he said, "I fell under her glamourie. I went into that hill for what I thought was a week or so . . . and when I came out, seven years had passed."

"I know," she said. "That was when the fairies gave you the gift of weaving. And later your son met them, too, and decided to stay with his true love—and so I was born, and you promised to take care of me. And now you can turn around and go home." She snatched at the reins, but he avoided her hand.

"The story I told you was not all the truth, Ellie."

"We have time for all the truth on the home to Kilcrennan. That way." She pointed. He ignored her and continued to drive toward Struan House.

"I made a wicked bargain that first time I went into the hill," he said. "I traded myself to her, to the queen. I did it to further my business, and I did it for my family, and for the wealth that would make them happy. She gave me the gift of the weaving in barter for my companionship. I was lured in by her charms, and believed it a fair trade—earthly riches earned through my own efforts, with a little help from the fairies. But I was wrong, Elspeth. I made a mistake, and I pay for it by returning there every seven years."

She looked over at him. "What are you telling me?"

"I became the queen's lover," he explained, "and she calls me back to her."

"Perhaps I should not hear this," she said uneasily.

"Perhaps you should, so you will understand what danger they can be, especially for those who dismiss their power. I am bound to the queen by a spell that I cannot break. I do care for her, but I do not love her. For years I have disliked being held fast by the glamourie she put on me. It is a wicked trap. Years ago I betrayed my wife . . . Niall's mother . . . for that bargain. That good woman died knowing that I was caught in the thrall of a fairy lover." He glanced at Elspeth. "And I would do anything to be free of it."

"Free of the Kilcrennan Weavers, and of all that you have worked for?"

He slowed, stopped the vehicle to look at her. "I would give all of it up," he said, "and never visit the land of the Fey again, never see my son again, he who chose their ilk over his own. I would give all that privilege up, Elspeth . . . for you, and for the privilege of living with my own love. Peggy Graeme," he said softly.

"Peggy!" Elspeth caught her breath. "Oh, Grandda, I did not know."

"Neither does she, not the whole of it at least. I am an old man, older than most suspect. Who knows how many years I have left, and I have many secrets. But Peggy, with her fine soul, accepts my past. She loves me in return, I think. Aye well." He sighed and lifted the reins again. "Ellie, I have made my mistakes. I want to right one of them by telling you the truth, and keeping you from making a mistake as well."

"What do you mean?" she asked, her heart thumping.

"Do not stay at Kilcrennan if it is only for me," he said. "Do not sacrifice your own happiness so that I can continue weaving in the manner that I do, and visiting the Fey world on my appointed day. Because I would rather be quit of it."

"So if I found someone to love—" She stopped, hardly daring to say more.

"Let the spells break, Elspeth. We cannot let ourselves live in fear of what the fairies might do, should they be displeased. Accept Lord Struan's proposal."

"But even if we could sort the rest, he prefers to live in the Lowlands and in the city, while I want to stay here at Kilcrennan. I love this place. And you, and Peggy."

"It is a problem, true," he said. "But surely there must be a solution. Go tell your laird that you love him, for he loves you, too, I think."

Feeling hope bubbling up inside her, Elspeth smiled, and suddenly wanted to jump out of the gig and run to the house. But she sat, twisting her gloved hands in her lap, and breathing faster. "If I did that, and all spells broke, what about the weaving? Your beautiful, magical work—"

"A weaver is what I am. I would just be a slower one." He smiled, and she saw a glimmer of sadness, and of courage, there.

"And what of the fairy treasure?"

"They insisted that it must be found, but I do not have it. We could bargain with them again. They do love to bargain," he said wryly.

"They will not trade with you again over this," she said. "I know it. I feel it." She tapped her upper chest. "They would be wrathful. It is too much risk for you to take."

Donal flexed the reins to turn the horse up the graveled drive to Struan House. "There is another reason for you to marry Struan. He saw me at the weaving, did he not?"

She glanced away, remembering what else had happened that night that only she and James knew about. "He did see you using the gift," she answered carefully.

"That secret must stay with us. So he must become part of the family."

Elspeth gasped. "You gave him the fairy brew deliberately!"

Donal chuckled in answer. Seeing that he was not about to stop and turn away from Struan House, Elspeth hastily smoothed her skirt, a light wool of indigo blue, and tugged at her shawl, a plaid of cream, blue, and green, her own weaving. As Donal slowed the gig near the entrance, she heard someone call out, and saw Angus MacKimmie walking toward them to greet them and take the horse.

Donal waved. "Greetings, Angus. Go on, Elspeth," he said quietly. "Go find your laird. Tell him," he said, leaning sideways, "that you want to be the new Lady Struan."

She was not certain what would happen, but she felt hopeful, at least. She leaned to kiss her grandfather's cheek. "Thank you," she whispered.

"The truth," he reminded her. "It is time."

Wondering how she could ever explain the truth, she rose to step out of the gig, and saw James walking down the steps toward her. He reached up for her, and she rested her hands on his shoulders. "Good afternoon, Lord Struan," she said, smiling.

"Miss MacArthur," he said, and she noticed how blue, how serious his eyes. He set his hands at her waist and lifted her down. A thrill went through to her bones as he set her lightly on her feet. "This is a surprise."

She looked up at him, suddenly nervous, for he seemed tense. He stepped back, and she saw others walking toward them. Among them were familiar faces—Sir John Graeme and Fiona. "John!" she said, startled. "And Miss MacCarran! I beg pardon, I had forgotten you might have guests," she murmured to James.

"Indeed I do," he said quietly.

"How good to see you again, Miss MacArthur," Fiona MacCarran said, stretching her hand forward to take Elspeth's briefly.

"Cousin Elspeth, how nice," John said, kissing her cheek. "I came north on business, and was not sure I would have time to visit Kilcrennan. Cousin Donal!" He walked away to greet Elspeth's grandfather.

James touched her elbow. "Miss MacArthur—you have not yet met my youngest brother, Patrick Mac-Carran." She smiled up at the young man who resembled the viscount, though his hair was darker, his eyes golden brown, his smile impish. As two others came down the steps, Elspeth turned again. Her heart pounded when she recognized the blond woman walking with a tall, dark gentleman.

"You remember Miss Sinclair," James said then.

"I do," Elspeth said. Smiling rather smugly, Charlotte Sinclair stood so close to James that her shoulder touched his arm. Feeling the jolt of that, and feeling she should not have come, Elspeth stepped back. "How do you do? What brings you to the Highlands?" she asked politely.

"We came with Lady Rankin to visit James—Lord Struan—and to tour your lovely Highlands." Charlotte turned her smile on James. "I'm determined to lure him away from his books and into the mountains to tour with us tomorrow."

"Lord Eldin," James said hastily. "please meet Miss MacArthur of Kilcrennan." Elspeth turned almost gratefully toward the stranger.

"A true Highland girl. I am charmed." He looked like a dark, avenging angel, his face stern and almost impossibly handsome, his physique as perfect as his neatly cut suit of clothing. Elspeth sensed something compelling yet unsettling about him. He inclined a nod and extended his gloved hand, and she rested her fingers in his.

Then the world went dizzy around her, and shadowy as if with smoke, and she could scarce breathe. *James*, she thought, *James*—and reached out for him, grabbing his coat sleeve almost blindly.

Chapter 18

Like ghostly images, she saw two scenes before her—the current moment, with James and Eldin both watching her, and at the same time, a little beyond where they all stood, she saw the two of them wearing the red jackets and dark tartan kilts of the Highland Black Watch, holding guns and surrounded by a smoky haze.

She stared at the two men in the vision, and then looked at James, who was watching her with deep concern—he wore a gray frock coat and waistcoat and buff trousers, his neck cloth neat and snowy, his thick brown hair gilded in the sunlight. He looked like a privileged gentleman. Beside him, Lord Eldin, a stranger to her until that moment, tall and severely handsome, also watched her, dark eyes narrowed.

James appeared in the ghostly image as a Highland officer in red jacket with white crossbands, and the dark blue-and-green tartan favored by the Black Watch. Soot smeared his face, and he had a bloody gash at the knee. He leaned on his upright bayoneted gun, planted in the road that was there—but not there. Beside him, Eldin held a bayoneted firearm ready. He fired it, threw it to the ground—and both men disappeared.

Mere seconds had passed. Breathing ragged, Elspeth tightened her fingers in Lord Eldin's, for he still gripped her hand. An earlier vision had shown James wounded on the field at Quatre Bras, and she knew he had lost a friend, his cousin. Now what she saw was more vivid.

She tore her hand from Eldin's. "You—" she whispered. "You were there! You saw Struan wounded, watched the other die—"

"Elspeth," James said, taking her arm. "Come inside."

"What did you see?" Lord Eldin asked her sharply. "Is it the Second Sight?" *Da Shealladh*, he said, the Gaelic surprising her.

"Come away," James said, and set his arm firmly around her to lead her up the steps to the house.

"What is wrong?" Patrick MacCarran ran toward them.

"Miss MacArthur is feeling faint. I'll take her inside," James answered. "Tell Mr. MacArthur that she is fine, only needs to sit down." Patrick turned away. Behind her, Donal MacArthur and Sir John stopped their conversation as Patrick went toward them.

The warm, solid pressure of his arm around her felt safe and good, and Elspeth let herself lean into his strength a little. He led her into the foyer and down the corridor to the library. The others, somewhat puzzled, wandered inside more slowly.

"What the devil happened?" His voice was quiet, patient rather than angry.

"Why did you tell them I felt faint? I am fine."

"Am I supposed to tell them that you are having

one of your fairy spells? They would never believe that, my girl." He sighed, looking at her sternly. Elspeth touched his arm, surprised and grateful that he had not denied it outright, as before.

"Do you believe it, now?" she asked.

He frowned. "Just tell me what happened."

She sighed. "Very well. I saw you and Lord Eldin together on a battlefield—your leg was injured, but you were standing, leaning on a bayoneted gun. Lord Eldin had a gun, too, and fired it, then set it down. Both of you were dressed for the Black Watch."

"My God," James said. "Sit down," he said, taking her arm. "You may feel fine, but you are shaking like an aspen tree. I do not understand this, but I will concede that something out of the ordinary happened." He led her to one of the wing chairs by the fireplace. "Would you take some whiskey, or tea, perhaps?"

"Not whiskey," she said with a half laugh. "Tea would be nice."

"Mrs. MacKimmie was already preparing tea for everyone, I think. Mrs. MacKimmie!" he called. "Drat. Stay here," he said, touching her shoulder. "I will be back. The others may descend upon you any moment. I promise to be right back." He lifted her hand to his lips and kissed her knuckles quickly.

She took in a deep breath. "James—" But then she stopped, for the time was not right. As he left, she leaned back in the wing chair, but felt uneasy. Hearing footsteps, she turned to see Lord Eldin crossing the library floor.

"Miss MacArthur." He came closer. "Are you well? I was quite concerned. We were just speaking, and you seemed overcome."

"I am fine. It was nothing." She rose to her feet.

"So you have the Sight," he murmured, looking down at her.

She felt wary. "Why do you say that?"

"I know something of it." He reached up to touch her brow with his gloved fingertip. "Ah. Fairy-held Sight," he said. "Interesting."

"That's madness, sir," she replied. But she felt something odd about Eldin—that he understood far more than he would say, and that he might be a threat to James—and might not. She frowned, puzzled, watching him. "Who are you?"

He laughed and turned just then, as James came striding across the room, his steps echoing with slight unevenness on the wooden floor. To Elspeth, that rhythm was welcome and dearly familiar. James approached and took her arm in a protective way, facing Eldin. Behind him, her grandfather, her cousin, and the others entered the room.

"Cousin Nick," James said brusquely. "I believe Mr. MacKimmie is bringing your barouche round just now."

"Excellent." Eldin inclined his head. "Good day, then. I regret that there is no time to take tea with you, though I am grateful for the hospitality. Miss MacArthur, do take care," he said smoothly.

"Sir," she replied, and felt James's grip on her arm tighten.

Eldin left the library just as Mrs. MacKimmie and a housemaid entered, carrying trays that held a porcelain teapot, cups, and plates of food. As Mrs. Mac-Kimmie set a tray down, the others gathered near the fireplace, murmuring their concern to Elspeth.

"Really it was nothing." Embarrassed, she felt heat rising in her cheeks.

"You seem fine," Fiona said gently. "Perhaps it was the chilly air."

"We are having autumn winds after so much rain," Mrs. MacKimmie said, as she set out the tea things. "The wind may have blown into her, wee lass that she is."

"Lord Struan was overly concerned. I am fine," Elspeth said. Her grandfather lifted his fingers to his brow briefly, and she realized that he was asking if it was the Sight. She nodded in answer.

Fiona sat in the chair opposite to pour out the tea. Elspeth accepted a steaming cup, as did most of the others. Once John Graeme was assured that all was well, he said farewell and left to join Lord Eldin in the barouche. The rest—Donal, the MacCarran siblings, and Charlotte Sinclair—remained in the library. Elspeth's incident seemed soon forgotten, which was a relief to her.

"This is a substantial tea," Charlotte remarked, looking at the generous spread of foods, including cold beef in small rolls, sausages, sweet and plain biscuits, a fruit compote, and slices of lemon cake.

"A Highland tea, miss," Mrs. MacKimmie said. "Near enough to a dinner, this. The laird often takes his tea this way now, with a small supper later. There will be soup later this evening, if that suits. Lady Rankin requested an informal meal for all this evening, as she is tired from her journey."

"We do need an early evening before our outing tomorrow," Fiona said. "This is excellent, thank you, Mrs. MacKimmie."

While they spoke, Elspeth glanced at James, who remained standing beside her chair, a cup and saucer cradled in his hand. "I'm quite mortified," she told him softly.

"It is forgotten," he replied. "My great-aunt is still napping, exhausted from traveling, and Sir Philip has wandered off to look at the gardens—or there would have been much more drama over your welfare."

"I should go," Elspeth said, setting her cup on a small table. "I only came by today to, ah, offer help with your work, as we had discussed."

"I'm glad you did." He leaned an elbow on the back of her chair, and she looked up to see that his eyes were the sincere blue of a summer sky. She wanted to stay, and yet felt uncomfortable, now that the house was full of others who were important in James's life, when she was uncertain of her own position.

"Struan," Charlotte called. "We want to hear about this beautiful library, and also about the curiosities in the display cases. Come tell us about them!"

"A moment, Miss Sinclair," he answered. "Fiona is quite knowledgeable about geological matters herself. My sister makes a particular study of the fossils that occur naturally in limestones and other rock," he told Elspeth, who nodded.

Charlotte Sinclair's stormy frown told Elspeth that his reply did not please her, but Fiona rested a hand on her arm and began to explain something about the stones and objects in the display case.

"I should have remembered that you were expecting guests. You are too busy to work today. We can discuss your grandmother's book later. I will leave with Grandda."

"Stay," James said quickly. "I'd like you to stay. You and your grandfather must at least finish your tea."

Donal MacArthur, who stood studying the painting over the fireplace, glanced over his shoulder. He was sipping a cup of tea in one hand, and nibbling at a bit of lemon cake held in a napkin. "Thank you, sir," he said, swallowing. "I do have some work to do this afternoon. Perhaps Elspeth could remain here until I return for her."

"She may stay as long as she likes." James glanced down and met her gaze.

Forever, she thought. She wished she could stay with him that long. But she was unsure how he felt about marrying her now. With Charlotte Sinclair here, perhaps he was glad to be free of his obligation. She wanted to tell him the truth as her grandfather had urged, but with the guests present, there was no chance for a private discussion. And Charlotte was so intently possessive of James that Elspeth wondered if his impulsive offer of marriage still stood.

And that hurt like a blow to the very heart—she had not thought of him with someone else. "Grandfather, Lord Struan already has several guests."

"If he does not mind, than we will not," Donal said. "I will be back later, Elspeth, which will give you time to assist Lord Struan with his paperwork, if he likes."

"Certainly." James began to accompany them to the library door, but Charlotte hurried over to take his arm, smiling.

"You're leaving?" Charlotte asked. "So nice to see you. Struan, you really must tell us about the pretty stones in the case." She tugged on his arm. With a quick glance for Elspeth, James walked away.

Donal leaned down as they walked into the corridor. "That one has the face of an angel and the manners of a magpie," he whispered, and Elspeth laughed.

"I had better stay to be sure the magpie does not claim your blue stone," she said.

"Aye, do that. I did not have a chance to look close at the stone, but I believe it is the one, and we must have it back," he said. "Best that you stay and claim your ground, hey? You do have an agreement with the man."

"I am not sure of that," she replied, "but I will not squabble over a man with another woman. If he wants me, let him show it, or I am gone back to Kilcrennan, where I will stay, no matter what he does." She lifted her chin.

"So you have changed your mind. Good. But you are still too stubborn."

She sighed. "Grandda, listen." Quickly she explained the vision she had seen earlier. "Afterward, Lord Eldin knew that I had the fairy gift, and he had the knack of it. He did this," she said, and put a fingertip to her brow.

Donal frowned. "There is something strange about the man, I admit."

She nodded. "I feel sure he is an old enemy to James, and he may still be a threat. He wants something, but I do not know what that might be."

"Well, Eldin is gone now, and we're better off away from that one. Elspeth, I will be back soon. While you are here, take a moment to look at Niall's painting."

"I know—James pointed out that some of the women look like me. I hoped that meant that they look like my mother as well."

"They do indeed. I met your mother once." He

touched her chin. "Go study the picture again. There is something more I noticed, and I wonder if you will see the same."

"Very well," she said, puzzled. When Donal left, she returned to the library.

James stood with the others by the glass-front display cases, talking about the rock samples on the shelves. Elspeth remembered standing there with him on an evening when they had been alone together—blissfully, passionately alone. And now Charlotte Sinclair pressed her shoulder against his, her blond hair shining in the sunlight beside the chestnut and gold gleam of his hair. They were beautifully matched, Elspeth saw, as they leaned together to look at the stones.

She went to the fireplace to gaze at her father's painting, admiring the landscape of a moorland rinsed by moonbeams, with the details of forested hillside and a doorway to the fairy realm. Here and there, the same lovely, dark-haired girl appeared, like a medieval painting showing different moments in the same picture.

Then she noticed a new detail. To one side of the painting, she saw a dark rock wall and the narrow mouth of a cave. Within those shadows was the glimmer of jewels and gold—tiny dabs and dots of color that depicted a cache of gold and treasure.

She stepped to the side for a better perspective, nearly stumbling into James, who had come up behind her. She grabbed his sleeve. "James, look," she whispered. "There, to the far right. Do you see the treasure chest?"

He studied the painting, then nodded. "Interesting. I had not noticed it before."

"My father included so much in the picture—the fairy riding, and likenesses of my mother, and now some hidden treasure. What if he meant to leave clues?"

"The legends are well known in the glen, so your father put them in the picture."

"Do not give me your logic. It means more, I know it." She tilted her head. "And that rocky outcrop looks familiar. I've seen it somewhere."

"Good. We will find the cave, the treasure chest will be inside, and the fairies will dance at our wedding." He had a wry edge to his voice, and she glanced up.

"You still do not believe."

"None of this is easy to accept, Elspeth."

"I wish you would trust me."

"I *do*," he murmured. "But do not expect me to accept clusters of fairies tromping about my garden, or at your home . . . or in our lives. I do not put my trust in fairy stories."

"Please, we must talk," she said. "About the lost treasure, and the rest."

"I am listening," he murmured. "Go on."

"Fairies and treasure! How exciting! Tell us all," Charlotte said as she came toward them.

His attention centered on Elspeth, James had not noticed the others coming to join them. He wanted—needed—time alone with Elspeth, but there was no blasted privacy to be found just now. He would have gladly sent the lot of them off on their Highland tour, but he also wanted time to confide in Fiona and Patrick; his siblings deserved to know that he wanted to marry Elspeth.

Despite her refusals, and his impatience with her the last time they had parted, he knew he was not done with this. He would never give up on her. Yet with guests at Struan, he would not soon find a chance to tell her so—and to tell her that he loved her.

"What about lost treasure?" Patrick asked. "We overheard you, so do not deny it. Fairies," he went on, "are such an interesting topic. Fiona loves them." He glanced at his sister, who nodded, tucking her arm in Patrick's.

"Have you discovered any fairies at Struan?" Fiona asked, smiling.

"Indeed," Charlotte said. "That might be the most interesting thing about this place. Missing treasure sounds so adventurous. Perhaps we could find it."

"It's only a local legend of a fairy treasure lost long ago," James said. "They say the fairies want their gold back, or some such. It's an entertaining Highland tale."

"There are fairies in that painting over the mantel," Fiona pointed out.

Charlotte moved forward, gliding between Elspeth and James to look at the painting. "What a pretty picture. Though it would be better in one of the bedrooms. With half-clothed frolicking sprites, it's not proper for a stately public room like this one."

"I like it where it is," James answered. "Miss MacArthur's father painted it, and the picture was also a favorite of my grandmother's."

"Your father?" Charlotte looked at Elspeth with surprise. "Then perhaps your family will want the picture back when James sells Struan House."

"Sells?" In Elspeth's glance, James saw a poignant

depth, vulnerable and distressed. He frowned, unhappy with Charlotte for speaking out.

"Yes, he has decided to be rid of it," Charlotte said, tucking her hand in his elbow with not-so-subtle propriety. "We all agree it is for the best. James has responsibilities in Edinburgh, and a house like this requires so much upkeep, and we—I mean, Lord Struan—will not spend much time in the Highlands."

"I have not yet decided what I'll do." James stepped away to make the point with Charlotte, who only smiled. She could be oblivious to the truth once she set her mind on something, and he was her renewed goal.

"Lord Struan, you neatly evaded a near marriage proposal there," Sir Philip said in a jovial tone as he came toward them, escorting Lady Rankin on his arm.

"Philip!" Charlotte blushed. "Only you could be so bold. Lady Rankin, I hope you are feeling more rested now."

"I am. Did we miss tea?" James's aunt came to kiss his cheek, and went toward the tea table while Fiona poured cups for her and Philip. "Miss MacArthur, how nice to see you again," Lady Rankin said, turning. "I heard you were visiting today. You live nearby, as I recall?"

"I do," Elspeth said. "My home is at the other end of the glen."

"Aye, Kilcrennan. I recall that your grandfather is a weaver," Sir Philip said.

"How kind of you to remember," Elspeth murmured.

"Not at all, I have some Kilcrennan tartan in my own wardrobe." Philip nodded.

"Weaving! I hope small children are not employed in your family's textile factory," Charlotte Sinclair said.

"Only myself when I was small," Elspeth said, mischief glinting in her eyes.

"You weave cloth in a factory? How . . . startling," Lady Rankin said.

"I am a weaver," Elspeth confirmed, while some of the others raised their eyebrows. "But I use a hand loom in the old style. Kilcrennan is not a factory. My grandfather and his grandfathers before him were weavers in this glen."

"Mr. MacArthur is a fine artisan," Fiona said. "The Highland weavers are gifted and dedicated to their craft. Weaving is near an art form in the Highlands," she added. "In the North, there are no factories such as exist in the Lowland cities. Tartan has become very popular now, thanks to Sir Walter Scott's devotion to restoring the national identity and cultural integrity of Scotland. And after the king's visit, everyone is mad for tartan plaid, indeed for anything Scotch." She smiled warmly at Elspeth, who returned it. James blessed his sister silently, and exchanged a quick nod with her.

"You have a true appreciation for the Highlands, Miss MacCarran," Elspeth said.

"My sister has always loved the Highlands, where we spent time as children," James said. "Now she gives her time to a Highland society, and travels about teaching English to native Gaelic speakers."

"How good of you to involve yourself in such important work," Elspeth said. "I have heard it called the Celtification of Scotland, this new interest in our country's culture. My grandfather, as a born Highlander, laments it, but he is grateful to those who are willing to help the less fortunate Scottish people affected by so much change. And he does admit that his weaving business has benefited greatly from Southron interest."

"Kilcrennan will continue to reap rewards, given the enthusiasm for tartan and all things Scottish," James remarked.

Mrs. MacKimmie entered the room again, coming forward to clear the tea table quietly and efficiently. James nodded his thanks when she took his empty cup from him.

"Philip tells me the gardens here are spectacular, even in autumn," Lady Rankin said, gazing out the window. "I would love to see them, and I'm sure Charlotte would, too. Your manservant told Philip that there are fairies out in your garden. How quaint! We must go look for them. Little statues, I suppose he means."

"Och, Mr. MacKimmie meant actual fairies," Mrs. MacKimmie said, looking up. Lady Rankin gasped; James knew his great-aunt was not used to household staff joining in a conversation. He, on the other hand, liked the sense of ease he had encountered between servants and residents in the Highlands.

"Mrs. MacKimmie is right. Fairies are abundant on this estate," Elspeth said.

At the stunned silence, James smiled a little and folded his arms. "I suspect you all will find Highland fairies just charming folderol, as I did . . . when I first came here." Elspeth looked up at him quickly.

"How fascinating," Fiona said. "Have you truly seen fairies at Struan House?"

"On the grounds, and in the glen," Elspeth said. "The fairies always visit Struan House around this time every year. It is tradition. If you go out in the gardens at midnight, you may see them riding through . . . as Lord Struan and I did."

Now that had gone a bit too far, James thought wryly, as the others stared at Elspeth. But he knew it was best to get this over with; perhaps Elspeth, too, had realized there was wisdom in it. Sooner or later, after all, he intended to marry the girl, and so his family would have to accustom themselves to her outspoken, slightly fantastical, views.

"You . . . and Miss MacArthur . . . did what?" Charlotte asked.

"Saw the fairies," Elspeth said.

"At midnight . . . when you and Lord Struan were together," Charlotte went on.

"Dear heavens," Lady Rankin said. "You were alone with Miss MacArthur so late in the evening?"

"As a matter of fact we were," he said. "Miss Mac-Arthur found herself in a bit of a predicament one evening, and I came to her aid," James said. "Though I cannot vouch for seeing fairies, I will not dispute the young lady's claim."

"He had kindly offered me a place to stay in an awful storm," Elspeth said. "And late that night we saw the fairies riding through the garden. Or at least, I did," she added.

"Good God," Philip said. "I was just there. I saw nothing near as good as that!"

"Alone," Charlotte repeated. "Here. In the gardens, after midnight."

"Och, and what a night it was," Mrs. MacKimmie said, holding the tea tray in her hands. "A fierce storm, rain for days, the roads flooded and the bridge broken. 'Twas good of Lord Struan to rescue Miss MacArthur."

"Then you were here, too, Mrs. MacKimmie," Fiona said.

"Struan House is my home, Miss MacCarran," she answered without flinching.

In silent gratitude, James inclined his head toward the housekeeper, who left the room smiling, tea tray in her hands.

"James, please enlighten us further," Lady Rankin said. "I am confused."

"Gladly. Miss MacArthur was stranded by a devilish Highland gale. Traveling through the glen would have been risky, so she accepted hospitality at Struan House."

"I see," Charlotte said coldly.

"I suppose that couldn't be helped," Lady Rankin decided, "and you had a capable chaperone in Mrs. MacKimmie, even if her manners are forward."

"She is a most excellent housekeeper," James replied. "A treasure."

"The fairies?" Patrick asked. "You saw them on the grounds?"

"A beautiful sight," Elspeth said. "Lord Struan says it was a figment of my imagination, but I saw them as well as I see you." She clearly saw Charlotte frowning.

Fiona took Elspeth's hand. "My dear, this is astonishing and . . . well, wonderful. What did they look like? Does it take a special power to see them?"

Touching Fiona's hand, Elspeth felt a quick dizziness, and then the knowing. "You will see them your-self," she said. "Very soon. But . . . oh, you must be careful if you decide to draw or paint them."

"Paint them!" Fiona looked at James. "Does she know—"

"She does not," James said, frowning.

"The fairy ilk dislike having their images captured," Elspeth went on. "I think you will see them, but they may try to cause mischief for you if you sketch them." She paused. "You made a vow to your family . . . Lord Struan did so as well. A promise to Lady Struan." She glanced at James, her brow furrowed. "Other than finishing the book."

He watched her calmly, astonished. Though he had not mentioned the specific conditions of the will to her—and had planned to do so—he had thought that Elspeth MacArthur could no longer surprise him, even with her gift. Yet once again she had.

"Miss MacArthur, you *do* have the Highland Sight, just as Sir Walter said." Fiona beamed at Elspeth, and then at James.

"This is all rather silly," Charlotte murmured. James saw that her angry glower made her beauty harsh. She was edging toward spinster, he realized; he knew she hoped to regain his affection, especially since his in-heritance had changed her mind. But while he could offer her friendship, he could never offer her love. He felt sorry for her then, realizing that Charlotte did love him in her way—possessive and superior, but to her, that was love. Even now Sir Philip Rankin stood close to Charlotte, his gaze drinking in her pretty charms. Philip was short, plain, and balding, but he was clever and entertaining, he had a good income, and he was smitten with Charlotte. She needed someone to adore her who was just thick enough to overlook her flaws. A reasonable match might be found there, James thought.

"Not so silly, Miss Sinclair," he said then. "Fairy lore is very much part of the Highlands." He was a bit surprised at his own lessening skepticism.

"Ask permission of the fairies before you sketch what you see," Elspeth was telling Fiona. "Otherwise they might try to steal you away. That happened to my father when he—oh!" She gasped, turning to James. "My father painted them, and fell in love with one—and they took him because of the picture!"

"Who took him? Highland savages?" Lady Rankin put a hand to her bosom.

"Fairies, Aunt," Patrick said. "They steal people away to their world."

"What?" Lady Rankin grew pale. "Are they out there in the garden now?"

"If the fairies become angry, they may take humans away out of revenge," Elspeth said. "And sometimes they—"

James grabbed her arm, knowing he had to remove her before she could say more. He had seen that glaze before in her eyes, the one that overcame her when she began talking too freely, mostly of the unbelievable variety. Genuine or lunatic, he would spare her a further predicament, because he loved her.

He loved her. He had no time for that revelation now, though his heart bounded with it. Grasping her elbow, he turned her firmly toward the door of his study.

"As you can see, Miss MacArthur is quite the expert," he told the others, while he guided Elspeth beside him. "I am reminded that she kindly offered to advise me on local folklore before her grandfather returns. If you will excuse us—we will not be long." He ushered Elspeth through the open study door and closed it behind them.

Chapter 19

"Best leave it open," Elspeth said. "Charlotte will knock it down in a moment."

"Let her," he said. "Tell me what you were going on about back there."

"First tell me why you dragged me out of the library so rudely. Lady Rankin looked as if she would fall over in a faint at our hasty exit."

"More likely she was afraid the fairies would come get her. I thought it wise to get you out of there before you told all your fairy secrets, or predicted something dire, or invited the damned fairies into the blasted room," he ended emphatically, leaning forward.

"Which fairy secrets might those be?" She leaned toward him as well.

"Your grandfather's peculiar weaving habits. Your father's fate. And more."

"So you believe me!" She smiled.

"I would not say that. I will admit that what is normal for others is perhaps not the norm for you. Will that do?"

She tilted her head. "For now."

Her eyes, just then, were the color of clear aquamarine, lit with silver. But he would not tell her that. It was too damn poetic to tell her that. "What were you saying about your father and the painting?" he asked instead.

"I think I know what happened to my father." She reached for his arm, and he took her hand instead, her supple fingers strong from years of weaving. He admired her skill, and the woman, and he wanted to take her into his arms and show her how very much he admired all of her. But he kept still, listening. "He was out in the hills, saw the *daoine sìth* and sketched them, then went home to paint them into his canvas. And they took him in forfeit. I know it now. I must tell Grandda," she added.

"How in thunderation do you know these things?" he asked, losing patience. This, after all, was not what he wanted to talk about.

She sighed. "Your language deteriorates so when you are upset."

"Casualty of the war, my vocabulary," he said. "Go on."

"You know how I know. Stop asking me as if the answer will change to something you like better. I saw it here"—she tapped her forehead—"and I just knew it."

James shook his head slightly, then huffed a laugh, affectionate and accepting. Despite his reluctance and initial resistance, he was indeed beginning to believe her. Though it shook the foundations of reason, he wanted to give credence to what she said, what she believed—because she meant so very much to him.

Dear God, he was more smitten than he had ever thought possible. Reaching out, he traced his fingers over the softness of her hair, cupped her chin. His body throbbed even at that simple touch. "Beg pardon. So you just knew, in your way."

"I saw, in my mind, your sister walking in the hills carrying a sketchbook, and I saw her discovering some fairies. She must take care to avoid my father's fate."

"Fiona is too pragmatic to see fairies, and if she ever did, they would have a devil of a time getting her to go anywhere with them. You do not know my sister yet, but you will. She seems serene, but she would give them such a fuss, they would be glad to escape." Was he talking about fairies as if they were genuine?

"I hope you are right. James, what promise did you and Fiona make to your grandmother?" she asked.

"And just when," he said with a resigned sigh, "did that revelation come to you?"

"When I was talking to Fiona. *Did* you make a promise to Lady Struan?"

He exhaled. "By the conditions of my grandmother's will, in order to inherit, I must find a Highland bride. To be specific, a fairy bride."

"A fairy bride." Scowling, she crossed her arms.

"So the will states. Without that condition, there is precious little inheritance."

"Ah." She watched him, standing so close, the warmth of her body penetrating his own. She was so much a part of him now, in ways he could not easily define, and his body remembered other moments, standing so close to her.

"Elspeth." Not waiting for an answer, he bent his head to kiss her.

She shoved him away, pushed him so hard that he knocked a shoulder against the door. When she lifted a hand as if to smack his face, he caught it.

"You!" She was breathing hard. "You knew this all along, yet said nothing!"

"I suppose we both have our secrets," he murmured.

Breath heaving, she glared up at him. "Secrets! I may not have told you everything about me, nor did I expect it of you—but I have not deceived you!"

"Nor have I, you." He still had hold of her wrist, and drew her close, and she let him, though her temper fumed. She felt confused, betrayed. When he touched her she could scarcely think—when he lifted a hand to cup her cheek, a host of thoughts and feelings collided within her, and wanting to be in his arms won out. She leaned toward him as if entranced.

"But you knew this, and asked me to marry you—"

"I did," he agreed, drawing close. "And I would again."

"But—but not from a gentlemanly obligation, as you claimed. It was really because you wanted your inheritance. I was convenient to your needs."

"I wanted to marry you," he said, placing a hand on the doorjamb beside her head, so that he trapped her against the door. "I still do."

"Because I am Highland, and know more about fairies than most."

"That did come to mind," he admitted.

"Why did you not tell me?" And why had her senses not told her? She was befuddled with love for him— she had not sensed the truth.

"First of all, I would not know a fairy woman from a fishwife," he said. "And since you adamantly refused my offer, no explanation seemed necessary."

"I told you, I have my reasons for not marrying," she said, looking away.

"And I have mine for asking," he whispered, so that Elspeth tilted back her head, aware that he meant to kiss her, and that she would not resist—could not. When he touched his lips to hers, she sank into what was a stirring kiss, her hand curling in his, her knees gone crazily weak. Yet she summoned control again, and pushed him away.

"I suppose I cannot trust you now," she said.

"Fair enough," he said. "But I would trust you with my life. Ellie"—he hesitated, sighed out—"I am falling in love with you."

Her breath caught. She wanted him to know that she felt the same, and she wanted to step into his arms—but she had to tell him the truth, and take that risk, as her grandfather and Margaret had urged. "Oh, James," she said, moving closer. "I do—I do love you. But before you say more, there is so much you must know. To begin with, my mother was a fairy."

"Good God," he said.

A knock sounded on the door behind her, and Elspeth leaped, startled. James scowled, his hand still propped on the doorjamb. "Who is it?" he asked in a gruff voice.

"Fiona. Patrick is with me. Let us in."

Sighing, he straightened, and Elspeth stepped free, smoothing her dark blue gown and shawl, tucking the hair strands that had slipped loose from the simple knot at the back of her head. James opened the door to admit his sister and brother, closing it again.

"Now then," Patrick said. "What's the kerfuffle? Aunt Rankin thinks vindictive fairies are lying in wait for her outside, and Charlotte took off in a huff, dragging Philip to the garden. And the two of you have been closeted alone in here far too long."

"Miss MacArthur, this may sound ridiculous," Fiona said then, "but do you have any ties to the fairies? Any fairy blood among your ancestors?"

Elspeth lifted her chin. "My grandfather claims that I have some fairy blood."

"Quite a bit, from what I understand," James drawled, arms crossed.

"Excellent," Fiona said. "James, you've found her!"

"I have." Struan leaned against the large desk behind him, arms still crossed. "But she is not happy with me over Grandmother's fairy scheme. And when fairies are angered—"

"Oh, hush. What do you mean, 'fairy scheme'?" Elspeth asked.

"Our grandmother's will requires something of each of us," Fiona said, "in order to restore the fairy legacy to the MacCarran clan."

"Or none of us can inherit," Patrick said.

Stunned by the scope of this, Elspeth regarded them, trying to sort it through. "Perhaps Lady Struan wanted to change your minds about the *daoine sìth*," she said, "knowing you might not believe unless you had true proof."

"The *dow-in-shee*?" Patrick asked.

"The fairies," Fiona translated. "The peaceful ones."

"Not so peaceful when crossed," Elspeth added. "Your grandmother knew that. She knew that if James—Lord Struan—was to reside here, he would need to understand the fairies of this glen."

Patrick nodded. "She knew more about fairy lore than most, and she may have regarded all of us as too practical, and sore in need of lessons in . . . well, fancy."

"Elspeth," James murmured then. "Are you the proof we seek?"

Hands clasped, Elspeth hesitated. They watched her, all three. She met James's eyes, like a tidepool drawing her in. "It depends on what you are willing to believe."

"When we met here at Struan House," James told his siblings, "circumstances were such that I offered to marry Elspeth for the sake of her reputation. As it happened, the prospect suited Grandmother's scheme."

"And I have refused him," Elspeth said. "I cannot marry . . . just now."

"Oh dear," Fiona said. "I hope you will change your mind."

"Miss MacArthur, at the risk of intruding," Patrick said, "if you have some trace of fairy blood, you would do our whole clan a service by marrying our brother."

"You will not convince her. She's as stubborn a lass as ever lived," James said.

A movement beyond the window caught her attention, and Elspeth looked out to see her grandfather's gig advancing along the road toward Struan. He was returning already. She had to make a decision to either tell all the truth and take the risk, or keep the rest of her secrets forever—and lose her chance at happiness.

Her birthday was but a few days away, and with that would come a crucial turning in her life. Donal MacArthur had been right, after all—Elspeth was already in love. It was too late. The fairy hold would break—but unless the treasure was found, she and her grandfather remained in danger.

She faced James. "I have fairy blood through my mother," she said. "I have seen the Fey, and so has my grandfather. I know you do not really believe it, James MacCarran. But for me and mine, it is so. I hope you can accept that."

"I can," James said quietly. Behind her, Elspeth heard Fiona sob out and smother it with a hand to her lips, a hand on her chest. Patrick beamed, watching them.

Elspeth nodded slowly. "Then I will marry you on one condition."

"A condition. My grandmother would approve of that." James took her hand, his fingers snug over hers, safe, warm, compelling. A fierce urge to be in his arms overwhelmed her. "Go on," he said.

She straightened her spine, tall as she could, heart beating fast, for she was keenly aware of the risk she was taking. It was as if she perched on a crumbling cliff edge, and only their clasped hands, their joined will, their combined love, could save her.

"I will marry you," she said, "if we find the lost fairy treasure tomorrow."

He huffed in surprise. "Tomorrow! That sounds like a refusal to me, my girl. More gentle than before, but a pitfall nonetheless."

Glancing at Fiona and Patrick, Elspeth shook her head. "I do want to marry you, but I cannot unless that treasure is found. Not for riches—not to marry a wealthy lord, or to bring a dowry of my own. Please trust me."

"Elspeth, we can marry and spend our leisure time looking for treasure in these hills. Why the hurry?"

"Because I do not know how long we have together," she blurted. "A lifetime, or only days. The treasure must be found, or a bargain that my grandfather made with the Fey may cause terrible mischief for all of us."

He stood, taking her hands in his, and dipped his head. "If we had only days, Elspeth MacArthur," he said, "I would marry you. If we have a lifetime, I would marry you, wealth or none between us. In that, you must trust me."

"I do," she whispered. "And I believe you can find the missing treasure. My father left us a clue, if we can only decipher it. I feel it is so, with all my heart."

"Whatever it is, we will try to find it, if that will ease your mind." He bent forward to kiss her lightly, and even with his siblings present—and Fiona gasping back another sob of happiness—she felt a heat like clear fire all through her. She tilted her head and kissed him, clutching at his coat, immersed in his strength, in his masculine mystery and tenderness. She knew with exquisite clarity how much she wanted this man, and she felt grateful that—providing great good luck found them—she would be with him forever. But the danger was still there—the final risk had not been met.

He pulled back, resting his hand on her shoulder, and she drew a breath, blinking as if emerging from a dream. Fiona came forward to hug her, and Patrick kissed her cheek, welcoming her to the family.

Yet she knew it might be too soon. She felt anxious beneath, for she had thrown down a gauntlet to fate, and the powerful forces of the Fey. Yet she felt as if this was right, as if she had known James and understood him forever, part of her own soul. The differences between them only made the match richer—like a clear lake mirroring a mountain, the same image yet

rendered in two ways, one shimmering and changeable, one strong and solid, earthlike.

"James, I must know," she said quietly, looking up.
"I must know that you take my request seriously. The
treasure must be found tomorrow, at any cost."

"Tomorrow, my aunt and the rest plan a tour of
Loch Katrine. Do you want me to stay here, with you,
and search in the glen?"

"I—do not know." Suddenly she felt doubtful, fear-
ful, having no clear intuition regarding the treasure,
much as she had tried. Nothing at all came to her,
though she furrowed her brow, closed her eyes. Effort
only chased the gift away. "I do not know where to
look, other than near Struan. And I know my grandfather has searched there."

"Your father's picture," James said. "Does it show
a specific location?"

"I remember that Grandmother called it a pretty
picture of Ben Venue," Fiona said. "She told me that
one summer. I thought it was the artist's name, but
could that be of help?"

"Ben Venue!" Elspeth gasped. "That is the mountain southwest of Loch Katrine. Your aunt's party will
go past there tomorrow."

"Then you must come with us, Miss MacArthur,"
Patrick said. "Elspeth."

"Ben Venue it is, then," James said. "We will go
with them. If your grandfather would come, too, he
could help us in the search. Though how we could
cover a mountain in a day, looking for hidden treasure—" He stopped, smiled. "We will do our best."

Elspeth frowned. "If I go, Charlotte will not like
it."

"Charlotte," James said, "is not my concern." He

drew her into his arms and held her, and she sighed, knowing how she would flourish in his keeping. If only they could meet the condition she had set for him— and that the fairies had set for Donal MacArthur.

She drew back and looked up at him. "It may not be right for me to involve you in this. What I am asking seems impossible."

"Now who is the skeptic?" He leaned down to talk quietly to her. "I met my grandmother's conditions, Miss MacArthur. And I will meet any that you ask of me."

He echoed her own thoughts. Tears stung her eyes, and she smiled. But she alone, of the four of them in the room, knew how dire the risk. If they failed, they would never again meet on this earth.

A rapping sounded on the door, and Patrick opened it to Mrs. MacKimmie. "Begging pardon, but Mr. MacArthur is here."

Slipping her hand loose from James's hold, Elspeth smiled at all of them, having no adequate words of farewell—or gratitude. She led them from the room to greet Donal.

Late that night, James turned the blue agate in his hands, watching the lamplight glow in its prisms. He had fetched the key from Mrs. MacKimmie to remove the stone from the display case, planning to present it to Elspeth the next morning. Her promise to marry him had affected him deeply, and even the condition she had set upon her acceptance had not dampened the hope, and the love, he felt.

He was not sure what sort of treasure they could find in the space of a day, but he would certainly try. What was the harm, he thought. If it was not found, he hoped to set her mind at ease over its existence. Perhaps some clue would come up if they got a chance to stroll the slopes of the hills depicted in Niall MacArthur's painting.

And he could only hope Elspeth would marry him no matter the outcome. Perhaps she set this Herculean task to test his sincerity and respect for her wild fairy beliefs. His respect and love for Elspeth was sure and intact, and needed no questioning, but he would go along with this. No doubt he could find stones and the odd crystal or two, perhaps a bit of fool's gold, in the hills tomorrow to suffice as "fairy treasure."

The MacArthurs had agreed to return to Struan House early in the morning to join the group setting off for the hills. Lady Rankin had persuaded Donal to act as a guide into the territory described in Sir Walter's poetry, and the weaver had been pleased to hear that his granddaughter would accompany them.

James did not know if Elspeth would tell her grandfather about their engagement now or later. Sooner or later, of course, everyone would learn of it. Perhaps Elspeth wanted to find some fairy gold first—or what might pass for it—for Donal's sake.

James still had not absorbed this fairy business, but he was willing to accept a certain amount of eccentricity in his future grandfather-in-law. As for Elspeth, he was puzzled by what she had called truth—a fairy for a mother?—but he would trust that sooner or later, the matter would sort itself out to the satisfaction of all concerned.

Leaning back in the leather chair, he lifted the agate again and held it to the light, studying the pattern formed by its wavy concentric rings of color. *Moonlight to midnight*, Elspeth had called the color range.

At the heart of the stone was a cluster of clear crystals so delicate and complex that the toothy formations looked like a miniature landscape of peaked hills and castle turrets.

He reached down beside the desk, where he had set the leather bag containing his tools, geological notebooks, and rock samples, and dug until he found the loupe. Switching the two lenses for magnification, he held it to the agate, tilting it to the light.

The blue striations were translucent hues of good clarity, and the lenses showed better detail in the central crystals. He hefted the agate in his hand, its outer casing of granite like a thick husk. When he turned it, the angle changed and the crystal-lined cavity now looked like a cavern—one he had seen recently.

"What the devil," he murmured to himself.

Frowning, he stood and took the lamp. Walking into the library, he went to the painting over the mantel, and held the agate perched on the palm of his hand to compare it with the painting.

The cavernlike crystal center seemed almost identical in shape and depth to the hillside cave rendered in the painting, where the spilling treasure was depicted. Even the turf of the hillside, painted in green tones, had a swirl pattern similar to agate rings.

Thoughtful, James returned to the study, uncertain how to interpret that odd coincidence. But he told himself, as he sat down again, that the blue agate had belonged to Donal MacArthur. The man's son might easily have seen it, and used its design in his painting.

Reminded of Niall MacArthur, he reached toward

the manuscript that he had meant to work on this evening, and had set aside. He remembered a few pages that mentioned Niall, but he had not had time to go through them. Flipping sheaves until he found that section, he settled back to read them.

> *A young man of the local gentry* [wrote his grandmother] *went into the hills for the day, and lay down on a hill at sunset, tired after walking for hours while sketching from Nature. That was the last he was seen, for a shepherd spoke a greeting to him not long before. He disappeared on that hillside, and none knew his whereabouts. His father searched for his son and never gave up, even after months. One evening, as the father sat weaving at his loom, the son appeared to him in a mist, and said he had been carried away by a beautiful fairy who had pressed him to love her and to forsake the earthly realm to be with her forever. He begged his father to meet him at a certain spot in the hills where rocks hid a portal to the Otherworld. There, the son would explain all.*

James stared at the page, covered in his grandmother's minute handwriting. He had read this chapter at least a week before he had met Elspeth, but he had not given it much thought. Now he was stunned. Had Lady Struan based this tale on the disappearance of Elspeth's father? Perplexed and intrigued, James turned the page over.

The father went to the rock at the agreed time, and used a certain stone as a key to open the portal. There he met his son, with the beautiful lady who had lured him into that subterranean realm. With them was the queen of those hills, who long ago had won the father's love. She still held the tether of his heart, calling him back to her every seven years, an appointment he could not refuse, for he had accepted from her a gift that aided him daily in his weaving craft.

His son and the fairy bride presented him with their infant daughter in exchange for his son's soul, and he made a bargain with them: he could keep the child with him until the fairies called her back on her twenty-first birthday. So the weaver raised the girl, who remains protected within the beautiful glen. Her fairy kin gave her the gift of the Sight, so that she might see what cannot be seen, and know what cannot be known.

Gripping the page, James's hand trembled. Either his grandmother had a wildly vivid imagination . . . or she knew the secrets of Kilcrennan. The hand script continued along the edge of the page, and James turned it to read the rest.

The child, now a young woman, has only one hope of dissolving the fairy bargain to remain in the earthly realm. If she falls in love, and that man believes and respects the

*fairy ilk for what they are, she may stay.
But it is at a price: for her grandfather will
forfeit his life in return for hers, and enter
the realm of the Fey forever.*

He sat up slowly, tilting the page toward the light.

*The only remedy for that wicked bargain is
the return of a treasure stolen long ago from
the fairy folk who inhabit those remote
and wildish hills. And that, says the weaver
from whom I heard this story, can never be
found.*

Carefully, he folded the page and tucked it into the inner pocket of his jacket.

Chapter 20

"Look! Highland natives!" Lady Rankin pointed as the open carriage rumbled toward Loch Katrine, having left Struan House an hour earlier. Elspeth looked where the woman indicated, and saw two Highland men and a young boy walking along the foot of a hill. They were dressed in tartan kilts, loose shirts, worn jackets, and flat bonnets, and as the coach passed, they paused to wave and doff their caps.

"Please do not call them natives, Aunt," Fiona said, seated beside her, across from Elspeth and James. Elspeth glanced toward Mr. MacKimmie, driving the open coach, dressed in his usual kilt and jacket, like many Highlanders; though he appeared not to hear them as he concentrated on his task, the vehicle swayed and lumbered up a slope along the rough road. Elspeth grabbed hold of the edge of the leather bench seat.

"Well, they look like Hottentots," Lady Rankin said. "Nice that they greeted us. Highland manners can be very fine, I hear. My gracious, your coachman drives fast," she panted, grabbing a strap beside the half door, her bonnet ribbons fluttering.

"The Highlanders are used to tourists in the area," Elspeth said. "Grandfather says that the coaches fly so fast through here on their way to Loch Katrine, or southwest to Loch Lomond, that you could set a tea table on their coattails." As the others laughed, she relished the velvet rumble of James's chuckle.

"What Sir Walter Scott calls the Brig o' Turk in his poem is the bridge at the end of your glen, James?" Lady Rankin asked, looking back at a stone bridge in the distance.

"Not the one that washed out and was recently repaired, but another," James answered. "I did not realize its association with *The Lady of the Lake* until you treated us to so many readings from it this morning, Aunt." He glanced at Elspeth.

She smiled, tucking her head down, view obscured by her bonnet's gray brim. She wished she could reach for his hand, but she kept her hands folded, demure and gloved in pale kid leather, resting in her lap over her gown of pale gray wool under her bottle-green spencer. A tartan shawl in the MacArthur pattern of blue and green with touches of yellow draped her shoulders, and her leather half boots were suited to hill walking. She was confident that her outfit was attractive yet practical for the cool autumn weather, until Charlotte Sinclair had appeared, fetching in a walking dress and pelisse of pale blue accented in black, with matching bonnet and black slippers. Though Elspeth had considered comfort over appearance, she was glad that Charlotte rode in the second coach with Patrick, Sir Philip, and Donal MacArthur.

Now she leaned forward to look over the countryside. The open coach was Struan's large landau, with a single driver and two horses, but had elicited a complaint from Lady Rankin, until Angus MacKimmie explained that a coach and four was out of the question for the terrain. "We will be lucky even to reach the loch in this carriage," he had said. "Ye will be walking soon after that, with no good roads over rocky ground."

"That's fascinating, and perhaps useful for James's geological studies." Fiona smiled, seated across from Elspeth and beside Lady Rankin. Elspeth felt she had found a friend in James's intelligent, delightful twin sister. The engagement was still their secret—Elspeth had kept the news from her grandfather and Peggy, uncertain what the next few days would bring. But Fiona, knowing, smiled often, though Elspeth herself could not relax enough to enjoy, and trust, her own romantic future.

"There is Loch Achray," Elspeth said, pointing as the coach rolled past.

Lady Rankin consulted a small guidebook. "But it is scarcely more than a pool. How disappointing. That is a Highland loch?"

"A lochan, a small one," Elspeth said. "And very beautiful this time of year." Autumn gold and russet in the oak and birch trees covered the hillsides all around.

Fiona unfolded the page that Sir Walter Scott had provided for them. "Sir Walter reminds us here that 'the impressive Trossach Mountains are not the whole of the Highlands, but merely the fringe of the great Highland fastnesses, wildish and remote, further north. The Trossachs are the great massive slopes west of Loch Achray, between that and Loch Katrine, in a dell of woodland and cliff.'" Fiona looked up. "It is noble and picturesque scenery. No wonder it is so popular, not only due to Sir Walter's poem, from which you have liberally quoted, Aunt, but for its own spectacular beauty."

"You must make some sketches, dear," Lady Rankin said. "I want a record of the magnificence we are seeing today."

"I will, providing my little skill is adequate to the subject, madam."

"It is," James said. He looked out the other side of the coach. "Lord Eldin is opening a hotel somewhere near here. I believe he said it was called Auchnashee."

"Oh, I know that place," Elspeth said. "It's an old castle ruin at the middle of the western shore of Loch Katrine. Lord Eldin has a good deal of work ahead of him if he thinks to open an establishment there."

"He has the funds for it," Fiona murmured.

"Does this road go all around the loch?" Lady Rankin asked.

"It ends near the loch," Elspeth said, "once we go through the pass of Achray, and reach a curving strand at the nearest end of the loch. Carriages can go no further without difficulty and danger to horses and passengers. There is a mountain horse track along the sides of the loch, and a trackless heath, but no roads."

"I had no idea the area was quite so rustic. I thought it was prepared for tourists." Sighing indignantly, Lady Rankin thrust her considerable bosom outward, and fanned herself with the little book of poetry.

"We can hire ponies or walk," James suggested. "And there should be boats."

"Boats are available to tour the loch," Elspeth said. "Many choose to do that. A ferryman, Mr. MacDuff, has a cottage by the lochside, and hires boats to tourists. He will take us round for a fee. His neighbor rents ponies as well, and the ferryman's wife will provide luncheon in their parlor, or luncheon baskets if we care to do that. Mrs. Graeme sent baskets of food for us, so we can choose to have luncheon at the inn, or explore on our own." She saw James nod soberly.

"I prefer to explore on foot," he said. Elspeth nodded.

"'Indeed, the Trossachs area of Loch Katrine has a striking majesty,'" Fiona read from Sir Walter's letter. "'Ben Venue towers on its southwestern shore with true grandeur, massive shoulders crafted of the most ancient of rock, from the Goblin's Cave at its foot to the great crystals in its crown.'"

"Goblin's Cave?" James shifted in his seat. "I would very much like to explore that. For geological studies," he added.

"I have heard of that." Lady Rankin thumbed through her well-worn copy of Scott's *The Lady of the Lake*. "Here it is."

> *By many a bard, in Celtic tongue,*
> *Has Coir-nan-Uriskin been sung:*
> *A softer name the Saxons gave,*
> *And call'd the grot the Goblin-cave*

"A grotto, as at Struan House," Elspeth said. "I wonder if there is some relation."

"My sister, Lady Struan, thought herself an expert on fairies," Lady Rankin said, "and as I recall, she said her own grotto at Struan was modeled after a natural one in the Highlands. Perhaps it is this one."

Elspeth and James exchanged glances. "Could be," James murmured.

"Well, you may go ahead and explore for rocks or little savage hill goblins," Lady Rankin said, "but I have no taste for mountaineering or hill walking, or even a pony ride. A sail on the loch sounds excellent. Fiona, come with me to sketch whatever I would like for a keepsake. I think we can persuade some of the others. Miss MacArthur?"

"I would like to see the mountain," Elspeth said. "Especially the grotto cave."

"Come with me, Miss MacArthur," James said. "I think we can easily persuade your grandfather to act as our guide. Mr. MacKimmie can go with the others." She nodded vigorously, as if none of it was planned, while Fiona smiled.

"Charlotte will be disappointed if she is not invited, too," Lady Rankin said.

"She is not dressed for hill walking," Fiona pointed out. "I will ask her to sail with us. It looks like rain later." She glanced at the sky, where pale gray clouds rolled overhead, swirling around the mountaintops at either side of the pass of Achray. The wind was brisk and cool, the view so wide, enormous, and awe-inspiring that Elspeth sensed the elemental power of it, and drew one deep breath after another, sitting straighter, as if to absorb that strength into her being.

Fiona began to read from the folded page again. "'Ben Venue will appeal to ardent admirers of great landscape beauty. Its black and towering sides have a certain rich glossiness, and its craggy dignity houses many mysterious caves replete with legends.' Glossy?" she wondered. "Why would that be, James?"

He glanced toward the black mountain whose multiple peaks were visible beyond the low hills that edged the pass. "Deposits of mica would be my first guess.

Beds of mica-schist, perhaps, with granite and crystal. I am most interested to find out." At his feet was the leather bag with his geological tools.

"Here, this is interesting," Fiona continued. "'One of Venue's Gaelic names means "mountain of caves." The one most easily found is *Uamn nan Uruiskin*, or the Goblin Cave, along its lower eastern slope near the *Coire nan Uruiskin*, or Goblin Corrie.' How intriguing. Too spooky for me," she added. "I will leave that to you two brave souls."

"You're not the least bit of a coward," James told his twin, "but I can understand if you prefer the lazy luxury of a ship while you sketch."

"You may not find a steamer at this end of the loch today, though there is one further up at Glengyle, I believe," Elspeth said. "The ferryman keeps a pair of rowing boats for use by tourists who wish to go out on the loch. If the wind stays down, the loch will be smooth, and in any case, exceedingly beautiful. The scenery alone is worth it."

"A rowing boat?" Lady Rankin frowned. "I did not come all this way to sit in an inn sipping tea and gazing through window glass, so I will take even a small boat."

"Well done, Aunt," James said.

"I shall read more about Ellen's Isle, named for the heroine of Sir Walter's poem," Lady Rankin said, and flipping pages in her book, began to read aloud.

Elspeth closed her eyes and listened, and tried to quell her fears. She did not know what the day would bring, and she could not use her Highland Sight to guess at her own future. She would turn twenty-one in a few days, a birthday she dreaded celebrating, for what it might bring. She sighed.

After a moment, she felt James's fingers, strong and sure, slide under the cover of her plaid. She savored the quick, warm interlacing of their fingers, and the silent message there—*love, strength, passion, hope*—until the coach drew to a stop, and the secret knotting of their fingers slipped free.

At the ferryman's cottage along a strand that rounded the loch on its lower end, both coaches drew to a stop. Mr. MacDuff and his wife came to greet them, and then the group was treated to tea in the parlor. They drank hot, fragrant, sweetened tea and warm oatcakes with rowan jelly, while seated in a small room that had little to recommend it beyond the furnishings and two large, clean windows that boasted views of the mountain masses of Ben Venue to one side, and Ben A'an to the east, their lower slopes bordering the pass of Achray, through which the coaches had come.

Sipping his tea, James gratefully accepted some whiskey from Mr. MacDuff's silver flask. "The best in the Highlands," the man said. "Made locally. You will not find finer." He winked, and then went to pour some for Mr. MacArthur and the other men. None of the women were offered, though none of them seemed to notice.

"Is this fairy whiskey?" James asked Elspeth quietly, while Donal stood near.

"Oh no," she said, "that's rare stuff. This is a very good local brew, though. Our cousin is not the only one who makes whiskey in these mountains." She smiled.

"Who will sail over the water with us?" Mr. MacDuff asked then, and negotiations began as to how many would sail and who would go hill walking.

"James, will you come in the boat?" Charlotte asked.

He shook his head. "I want to explore the mountain slopes for rock samples," he explained, giving his leather bag a little kick to demonstrate his intention to work.

She scowled. "What about your leg? Can you walk that far without trouble?"

James shrugged. "I do not mind the exercise," he said easily, aware that Elspeth and his siblings glanced toward him. None of them would have made so blatant a reference to his lame leg, he knew.

Philip came toward them. "I would be happy to accompany you, Miss Sinclair," he said. "I'm interested in seeing Ellen's Isle with Lady Rankin and the others, and I hope you are, too. Struan can see the isle from the mountaintop, but he will miss its sublime effect from the water."

"I will see it another time," James said. "I am more interested in the geology than the scenery on this trip." He was anxious to go, and thought Elspeth and Donal were, too; they had their heads together in earnest conversation.

Patrick came toward them. "We've hired two boats, as most of us want to see the views from the loch, and Aunt Rankin is keen to see Ellen's Isle. James, you and Mr. MacArthur are for the mountain, is that so?"

"Aye," James said.

"My granddaughter will accompany us," Donal said, having overheard.

Charlotte whirled. "Miss MacArthur is going hill walking with you?"

"My dear," Fiona said gently, leaning toward them from her chair nearby. "Miss MacArthur is used to rugged Highland terrain and is dressed for it today. And naturally she may want to accompany her grandfather. You will be more comfortable on a boat outing, where you may relax at leisure. I plan only to sketch, and be lazy, and take in the beauties that surround this loch."

"I did think today would be a coach tour," Charlotte complained.

"We will make it a Sir Philip tour. Allow me to escort you around the shores of Ellen's Isle," Philip said, offering her his arm. He bowed. She laughed.

Relieved at minimal histrionics, James picked up his leather bag and followed Donal MacArthur and Elspeth outside. There, the wind was brisk and damp, and glowering clouds hovered over the mountain peak, visible from the inn yard.

Donal came forward and offered him a walking stick. James saw that Elspeth had one, too, a thick gnarly stick somewhat shorter than his own. He accepted it, knowing the day would involve strenuous walking and climbing. Though his leg often ached in rainy and cold weather, he had noticed lately that his injured leg had felt close to normal much of the time, perhaps a result of the beneficial Highland atmosphere, said to be excellent for one's health. He had first noticed it after the night of the wild storm, and whenever he was with Elspeth. Whatever caused it, good air or exercise, he was glad of any improvement. Although the doctors had long assured him that he would limp and be in pain all his life, he had tried not to let the injury, or his expectations of it, restrict him.

"This is fine," he said, tapping the walking stick, looking at Donal and Elspeth.

"We will meet you back here in the late afternoon,"

Patrick said, having just consulted with Mr. MacKimmie. "We will drive back in darkness, but there should be no trouble. Best of luck with your rock hunting, James."

"Bring back souvenirs," Philip called. "Diamonds and sapphires!"

James laughed. "More likely dirt-encrusted rock crystal if we're lucky. Late afternoon it is." He turned to Elspeth and Donal. "Are you ready, then?"

"We are," Elspeth said, though he heard a slight tremor in her light, clear voice.

Elspeth was quiet as the three of them walked over heathery moors for more than a mile. The foothills of the mountain sloped rather abruptly away from the heath, and as they climbed, little was said between them. Partway up the slope, Elspeth paused to catch her breath, standing on scruffy, rock-studded turf.

The view from that spot was magnificent, the steely surface of the loch smooth, the whole of its length visible below them, fringed with heathery moorland and blazing autumn-toned trees to one side, and the dark slopes of the mountain to the other. Above, the high peaks of Ben Venue, on whose slopes they stood, were obscured by the angle, and by a heavy ring of clouds and mist at the top.

James and Donal stopped, too, and James shaded his eyes with a hand. "Mica and schist," he said. "Up there. That glossy black rock. Even from here, the upper slopes seem to be made up of mostly that, with shale scree along the sides. The schist indicates massive heat early in the mountain's formation. A good sign for my research."

"We are not here for your research," Elspeth said.

"I am aware." Shouldering his leather pack with its long strap, he walked ahead.

"Then why are we here, if not for rocks?" Donal called from several feet ahead.

"To find the Goblin Cave. Do you know of it, Grandda?" Elspeth asked.

Donal waited for James and Elspeth to come closer. "Coire nan Uruiskin," he said. "Why do you want to go there? Is it for the rocks, Struan?"

"That, and because I promised your granddaughter that we would look for the fairy treasure."

"Grandda, we have something to tell you," Elspeth said then.

Folding his hands on his walking stick, Donal looked stern. "I am listening."

"I have agreed to marry Lord Struan." She lifted her head. "As you wanted. As we all want." She smiled at James, who touched her arm briefly.

Donal broke into a smile. "Excellent! But will you take her to Edinburgh?"

"We have not yet decided that," Elspeth said quickly.

"Elspeth has charged me with a condition," James said. "I promised to look for the missing gold while we are out today."

"That gold will not be found, I think, nor is this the place. It is not here. Do you know what they say of Coire nan Uruiskin?" He waited, and they shook their heads. "Cave of the Goblins, they call it. The urisks are small goblin creatures who haunt rocky places and cause mischief. Some say they are fairies, some not. They can be helpful to humans if treated politely. But the Fey, the older *Sidhe*, come here, too. It is one of the places where they live. Inside that cave is a portal to the fairy realm."

"Then it is a good place to search for the treasure," Elspeth said.

"Why would their missing treasure be just under their noses, in their own parlor?" Donal huffed. "Then they would have it. So it must be hidden elsewhere."

"Grandda," she said. "It is time we told James why all of this is so important." Donal MacArthur nodded gravely.

James reached inside his coat pocket and drew out a folded page. "I believe I already know the story, or part of it. I found this account among my grandmother's papers. It tells of a weaver and his son, and their meetings with the fairies—and tells of the girl-child given into the weaver's care."

Stunned, Elspeth reached out her hand. "Let me see." He gave her the page, which she read quickly, seeing her story summarized there. Silently she handed the sheet to her grandfather, who read it also, and circled it back to James. "That is the story you always told me, Grandda."

"Aye so," Donal said. "Lady Struan did write it down after all. I told her part of it myself. How she knew the rest about Niall, I cannot say. It is true, what is written there."

"I am not sure what to think about all this," James said. "But I trust you both. If you say it is so—well, then, I will do my best to believe it."

"Thank you," Donal said quietly.

James nodded and tucked the page back into his pocket. "And Elspeth's birthday? When is that, exactly?" He looked at her. "You have never said."

"October the twentieth," she replied. "Two days from now."

"I would offer felicitations," James said, "but I think you will not be happy until you see the twenty-first."

She smiled wanly, dreading to talk of it. Suddenly anxious and shivering, she pulled her plaid higher in the chill wind. "Grandda, where is this Goblin Cave?"

"I tell you, the treasure is not hidden there. We should stay away."

"I would like to see it, if only for geological reasons," James said. "If there is no treasure, there may be something valuable for my work." He reached into the leather knapsack he carried, and drew out a stone. "There may be more stones like this one."

"The blue stone!" Donal reached out for it, and turned it in the dim light. "This is the one," he confirmed.

"It was in my grandmother's collection, but it really belongs to you," James said. "I would like to know where it came from originally. Blue agate is rare, and a deposit of it could be important for many reasons."

"I did not find this stone. It was given to me by a fairy queen years ago, to use as a key to their realm on the appointed days when I go there—"

James frowned. "To the fairy world?"

"I tried to tell you," Elspeth said, thinking back to their evening at Struan House.

Donal nodded. "I have seen similar stones in this mountain, and in the hill behind Struan House, where the grotto now lies."

"Then I shall look there. For now, let us proceed to the cave, sir."

Donal nodded and led them up the slope, James

walking steadily using the stick as an aid, his stride long and sure, though Elspeth noticed his uneven gait. But she knew that even if his leg made the strenuous walk difficult, he would not complain.

Though it was barely noon, the sky clouded over in a cool mist. Elspeth felt a few raindrops on her cheeks as she looked up. She continued behind the men, whose longer legs covered the upward slope more quickly, belying any impediment. They advanced up the mountainside following in a narrow dip between two foothill slopes, a natural ditch like a tuck in a quilt. A slim runnel trickled downward between slopes of rock spotted with turf and brush. Ahead, on one side of the mountain, Elspeth saw a vast piling of rock and scree, as if it had tumbled eons ago from the massive black shoulders of the mountaintop, more than two thousand feet above them.

Now and then as they advanced, James would stop—not to rest his leg, unless that was his underlying reason—but to pick up rocks and examine them, sometimes dropping small samples into his sack, sometimes skittering them down the mountainside.

"Limestone with marine fossils, and signs of the Old Red Sandstone layer," he told them at one point. "Yet it seems volcanic beneath," he murmured a little later, to no one in particular. He drew out pencil and small notebook and wrote something down. "Granite and basalt. Fascinating."

Donal looked back at Elspeth. "He may not understand about fairies, but I do not understand what is interesting about a lot of old rock." She laughed.

Along the way, he stopped to brush his hand over a section of what looked like plain rocks to Elspeth, and then he stood and handed her a few small stones.

She gasped to see the glitter of a few perfectly formed crystals, both clear and peat-colored.

"Rock crystal and cairngorm, or smoky quartz," he explained. Appreciating their simple beauty, she thanked him, tucking the crystals in the pocket of her skirt.

"This way," Donal said, and led them sideways across the slope, which was easier than heading straight up. The ground was still turf and rock, rough and runneled, and they used the walking sticks liberally, with an occasional helping hand thrust out, one to another. Ahead, Elspeth saw a desolate expanse of fallen rock. Overhead, mist gathered thick, and raindrops began to patter their heads and shoulders, splattering on the rocks.

"The Goblin Cave is there," Donal said, pointing again. At the base of a cliff among the scree, Elspeth saw a dark opening in a fold of rock. "Now you have seen it. But we cannot go inside. It is not safe there."

"Grandda, we came all this way. What if this is where the gold is hidden?"

"The power of the Fey is strong here. We should stay away. Though you two have protection against them, more so than I."

"What is that?" James asked.

"Love," Donal said. "The bond of your love guards you, and that is what will break their hold over Elspeth—if that treasure is found. It would be stronger if—"

"If what?" Elspeth asked.

"If you were already wed. Though the love is there for anyone to see between you," Donal said. "It should be enough."

"Should be?" Elspeth said, again feeling nervous.

The rain began in earnest, and she reached out to James, and he took her hand. "Grandda, come with us. We will search together for the fairy gold. We will not be long."

"It is not there. Why would they have it there, in their own place?"

"Mr. MacArthur, may I see the agate?" Taking the rock, James held it up to the light, and looked around. "Ah, as I hoped." He offered the stone to them. "Look at the stone. There is a resemblance to the landscape—can you see it?"

Elspeth took it and studied it. Suddenly the shapes and points seemed to form an image. She gasped. "The crystal looks like the cave opening, but in miniature! But how could that be?"

Donal frowned, looking at the agate next. "I have held this stone many times, and have seen this cave, but I never noticed that before. How did you discover it?"

"Elspeth noticed the cave in Niall's painting, and last night I compared the agate geode to the picture, and saw distinct similarities. Now that we're here, the Goblin Cave seems like the place to look for this treasure."

"Why would Niall paint that cave in his picture?" Donal was still frowning.

"It may be a sort of clue," James said. "Perhaps he wanted to help his daughter, sir—and his father. Perhaps he wanted to lead you to the treasure, so that you could both be free."

"Oh, Grandda," Elspeth said, tucking her hands in the crook of James's arm. "Oh, what if James is right? My father may have meant this to help you one day, knowing he might not be with you."

Donal sighed aloud, sighed again. "So you think Niall left us a map? Huh," he said. "But there is nothing inside that cave but more rock, and some signs of the smugglers who come here now and then. And the fairy portal is there, invisible to all, but dangerous. We must stay away."

"Nonetheless," James said, shouldering his pack and grasping his walking stick, "I intend to go inside."

"For the rocks?" Donal asked.

"For the promise I gave Elspeth. You two wait here."

"I am coming with you," she said.

"If there is any real danger in this situation," he replied, sounding unconvinced of that, "it is to you, not me. Wait here, or go back with your grandfather, and I will meet you later." He kissed her brow and turned away. Elspeth grabbed his coat sleeve.

"I will come with you. Grandda—" She turned, the rain now pattering the slope.

"Go ahead," Donal said. "Go with him. Keep the stone with you," he said, for she still held it. "You may need its power. I will wait here." He tugged his flat blue bonnet lower and drew his plaid up over the shoulders of his worn jacket.

She could not bear to leave him sitting there alone in the rain, but she knew he would not come with them, once he had refused. "Go back, Grandda," she said. "Do not wait here for us, in the cold and the rain. We will be fine—but I do not know how long it will take us in the cave, with James collecting his rocks, and having to search for any hidden treasure. Walk back, and we will meet you at the ferryman's house."

He shook his head in protest. Then suddenly he

sighed out. "Perhaps it is best if I do not stay here alone for the Fey to find me. But you are in more danger."

"Not until my birthday," she said with a brightness she did not feel. "I am safe until then, and I am safe with James. Go on." She hugged him and stepped away.

"Eilidh," he said. "Guard yourself the best way you can."

Surprised, she turned. Her grandfather had rarely used her Gaelic name, claiming it had an unpredictable power if spoken aloud. "What do you mean to say?"

"I wish you were married to the man already. He is a good man, and your love will protect you both. That way they can have no hold over you. But there is an even stronger bond that they can never break, and that is a love that is not only devoted but united. If only you had married him before this," he said again, shaking his head.

"That will come soon enough," she replied quietly.

Donal stood, took up his walking stick. "Marry him now," he said. "Go take his hands in yours and wed him now, in the old way, before you go in that cave."

She stepped backward, her grandfather's suggestion alarming her, ominous rather than joyful. "I will be fine," she said. "We will have a wedding that all can celebrate."

"Now," he said. "Give him your forever pledge before you go into that place; form that bond now. I will wait and witness it, do you like."

Elspeth felt a cold grip of fear suddenly. The wind whipped hard, pushing at her back, but she stood firm. "That is not necessary, but thank you. Go down the slope, Grandda, and be careful in the rain," she said. "We will meet you at the inn by the loch."

She turned to hurry after James, who was already proceeding up the slope toward the boulders that framed and nearly obscured the cave entrance in the cliff.

As she came closer, she heard grumbling thunder overhead, and rain pattered down. As she approached the cave, the dark opening looked foreboding.

"James!" she called out, coming closer. He was kneeling, examining some rocks while he waited for her. Waving, he seemed in no hurry as he used a hammer to break off a bit of stone.

Hurrying toward him, she noticed the cluster of black boulders that framed the entrance, shaped like granite sentinels to either side of the cave. Feeling wary, she turned to see her grandfather walking steadily downhill, following the course of another runnel track. He would be safe soon, she knew, once he reached the lower slopes, where there were cottages and shepherds, and the loch below.

She stood for a moment, thoughtful as she recalled what he had said, and the gravity and concern he had shown. Then she turned to walk toward James. He glanced at her over his shoulder. "Much of this is limestone, but there are excellent patches of granite," he said, "showing traces of chalcedony, of a translucent variety. Some flecks of obsidian, too, with mica and quartz as well. Granite is a composite rock," he went on, "and the degree of chalcedony in the rubble here indicates that there could indeed be agate somewhere."

"That's wonderful." Her heart was beating strangely fast, and she felt a bit disoriented. "They are lovely rocks."

"Indeed. There could be something of real geological significance in that cave. The limestone layer is above a layer of granite, indicating a marine era with an earlier heat era. Quite possibly, heavy volcanic activity transformed this mountain eons ago. Did your grandfather decide to go back so soon?" He looked past her.

"I sent him down. There is no need for him to wait alone in a place where he feels unsettled. You and I will be safe, especially if—" She stopped, watching him.

He aimed the double magnifying lens toward the rock and peered through. "Excellent example of a trilobite—Fiona will love it. Aye, we will be fine, if what?"

"If we marry before we go inside there."

Chapter 21

"If we do what?" The rain pattered on the rock and scree, and James thought she said something else—*marry*—but he must have heard it wrong. "Did you say hurry?"

She stepped closer, the hem of her gray gown brushing over the rocks that he was examining, and then she knelt beside him. "I said marry."

James set aside the loupe and the hammer and stared at her. Then, with the aid of his walking stick, he rose to his feet and took her hand to pull her up with him. "Now?"

She nodded, her eyes beautiful in the cloudy light. "Here and now, for protection before we go inside the cave."

"I see." He spoke slowly, trying to take it in. Marry—when he had pushed so, and she had resisted. He had let it go, resigned to wait, and then she came to him like this, so earnestly that his heart wrenched with love. She was a marvel to him. He shook his head, huffed a laugh, almost disbelieving. "And the condition I must fulfill? My Herculean labor, finding the fairy treasure before I win the hand of the princess?"

"We have no time for that. I want to marry you now, here, in the old way."

He drew in a breath, stirred deep, but cocked his head. "You are a fickle creature, Elspeth MacArthur."

"It is my fairy blood, that changeable nature." She lifted her head. "I want us to pledge now, here, if it is marriage you truly want. That will guard us both. No one can sunder us or harm us that way."

James felt overwhelmed for a moment, unexpected and powerful emotion rushing through him. He loved this girl above all else—loved her full and deep, but he had not expressed it well, or even adequately. He set his hands on her shoulders. "Whatever you want, I am your man for it. I love you," he murmured, pulling her close.

"And I love you as well," she murmured. "And this feels right to me. But are you truly willing, here and now?" she asked again.

"I am. I doubt we are in danger from the fairy kind," he said softly, "but if this is what you want, then we shall do it without delay."

She tipped her head. "What if I say, once we are wed, that I want to live in the Highlands? We have not settled that, and it is a concern. Will you do as I say then?"

"I will do your bidding in the matter of marriage, now and gladly. In the other matter—let us negotiate. Fair enough?" She nodded. "Good. How, and where?" He held her hand in his, and looked around. "What spot would you choose for your wedding?"

She tugged on his hand to lead him toward one of the streams of water that cut down from the mountaintop, carrying rain and melted snow to the lower levels, thus transferring the power of the mountain and sky to the earth. "Here," she said. "Step over the water, and stand there, if you will, and I shall stand on this side."

He crossed the slender runnel and turned to face her. He had heard of such things, read of them here and there. "The old tradition of handfasting," he said. "We join hands over running water, and speak our vows." He took her hands in his, and noticed that her fingers were trembling. Letting go for a moment, he drew off her gloves—his hands already bare—and tucked the small kid gloves into his pocket.

Elspeth then placed her right hand in his right, and her left in his left, so that their forearms were crossed. "It is a very old Gaelic custom, I have heard, to form a love knot over running water. The union will be strong, and last forever, with such a blessing. And then the vows—just say what comes to you," she whispered. "Whatever enters your heart, let it come through your words."

James took a breath, let the feeling swell within, heart and soul. The force of what gathered in him filled him with humility, with awe. Feeling solid earth and rock beneath him, and aware of the power of water and the infinite symbol of their crossed hands, he felt so moved that for a moment he could not speak. And then he did.

"I, James Arthur MacCarran, take you, Elspeth . . ."

"Eilidh," she whispered. "My birth name is Eilidh."

"*Ay-leth*," he repeated softly, gazing at her through a misting rain. "Beautiful. I, James Arthur MacCarran, pledge my troth to you, Eilidh MacArthur. I take you as my wife and my lover, forever and a day."

"I, Eilidh MacArthur," she murmured, "pledge my troth and my heart to you, James MacCarran. I take you now as my husband and my lover, forever and a day."

He leaned forward, drawing her crossed hands toward him, and he kissed her. The water burbled between them, the rain fell upon them, and he kissed her slowly and deeply, his heart thumping hard for what he had just done, what he felt, what he had promised. She lifted on her toes and leaned in, their hands still crossed, and then gently drew back.

He stepped over the water to join her, and took her into his arms. "There we are, Mrs. MacCarran," he murmured. "Now we will be safe inside the cave."

"Good. And safe always," she said. "And I will keep my name, if you do not mind, Mr. MacCarran. It is my right to do so, as a Highland wife. Come, we may as well get this over with." She tugged on his hand.

"Oh, my insulted manliness, madam."

"Not that," she said, laughing a little. "The cave. The search."

"I thought the condition might be excused with our change in marital status."

"But the gold must be found. We have no choice," she said earnestly, wrapping her hands around his forearm. "We must save Donal MacArthur."

"And ourselves as well, so it would seem. Aye then. Come ahead." Buoyed by the power of the last few minutes, he kissed her again, then pulled her close and walked with her toward the cave.

Elspeth shivered in the cool darkness as they stepped inside the cave. She looked around, drawing her plaid close and gripping James's hand tightly. She saw only an ordinary cave, irregularly shaped, not very large, with rough curving walls and shadows deepening near the sloping back, where there was another opening, leading beyond.

No fairy halls painted in gold, no tall, luminous fairies waiting for them. She breathed a sigh of relief.

James reached out to brush his hand over a span of pale rock wall. "There's a good bit of metamorphic dolomitic limestone here," he said. "Limestone deposits," he explained, "when large enough, often contain caves and caverns, like pockets of air as the stone formed and cooled. This is a very fine cave," he went on, and let go of her hand to walk deeper inside, looking around.

Elspeth held back by the threshold, chilled and wary, as James moved around, stroking his hand over the undulations and textures in the rock walls. He glanced back at her. "I've a tinderbox in my satchel," he said. "We can make a fire and warm up if you like. We can spend some time looking about this place, with your grandfather gone, and the others not expecting us for hours. What is wrong?"

Without realizing, she had wrapped her arms snug about herself, shoulders tensed. "I am a bit nervous, wondering if there are . . . others here."

"Your grandfather's remarks were a bit unsettling, I will admit. But we're safe. We ensured that just a few minutes ago." He came back to take her in his arms and kiss her gently. "Do you want to stay here and wait while I look around?"

She shook her head. "I do not want to stay alone." He took her hand in a firm grip, and she walked with him toward the back, where he ducked his head, being taller than she, and stepped ahead to peer into the shadows.

"The cave has at least two chambers," he said then. "There's a smaller inner room back there. And this larger cave has been in use recently. Look," he said, gesturing toward the side wall. "Accommodations for a horse—that's a stone trough over there, with . . . huh, some oats still in it," he continued, letting go of her hand to step in that direction. She saw that some stacked stones formed a feeding trench, and iron hooks had been hammered into the wall for reins and other items.

"Who would bring a horse in here?" Elspeth asked. "We should go."

"Not fairy riders," he said wryly, "but smugglers."

"Ah, true, Grandda mentioned that." She laughed at her own nervousness. "A fair amount of smuggling goes on in this region. They often stash their goods in caves, and hide men and horses as well from excise men and sheriffs who may be after them. Our cousin—" She stopped.

"Your smuggling kinsmen will be snug in their homes on such a dreary day. Even if they're about at night, it's not a concern for us." He walked toward the inner chamber entrance, and peered into it. Elspeth followed. The dark, close space was deserted, she saw with relief. Faint light spilled there from the outer room, revealing shadowy objects—boxes, a chest, stacks of blankets, a natural rock ledge used as a shelf for bottles, bowls, candles, tins.

"They were definitely here at some point," James said. Elspeth stepped tentatively into the smaller cave, her curiosity getting the better of her. She followed a natural ramp of rock, since the second cave was below the outer one, set deeper in the earth. The space was smaller than the other cave, though tall enough for James to stand upright.

"These wooden crates stacked against the rock wall are empty," he said, looking into them. "Nothing here would be of current interest to smugglers." Taking his tinderbox from his leather satchel, he knelt, and flashing steel to flint, made enough sparks on dry wood shavings to create a little flame.

He lit one of the candles that sat on a ledge, and stood to hold it high, the golden glow spilling down. Elspeth saw that the cave had been transformed into a crude nest with blankets. Poking about, James found a crate that contained two whiskey bottles and a small sack of oats.

"The rock here is a bit different than the outer cave," James said. "Those are mostly limestone, with basalt and granite in the floor, while this one has much more granite composition. Interesting."

"So that means the layers show different ages in the rock," she said. "This cave is below the other, so this granite layer formed first."

"Very good! I did not know you even listened to my ramblings." He smiled then, with his eyes, warm and sparkling.

"I was listening to you all along," she said. "And I am a little curious about the rocks now, to be sure. Oh, it is cold and damp here." She rubbed her arms.

"There is a devilish chill in some caves, and we're damp from the drizzle," he agreed. "The whiskey and those blankets are tempting."

Seeing a wooden chest in a dark corner, she knelt to open it, sifting her hand through piles of fabric inside. "Plaids, some shirts. No treasure," she added.

"Did you think it would be so easy?" James chuckled. "No wonder Donal said there was nothing in this cave. The smugglers would have found any treasure that was here. And if there was treasure at some point, it was probably owned by men and stolen from them long ago, and simply attributed to the fairies."

She stood. "You still do not believe us, do you."

"As long as it can be explained," he said, "it is hard to accept some aspects of the tale. Fairy treasure makes a better legend than a dispute among thieves, for example."

She shivered again, and in the shadowy space, undid the ribbons of her bonnet, for it obscured her vision a bit. She set it by the door, her dark hair slipping free of a few of its pins; she pulled the rest out and dropped them into her pocket. When James picked up one of the plaid blankets and draped it around her shoulders, she smiled in thanks.

Raising the candle to shed the light on the back part of the cave, James went toward the shadows. "There is another cave back here, I think," he said, and as he explored the back wall, his hand and arm disappeared into a crevice. "Aye. This way." He slid into the space he had found, and Elspeth hurried to follow, eager neither to be left alone, nor to explore the place much. Her shivers were not entirely from cold, for a dread feeling still had not left her.

Yet James was her husband now, newly committed, the promises they had made still warming her heart and buoying her spirits. Wherever he went in this place, she would call up equal courage and go as well.

The cleft in the rock was narrow, but the opening widened, and she found it easy enough to slide through, following the light of the candle James held aloft.

"What is this?" she asked, looking around. It seemed to be a long tunnel, narrow with a low ceiling, that vanished at the far end into pure blackness. She heard the faint drip of water somewhere, and heard no other sound but her own breathing, and his, and the soft sputter of the flame on the wick as a draft went past. "Another cave?"

"More like a channel in the rock, or a subterranean passage of some kind," James said, walking ahead to explore, the curve of the ceiling so low that he stooped, and then crouched, running his hands along the rock to examine it. She saw other pools of shadows, narrow and low, like nooks and recesses, where James could stretch a hand, even an arm and a shoulder.

She saw him pick up a loose rock and pound at other rock encrusting one of the shadowy recesses. The sound echoed in the small chamber as he broke something away. He came back to join her, stretching out his hand.

"What have you found?" she asked, and he opened his palm to show her a chunk of dull stone. "What is that?" When he shone the candlelight on it, she saw a green glow.

"Agate," he said. "Not the blue sort, but agate nonetheless. An excellent find!"

"Oh!" she said brightly, covering her own disappointment, having hoped, however foolishly, for the chest her father had painted, with dripping handfuls of pearls, gold, and jewels. "That's wonderful for your work."

"Aye," James said. "I will come back here to work. As for the rest, caves and passages are often in clusters, as in this place. But this subterranean corridor leads nowhere. There is agate and common quartz, but little else. I doubt the smugglers have even been back here, for the stones are undisturbed."

She turned slowly. "This does seem a good place to hide a hoard, though."

"Aye, but not the case. I looked along all the crevices in here, and we've checked the outer caves." He shook his head. "There's nothing here, Ellie. I wish it were otherwise. I know you and Donal want to find the gold."

Elspeth sighed. "Perhaps we will never find it."

Gently he set his arm around her shoulders. "But we are handfasted now, and that alone was worth the climb up here."

"Aye," she said. "Worth more than agates and granite layers?"

He pressed his lips against her hair. "I know you are disappointed, love."

"A bit," she said, keeping secret her remaining dread over her upcoming birthday, and the possible trouble that could result from that in two days. "Well, Grandda will know what to do. He made the bargain with the fairies when I was born. Should we go back now?"

"No one expects us for a while yet," he murmured, pulling her closer. "And we are so nicely alone here, with plenty of time on our hands, it seems."

He flexed his fingers on her arms and skimmed his hands downward. The shivers she felt then were the delicious, enticing sort. She rested her hands on his chest, feeling a wonderful, tender pulsing inside, in rhythm with her quickening heart.

"We do seem to be very alone here," she said. "No smugglers. No treasure."

"No fairies but the one in my arms," James whispered, laughing softly, the dark velvety sound thrilling through her. Elspeth laughed, too, a mixture of relief and arousing interest. She pressed closer as his arms encircled her, and he kissed her, deep and slow.

When he slid his hand under the blanket over her shoulders, he pushed it to drop it away to the ground. Then he reached out and set the flaming candle on a natural niche in the rock wall. Breathing deep and quick in sudden anticipation, Elspeth shrugged off her plaid shawl and began to unbutton her dark green spencer, letting it drop down with the plaid. The neckline of her gray gown was low enough to show the ruched layer of her shift and lace-edged corset beneath, and James reached out to trace his fingers over her collarbones, sliding his fingertip into the hint of the dip between her breasts showing just above her underthings.

She lifted her hand to his chest and felt the heartbeat all through him like thunder, and stepped close again. He opened his arms and drew her into his embrace.

"What is this?" he asked, low and husky, nuzzling his lips against her hair, her cheek. Lifting her face to his, she felt sultry with early excitement. "What sort of treasure hunting do you have in mind, madam?"

"Did you know," she whispered, "that handfasting is legal in Scotland by the old laws, but is not a true marriage until it is consummated? Until then, it is no more binding than an engagement."

"Consummation," he murmured, "is a lovely idea.

We should remedy the situation before any more time slips past us."

"Are you sure we really have time here?" she whispered against his lips.

"Absolutely," he answered, slipping his mouth to her ear, blowing soft there, so that she groaned a little, arching against him. "It is as if time has slowed inside this place, do you feel it?"

She closed her eyes, breathed. She did feel it—whether it was magic or pent-up desire, or the relief of finding nothing to threaten them here, she sensed it—a leisure, a relaxing of time, especially now that there was no hint of treasure, and nowhere else to look, or to go, for now. She would have to sincerely trust that all would be well, a revelation of sorts to her, but the fear and concern lifted, dissolved. She wondered, once she set foot outside this almost magical cavern, if it would return.

He kissed her then, and thoughts vanished like shadows before light. She bent back her head to accept it, sighing, feeling so good and so safe, no matter where they were—she was with James, and she felt loved and cherished, body and soul. And strangely, it was as if the intimate space in the rock had opened just for them, with time dissolving away, and passion warming the atmosphere.

When he kissed her again, she felt a tenderness so strong that her limbs trembled as if they might melt, hot and buttery, and no longer support her. Moaning, she let her knees sink, and James sank with her to the plaids on the ground, still warm from her body. From the press of his hard length against her own, she knew that he felt as she did, growing urgent with passion.

He cupped her jaw, traced his fingers down her throat and over her upper chest, so that her heart leaped. She arched, hungry for more, savoring his lips, the supple touch of tongue to tongue, the graze of his fingertips over throat and collarbone, all of it made her breath catch, her heart pound. When his hand moved down over her bodice, she moaned softly, moved toward him.

His hands were compelling, gentle, and desire went through her like lightning. She pressed her hips against him, aware of the hard evidence that he wanted her as much as she ached for him. Handfasted, married, they were pledged, and she felt such a surge of love and compassion for him that it nearly started tears in her eyes.

She slipped her hands over his shoulders, and up, sinking her fingers into his thick chestnut, gilded hair. There were no words to express what she felt in that moment, and she could only let hands, lips, body tell him what she felt.

His fingers found the hidden buttons of the front flap of her bodice, and she sucked in a breath, anticipating, as he drew away the cloth and slipped his fingers over the chemise beneath, his fingers working deftly at her short corset. Finally, at the exquisite touch of his fingers over breast, she moaned softly, breath coming faster. Her nipples pearled for him, and when he bent to touch his lips to her breast, she clung to him, running her fingers deep in his hair.

"James," she whispered, "this is right, what we have done, marrying between us. It will make us safe forever; I feel it is so."

He lifted his head to kiss her, drew back. "Aye," he said, and took her down to the hard earth, and the pile of plaids hastily spread there. "And we will make sure of it."

Passion rocked through him, all the feeling he had saved for her, and all the deepest emotions so long restrained, years of it coming to the surface now like steam, for she fired his blood, his soul, and drove him to come out of himself, to open mind and heart. No other woman would ever have done that for him—she delighted him beyond measure. He kissed her, driven mad by her sweet, lush charm, by the delicate flowery scent of her hair, the warmth of her arms around him, the taste of her lips, her skin. She opened her mouth for him, and he tasted the inner moisture there, and when she pressed her body against his, he pulsed so hard, so hot for her, only for her.

She held magic in her—she was like magic, and a miracle, to him. She kept his soul bright, made his blood pulse, had done so since the first. He swept his hand over her breast, and she breathed against his mouth, and he ached deeply, hardened further for her.

He adored her, wanted her so intensely that it whirled through him like a storm. The urgency of the desire built inside him, yet he knew they had only moments here, and must return soon. But he could no longer restrain his desires, and she wanted this, too, as he did, and with these moments of peace and privacy in this strangely enchanted place, he would take her, and give to her.

"Ellie," he whispered into her small and perfect ear. "Are you sure?"

She nodded, put her hands to his face, kissed him, and it was all the answer he needed. Tenderness whirled through him like a thrill, head to sole, and he pulled her to him, and their kisses went to wildness, fiery and deep as fine whiskey, the fire sinking straight to his heart, and into his soul.

Moving a little, lying beside her, he braced his back against cool, dark rock, and felt himself draw strength from its massiveness, the nature of rock in harmony with his own nature, silent, restrained, patient. She leaned against him, and he slid his hands down to her hips, up and under her skirts, pushing cloth aside, felt her hands tugging at his own clothing. He slid his long fingers over the incredible softness of her bare hips, and pressed her tightly against his aching hardness, though he slowed himself deliberately, not wanting to rush her or this moment for them both.

But she was impatient, capricious, slanting herself against him, boldly, so that he could feel against him the soft place his body sought, and he near went wild, dipping his head against her shoulder, breath coming fast, so fast. "Love me," she whispered against his hair. "Love me now, here, for tomorrow everything could change forever."

He groaned soft, hearing those words, understanding the sadness and the joy in them, and he flared his fingers over her slender hips, and pulled her against him. She looped her arms around his neck and kissed him, deep, tender, till he knew he would burst without her, and he lifted her slightly and she knew, she opened for him, warm and moist, and he surged into her, deep and sure, honey and fire. She moaned against his mouth, and he felt all the desire he had saved for her sweeping, pouring through him like a torrent, and he moved slowly, carefully.

When she found the rhythm of it and pushed

against him, he felt himself sink deeper, thrusts powered by his love for her, his utter need for her, body and soul. As she shuddered sweetly against him, pent-up need and fire burst through him, taking him past time and reason, into pure feeling like iron in a forge. Her mouth moved over his, silently pleading, and he kissed her, taking her breath into himself and giving her his own.

Chapter 22

"There's no trace of a legendary treasure here," James said. "But the place is a great geological find." He held Elspeth's hand as they walked out to the outer cave again. While the caves held no promise of fairy gold and only ordinary traces of smugglers, he was excited at the reliable geological evidence, and planned to return. Every moment here, for him, had been worthwhile, for he had found his bride as well. Fairy or none, he knew this was right, between them, and he felt deeply grateful for that.

"We could search the smugglers' things before we go," she suggested. "Perhaps they've hidden something away." She hefted the blue agate in her hand, and lifted it. "Why would my father leave us a clue that led to this cave—and then nothing?"

"Well, the agate led to more agate. Very well, no more talk of rocks," he said, when Elspeth slid him a glance. He ran a hand through his hair, considering her question, his fingers still entwined with hers. "I wish I had an answer."

"Perhaps we should go now," she said, sounding weary and discouraged. "The others will wonder if we do not meet them in another hour or so. At least we have some plain crystals and small green agates to bring back to them," she added, smiling.

He did not like seeing her defeated, but he did not know how to help her find what she most wanted. And the blue agate still puzzled him—it had seemed a deliberate resemblance, but now it was indecipherable, beyond the entrance to the cave. Perhaps he would discover a pocket of blue agate on his return here—he certainly hoped so.

"Give me a few moments to record some geological information, if you will," he said, and left her to fetch his leather satchel. Rummaging for the notebook and pencil, he resumed note taking. "A good deal of trap rock under all," he murmured, jotting down further thoughts, "with much of the interior walls formed of limestone. Evidence of shell fossils even at first glance." He looked over at Elspeth. "We should bring my sister here some other time, to look at the fossils. Her eye for those is much better than mine."

"We may as well bring her up here. The place seems safe enough. Even the fairies are not here. I wonder why Grandda said they were here. Perhaps they inhabit some other part of the mountainside, far below these caves."

James hardly heard her, scribbling more thoughts. "In the smaller, inner cave, there are traces of granite composite, with rock quartz, feldspar, mica," he said to himself. "Basalt, other compressed rock. Flecks of crystal formations throughout. Heat once occurred beneath the limestone layers, as the inner cave is set well below the outer one, with a subterranean passage closed off, but pitted with niches where crystals occur. Pocket formations indicate bubbles in ancient lava or magma flow. Good green agate . . ."

Elspeth waited patiently as he wrote down the rest of his observations. "You and Fiona can come back here later, James," she said finally. "Oh—I left my bonnet." She disappeared into the smaller chamber, walking down the rocky slope there.

After tucking away his things, James left his leather satchel and his walking stick with Elspeth's by the outer entrance, along with her plaid shawl and his coat, and then he walked back to find her. He did not see her in the small chamber, and for a moment panicked, until he noticed her on her hands and knees in a dark corner.

"James," she said. "Come look! I found another little cave here. There's an opening, but these rocks are in the way."

He joined her, bending low to look past her. Several rocks were piled up near a low cleft in the wall, and Elspeth was trying to shove one of them out of the way. The rocks were not large—no bigger than bread loaves and Yule puddings, most of them, and some were dark and quite lightweight, while others were surprisingly heavy, given their size. He had expected them to be made up of limestone or shale, but on closer inspection, he realized that these were odd, indeed, for this area of the cave.

"What the devil—these rocks are mica, schist, biotite," he muttered. "Much of them are iron ore, all stacked here. It is not a natural rockfall, given the other rock in here. I believe your smugglers mean to hide something. They've blocked off the opening. Perhaps they have a little niche here for their best fairy whiskey—or French gold."

"Gold?" Elspeth looked up.

"New-minted coin," he said wryly. "Earned by smugglers. No fairy treasure, I'm afraid. What in thunderation is this," he said under his breath, and guided her out of his way so that he could shift more stones. "Light the oil lamp on that ledge, my darling."

She hastened to do that, using the flint from his leather pouch, and came back with the smugglers' lantern glowing in her hand. James took the light and held it close to the rocks that he had shifted, and the ones still piled up against the back wall.

"Someone has piled mica, biotite, and even chunks of hematite—pure iron ore—against this crevice. Well, they must have had it to hand, and it makes an effective barrier. Here, roll this away. Do you have the strength? Aye, bonny girl," he murmured, as he and Elspeth began to move the stones out of the way. He took the lamp again and got down on his knees. With several of the stones cleared away, he saw that the opening was large enough and deep enough for a person to pass through.

Kneeling, he leaned into the opening, shining the light around. And suddenly, as if the very earth gave way beneath him, he was sliding, tumbling, striving to hold the lantern without dropping it, as he fell into blackness.

Elspeth screamed behind him and he felt her grab for his shirt and miss, and he knew she fell after him. He slid over rough stone, pitted and studded and toothy, and came to a stop on a fairly level surface. Elspeth tumbled down after him, knocking into him, and with one hand he helped her right herself. Then he came to his knees, still holding the lantern, which thankfully had not spilled.

The light glowed in a small space, like a snug pocket in the greater rock, no bigger than the most snug of cottages. Tall as he was, he would not be able to stand upright. Elspeth, however, did, brushing at her skirts, gasping a little after her fall.

"Are you hurt?" he asked. She shook her head. He lifted the lantern high, and looked around. "My God," he said.

All around, studded in the curving walls and ceiling of the pocket, were crystals and gems, glittering in prisms and rainbows of sparkling color.

Elspeth slowly turned. "What is this place?" she asked. "Where are we?"

"A natural gem pocket, I believe," he said. He stood, forced to crouch down, and he went round the little space, running his hand over the walls, holding the lantern up. Elspeth took the lantern from him and held it high so that he could look in more detail.

"Aye," he said. "Tourmaline in a range of colors, natural clear crystal—look at this," he said, and snapped off a crystal rod a couple of inches long, and handed it to her, a pure and sparkling thing. "And this." He took the small chisel from his pocket and with another wrench and snap, he held out a glowing purple stone. "Amethyst."

"All in one place?" she asked. "How can that be?"

"They are all crystals, formed in a bubble in the earth, planted and growing here in the rock bed over eons. Crystal quartz, tourmaline, amethyst . . . beryl . . . aquamarine . . ." He named them as he found them, each a different color, while Elspeth held up the light.

"Amazing," she said. "Beautiful."

"It is astonishing to find them all here like this, so pure and in such variety, in such profusion and size. Yet it is geologically possible." He crouched. "We need to be careful of the sharp points of the crystals under-foot as we walk—and do not kneel, or it will hurt. And we'd best not crush or break them, though some will naturally snap free with even the lightest step." He examined some crystals he had pried loose, and scattered them on the rock floor, where they gleamed like a royal ransom.

A chill of realization went through her. "This place . . . is like a treasure chest."

"It is," he agreed, and stood. "My God, it is indeed. A living treasure hoard, a subterranean chamber, held in the earth itself all this time."

"Could it be?" She knew he would understand, and he nodded.

"Aye," he said thoughtfully. "Aye, it could be that indeed. Perhaps it was not a treasure chest we were searching for all along, but a treasure chamber. A pocket mine, filled with natural gemstones."

"But if this is it, and my grandfather said they have a portal to their world somewhere in these caves, then it was never hidden. I do not understand."

"Fairies need not be the explanation. This is a very exciting geological discovery. And I'll find you a gem for the ring that I owe you now." He smiled, and held out his hand to show her a gleaming, perfect amethyst, and another glittering aquamarine. "If these do not suit, we will keep looking."

She gasped at their beauty, then stopped as another thought came to her. "James, what if this place was hidden deliberately, to keep anyone from finding these beautiful stones? What if it was hidden from the fairies themselves?"

He frowned, considering. She thought he would point out the lack of logic in her question, but instead he went back to the ramp down which they had fallen. She saw that it was not so difficult to climb back up, which was a relief—she had wondered how they would manage to get out of the jeweled cave.

He quickly made his way up the rampart, and eased through the small opening, leaving her alone in the pocket. "Just a moment," he called back.

Shortly after that, he came back, walking half-crouched down the little ramp this time. He sat on a crude ledge in the rock, while she stood with the lantern. "It must have been the iron," he said.

"Iron? I do not understand."

"Donal said an ancestor of his stole the treasure and hid it away."

Elspeth nodded. "The Fey were very angry, and have been for hundreds of years, wanting it returned. So what they are looking for could not be this place, right under their noses, as it were."

"Iron," he said again, thoughtfully. "Someone blocked off the entrance with the rocks, most of which contain iron and iron ore. Perhaps it was done by that MacArthur ancestor of yours, three hundred years ago."

"Oh! Fairies cannot cross over iron! They would not be able to come in here. Oh, James! It was not a chest of gold at all that they lost. They lost access to this mine, because they could no longer come here. Perhaps, with so much iron piled there, they could not even see the place," she added. "It disappeared from sight, as far as they knew."

"Fairies." He scowled, and she knew he struggled with her theory.

But the idea exhilarated her. She felt certain it was true, so certain that she laughed with delight. "This has to be it!"

James gave a long sigh, hands to his hips, looking around. "I suppose anything is possible once we start talking about fairies. And marrying them," he added. "Well then, if we are to return the treasure to the fairies, and free you from their wicked spell," he said, sounding wry, "we had best roll up our sleeves and move all that iron away from the opening."

She laughed again, the sound echoing in the little chamber like a harmony of bells, and she followed James, who handed her up the little ramp.

An hour or so later, James wiped the back of his forearm along his brow, and stood back to survey what he and Elspeth had done together. The opening of the little pocket mine was cleared, all the smugglers' goods moved to one side of the inner chamber. The various rocks had been moved, some of them easy enough for Elspeth to carry alone, some of them so heavy that he had strained to lift and transport them. But each one had been moved.

They had taken the stones outside the cave, and one by one, had rolled them down the mountainside away from the Coire nan Uriskin. Now James nodded to himself, seeing the little crevice clear, and he walked out to the larger chamber, where Elspeth stood by the entrance, surveying the view. He joined her there. The rain continued, and heavy mist clung to the slope. Darkness gathered as well.

"We had best leave," James said. "Could take us quite a while to find our way down to the moor and the lochside inn. The others will be getting anxious."

She nodded, crossing her arms, sighed as she leaned against him. "I wonder if we have fulfilled the bargain. How will we know?"

"If that is indeed the fairies' treasure, then we have made it available to them again. And you fell in love," he murmured against her, "at least I hope so."

"I have," she said, slipping into his embrace.

"Then it is done, and the proof will be that you and I will stay together always," he said. He bent to gather his coat, and Elspeth walked away to gather her own things. "Come ahead. Elspeth?" He turned. "Elspeth!"

He saw then that she had disappeared. Running to the second cave, he did not see her there, either. "Elspeth!" The sound echoed against the walls.

Eilidh . . .

When she turned, they were standing there at the entrance to the pocket mine.

Three of them, a man and two women, tall and beautiful, looked at her, and she seemed to see well into their eyes, and fall there somehow, and she was drawn forward. Out of the first chamber she walked, and through the second, and down into the gem pocket she went, following them. Vaguely she realized that she was not walking on ramps or rock, but passing through walls, through stone, like a wraith, following them.

You can do this because you are fairy blood, one of them told her.

Who are you? she asked, and she spoke but did not speak.

We are your kin, they said, all of them in unison.

And then she knew, for she stopped, found her willpower and made herself stop and look at them. They were standing in the pocket mine with her, and though it was not a large place, and she was not tall, the ceiling and walls seemed to expand to allow ample room for all of them.

One woman was flaxen-haired, her features beautiful but harsh, somehow, and eyes a deep violet. The man was tall and dark-haired, and looked oddly familiar to her. The other woman was small, with hair like ebony and eyes with a crystal sheen.

Eilidh, the man said, and then she knew.

"Niall," she said, her heart pounding, and she was glad to know she was still flesh and blood. "Niall. Father—"

"My daughter," he said, reaching out to her. His hand was warm. He was flesh and blood, too, after all, though he lived with the Fey now. "This is your mother, Riona."

The dark-haired, delicate fairy woman stretched out her hands, and her crystalline eyes filled with tears, and Elspeth was enfolded in her embrace.

Curiously, she felt little more than wonder, and a strange sense of relief and ease. She stood back, looking at them, and felt herself trembling all over. "Mother," she said, trying out the word she had never used in her life for anyone. "Mother. And . . . Father."

They smiled, the one handsome, still a young man, for he had scarcely aged; the other inexpressibly beautiful, like a jewel come to life. "And this is our queen," her father said. "She rules over all the fairies of this region—there are many such queens and kings, and she holds this part of the land in her thrall. We are hers."

"Eilidh," the queen said, and held out her hand, beringed, long-fingered, milky. Her hair was long, like spun gold, and woven with diamond-scattered ribbons, and her gown, cream and white and embedded with crystal, seemed to glow.

Elspeth stared at her, entranced by such beauty and dazzle, for she seemed to sparkle, every part of her, as if she held a luminosity that never abated. Then she remembered meeting the king of England months before, and dropped in a low curtsy. And straightened.

"Am I . . . have you taken me away?" she asked them.

"We lured you here, and we have taken you this far, yes," Niall answered.

"I cannot go with you," Elspeth said, and took a step backward. "I cannot."

Her fairy mother lifted her hands expressively. "Stay with us."

"I will not," she said, walking backward again. "I want to be with James. I have married him," she said. "Our souls are joined. I love him, and I will not go with you." The words sounded odd—her voice, her being, all seemed strange, as if she were here, as if she were not. She took a risk, she knew, in countering what the Fey wanted.

"Eilidh," her father said, and reached for her again.

Elspeth!

She turned.

James circled the little chamber, and the outer chamber again, even looking outside to see if she had started down the mountainside. "Elspeth! Where are you!"

He dropped to his knees and peered into the pocket mine, but it was completely dark, black inside, and he heard nothing. Afraid she had fallen in there, perhaps gone to fetch another crystal to bring with her, though he had taken a few for both of them, he eased head and shoulders into the crevice. "Elspeth!"

And he thought he heard, in the dark, her voice. *James.* "Where are you?" he called. *Here.* She sounded far away, even strangely ethereal.

Walking down the little ramp, he groped in the darkness, feeling the walls, sharp with crystal points, rough with the granite and basalt that supported them. "Elspeth, where are you?" He wondered if there was some other pocket they had not found, for he heard her voice, somewhere. Hands roaming over the walls, he called again.

And suddenly behind him, a light flared from nowhere, and he whirled.

She was there, standing with others—three people with her, strangely clothed like out of some medieval play. They shared great eyes, all of them—pale and large in their narrow faces, glittering eyes colored like jewels. Elspeth's eyes, too, had that silvery sheen he sometimes saw in them.

"My God," he said, striding toward her—what happened to the ceiling, he wondered vaguely; earlier he had not been able to stand to his full height in here. He circled his arms around Elspeth, and she tucked into his embrace. James looked at the others, who stood still and silent, regarding him calmly. "Who—"

Elspeth's fingers came to his lips to dispel the oath. "This is the queen, and this is my own mother. And this is Niall MacArthur. My father."

He nodded to the females, and reached out to grasp

Niall's hand, feeling a thousand times the fool, wondering if he had fallen somewhere and hit his head. Surely that. Then the dark-haired woman touched his hand, her fingers slim, cool. He was shaking hands with a fairy.

A fairy.

"Elspeth—" he said, drawing her backward with him. "We must go—we must leave here. The others will be looking for us. Donal will be looking for us," he added, gazing at the man's own missing son.

"Donal," Niall said. "We will see him soon, when he visits next, for the seven years are nearly up again."

"But the fairy spell is broken now," Elspeth said. "Love . . . its magic is strong." She glanced at James.

"The girl is right," the queen said. "We will call Donal back to us again, and hope that he will choose to stay with us."

"He has the right now to make his own choice," Elspeth said.

"That is true." Her father had a dignity and beauty that showed regal, even the slight incline of his head. And she saw Donal there, in that pride. "Eilidh," he said. "We owe you a great deal, both of you. The treasure is found. Once again we can enter the place where so long ago the Fey mined the riches and magic and beauty of the earth. You found what the Fey could no longer see, after the treachery of the thief who did this. Thank you both."

"You are welcome," James said, feeling distinctly odd. This could not be happening—and yet it seemed as real as anything he had ever experienced. He reached out, touched Niall MacArthur with a finger, pushed against his shoulder, felt the solid muscle there.

Niall smiled. "I am real. I am human. It is magic that maintains me."

"What is going on here?" James asked.

Niall shook his head gently and gathered his wife under his arm, in much the same way that James held Elspeth, safe and close. "Once you learn to believe in what seems impossible—to believe, and trust—then all things, even magic, are possible."

James let out a breath, and the exhalation echoed around the chamber. It seemed genuine, all of it. Elspeth set her arms around his waist, hugged close.

"James MacCarran," the queen said. "Do you have fairy blood?"

He looked at her, a shining creature of a woman, lithe and gorgeous, ageless and elegant. "So it is said in my family," he answered.

"Good. Then you may come with us as well. Hold my hand." She reached out. "Do not be afraid."

Well, he was not going to show any fear, for certain. He took her cool fingers in his own, and held Elspeth with one arm, protecting her, for he had no idea what might happen next. She wrapped her arm around his waist.

Come, the queen said, and all seemed to go to mist and light. James moved forward, touching her hand, and Elspeth took her mother's hand, and Niall turned with them. And they all stepped through the wall.

Corridors of granite and limestone arched overhead, deserted, and James walked beside Elspeth. He heard the muted echo of their footsteps, of voices, but saw little beyond the wonder of the subterranean passages, tunnels into the heart of the earth. He felt awestruck, astonished, looking around.

Elspeth walked with him, holding his hand, and they followed Niall and his fairy wife, for the queen had left them. They moved down the corridor's sloping floor toward a blaze of light. James went cautiously, curiously. He heard a carillon of laughter, the strumming of harps, a steady drumbeat, and voices raised in song. Farther along, he heard the skirl of pipes, and his heart swelled at the sound.

Niall turned. "Do not go anywhere, but only follow us. Do not eat or drink anything that you see, do not speak to anyone but one of us." He turned back.

There were rooms along the corridors, and James peered inside as they passed. The rooms glittered with light and crystal, with gorgeous fabrics and finely crafted furnishings, though they were empty of people. Small tables in the hallway held dishes filled with fruits, sweets, breads, and cheeses. Wine trickled from golden fountains into crystal goblets. James felt intensely thirsty, suddenly, and wanted to drink. He was hungry, wanted to pluck an apple from an arrangement, but remembered Niall's admonishment, and moved on.

The tunnel they were in split into three pathways, two narrow and one broad, all channeled through the heart of the stone, which glittered with crystalline detail. One way, James saw, led to a spacious room, partially visible along the curving corridor. Light, music, and laughter came from there. The left corridor was brightly lit as well, and he heard the sounds of hammer and metal, as if from a forge. The center pathway was dim, and they followed its course.

The walls of the tunnels glittered with flash-fire colors that traced through the rock: ruby and gold, emerald and silver, sapphire and bronze. He touched a hand to the cool wall as they passed, and his fingertips came away with sparkling dust.

"Do not," Niall reminded him. They walked on.

Then he realized that the floor of the corridor was sloping upward, leading upward, and they climbed. And then it occurred to him that his left leg, which, after the climb up Ben Venue to the Goblin's Cave, had ached with the effort, did not hurt at all. In fact, he was not limping—not the least.

He reached for Elspeth's hand, pulled it upward to kiss it, smiling. She tucked her shoulder under his, her arm about his waist, and they walked upward, to where the light was now shining, and he could see, finally, a doorway, with trees and blue sky beyond.

"Here," Niall said, and stopped, "we will leave you. Go on, the two of you, back to your world. We have no hold over you any longer. We are only in your debt."

"Father," Elspeth said. "Oh, Father—" and James stood back as she went into Niall's embrace, their heads tucked together for a moment. Then she turned to her mother as well, their shining dark hair and delicate faces so very much alike. Finally Elspeth stepped back, tears streaming down her face. She took James's hand.

"Go on," Niall said. He clasped James's hand, let go. "Take care of her. She is precious, not only for who she is, but for what she can bring to your family. Great joy and enrichment will come to all of you through the fairy ilk. Eilidh was born to be with you, not with us. My wife and I knew that from the first. We knew she had a destiny of love and a responsibility to the family that you and she will create. We did what we could to make sure that you found each other."

James nodded, listening. "My grandmother," he said. "You knew her."

"I did," Niall said. "We were friends. We met before I went over to the Fey—and afterward, we met in the hills, and I taught her much of what she knew about the fairy legends. We spoke of you—of my daughter, of her grandson—and we planned this, Lady Struan and I. She would be pleased to know that it has all turned out so well."

"Planned it?" Elspeth asked. "What do you mean?"

Niall glanced at Riona, then at his daughter. "Lady Struan did not know what to offer her eldest grandson when she was deciding on her final wishes. She knew he was unhappy, that he had a darkness in his heart. And she wanted to renew the fairy blood of the Mac-Carrans through him, and each of her grandchildren." He paused, laughed a little. "They will each have their adventures, the others. Lady Struan and I wanted the greatest happiness for all of you, though such happiness must be earned."

"Did you make plans for my brothers and sister as well?" James asked.

"Not I," Niall said. "But the lady made certain that each of her grandchildren have their chance. Though there is no guarantee. There is never a guarantee, where fairy magic and human will come together. Sometimes there is clash, and sometimes there is . . . bliss."

"Father," Elspeth said. "You knew all along that I should be with James?"

"We felt it was so, and hoped. But it was up to you," he said. "I am only human."

"And the treasure?" she asked.

"It had to be found," he said. "There was no bartering where that was concerned. Without that discovery, you would have had to return to us forever."

"Dearest one, you must go," Riona said, her voice gentle, sad. "You cannot stay here longer, or the fairy thrall will take you, despite all our wishes for you. Go."

Elspeth nodded and reached out to embrace them, but they stepped back quickly, and she gave a little cry as they vanished. James took her hand then, firm and reassuring and in silence, aware that she felt hurt and joy all at once.

He walked with her up the remaining slope, and stepped out into the sunshine.

And he recognized that he stood at the top of his own garden, overlooking the back of Struan House. He and Elspeth had emerged from the grotto that his grandparents had built, and where Donal MacArthur had once found a portal to another realm. Turning, James saw the rock wall behind him was solid, as if it had never been open.

"We met, for the second time, here in this garden," Elspeth said. "Just there, I fell and landed at your feet, in that drenching rain."

He hugged her close. "And a better day than that," he said, "there never was. Come ahead, love." He led her down the slope toward the house.

Hearing dogs bark, then hearing shouts, he saw the back door of the house open, and his brother and sister rushed out and onto the lawn. James grinned and waved, keeping his arm snug about Elspeth's shoulders.

"Where the devil have you been?" Patrick asked, clapping him on the shoulder. "By God, we were worried!" He leaned to kiss Elspeth, while Fiona embraced James, then Elspeth as well.

"We have all been so terribly worried, James," Fiona said. "I dreamed that you were lost in the caverns under the earth, wandering. Where have you been?"

"Dreams?" James said. "Did you nap while waiting for us to get back?"

"Nap?" Fiona blinked and looked at Patrick, who frowned. "Not at all. I've hardly slept at all, with you gone so long!"

"It was a few hours only," Elspeth said. "And then we found our way back."

"A few hours!" Patrick shook his head. "You have been gone for three days."

"Three days," James repeated, and Elspeth gasped softly.

"Such a relief to see that you're not hurt," Fiona said. "The others have been so frantic. We've been searching for you. Donal MacArthur said the cave was empty, but for your coats and things. He went to look for you, and came back very concerned."

"So Donal, Angus, and I went out each day, walking the hills and the mountain by the loch," Patrick said. "Cousin Nick met us there just yesterday to help as well."

"Eldin helped you?" James asked.

"He muttered something about finding fairy gold, but he seemed interested in your welfare, especially Elspeth's, I think," Fiona said. "Though if you found any treasure, do not tell him. He asked so often about it that greed may be his real reason."

"No treasure," James said succinctly. "A few crystals." He pulled his hand from his pocket and opened his palm. "And a few beautiful gems perfect for a ring."

"A ring?" Fiona asked. "Why are we talking about

jewelry, when your lives were in such danger? You're tired and in need of water, food, and rest. Come inside."

"Thank God you are safe," Patrick said. "How on earth did you find your way back here through the grotto?"

"Connected underground caves," James said. He looked down at Elspeth, into her eyes, like silver and aquamarine in the sunlight. He drew her close again, leaned his head against hers, savoring the feel of her in his arms—real, warm, his own bride. "Just that."

She smiled, her eyes sheened with tears. "Shall we explain it, James?"

"I doubt they would believe it," James said, and glanced at his brother and sister. "We were a bit lost, I suppose. That's all."

"See, it's what I told Donal all along," Patrick told Fiona.

"But we were not in danger, after a point. We took our time, and oh—we got married," James said.

"Married! How, without a license, or a pastor, or—or guests!" Fiona said. "Aunt Rankin will have a conniption." She smiled.

"There are ways to marry in the Highlands," Elspeth said.

"Not terribly legal," Patrick grumbled. "You will need a proper wedding."

"That would be lovely," Elspeth said, tucking her arm around James's waist.

"Well," James said, "I did need to find myself a Highland bride, one with fairy blood. I've done just that." He kissed Elspeth's brow.

Fiona laughed merrily. "Grandmother would be so pleased to see this."

"Come now, neither of you believe in fairies any more than I do," Patrick said.

"Do I not?" James asked. "You will each have your turn to find out for yourselves, William as well. But I will warn you"—James could hardly keep from smiling—"though it may not prove easy . . . it will certainly be an adventure."

Epilogue

January 1823

"**S**urely we cannot fit another blasted thing into that carriage," James said, stepping back to survey the old Struan landau, packed full with belongings—most of them not his own. His breaths blew misted in the chilly air, and his boot heels crunched on the snow-pack that lined the drive. "We may have to take two carriages for this trip. Are you certain the loom has to come with us?"

"It does, my dear," Elspeth said, coming to stand beside him. "If we are to spend the winter in Edinburgh and stay through to spring so that you can finish your lecture series, then I must have my loom to keep me occupied, or I shall be insanely bored." She smiled mischievously, her face framed by a black velvet bonnet and the high neck of her dark plaid redingote, her gloved hands deep in the ermine muff he had presented her for Christmas.

Hidden inside her gloves and the muff was the amethyst and diamond ring he had commissioned for their wedding two months previously, but he knew she wore it with pride, and joy for what it represented, and delight in its fairy-gem sparkle.

"Insanely bored!" He laughed, feeling good-natured despite the loom dismantled and strapped rather conspicuously to the back of the landau—Lady Rankin would no doubt call them Gypsies when they arrived at the Edinburgh town house. He reached out to hug Elspeth close. "I can think of ways to keep you occupied, none of them boring." He nuzzled at her cheek, where pink bloomed from cold and a blush.

"I would dearly love that," she murmured. "But whenever you are busy with your classes, your writings, and your beloved rocks, what will I do with myself?"

"Lucie Graeme will be dragging you off to teas and parties to introduce her dearest cousin, the new Lady Struan. You will have little time for weaving."

"The eccentric Lady Struan will make time for weaving," she said. "And when word gets round of it, there will be no more invitations."

"Nonsense. The eccentric, unique, brilliant, and ravishingly beautiful Lady Struan," he said, "will make weaving a new rage among the ladies of Edinburgh."

She laughed. "I will have no time to teach them, for I must complete a MacCarran plaid for my husband—it is Highland custom for a new bride. It should be woven in their Highland home. However, we will make an exception this time—"

"You are always the exception, my girl," he said, teasing.

"And by early summer, you have promised that we will be back at Struan House, to spend the months through until winter comes again. And hopefully Lord Struan will find enough to do for a few months, until the university opens in September."

"I will have more than enough to do on the estate, having been away so long. Though Angus MacKimmie will do a fine job watching after everything until then." He nodded to Angus, who nodded back, busy tying the last of the luggage to the back of the landau. "I think this may be my last semester lecturing for a little while."

She turned to him with a little gasp. "Is it so? We will live here at Struan House?"

"Well, moving between homes does seem our best arrangement for a while," he said. "But Grandmother's fairy book is complete—with the invaluable help of you and Donal—and now that it is in Sir Walter's capable hands, I must work on my book about geognosy. I plan to begin a study of Scotland's ancient rock layers as well. That latter project will keep me exploring, and living, in the Highlands."

Elspeth leaned her head against his shoulder. "That is wonderful. I need to be here more than in the South, for my grandfather."

"I know," he murmured. "And I would not mind being a Highland laird most of the year. I can arrange to act as a visiting scholar at the university rather than a resident lecturer."

"It is good for me to be near Grandda most of the year. With the fairy spell off him, he has slowed at the weaving, and there is a great deal of work at Kilcrennan."

"He has Robbie Lamont to help. Besides, Donal has more on his mind these days than weaving, with a new wife to keep happy. Though I've never seen such contentment in a couple—as if Peggy and Donal have been wed fifty years instead of two weeks," he said. "I have every hope we will continue as happy as they are in our later decades."

"What, with me going off to the fairy realm every seven years for a day or two, and you accepting of it? That is what Donal agreed to do just to see Niall. Oh, but I think you might like to go there to see what rocks and gems they're hoarding there."

"Do not ask too much of my tentative acceptance," he said wryly. "I have not decided what happened, though I have ceased to question. I still wonder if I struck my head on a rock that day, and dreamed the whole incident."

She tugged his hat lower, and made a face at him. "That was no dream. But the rest, oh, may this all be a dream we will enjoy forever. The others are coming now," she said, turning. "They said they would be here in time to bid us farewell."

He glanced around, but saw no one on the lane leading to the house. "Odd."

"Coaches coming," Angus called then, from his higher post, balanced on the carriage frame. "Two of them, a gig and a barouche."

"Barouche?" James asked quickly.

"Black barouche, sir, and very fine," Angus said. "Same as was here before."

"Nick," James muttered. "What the devil does he want?" He walked a little along the lane, and Elspeth came with him. "Ah. There they are. We expected Donal and Peggy, but what business does Eldin have here? He withdrew his offer on the property, of course, and until the will is finalized—all four siblings must meet our conditions before the moneys would ever be transferred—he has no business coming here, or see-ing any of the MacCarrans, so far as I'm concerned."

Elspeth tucked her hand inside the crook of James's elbow. "Remember, he did help search for us when everyone thought we were lost."

"He wanted the treasure," James said. "And no one knows, but your grandfather and we two, where that is. We told no one about that pocket mine, and it will stay so."

"It would be invisible to anyone who looked in those caves anyway."

"If you say so, my darling. Though if I went there, I know I could find it."

"Because they would let you inside," she said blithely. "We three, and no others."

"Rationalize it how you will, we are still talking about fairies. I remain undecided. But intrigued," he added. "I will give you that."

"Here they are," she said, leaving his side to dash forward on the snow-packed road, so that James hur-ried alongside her, not wanting her to slip. His own balance was quite improved, and on all but very cold and rainy days, or long strenuous walks, he managed without a cane. Highland air and exercise—or fairy magic, as Elspeth claimed—had been excellent for his leg. And his heart, come to that, he thought, smiling to himself.

The gig that carried Donal and Peggy rolled to a halt, and the newlyweds climbed down, wrapping Elspeth in embraces and warm, loving conversation. James stepped forward for handshakes and Peggy's kiss, too, all the while distracted by the black ba-rouche as it came closer.

"We will see you in Edinburgh," Donal was saying.

"I will meet with the tailors to deliver new plaids next month, and go over the next group of commissions. Whatever is that raven-hearted rascal doing here?" He looked around, too.

"I do not know," James said grimly, and walked away to meet Eldin's barouche as it rolled to a halt, crunching on snow. He noticed a riderless, saddled horse tied to the back of the carriage, and wondered at that.

"Eldin," he called, stepping forward as the coachman jumped down to open the door; he glimpsed his cousin in the shadows. "May we help you on this cold morning?"

Nicholas MacCarran, Lord Eldin, stepped smoothly from the carriage, his height equal to James's, his greatcoat black as raven wings, indeed, James thought. He doffed his hat and murmured a greeting. "Struan," he said then. "It was I who came to help *you*."

James frowned. "How so?" Behind him, he heard footsteps, and then Elspeth placed her gloved hand on his arm. He pressed her hand to his side, all the while looking at Nick. "We are about to leave. I wish we could offer you hospitality, but—"

"Good morning, madam," Eldin said, taking Elspeth's gloved hand. "Excellent to see you again. You are looking in fine health. Both of you," he added, his gaze dropping to James's leg, no doubt noting the missing cane.

"Lord Eldin, welcome. May we offer you coffee or chocolate this cold morning? We have time," Elspeth said, glancing at James. "Donal and Peggy are here, too, and Mrs. MacKimmie is preparing a small repast before we depart."

"I regret I cannot join you, as I must return to

Auchnashee. The refurbishments to the castle are going well, provided I supervise. Today I came here only to ask, Struan, if you would convey my best to Miss Fiona, and extend her my invitation to stay at Auchnashee when she comes north again. Free of charge, of course," he said, though his tone was stiff. "We are family."

James stared at him, unsure what to say, probing in his mind any possible motive. "I did not . . . realize Fiona was coming north anytime soon."

"I believe so," Eldin said, smiling—that tight little smile never seemed to leave his lips—and yet James saw something in his cousin's dark eyes, something he had not seen before, a flash of hope or vulnerability somehow, and gone.

"We will be sure to give Fiona your generous offer," Elspeth said.

"The other reason I am here," Eldin went on, "is to offer you the use of my barouche for your journey. I will not need it for a while, and your ghillie can drive it back to Auchnashee after you ride in style and comfort to Edinburgh. It does not do for the Viscount Struan and his new viscountess to travel like Gypsies."

Now James gaped. "How did you know—that we were even leaving today?"

"I had a letter from Lady Rankin," he answered. "She suggested the loan of the barouche. She feared you would lash all your belongings to the landau like a pair of tinkers. It seems she is uncertain what a girl with fairy blood might do." He smiled at Elspeth. "I assured Lady Rankin in reply that the new Lady Struan would be exemplary."

"Thank you," Elspeth said. "We are honored by

the loan of your carriage. Are we not, James?" She pressed her elbow against his side.

"Of course," James said. "Thank you."

Eldin inclined his head and spoke to his driver. Politely refusing an offer of hospitality again, he mounted his horse and rode away. James stared.

"What the devil was that about," he muttered. Elspeth slipped her arms around him and rested her head on his shoulder.

"We cannot puzzle him out now," she said. "Let us go inside for a little while, and have some hot drinks with Grandda and Peggy and the MacKimmies, before we take the barouche and landau on our tinker parade across the Highlands."

James laughed, hugging her close, standing in the middle of the snowy road, his breath coming in foggy clouds. Elspeth's nose was pink in the cold, and he kissed it. "I suspect you are in no hurry to leave Struan House."

"I would prefer to stay in the Highlands," she said. "But I will go anywhere with you, Lord Struan. Anywhere at all, to the city or the hills, even if all you do is talk about your dear old rocks. You know that, I hope."

He kissed her then, taking time for it, tender and slow, despite the cold. "Aye," he whispered. "I know it well."